D0553942

Wizard Girl

by

Karen Eisenbrey

Published in the United States by
Not a Pipe Publishing, Independence, Oregon.
www.NotAPipePublishing.com

Paperback Edition

ISBN-13: 978-1-948120-31-9

Dedication

For my sister Yvonne,

who long ago pointed me toward
fantasy novels by women authors,

and who brought up four wizard girls.

Wizard Girl

CHAPTER ONE

A true healer's power lives in her hands, ready for use when it's needed.

Luskell's power clearly lived somewhere else. The night was only half over, but her feet hurt and her legs trembled with fatigue. She stumbled into the corridor, sank onto a bench and closed her eyes. Her back ached enough that she probably wouldn't fall asleep sitting up on the hard wooden seat. Probably.

"Luskell. Don't you usually work days?"

Luskell forced her eyes open and cast a weary smile to the small gray-haired woman beside her. "Hello, Balsam. I traded with Hanny. Her brother's in town and she wanted to see him tonight."

The broad corridor, with its dark wood paneling and lofty ceiling, hinted at the house's past as the grand residence of a wealthy merchant. It used to be Balsam's home when she was a girl. Now it was Balsam's House, a place of healing. Luskell had been working there for almost a year, honing her skills. She had the power and some training, but she wasn't a natural healer. Not like her mother.

"Her brother. Is that what she told you?" The corners of Balsam's mouth pulled up against her efforts to keep her lips straight. "Maybe she didn't want to scandalize an innocent."

"I'm not an innocent!"

Balsam raised an eyebrow. "I'm fairly sure you haven't been with a man yet."

"Oh. That way." Luskell's cheeks blazed. "Anyway, I might have. I'm not a baby, you know."

Balsam patted her hand. "No, you're not, and I guess I shouldn't assume. If you lived in Deep River, you might be betrothed by now, if not already married."

Luskell shuddered. "Then it's a good thing I don't. But maybe Hanny didn't lie. If my brother were in town, I'd spend all the time with him I could."

The old woman chuckled. "Your brother isn't even two. I hope he's not up this late."

Luskell smiled. She wasn't thinking of baby Crett, but of Ketwyn. The brother who died at birth, four years before Luskell was born. She hadn't seen him in a long time.

"You look like you're regretting your swap," Balsam said.

Luskell stretched to ease the soreness. "I tried to sleep during the day, but I'm not used to it. And I didn't know it would be this busy at night!"

"It isn't always, but this is winter wobbles season, and it's bad this year."

"You don't have to tell me."

Winter wobbles. It sounded inappropriately comical for such a serious illness. Named for the muscle weakness that caused sufferers to totter and reel, most years it was a minor seasonal annoyance—miserable but not dangerous. Luskell's first winter at Balsam's House hadn't seen anything like the number or severity of cases they were dealing with now. A harsh cough drifted down the wide hallway. The contagious ward in the former ballroom was filled with wobblers, mostly very old or very young.

Luskell's mother had gone to care for her own sick father in Misty Pass. Luskell hadn't heard how Grandpa was doing, but here in Eukard City, the theaters and concert halls were closed because of the epidemic, and the annual Governor's Ball had been canceled. Children went to school with handkerchiefs tied over their faces. You couldn't close the taverns and markets, but most people avoided crowds.

Luskell had been busy most of the night, bringing down dangerous fevers, soothing coughs and body aches, and trying to strengthen her patients' own defenses all while keeping up a protective charm so she wouldn't get sick herself. Every effort cost magical power and physical strength. As if that weren't enough, a healer who was sensitive to emotions, as Luskell was, had to remain open to her patients' feelings—the anger, the fear, the misery of the sick or injured. Everywhere Luskell turned, the flame or darkness of someone else's feelings overwhelmed her. And all on not enough sleep.

Luskell yawned. "There was a knife fight at one of the taverns, too." In spite of her best efforts as she cleaned and closed wounds, someone's blood stained her sleeve.

"The Otter. I heard." Balsam's words slurred into a yawn.

"Sorry. It's catching, isn't it?" Luskell turned to look at Balsam more closely. "Why are you working tonight?" Balsam was old enough to be her grandmother, but usually strong and vigorous. Tonight, she seemed spent.

"I sat with Mirion all day. She's dying."

"She's been dying for weeks."

"Years. I thought she'd pass this afternoon, but she's still holding on." Balsam sighed. "Would you mind sitting with her? I need to close my eyes for a bit, but I don't want to leave her alone."

"What do I need to do?"

"Nothing. Just ... be there." Balsam studied Luskell. "It might not happen, but have you ever witnessed a death?"

"Yes, one." Luskell shivered. One kind of innocence was long gone. "I'm not afraid, if that's what you mean."

"All right, then. Let's go."

They got up and moved to the chronic ward. Lined with tall arched windows hung with velvet drapes, this had once been an elegant reception room. A low fire burned in a tiled fireplace. No one here was contagious, so Luskell didn't need the protective charm for herself. A magical barrier in the double doorway kept infection from spreading to the vulnerable patients inside. It had to be refreshed daily, but the healers shared that duty, keeping it light.

The dimly-lit room was quiet. Only about half the pallet beds were occupied, and most of the patients were asleep.

Mirion lay awake, propped up with pillows to ease her breathing. She was about the age of Luskell's parents, forty or so, but worn beyond her years. She'd lost her family in a fire years ago. Her own lungs were permanently damaged by the heat and smoke, and she came to Balsam's House several times a year for a few days of treatment. The healers could relieve her suffering some, but the damage was too severe to be completely healed. This time, they hadn't sent her home.

"Mirion, you know Luskell, don't you?" Balsam asked. "She'll sit with you."

4

"Don't leave me!" Mirion whispered, and gasped for breath.

"Shh, don't try to talk. I'll be back at sunup, and Luskell will stay with you till then." Balsam gestured toward a small table beside Mirion's bed. It held a water jug, a cup, and a small vial of a clear liquid. "Luskell, you can give her drops if you need to, to ease the cough or help her sleep. Two should be enough."

"No drops!" Mirion struggled to sit up, then fell back against her pillows, exhausted by her outburst

"Well, if you change your mind ..." Balsam gave them both an encouraging smile and left the ward. She lived in her own apartment upstairs. As late as the sun rose this time of year, she would probably manage close to a full night's sleep in her own bed. Luskell envied her, but didn't begrudge her the rest.

Luskell smiled nervously and sat on a cushion next to Mirion's low bed. She wasn't afraid of death. It was one of the things that happened in a place like this. Luskell had helped wash and move bodies. But the only person she'd seen die had gone violently, and by his own hand. She'd had nightmares for weeks afterward. Still, Mirion had held on all day. Maybe she wouldn't die before Balsam returned. Even if she did, it wouldn't be like Trenn.

"Are you sure you don't want the drops?" Luskell asked. "They'll help you feel better."

"What if I don't wake up?" Mirion rasped. "I don't want to go into the dark!"

"What dark?"

"I don't want to be alone."

"You won't be." Luskell took her hand. It was cool, and Luskell could feel Mirion's life leaving her. "I'm here."

"I ... don't mean ... now. I'll be alone ... in the dark."

"But you won't be. Your family will be waiting for you on the Other Side."

"You don't know that."

Luskell went on as if Mirion hadn't interrupted. "And it isn't dark. There's no sun, but it's bright and warm."

"I'm afraid ... to go."

The woman's hoarse voice died away as she struggled for breath. Healing was hard work. Dying was harder. Mirion's eyes grew wilder and more desperate with each gasp. Luskell laid her free hand on Mirion's chest and tried to give her some relief. She felt the magic as a warmth at her core, in her chest and belly. It traveled down her arm to her fingers, a tingle somewhere between pain and pleasure. Her power revealed the extent of the damage. There was no relief that way.

"May I use a sleep charm?"

Mirion didn't try to speak but shook her head, refusing.

"What if I sing to you, then?" Luskell stroked the woman's hair and began to croon Aku's Lullaby. She knew from experience it calmed fussy babies and skittish horses, and by reputation that it quieted restless volcanoes. Mirion closed her eyes and fell into a shallow doze, restless as she struggled for breath. Luskell left off singing and whispered a sleep charm, into which she pushed a little extra power. Under its influence, even a healthy person would sleep undisturbed and wake refreshed.

But someone as sick as Mirion might not wake at all. Which could be a mercy; Mirion's life had become nothing but misery. It hadn't been Luskell's choice to make, but it was too late now to undo the charm. Mirion was already slipping away.

She was afraid to go alone. Luskell wasn't supposed to do it. She'd been warned not to, though she didn't know why. And it was one thing she was good at. She could make this right.

"I'll go with you," she whispered.

While holding Mirion's hand, Luskell stretched out on the floor with her head on the cushion and closed her eyes. She imagined the place she'd described, a grassy meadow, bright and warm. She'd never met Mirion's family, but she imagined a man and two children, lost in a fire. They'd know.

She pictured one other person, then gave herself over to sleep. Tired as she was, it took no time at all. When she opened her eyes, she was there, but Mirion wasn't. Luskell had never tried to accompany anyone to the Other Side. She'd arrived first.

Luskell wasn't alone, though. A tall young man waited for her. He had unruly red hair and pale, unfreckled skin; he'd never seen the sun. His wide mouth stretched in a smile and his bright blue eyes sparkled.

"Luskell!" He folded her in a barely substantial embrace. "Why are you here, little sister?"

"If you won't come to me, I have to come to you."

He held her shoulders and looked at her. He wasn't much taller; they were almost eye-to-eye. "There should be a need. This is no place for the living."

"I need my brother, Ketwyn. Isn't that enough?"

Ketwyn grinned again. "I wish it were." He continued to gaze into her eyes. "I'm glad you inherited Knot's blue eyes. With that and your height, people might believe we're brother and sister, if they saw us together."

Luskell sighed. "I wish they could." He got his height and eye color from his father, who was not hers. Her eyes were much darker than his, as were her skin and hair. Although they were half-siblings, they didn't look related.

"What's that in your hand?"

Luskell held a blackened wooden staff taller than she was. She'd never seen it before and didn't remember picking it up. A slight vibration in the wood reminded Luskell of her late grandfather's nearly weightless touch when he visited her dreams.

A movement caught Luskell's eye and she looked up from the staff. Far away downhill yet perfectly clear, she saw the room in Balsam's House, and her own body as she lay asleep next to Mirion's bed. A lone figure stood uncertainly at the bottom of the slope.

"Wait a moment, Ketwyn. Don't go anywhere."

Luskell descended the slope, her feet barely touching the soft grass. In no time, she was at Mirion's side.

"It isn't dark."

"I told you." Luskell took Mirion's hand. "Come on, this way."

They climbed the slope together, not laboring, moving easily. Mirion seemed to grow younger, the years of illness falling away. A man and two little girls waited at the top. Mirion ran the last few steps into her family's embrace. Luskell rejoined her brother.

"Ah, that's why you're here," Ketwyn said. "Well done; but you should go now." He kissed Luskell's forehead and was gone.

Luskell stayed a moment to watch the reunion. She suspected the man and children looked as they had before they died. Adults generally appeared that way. The spirits of children could choose to appear the age they would have been had they lived, as Ketwyn did. They were allowed to grow up in the afterlife. It was kind of these girls to let their mother see them first as she remembered them.

Mirion turned toward Luskell. "How did you know? How are you here?"

"I'm dreaming."

"But how—?"

Luskell gripped the staff. The scene was already fading, and she answered in the faintest whisper. "I'm a wi—"

CHAPTER TWO

Luskell woke to the winter sunrise slanting through the south-facing windows. Mirion held her hand in stiff, dead fingers. Balsam perched on the edge of the bed.

"Good morning, Luskell, and thank you. I had hoped she'd wait until I came back, but death isn't always predictable."

Luskell sat up and rubbed her eyes with her free hand. "Is it all right that I helped her sleep?"

"In her case, I believe it was a great kindness." Balsam glanced at the little bottle on the table. "How many drops did you use?"

"None, she wouldn't take them. She didn't want a sleep charm, either, so I sang to her. She was so restless, though. I worked the sleep charm before I thought about what it might do." Luskell forced out the next words. "I didn't mean to kill her."

"You didn't. The fire killed her, only it took all these years to finish the job. You did right."

"She was afraid to go." Luskell's voice was gummy with sleep. She cleared her throat. "She thought it would be dark."

"I hope you at least stayed awake until she was gone."

"Not ... exactly." Luskell glanced to the side.

Balsam frowned. "Luskell—"

"I went with her."

That silenced whatever scolding or advice Balsam was about to give. She gently pried Mirion's fingers open to free Luskell's hand. The dead woman's eyes were closed, her expression more peaceful than Luskell had ever seen her, at least on this side. "You crossed over to the Other Side? I didn't know you had that ability."

"I'm not supposed to use it." She rubbed the life back into numb fingers.

"According to whom?"

Luskell glanced up. "The dead. But she was afraid to go alone, and I knew the way..."

Balsam stared at her, shaking her head. "You're full of surprises. I've never known anyone who could do it; or anyway, that would admit it. It could be a useful skill in a healer, though—like a midwife, but at the other end."

"I don't think I'll make a habit of it."

"Perhaps not. You don't want to risk becoming a bad witch like Old Mother Bones."

Luskell laughed. "She's only a story. And not my favorite." Luskell had never cared for the tales of the skeletal hag who could drag a living soul to the Other Side and hold it there until the body perished. There had to be kinder ways to make naughty children behave.

"Nor mine. Your mother's the only woman I know brave enough to call herself a witch, at least since my bad-girl days." Balsam smiled and winked.

Luskell got to her feet, as did Balsam. Standing, the old woman barely reached Luskell's shoulder. "I could work today, if you need me." She tried to sound more enthusiastic than she felt.

Balsam smiled. "Don't you know what day it is?"

Luskell started to shake her head no. Her eyes widened as she remembered. "Short Day? Already?"

"Happy birthday. You're seventeen, and you've fulfilled your contract. We can make up a new one if you want to keep working here, but take today off, at least. You've earned it."

"Thank you. I will." Several hectic days in a row and her one night on duty had disoriented Luskell enough that she'd forgotten this long-anticipated day. She didn't have to come back unless she wanted to. And she didn't think she wanted to.

Luskell left the chronic ward and walked to the healers' dormitory at the end of the hall to collect her things. During the summer, when she could come and go in daylight, she'd slept at home. Since Fall Balance, she'd stayed at Balsam's House when she was on duty. She went home for her days off, but most of her clothes were here. She packed them all into a satchel.

Although healing was not her greatest strength, Luskell had nothing against Balsam or Balsam's House. She wasn't sure what the community would do without this place that provided care to victims of accident or violence in the general neighborhood; those too sick to be cared for at home; and those with no one at home to care for them ... or no home. It was a good place for a young healer to get training and experience. Collaboration built confidence in newly-acquired skills, and the other healers provided a supportive community. A healer from Balsam's House had everything she needed to either go out on her own, or stay to serve (and help train the next generation). As far as Luskell knew, it was always *she*. It had been a women's enterprise from the start. Balsam made the initial endowment from her own inheritance, and other well-off women had continued to fund the work. Men could have healing power, but generally preferred to work without help—at least, not from women. Luskell's father was the only man she knew to volunteer at Balsam's House even occasionally.

Luskell stopped by the dining hall, though she hadn't been awake long enough to have an appetite. The morning meal was the only one everybody took together, the night shift as they came off duty, the day shift as they came on. She poked her head in and waved to her old school-friend Cedar. When Luskell first started at Balsam's House, she'd appreciated having a friend on staff.

"Morning, Luskell! Coming on or going off?" Cedar grinned and smoothed her short, sandy hair with her hands. Unlike Luskell's mother, Cedar had no magic to project illusion hair styles, but she found short hair more practical. She wore trousers for the same reason. Although only eighteen, she was developing into a capable midwife with a steady temperament that calmed the fears of first-time mothers.

"Off. I swapped with Hanny."

Cedar patted the bench beside her. "Have some breakfast before you go."

Luskell shook her head. "No, I need to get home."

At that moment, Hanny walked in, pink-cheeked as if she'd just come from outside. She was a few years older than Luskell, golden-haired and curvaceous. She was a capable healer, in spite of a flirty nature.

"How's your brother?" Luskell asked.

Hanny blinked, and her color deepened. "He's ... fine."

"I'll say," someone murmured.

Hanny glared at her, then turned back to Luskell. "Can you work for me again tonight?"

Luskell smiled. "Sorry. I'm going."

"How many days do you have off?"

"I don't know. I fulfilled my contract, so as many as I want, I guess."

"You did?" Cedar asked. "Don't forget about us."

"I won't. See you later."

Luskell collected her last pay, then hurried out into the cold bright morning. The weather had been mild, but now it felt like winter. She wrapped her cloak around her. It was new this winter, thick and warm. The wool was a beautiful dark blue that her mother chose because it matched Luskell's eyes. It was long and full enough to cover anything she wore, from her boyish travel clothes to a ball gown. Better still, the front panels were lined with pockets of varying sizes.

Luskell hefted her bag and set out into the just-waking streets of Old Town, the neighborhood around Balsam's House and the library. When she walked home at a busy time, she liked to travel without being seen—not truly invisible, but under a spell that deflected notice. It required less power than true concealment, and worked almost as well in a crowd. Luskell enjoyed watching people and listening in on conversations without drawing attention herself or enduring glances from strange men. But this early in the morning, there was hardly anyone out and no need to hide.

As Luskell crossed the square, the library's tall spire gleamed. The early light glittered on frosted windows, and every puddle had a glaze of ice. She was careful to avoid slick spots, but hurried all the same. Across the square, a boy about her own age swept dust out of the Wizards' Hall, another former mansion but less ornate than either the library or Balsam's House. Luskell didn't recognize him; probably a servant or a new apprentice wizard.

He looked up from his chore. "You! Healer girl!"

Apprentice, then. They all seemed to pick up a bossy attitude. But how did he know? Had he been watching her? Still, Luskell wasn't afraid of boys.

"What?"

"Come over here. I've got something for you." He winked.

She wished she'd gone unseen, after all. Too late now. And there was something else. She didn't wish to know his thoughts or feelings, but a hint reached her, anyway—an impression of an actor in an ill-fitting costume playing a part he didn't know. If she played along, would he know his next line?

She held her voice steady. "Bring it here, then."

He hesitated, then grinned like a little boy and took a step toward her. His childlike glee almost changed her mind, but not quite. She called up a tiny amount of power and flicked her hand to direct the repelling charm. With a startled cry, he fell backward onto the stones of the square.

"Careful, wizard boy. The going is treacherous today." She left him there, cursing ineffectively. She wanted to laugh, but chose a mature silence instead.

Balsam was correct that Luskell hadn't been with a man yet. She doubted she was the only one; the other healers-in-training weren't any older than she was. But women of power had freedom in that regard that most women lacked. Some married, but few saw the need to wait once they felt ready for a lover. Luskell didn't know if the story was true, but rumor had it when Balsam was a young itinerant healer, she'd had a different fellow in every town.

Luskell found the idea of a lover thrilling. She longed for the experience, though not enough to take up with a rude apprentice wizard. She wanted the first time to be *right*. She'd overheard enough from the other women at Balsam's House to know it wasn't always—everything from clumsy fumbling, to impatient lovers in too much hurry, to unwanted, forced encounters. So Luskell didn't plan to go with just anyone.

A warm, yeasty aroma reached out to Luskell as she passed a baker's near home. Her appetite arrived with a growl. A month's pay jingled in her pocket; she went in and bought a loaf, fresh from the oven.

The baker wrapped the warm bread and passed it over the counter. "You go straight home, now. It's not safe for a girl on her own."

"It's daylight! What's not safe?" Luskell asked.

"They found another body—strangled."

"That's two in one month! Near here?"

"No, in the Garden District again. But still ..."

Luskell nodded. She knew the Garden District, but hadn't been there lately. It took its name from the large public garden that honored King Braffin, the long-ago last king of Eukard. It wasn't a wealthy area, but had never seemed unsafe. Now it was the site of at least two recent murders, whose frequency seemed to be increasing. "I promise I'll be careful."

Luskell's family rented rooms over a textile merchant's shop several streets away from Balsam's House. The merchant, Wyll, was married to a woman who had grown up with Luskell's father in the remote village of Deep River. Wyll and Kiat lived with their children Wyllik and Keela behind the shop, so they were neighbors as well as landlords.

As Luskell left the bakeshop, she met Wyllik and Keela coming in. "Happy Short Day," she greeted them. "Since when does it take both of you to buy bread?"

"Happy Short Day, Luskell," Keela said. She was only a year younger than Luskell, but Luskell would have made two of her, at least in height. Daintiness, like dark hair and eyes, ran in Keela's family. "Since Papa heard about this latest murder, I'm not allowed out on my own, even in daylight!"

"I just heard about it myself," Luskell said. "Do they know, was it another prostitute?" She felt sorry for women who had to earn a living that way, but if the murderer was targeting them, maybe the rest of the female population was safe.

Wyllik shook his head. "Midwife, I heard. Probably on her way home after a delivery."

Luskell shivered. Healers and midwives were another category of women with an independent living who might be out alone at night. Luskell felt capable of defending herself, but not every healer could say that. "Still, you're probably safe."

The siblings exchanged a glance. Keela's pink cheeks reddened further. "Um. I might have some power. Maybe."

"Look at this." Wyllik held out his left hand. The palm was pink, like the new skin after a bad sunburn peels. "I stumbled against the stove last night and burned my hand—burned it bad. But Keela grabbed it and kind of ... stared at it, and the pain went away. By this morning— almost nothing."

"Keela, that's wonderful!" Luskell exclaimed. "So you take after your Auntie Brynnit. I'll bet you slept well last night."

"Like the dead!" Keela laughed, then sobered. "But I dreamed I couldn't breathe. Do you suppose...?"

"You couldn't have helped that woman," Luskell assured her. "Will you go to Balsam's House for training?"

"Mama would rather I study with Brynnit in Deep River, maybe in the spring. Are you on your way to Balsam's House now?"

"No, home. I worked last night, but now I've fulfilled my contract and I'll have some time off." Luskell was happy to change the subject. "I'm seventeen today."

"In that case ..." Wyllik grabbed her and planted a rough, sloppy kiss on her lips. He was shorter and had to stand on his toes. "Happy birthday. Now you can't say you've never been kissed."

Luskell shoved him away. "I've been kissed before, much better than that." She wiped her mouth on her sleeve.

"What haven't you done, then? I'd be happy to help."

Luskell shook her head, but couldn't help smiling. Wyllik didn't mean any harm. He had been an incorrigible tease for as long as she could remember. He was nice enough looking, with his brown eyes and wavy, dark hair. It was hard to ignore how he'd filled out in recent years. But there had never been any spark. He was too much like an irritating but lovable relative.

Keela punched her brother in the arm. "I'm sure there's nothing she wants to do with you. Now, maybe if Jagryn were here ..."

Luskell's mouth went dry. "What about Jagryn?"

Keela grinned. "When he was here over the summer, there was hardly ever daylight between you two."

"That isn't true! I was working most of the time, and when we were together, we were studying."

"Is that what you call it?" Keela laughed out loud at her own joke, and Luskell couldn't stay angry. Keela controlled her mirth. "Crane will be glad to have you home. He misses your mother already, and it's only been two days!"

"I should get home, then," Luskell said. "I'll see you later."

She used the hiding spell as she walked on. There were enough people out now to be a bother. She wanted to be alone with her thoughts. The bread was a warm load against her chest, and thoughts of Jagryn warmed her from the inside. He was Wyllik's age, eighteen now, with similar looks, though Jagryn had a slighter build. He almost always wore a smile, and it was never fake. He had talent, but wasn't conceited; he worked hard to use his skills well, and enjoyed the effort. Luskell had known him all her life. Their families had been close for generations: his grandmother and hers were best friends; his father and hers, likewise. He was the one who should have seemed like a relative, but with Jagryn, there had been a spark. She wasn't sure of what.

Perhaps only the magic they had in common.

CHAPTER THREE

Luskell had kissed Jagryn for the first time the day she discovered her magic: an impulsive outburst of delight, and Jagryn, the most convenient target. That was over two years ago, when she spent the summer in the Dry Side village of Deep River, her father's hometown as well as Jagryn's. She hadn't known he was infatuated with her until it was too late to discourage him. She wasn't sure she wanted to. But they were both too young then for anything serious. And Jagryn wasn't the only boy in her life.

They were a team of three then—Jagryn, Luskell, and Laki—teaching themselves magic in secret. Luskell had known Laki all her life, too. He was a few years older. She had always looked up to him, admired him, and was maybe a little infatuated herself. He taught Jagryn and Luskell the magic he already knew — mind-talking and transformation — and the three of them learned as much as they could from an old book. But Laki had more responsibilities. His father was Aklaka ambassador to Eukard, and Laki was his aide and translator. His mother was Uklak—chief—of their band, and Laki was her heir. He went his own way after their summer of magic. Before they parted, he had hinted that he wanted to marry Luskell someday, and gave her a kiss that made her insides twang like a plucked string. She didn't give him an answer, but she couldn't forget the kiss if she tried.

As for Jagryn, he was her father's apprentice. Once Dadad knew what Luskell could do, she and Jagryn studied openly together in Deep River, before baby Crett was born. They were an odd team. Luskell had more raw power, Jagryn had finesse. Dadad taught them together, tailoring individual instruction to each student's strength. He encouraged them to work together, combining their power, and when they succeeded, they were formidable. When they didn't...

When they'd been working together for several months, Dadad took them out one breezy spring day to a remote hilltop and taught them for the first time to work weather. Clouds hurried across the sky, and the new grass lay flat before the steady wind.

"Weather is complex, with many strands," Dadad explained. "It can be controlled, like a horse with reins ... if you have a deft touch. We won't try that today, but reach out with your power and see if you can feel the strands."

How could she reach out to the weather? The wind tugged at Luskell's skirt, filled it, twisted it around her legs. Stray tendrils of hair blew across her eyes and mouth. She pushed them back impatiently and tried to focus on the lesson. Weather happened in the air. Maybe if she regarded the air as a creature, with a mind.

Luskell closed her eyes and imagined an arm emerging from the top of her head, extending as far as it needed to with fingers so sensitive they could detect a thought, a feeling. In an unforgettable moment, she felt what Dadad was talking about, like many silken threads in the fingers of her mind's hand. She wanted to do something with them.

Jagryn! Let's change the weather! Mind-talking was second nature by this time.

I don't know. Crane said not to.

He only thinks we need more practice, but I can feel how to do it. If we work together, I'll bet we can change the wind's direction. Where's the harm in that?

It's kind of hard not to give the strings a tug, isn't it? All right, let's.

They moved closer together in order to blend her power with his precision. They pulled on the strands, tentatively at first, then with more confidence. And the wind changed. One moment, Luskell felt the elation of triumph; the next, she spun wildly through the air, blinded by dust and wind. She thumped against another body.

Jagryn? What—what—? Luskell couldn't pull her thoughts together enough to ask a question.

Whirlwind. In it.

Jagryn's voice in her mind calmed her some. When she banged into him again, she held on tightly. They fell to the ground and tumbled to a stop, dizzy, bruised, scratched ... and naked. The whirlwind spun away, triumphantly bearing the tattered remains of their clothes.

Luskell released her grip on Jagryn and turned away. She drew her knees to her chest and wrapped her arms around them, hunched forward to shield her modesty. After a moment, she risked a glance over her shoulder. Jagryn had assumed the same posture and was studiously not looking at her.

Dadad ran across the grassy prairie to where they'd come down. As soon as he saw that they weren't dead or injured, he turned his back. Luskell thought he was shaking with anger, until she heard him laughing.

"No punishment I could devise is heavier than what you've done to yourselves," he said when he'd recovered. "This is why I don't want you working unsupervised. See the trouble you've made with me right here?" He shook his head and sighed. "I should make you walk back to town in your birthday clothes."

Luskell stared at him in horror. Would he do that? Besides the humiliation, it wasn't a warm day, and she was already shivering.

"But I won't. If you've recovered enough, I guess we'd better fly back."

Transformation was one of Luskell's talents. The chance to become a bird and fly took the sting off the weather debacle. But after that, Dadad continually delayed any more weatherworking lessons. And they weren't allowed even a moment alone.

When Luskell's family left Deep River to spend the summer in Misty Pass, Jagryn had to stay behind temporarily while they adjusted to life with the new baby. In the fall, they returned to Eukard City so Luskell could train as a healer at Balsam's House. By then, it was already wintry in the mountains, not the best time to travel. Jagryn would join them the following spring or summer, practicing on his own in the meantime. Dadad trusted him not to do anything rash. He wasn't Luskell.

On Short Day (and her sixteenth birthday), Luskell had signed a contract to work at Balsam's House for a year. Half a year later, on Long Day, Luskell had stepped out of Balsam's House for the walk home and found Jagryn waiting for her on the porch.

She threw her arms around him, laughing with delight. "I didn't know you were coming! When did you get to town? Where are you staying?" She tried to picture their cramped rooms with one more person.

"I came in on the afternoon coach, and I'm staying at Wyll and Kiat's."

That made sense. They were kin by marriage—his uncle Jagree was married to Kiat's sister Brynnit. And he'd be right downstairs. "Perfect! Why didn't you tell me?"

"I wrote to Crane, but I decided to surprise you." Jagryn wiped his brow. "Is it usually this humid?"

"It can be rainy this time of year, but it's not usually this warm at the same time."

"Crane says there's a storm brewing. He asked me to make sure you got home safe."

Luskell laughed. "Does he think you can protect me from lightning?"

"Perhaps he thinks I have enough sense to duck indoors." Jagryn smirked.

Luskell gave him a playful shove. "I have a better idea. Let's move the storm away from the city."

Jagryn stared at her. "I'm waiting for you to say, 'Only kidding.' But you're not going to, are you?"

"We know how to do it! We just need to be careful this time, and coordinate what we're each doing." She stepped down off the porch and studied the dark, low clouds that made early evening as dim as twilight. "We should be closer to the sky. Come on."

Luskell didn't know whether it was true, but it sounded like the sort of thing Dadad would say. And she remembered the hilltop in Deep River. She ran into the maple grove that grew between the library and Balsam's House and scampered up the tallest tree. She climbed as high as the thinning branches would allow before she looked down. Jagryn stood at the base of the tree, staring up at her.

"This is no good," she called down. "Not high enough."

"Good, because I'm not part squirrel like you. Now come down here—you make me nervous."

Luskell laughed and transformed to a pigeon. Instead of climbing down, she fluttered upward. Although not as forested as some parts of the city, this neighborhood boasted a few towering firs, taller than the maples. But a tree wouldn't do for what she had in mind. There was another high point, both convenient and suitable: the roof of the library. Luskell lighted near the domed glass-and-copper skylight with its proud spire. As Luskell transformed back, another pigeon landed next to her and became Jagryn.

"This is such a bad idea," he said, then grinned. "What do we do first?"

She pushed stray curls out of her face; her hair always came loose when she transformed. "We push the storm out over Eukard Sound—not that far, but away from the city."

Luskell reached out for the multitude of strands. They felt familiar, but different. Many sparked and hummed. "Feel that?"

Jagryn nodded. "It's alive!"

"Here's what we do: we gather up all the sparking threads and send them away."

It was an intuitive guess, and it seemed easy. Luskell gathered the sparking, vibrating strands into a growing bundle; Jagryn did the same. His hair stood up and she felt a tingling over her scalp and arms that had nothing to do with her own power.

"That's probably enough," she said. "Let's push it a—"

She was still speaking when CRACK! A huge lightning bolt struck the spire. The heavy glass of the dome rang like a great bell, a sound more felt than heard. Luskell staggered against the parapet and collapsed onto the gently sloped rooftop. Her ears were filled with a noise like a rushing river, with a piping whine on top. Her vision held a jagged after-image surrounded by black dots. She didn't know where Jagryn was. When she tried to get up to look for him, the world spun crazily. She fell back and lay still until she could see again. Her ears still rang, but when she sat up, the world held still.

Luskell crawled over to the skylight. The few people inside the library all stared upward. The lightning strike must have made an incredible din inside. She doubted they could see her. It was lighter inside than out. But where was Jagryn? She pictured him burned to a cinder, or fallen over the edge. He'd said it was a bad idea; why hadn't she listened?

She found him lying on another part of the roof, not moving. If he was dead ... As she reached out to feel for a pulse, he opened his eyes and slowly sat up.

He rubbed at his ear. "We're alive, right?" His voice sounded distant and distorted, like he was talking underwater.

"Yes! Are you all right? Your eyebrows are smoking!" Luskell patted them with her fingers. Scorched bits of hair broke away. "I think I'm fine, but your hair's all on end."

He reached to smooth her hair, an impossible task under the best of circumstances. She pulled him into a tight hug and their mouths met as if by prior agreement. Tiny lightning cracked between their lips. When they separated, Jagryn chuckled. He still looked dazed. "This was such a good idea." He kissed her again, longer than before.

She liked it. A lot. "Let's stay up here." A few fat raindrops splattered on the roof and on their heads. Then the heavy dark clouds opened up and spilled over. Luskell stood. "All right, let's not."

They transformed again and fluttered down to the square. It was raining too hard to fly home. They ran instead, but still arrived soaked.

Luskell opened the door and found herself engulfed by worried parents. Mamam hugged her, then Jagryn. "You're so late! I thought something must have happened."

Luskell gestured toward the rain outside. "Well ... this storm ..."

Dadad built up the fire in the stove and brought towels. "Only one thunderclap, but it sounded close."

"Lightning struck the library," Luskell replied. She rubbed her still-ringing ear. "We were right there."

Mamam made a worried clucking noise. "I hope you were somewhere safe."

"That's why we're so late. When it seemed like the lightning was past, we made a run for it." Luskell hoped if she didn't provide details, they would fill in what they wanted to believe. Her hair was now plastered to her head, and Jagryn's covered his singed eyebrows, so there wasn't much evidence of what had happened.

Jagryn didn't seem inclined to tell, either. He handed his damp towel back to Dadad. "I'd better get downstairs and change."

"We'll see you soon," Mamam said. "Kiat invited us to supper."

For the rest of the summer, Luskell worked with Dadad and Jagryn when she wasn't on duty at Balsam's House. She and Jagryn exchanged furtive kisses whenever they could grab a private moment, trying to recapture the thrill of the Lightning Kiss. Not as private as she'd assumed, if Keela had seen them.

But Luskell wouldn't change anything, even so. She treasured those moments of exciting discovery—one more thing they were learning together. She knew how much

Jagryn liked her; she could read thoughts and feelings, and he wasn't good at hiding his, or didn't try with her. Maybe he could have been her first, though he seemed less interested since he'd returned to Deep River. Besides, for all his talent and good looks, he was an unsophisticated country boy. He'd want to get married. Luskell couldn't imagine settling down in the middle of nowhere for anyone. Or settling down, period. She wanted something different.

CHAPTER FOUR

Luskell crossed the cobbled street to Wyll's shop, climbed the outside stairs to the upper level, and dropped the hiding spell. Inside the cozy room, the warmth of the small wood-burning stove enfolded her like a favorite quilt. Between the door and the stove stood a table and four chairs. A rocking chair sat near a window across the room. Her parents' big bed filled one corner. On the wall next to the window, shelves held dishes, cooking staples, a few books, and her mother's extensive collection of medicinal herbs.

"Dadad? I'm home."

Her father turned from the stove, his habitual stern look warmed by a welcoming smile. He had his straight black hair tied back. Both it and his neatly trimmed beard seemed to have more gray in them than Luskell remembered, though she had seen him only a few days before. "The birthday girl! I thought you might be home today." His smile widened when she held out the bread. "A birthday girl bearing gifts? Even better. I didn't have a chance to buy bread yet." He took the loaf from her, but his attention was no longer on the bread. "You have blood on your sleeve. Are you all right?"

Luskell glanced at the smear. "Knife fight at the Otter last night."

"Who won?"

She barked a laugh. "Everybody lived, if that's what you mean. We patched them up and sent them home."

"You did your job. That's my girl." He pulled her into a hug that warmed her better than any fire. He was one of only a handful of people she knew who were taller than she was. She came up to his chin and fit neatly into his embrace.

"Have you eaten?" he asked.

"No, I'm starving."

"Good, we can break our fast together."

His smile was genuine, but a little too bright. Luskell reached for his feelings. There was no question of Dadad's affection for her, but her presence also relieved a sharp loneliness.

She sat at the table. "You miss them, don't you?"

He sighed and gave her a half-smile, less forced than before. "That obvious, is it? I lived alone for years. You'd think I'd remember how!"

"You're domesticated," Luskell teased.

"And a better man for it." He set a skillet on the stove to heat.

"Did they get to Misty Pass all right?"

"Yes. I heard from your mother this morning." He tapped his head to indicate mind-talking. "Grandpa Eslo caught this terrible winter wobbles that's going around, and it settled in his lungs."

Luskell's heart lurched. "Is he all right?"

"He's still very sick, but out of danger now. She got there just in time."

"That's good to hear, but Crett must be underfoot."

"Nari is tickled to care for him. She views it as a privilege."

Luskell smiled at that. Grandma Nari was really their step-grandmother, but she loved them, and their parents, better than many a blood relation would have. "I'll answer Mamam for you, if you like." Dadad could mind-talk over short distances, but not all the way to Misty Pass.

"I'd appreciate it. And she'll want to know you fulfilled your contract." He laughed. "Did you think I'd forget? It was a big commitment, and we're both proud of you. Balsam speaks highly of your diligence."

"'Diligence' sounds like another way of saying, 'She has little talent but works hard to make up for it.'"

"Raw talent did this." He held out his disfigured right hand, scarred by his first use of magic. "I think I prefer hard work."

"Maybe. I do understand that Balsam's House is no place for fooling around. And I was usually too tired for anything like that, anyway. But it was good to work at something practical."

He added a knob of butter to the skillet. When it was melted and sizzling, he broke two eggs into the pan. "Will you do another year, then?"

"I haven't decided. I might volunteer from time to time, the way you do."

"It's steady, respectable work." Dadad sliced the bread. When the eggs were cooked, he removed them from the skillet to a pair of plates, and added two slices of bread to toast in the remaining butter. When all was ready, he set a plate of egg and toast in front of Luskell.

She had a healthy appetite by this time, and started to eat right away. It was a good excuse not to respond to his statement. What he said was true. There weren't many safe, respectable opportunities for a woman to use magic. Luskell recognized the value of the skills she'd learned and honed at Balsam's House. The fact remained, she had little natural aptitude for healing. She compensated with sheer power, which made for tiring and unsatisfying work. She didn't want to spend her life at it. She wanted something ... different.

She gazed across the room, where her father's staff leaned in the corner. To most eyes, it was an unadorned walnut walking stick, worn smooth and darker at the grip. To Luskell, it glittered with the magical power that infused every fiber of the wood. Something about it nudged a foggy memory. "Did Knot have a staff?"

Dadad followed her gaze. "Yes, the one his master made for him."

"Where is it?"

He shook his head. "Lost in the fire. And if it hadn't been, I would have buried it with him."

Lost in the fire. Luskell's hand gripped on nothing as she remembered her dream visit to the Other Side. She had been thinking of people lost in a fire, but maybe the staff heard the call, too. "So you'll make a staff for Jagryn?"

"Yes, when he completes his quest. Then he'll be a wizard, not an apprentice anymore."

Luskell nodded. "In Deep River, they called him a wizard already."

"The term is often used loosely, for any boy with some power. But really, was I a wizard when I set my own hand on fire? I might charitably have been termed a wizard-in-training. The magical community here prefers to reserve the title for those who've studied with a master and proven ability and wisdom."

"I know. What's Jagryn doing for his quest? Does he have to go somewhere?"

"Not necessarily. He needs to learn how to do some kind of magic without help from me—an independent experience." Dadad raised an eyebrow. "But in Jagryn's case, he does have to go somewhere. He wants to learn to visit the dead."

"But that's easy!"

Lines deepened in Dadad's forehead. "It disturbs me to hear to you say so. Few have the ability to cross over, and I've never known anyone to do it as readily as you do." His stern look softened. "But I trust you to be careful."

"I'm always careful." With that, anyway. She chose not to tell Dadad what she'd done for Mirion. Luskell wondered if he was right about the uniqueness of her ability. The dead could appear in dreams to anyone with power, but the dreamer didn't always remember or understand. Luskell hadn't even known she had power when she received those first visits from her brother and grandfather. But even then, she could control her dreams to some extent. It hadn't taken her long to work out how to visit them in return.

Luskell wiped up the last of the egg yolk with her bread crust, then crossed the room to the staff. She touched it with one finger, and the power vibrated through her. She felt dizzy and leaned against the wall. Dadad wagged his finger at her. She had touched the staff many times, always with the same result.

"Why does it do that?"

"It's tuned to my power, not yours."

"So another wizard can't take it from you?"

"Could and did." Dadad laughed and shook his head at Luskell's open-mouthed look of disbelief. "He was more powerful and I was naive. Anyway, he gave it back. But it was the first lesson my father taught me—don't give your staff to another wizard. Even if he can't hold it, he'll take it from you if he gets the chance, and then you can't use it."

She gave him a mischievous grin and wrapped her fingers around the staff. She had never tried to grip it with her whole hand, as she had the staff in her dream. The out-of-tune vibration nearly brought up her breakfast. She dropped the staff and slid down the wall to sit on the floor. "I've seen Mamam hold it. She doesn't have a problem."

He considered this. "I gave her permission the first time."

"Did Knot make your staff?"

"I made it myself. I guess that's appropriate, as I was self-taught. But I did everything backwards. I needed the staff just to have enough control and confidence to use my power at all."

"So it was all your quest?"

He chuckled. "Right up to finding my teacher. As I said, backwards." He winked at her. "Keep that to yourself. If the other wizards knew, they might decide I'm not one."

"But you're better than any of them. They ask your advice; they listen to you."

"That doesn't mean they need to know everything about me." Dadad got up from the table and held out a hand to Luskell. "Will you answer your mother's message for me now?"

She grinned and let him help her up. "What's in it for me?"

"I'll wash the dishes."

"Done." Luskell sat in the rocker by the window and closed her eyes. She reached with her mind to Misty Pass, to the Fogbank, and almost immediately touched a complex, busy mind.

Mamam? Do you hear me?

Luskell! Yes, I hear you. Is anything wrong?

No, I wanted to let you know Dadad got your message. And he misses you.

I miss him, too. And you. Oh! It's your birthday, isn't it? I can't believe I almost forgot.

You have a lot to think about. I fulfilled my contract at Balsam's House.

And I'm so proud of you. I knew we'd make a healer of you eventually. Will you go back?

Not right away.

I was going to suggest you join us in Misty Pass, but maybe you should stay with your father until he's free to come, too. I don't want him to get lonely.

We'll come up together. Give Grandma and Grandpa my love, and kiss Crett for me.

I will. I have to go now. I love you, Luskell. And I really am proud of you.

They broke the connection. Her mother's pride warmed Luskell and chafed her at the same time. There was no good way to tell Mamam she didn't want to be a healer.

She. Wanted. Something. Different.

Luskell opened her eyes and yawned before she could speak. "I was up most of the night," she explained. "Now that I've eaten, I need to sleep. What are your plans today?"

"Do you remember Dalmer?"

"Sure. What's happening?" Dalmer was an apprentice wizard, a year or so younger than Luskell. He'd been studying under Drikkum, but the old man had died of winter wobbles a month before, in spite of Balsam's best efforts.

"He has a new master, but they're not seeing eye to eye," Dadad explained. "I was going to meet with them this morning and try to sort things out. And then there's something I want to check on. But if you'd rather I stay here ..."

"Go on. I'll see you when I wake up."

"I'll be here."

She felt again Dadad's affection, and a whiff of disappointment. He wanted her company, but she wouldn't be much good to him yawning and dozing off. She went into her room and closed the door behind her. It was little more than a closet, mostly filled with the bed, though there was room for a washstand in the corner. Luskell's mother had insisted that a girl her age needed privacy. Luskell appreciated the thought, but closed off from the stove, the room was freezing. She didn't waste time getting undressed, but slipped off her shoes, crawled under the covers, and fell asleep moments later.

CHAPTER FIVE

Luskell stood on the roof of the Governor's Mansion, clad in her mother's best summer dress. The pale blue silk whispered in a warm breeze, and Luskell stretched luxuriously. She had assumed she'd never get to wear it; she was too tall, and didn't have the bosom to fill out the bodice. Besides, the dress was ruined when ...

Luskell frowned. It was just past sunset, and the rooftop terrace was arranged for a fancy dinner party. Chairs with colored cushions surrounded a long table, where lantern light gleamed off dishes and glassware. But Luskell was alone; she saw no other guests. Then a young man appeared from the shadows. There was something familiar about his angular build, his serious expression, his blue eyes. Luskell feared him, but she couldn't remember why.

"Stay back!" she tried to shout. Her voice was barely audible.

He held out empty hands. "I can't hurt you now. I only want to talk."

"Trenn?" she whispered. He nodded. "Of all the dead men who could visit my dreams, why you? And why now? It's been over two years." And in this place. He had attempted to murder Luskell's mother and father, threatened Luskell, and finally killed himself rather than go to prison.

"It's not that easy to visit dreams. But I've been watching you."

Luskell crossed her arms. "Well, don't."

"There's little else to do. Have you any idea how dull it is to be dead?" Trenn dragged a chair back from the dining table and slumped into it. The dejected posture rendered him even more harmless.

Luskell took a seat near him. "I guess I don't."

"Sometimes those of us who died young can learn something from the more experienced, but beyond that, we watch the living."

"But why watch me? You don't even know me."

Trenn closed his eyes and pressed his hands against his knees. He sat straighter and opened his eyes. "I promise I don't mean you any harm. It's just, you have— you are—everything I wanted to be. You have power, you have training. Your family loves you. But you have the same problem I did."

"What problem is that?"

Trenn glanced away, into the darkening city. "Your father is doing good work."

Luskell knew he didn't mean Dadad's work with Jagryn, or not only that.

"Masters don't always know what their apprentices need," Trenn went on, "and apprentices certainly don't know how to ask. Crane has a talent for seeing past the misunderstandings."

"All those years helping the Aklaka ambassador have paid off, then."

Luskell only pretended not to understand. Not every self-taught wizard turned out as well as Dadad. Trenn had used his ill-gotten magic in service to a corrupt governor. When Luskell and her friends helped stop his plot, he killed himself in front of her—and she couldn't save him. None of them could. But that incident led some of the city wizards to invite Dadad to help them identify hidden magic users so they could be properly trained. He also mediated between masters and rebellious apprentices to help them work together and draw out the apprentices' talents without crushing their spirits. He remembered better than most what it was like to be young, with more drive than wisdom.

Trenn smiled in spite of Luskell's sarcasm. "Powerful wizards are rarely so diplomatic. It's possible he averts great danger every day."

"My father doesn't need your flattery. Why are you telling me this?"

"He works with boys who aren't being heard, whose power is overlooked and might otherwise not develop fully, or might develop warped."

"Yes, but what do you want with me?"

"He works with boys," Trenn repeated.

"I still don't—" Luskell stared at Trenn. Boys with magical power sometimes received incomplete training because of poor communication. But if not for Dadad's unusual attitudes, she herself might have received no training at all beyond healing, the area where she had the least talent. And yet, if she put her magical talents to open use, she ran the risk of being labeled a witch, a role in

which she would receive grudging respect at best. Those stupid Mother Bones stories had ruined it for everyone.
"Why are you telling me this?" Luskell's voice quavered.

"Because I knew you'd see the unfairness."

"I do, but—" An idea struck like a lightning bolt. "Are you saying I should ...?" Her throat dried up and her voice trailed off.

"Someone needs to be first."

She nodded. It seemed ludicrous, but there might be a way. It would take time, and more ...

"Thank you, Trenn. I'll think about it."

"It's the least I could do, to make up for the wrong I did before. I'll go now."

"Give my love to Knot and Ketwyn."

He bowed slightly and vanished. The rooftop and the summer night faded.

Luskell woke in her room. Short Day's noon sun slanted through her window. As she got out of bed she noticed again the bloodstain on her sleeve. She should have washed it out right away, but there hadn't been time. She stripped off the blue dress—wool, not her mother's silk; that dress had, in fact, been ruined the night Trenn died. She shivered into a clean one of gray flannel. She wanted to return to the warm sitting room, but first washed out the blood with cold water and soap, and a touch of magic when the stain proved stubborn. While she scrubbed at it, she thought about her dream. When she had been in that place for real, there had been a lot of blood, but the dream was clean and peaceful. And Trenn's message hadn't faded.

She returned to the sitting room, where Dadad sat at the table, writing something. He looked up with a smile.

"There she is, her old self again."

"How was your meeting?" She went to the window and opened it. A box on the outer sill kept perishables cold. She took out a pot of half-frozen soup, enough for two bowls.

He frowned. "It didn't happen. Dalmer was there, but he didn't know where Slake was. Based on Dalmer's interests, I'm making a list of spells and lore that should satisfy both of them, for when we do meet."

"That's something, anyway. What about your other errand?"

"Even less satisfying." Luskell waited for more details, but he seemed to regard the subject as closed. "Did you sleep well?"

"Mm." She set the soup pot on the hot stove and sat across from him. "Do you remember Trenn?"

Dadad lost his smile. His dark handsome face sagged and he looked ten years older. "I could hardly forget a man who threatened those I love the most. Whose death I caused."

Luskell reached across and squeezed his hand. "No. He did that himself."

He straightened himself and was her strong Dadad once more. "I keep telling myself that. I wish I could have gotten to him before he went wrong."

"He admires the work you're doing now." He frowned, and she scrambled to cover the slip. "I mean, he would admire it. I imagine."

Dadad shook his head. "You dreamed of Trenn? What do I have to do to protect you from that ... that ...?"

"Trenn can't hurt me now. He says he wants to help me. He offered advice."

Dadad's smile returned like the sun from behind a cloud. "I can't fault him for that, but I worry—I thought you didn't visit the dead anymore."

"I don't! Trenn came to me." Dadad seemed to accept that, but she didn't want to lie to him. "But... I helped a woman die last night. I went with her to the Other Side."

Clouds covered the sun again. "I know you meant well, but that's dangerous. What if you can't get back?"

"It hasn't been a problem. I wake up, and I'm back."

"Did you ... see my father?"

"No, but I think I held his staff."

He nodded thoughtfully. "That's why you asked."

"Will you make me a staff?" she blurted.

"The last thing you need is something to amplify your power."

"But it helps with control, right? I could use that."

"A healer doesn't need a staff. "

"I already told you, I don't want to be a healer!" Luskell sputtered. "Why should I be limited to the thing I'm worst at?"

"A witch, then?"

"Please. No."

She wasn't sure why she cared so much what she called herself or whether she had a staff. She'd never thought about it before, but all the female magic-users she knew were healers. Her mother was a lot more than that, and had chosen to call herself a witch. It wasn't a title that got much respect, though Mamam had a compelling personality to go with her power. She could call herself whatever she wanted. But Luskell didn't want to use that name. It didn't fit.

"All right," Dadad said. "I didn't know you felt so strongly about it. What do you want to do?"

"I want to use all my power, the way you do. I want to be ... a wizard."

CHAPTER SIX

The fire popped. Faint voices drifted through the floor from the rooms below. The silence stretched out as Dadad stared at Luskell. He blinked several times and started to answer, then changed his mind. He shook his head and looked to the side, as if a wise adviser stood at his left.

"You didn't answer my question," Luskell prompted. "Will you make me a staff?"

"No. I won't." His voice was firm and decisive, but he wouldn't look her in the eye.

She folded her arms. "But you'll make one for Jagryn?"

Dadad's adviser must have had wings, because he looked to the ceiling. "He's my apprentice."

"And what am I?"

"My daughter." At last, his gaze rested on her. He wasn't in the habit of shielding his emotions at home. A complex stew of pride, bewilderment and worry rolled over Luskell.

"Yes. So why not?"

"A father can't make his own child a wizard. It keeps things ... honest."

Luskell frowned. "But your father was your master."

Dadad snorted and one side of his mouth quirked up. "He wasn't much of a father. Besides, I already had my staff by the time I met him. I made myself a wizard. Knot only polished the rough edges."

Luskell leaned toward him. "You did more than that for me. You taught me everything."

"Maybe I didn't know any better." He gave her a wry smile. "No, I knew you had enough power to be dangerous if left to yourself. But I can't make you a wizard."

"Fine. Who can?"

"No one."

"Why not? You said yourself I have the power, and we've done all this work—"

He huffed impatiently. "Luskell, you're a girl!"

"So what?" In spite of his rare show of frustration, she had to ask.

He held out his hands as if laying something obvious before her. "A girl can't be a wizard."

Luskell clenched her jaw and looked straight into his wide hazel eyes. "Who. Says?"

Dadad opened his mouth to answer, then closed it again. His brow furrowed.

"Who says?" Luskell repeated. "Is it a rule? Is it written down somewhere?"

Dadad's smile slowly returned. "I don't believe it is. Probably more tradition than rule. I should say no girl *has been* a wizard. Why are you so interested all of a sudden?"

"Everybody keeps asking if I'm going to work for Balsam, but I'm no healer. I want to use my power for something different. And then, what Trenn said ... So I want to be the first woman wizard. But before I can do that—"

"You'd have to find a master, and earn your staff." He puffed out a breath. "I can't believe we're having this conversation. On the one hand, I want to encourage you." He held out his left hand, which he used for writing and intricate magic. "You have a great talent, and you've made impressive progress in learning to use it. I couldn't be more proud." He extended his right hand, scarred and clumsy since his first act of magic. "On the other hand, I hate to expose you to the kind of attention this ambition of yours will attract. The danger."

"Somebody murdered a midwife last night," Luskell pointed out. "There's danger either way."

Dadad sighed. "I should have guessed you wouldn't listen to me."

"I always listen to you." Luskell nodded decisively. "So how do I find a master?"

"I guess you go to the Wizards' Hall and ask, like anyone else. There's a good chance they'll laugh at you, but you never know." He reached out his hand and brushed back a few dark curls that had come loose from her braid. "You could cut your hair and disguise yourself as a boy. Or with your height, a young man."

Luskell considered that. She had often worn trousers when hiking in rough country, but she'd never pretended to be a boy. Even with her slender build, she had enough curves that it would have to be an elaborate disguise. And cut her hair? Her mother cut her own hair short. Luskell had been tempted a few times, but her hair was like her grandfather's, and he'd always worn it long. As her father still did, though it was no longer the fashion in the city.

"The whole point is to do this honestly: to be a girl and a wizard at the same time." Luskell stroked her chin.

"Besides, at my age, a boy would probably need to shave once in a while. And most of the wizards and apprentices already know me. It would be hard to fool them."

Dadad nodded. "I guess if I can't talk you out of it, I'll give you my support. It won't hurt to ask. Just don't expect anything."

The soup pot steamed and bubbled. Luskell dished it into two bowls and set them on the table. "I'll go after we've eaten."

"Do you want me to come with you?"

"No. I'll do this myself."

Dadad put on an obviously fake frown. "So I'm to see you only at mealtimes?"

She laughed at that. "I suppose that depends on my master."

"If you find one."

"I will! I already have more power and skill than any of those apprentices. How can they turn me down?"

Dadad shook his head. "You have a lot to learn about people. If only it required nothing more than ability and stubbornness!"

"Who's stubborn?"

He laughed. "You're your grandfather's grand-daughter and your mother's own child."

"Sounds like a recommendation to me."

After lunch, Luskell rebraided her hair to contain any stray tendrils. The gray dress, though not her favorite, seemed appropriately sober for her errand. She stood before her father. "Do I look serious? Mature? Maybe wizardly?"

"I don't know how to judge," he admitted. "I do know it gets dark early. Wait at the Wizards' Hall. I'll meet you and walk you home."

Luskell gave her word reluctantly. It seemed unfair that women had to be protected by men ... from other men. But if agreeing to protection brought her closer to independence, she was willing to accept it for now.

It was a bright, frigid afternoon. Luskell walked fast to stay warm. Although she had visited the Wizards' Hall many times, this was her first time on her own. Rather than walk in as she would with her father or Jagryn, she rang the bell and waited. To her dismay, the apprentice who answered the door was the same she had seen in the morning. Close up, he looked older than she'd thought him then. He was about her height, with dark blond hair and pale stubble on his jaw. He had hazel eyes, like her father. That detail irritated her more than it should have.

"If you're here about the kitchen job, the entrance is around the side and down the stairs." His rote delivery told her he'd been giving this answer a lot today.

"I'm not. I'd like to talk to—"

"I know you!" he interrupted. "You're that healer from this morning. Did you come back for what I offered?" He seemed more puppyish than worldly, but no less annoying. Before she could say anything, he said, "I didn't, um, notice then how tall you are. How far do your legs go?"

"All the way into my boots," she replied in the iciest tones she could manage, and stamped for emphasis.

Another youth appeared behind the boy at the door. "Hey, Luskell. What can we do for you?"

Luskell closed her eyes in relief. At last, someone sensible. "Hello, Dalmer. Sorry about Drikkum."

"Thanks. Having a new master, it's almost like starting over at the beginning."

"Your new master is difficult?"

"Slake is ... he has a different style from Drikkum." Dalmer didn't offer details, but it was easy to imagine the conflict. Luskell hoped her father could make peace between them.

The older apprentice looked back and forth between them. "So you two know each other?"

"I forgot! You're new," Dalmer said. "Luskell, this is Fandek. He started here a few days ago. He's going to study under Breet. Fandek, this is Luskell. Be polite to her."

"Um." Fandek looked at his feet.

"Was he rude to you already?" Dalmer asked.

Luskell studied Fandek's red face. "Maybe Fandek would like to answer that."

Fandek gave her a sheepish look. "I didn't mean to be. I'd heard the other fellows talk to some of Balsam's girls, and ..." Under her cold stare, he trailed off and tried again. "I didn't know you were anyone special."

"It shouldn't matter. Now, are you going to keep me standing out here in the cold or let me in?"

Fandek stepped aside and Luskell passed through the entry into the wide front hall. Through an arch to her left, a few men and boys ate a meal at a long table. To her right was a large room where two maps, one of the city and another of Eukard, hung on either side of a big stone fireplace surrounded by comfortable armchairs. Luskell glanced longingly toward the fire blazing there.

Dalmer closed the front door, shutting out the cold. "So, what can we do for you?"

"Do you know of a wizard who needs an apprentice?"

Dalmer nodded. "Do you have someone to recommend?"

"I ... yes, I know someone."

"That's good timing; Bardin graduated his apprentice recently. Have a seat, and I'll see if I can find him for you."

At the mention of Bardin, Luskell felt her chances improve. He was one of the oldest wizards in Eukard City. Eccentric, but less set in his ways than many half his age. He had a habit of devising projects that required the combined efforts of several wizards, always a tricky proposition. But Bardin had experience and a calm nature that led people to listen to him. More than that, he had imagination.

She took off her cloak and handed it to Fandek, then swept past him and settled into one of the armchairs by the fire. She could already feel the staff in her hand.

CHAPTER SEVEN

Luskell doubted anyone would question her ruse about helping a friend find a master. Her father often identified candidates, and it wasn't a stretch to imagine one might be her friend.

The Wizards' Hall wasn't a formal school, but served as a convenient meeting place for masters and apprentices, as well as a social center where they could have a meal and catch up with other practitioners—either local or on a visit from elsewhere. Outside Eukard City, many wizards stayed in a place only as long as their skills were useful, then moved on. If an itinerant wizard met a boy who showed promise in magic, he might take him as apprentice or bring him to the city to be matched with another master. There was nothing to stop a wizard from seeking an apprentice in the city, but more often the apprentice came to the Wizards' Hall, looking for a master.

Even if the apprentice never became a fully qualified wizard, a little training went a long way toward keeping potentially dangerous power under control, as Dadad had done with Luskell. She already had the power and the skill to be useful, if anyone would let her. All she needed was a stamp of approval. It was a matter of making her request sound so logical, no sensible wizard could turn her down.

Luskell waited by the fire, fidgeting as time stretched out. Where was Dalmer with Bardin? She saw several master-apprentice pairs head outside or upstairs to the workrooms. Fandek appeared to be on some kind of chore detail, but he wasn't all that busy. She suspected he was watching her, though she couldn't catch him at it.

A man of about thirty and a boy around Luskell's age got up from the dining table and approached the fire. The wizard had straight hair so blond it was almost white, and gray eyes like dirty ice. His apprentice was a skinny boy with unruly black hair and large, dark eyes in a pale face. He kept behind his master and smiled uncertainly at Luskell.

The man fixed Luskell with his cold stare. "You don't belong here."

The apprentice tugged the wizard's sleeve. "Master Larem, I've seen her here before, plenty of times."

Larem turned and scowled at the boy. "Have you, Terulo? As a wizard's guest, perhaps. She shouldn't be here on her own."

Luskell couldn't decide whether she objected more to being asked to leave, or being talked about as if she weren't there. "I'm just waiting for—"

"It's time for you to leave, young woman. This is a place for men."

Without thinking, Luskell blurted, "It wasn't always."

The wizard blinked. "What?"

"Men and women used to meet here to share knowledge, techniques, probably meals. A long time ago, but still—"

Larem frowned. "That's not true. Where did you hear such a thing?"

"I read it in Soorhi's diary."

"Never heard of it. Who's this Soorhi?"

"My grandfather's uncle." Luskell wished she'd kept her mouth shut. Too late now. "He started the first free school in the city, and he used to visit here sometimes. A wizard cursed him over a woman."

"Well, that's a nice story, but I doubt it's true. Was this Soorhi a wizard?"

Luskell's face warmed. "I don't think so. He was a teacher."

He smirked. "There, you see? So why would he be here at all?"

"He had some power. Eyes in the back of his head or something."

"A likely story. But you see what would happen if we let women in here? Fights and curses." Larem chortled smugly.

"It was a diary, not a storybook!" Luskell growled. "Soorhi raised my grandfather, and *he* was a wizard."

"I'm sure he was, dear. What was his name?"

Luskell narrowed her eyes and glared at Larem. "Yrae."

That name was usually met with discomfort, fear, sometimes great respect. Luskell was unprepared for the roars of laughter.

"Oh, of course it was! You do have a good imagination! Yrae was not a real person, my dear. Everyone knows that." He collected himself and gave her a patronizing smile. "You've had your fun. Now it's time for you to leave."

Before Luskell could continue arguing, Fandek joined the conversation. "No, she's waiting for Bardin. He'll be right down."

Larem seemed disappointed as he turned away. Terulo gave Luskell a little wave and mouthed, "Sorry," before hurrying off in his master's wake.

Fandek stood with his back to the fire. "Healers work outside a lot, do they?"

Luskell looked up at him with a puzzled frown. "Not really."

"Then how do you get so brown in winter? You could pass for Mountain Folk!" He grinned.

"No, I'm too short, and they're a lot darker." Luskell studied her hand. The skin was a soft golden brown, dark compared to Fandek's typically Eukardian winter pallor. "But that's where I get my coloring—from my Aklaka heritage."

Fandek swallowed. "Sorry. I don't mean to be rude."

"No, you just talk without thinking. Have you always had that habit?"

"I guess. Except around my pop." He looked away from her and stared across the room.

Luskell glanced up at him. "You're older than most beginning apprentices."

"Late bloomer," he said. "Nobody recognized my ability until I was fifteen."

"Did you set yourself on fire?"

Fandek's eyes widened and his mouth dropped open in horror. "Does that happen often?"

"I hope not. Some wizards discover their power through accidents, that's all. So how did you find out?"

"My father was about to hit my brother, and I yelled, 'Stop!' He couldn't move until I released him."

Luskell nodded. It was usually something like that—an emotional moment that let the power out, sometimes helpful, often damaging. "But you're not fifteen now."

"No, eighteen. Almost nineteen."

"Why didn't you come here sooner? Do you live far away?"

Fandek shook his head. "Just down in the Garden District, but I couldn't leave Deklyn alone with Pop."

"Deklyn's your brother?"

He nodded. "My younger brother."

Luskell smiled. "I have … one of those." She'd almost said "two brothers," but most people wouldn't understand about Ketwyn. "He's still a baby, not even two yet."

"Deklyn's sixteen, but he's … slow. Sweet tempered, though, and good with animals. As soon as he was old enough, I got him a job in the stables at the coach office, and then I came here."

"So your father's all alone now?"

"No, he's dead."

Luskell clapped her hand over her mouth. "I'm sorry!"

"Don't be. I'm not."

Luskell was tempted to read Fandek's thoughts and get the rest of the story, but that would be hypocritical after all the talk of politeness. "Where's your master today?"

"Down with the wobbles."

Luskell blew out an exasperated breath. Now that she thought about it, she had seen the wizard Breet at Balsam's House. He was not in danger now, but too sick to go home yet. "Do you at least know how to protect yourself?"

"No. Is that even possible?"

"It's the first thing a healer learns. Come here." She patted the chair next to hers, and he sat. He jerked when she placed her fingers on his temples, but then held still. She closed her eyes. He was in good health, not yet infected. She carefully avoided his thoughts; she didn't want to know, and had no right, anyway. She opened her eyes and removed her fingers from his head. He was staring at her with his mouth half open, and his cheeks were red. If she hadn't known better, she'd have said he had a fever. "You haven't caught it yet. If you want to stay healthy, there's a charm that'll protect you. Always use it if you're around people you know are sick. The way things are this winter, you'd do well to use it whenever you're in a crowd."

She instructed him on the words to the spell and how to apply it. It took him a few tries, but with practice, he got it. The wizards at the lunch table had turned to watch through the doorway. Luskell tried to ignore them. She was saved awkward questions by the arrival of Bardin.

Luskell stood as he approached. Although a small man with a lined face and a fringe of white hair around a bald head, he crossed the room with brisk steps. The corners of his mouth naturally turned down, though Luskell knew him to be more amiable than his perpetual frown would indicate. He took both her hands between his. "Good to see you, Luskell. It's been too long. What can I do for you?"

Luskell allowed herself a smile, wishing Larem could have seen the greeting. "May we speak privately?"

"Let's see if one of the workrooms is available." He glanced at Fandek. "Thank you for entertaining our guest. You may return to your duties."

As she left the room, Luskell glanced back. Fandek stared after them, his mouth open. Even without trying, she could hear his thought: *Who are you?*

CHAPTER EIGHT

Luskell followed Bardin upstairs to a sparsely furnished room. Two chairs faced each other across a narrow table, its top marred with scorch marks and dents. He ushered her in and sat in the chair facing the door. Luskell moved to close it.

"Leave it," Bardin said. "Appearances, you know. Please, sit down."

Luskell wasn't sure what he meant by *appearances*, but an open door defeated the purpose of a private meeting. She took the seat facing him, unsure how to open the conversation. She was thankful when Bardin spoke first.

"It's good to see you again, Luskell. I hear excellent things about you from Balsam."

"That's ... kind of her."

"How's your friend Jagryn?"

"I think he's all right. He's doing his quest work in Deep River, but I haven't heard much from him since he went back there."

"He's a young man with great potential. A shame he couldn't finish his work here." Bardin gave her a sidelong glance. "I assumed you would agree, until I saw you getting so cozy with our newest apprentice."

She flinched, then faked a laugh to cover her shock at both assumptions. "Fandek? I was only teaching him a charm to keep him healthy during this epidemic. I couldn't believe he didn't know it already."

"Thank you for your interest. He hasn't had much instruction yet. But that's not what you came to talk about, is it?"

"No." This was it. Luskell scraped a fingernail across a burn on the tabletop and tried to marshal her logical arguments. "I ... know someone who wants to be a wizard, and I heard you might be looking for an apprentice. Is that true?"

"It is. Dalmer said you had a recommendation."

"Yes, but the situation is—" Luskell took a deep breath to steady her nerves. "—unusual. Tell me, what makes a wizard?"

"Why are you asking me, when you live with the greatest living wizard in Eukard?"

Luskell smiled to hear such a thing about her father. "His experience is unconventional. You might have a more complete answer."

Bardin rested his elbows on the table and tapped his fingers together. "All right. There's power, obviously. Skill to use it. Experience. The main element is there in the name—wisdom. Discernment. Common sense. Someone who can demonstrate all those elements earns a staff."

"But who decides?"

"In the usual way of things, if a youth shows promise, he is apprenticed to a mature wizard who trains and nurtures his ability and helps him develop wisdom.

Presumably, the master knows the apprentice well enough to judge when he has earned his staff."

Luskell nodded. So far, this was familiar, but it was helpful to hear it all spelled out at once. And encouraging; many of the qualifications already described her. "But say someone comes here, almost grown and with power and skill, but little formal training. Or trained by a family member. How does that person earn a staff?"

Bardin smiled. "It happens. Young Fandek is such a case of someone arriving relatively late in life. We try to match him with an appropriate master to examine his abilities, fill any gaps in his knowledge or practice, and help him design a challenging independent experience—his quest. If he completes these tasks to his master's satisfaction, he receives his staff like anyone else."

"Does it take long?"

Bardin chuckled. "It takes as long as it needs to. A boy starting from nothing might need five, six years to mature into a wizard. Longer, even. How old was your father when he earned his staff?"

Luskell mentally substituted *made* for *earned*. "Seventeen, I think. Almost eighteen. He'd been working at it since he was twelve, but most of his progress came late."

"There, you see? That's fairly typical—my master took me on when I was twelve, and I received my staff at eighteen. My old apprentice, Virosh, is twenty. But if a youth is powerful and already skilled, his apprenticeship might be more of a formality."

Those were the words Luskell was waiting for. "And what if he's a she?"

Bardin stared at Luskell. His eyes widened further and he bit his lip. He shook with silent laughter until he couldn't hold it in, then released a deep, rolling chortle so contagious, Luskell smiled though she wasn't sure what was funny.

Bardin held his sides and slapped the table. "She? A girl! Who wants to be a wizard!" As the fit passed, he wiped his eyes and shook his head. "You had me going there! For a moment, I thought you were ... thought you were ... serious?" He sobered when he met her gaze. She wasn't smiling anymore and blinked back tears. Bardin reached across and patted her hand. "You really meant that? Oh. This isn't about someone you know. It's you, isn't it?" Bardin leaned back and gazed up at the ceiling a moment before he looked Luskell in the eye again. "My dear, I am sure you're quite able in your way, but you're no wizard. Females simply aren't constituted for it. The power required—the learning—it's just too much. You show great fortitude even to ask. I'm sorry. You should go back to Balsam."

Luskell shielded her emotions and kept her face impassive. Dadad had warned her this might happen. "Or maybe I should run for Governor."

"In twenty or thirty years. But even Klanya wasn't elected to the position."

"And the man who was is now in prison for conspiracy and treason." Luskell wanted to add that she'd helped put him there, but then she'd have to include Laki and Jagryn, which in Bardin's eyes would diminish her role. Or eliminate it entirely.

"True. But remember, Klanya is from an old political family. Her father and grandfather served in a number of offices. And did you know she first joined the Legislative Council to complete her husband's term after he died? Even with women voting these past fifty years, not many have been elected to high office."

"I didn't know that," Luskell allowed. "I'm not really interested in politics. But I suppose you could say I'm from an old magical family. So it follows—"

"I'm afraid it doesn't."

Luskell rose from her seat. "Well. Thank you for speaking with me."

"Any time, Luskell. I wish you all the best, and I'm sorry to puncture your ambition."

As Bardin escorted her downstairs, Luskell was already making plans to come back another day and talk to someone else. Dalmer and Fandek looked at her questioningly, but she ignored them. She was on her way to the door when it opened and a different small, bald-headed old man entered. His step was nowhere near as steady as Bardin's. "You! Kitchen girl! Fetch me some tea!" His voice was hoarse, and he broke into a fit of wrenching coughs.

"Slake, she's not—" Bardin began.

Slake staggered against Luskell. By reflex, she caught him. He sagged in her arms and she helped him to a chair by the fire. Even without the cough, the fever heat revealed his illness. With a few words and a swift gesture, she threw a protective charm over herself and everyone else in the room. "He has winter wobbles," she said to Bardin. "Has anyone else been coughing like this?"

"Only Breet, as far as I know."

"To be safe, have everyone use a protective charm when they're in a group. Slake, do you have anyone to take care of you?"

"I live alone," he rasped. "I take care of myself."

"Not today." She reduced his fever and body aches enough that he could walk comfortably a short distance. "I'll take him to Balsam's House."

"No," Bardin said. "Dalmer, you take him. Luskell, come with me. Now."

He gripped her elbow and propelled her up the stairs with surprising energy for someone his size and age. They returned to the upstairs room. This time, he closed the door and resumed his seat at the table. After a moment, Luskell sat, too. She'd thrown a lot of power around and felt unsteady.

Bardin studied her in silence for long enough to make her nervous. She was tempted to read his thoughts, but that was rude. A wizard like Bardin would probably know what she was doing anyway and shut her out if he didn't want her to know. She didn't have to do anything to detect his emotions, but they weren't very revealing. He was both excited and distressed about something, and seemed to wrestle with a difficult decision. Luskell couldn't imagine what any of it had to do with her.

"What did I do? Am I in trouble?"

He smiled and shook his head. "Not at all. I'm sorry I gave that impression." He got up and paced back and forth with his hands clasped behind his back. "It's just that sometimes the thing we're looking for sneaks up from an unexpected direction." He paused and faced her, his hands resting on the table. "This will sound strange. I would like to ask for your help, Luskell. I know I turned down your request, so I won't blame you if you say no. But I hope you won't."

"Help with what?"

"I've been thinking of getting together teams of wizards, or wizards and healers, to go into the more crowded areas of the city and try to protect people from this epidemic."

Luskell picked up the thread. "If fewer people are infected, the disease won't spread as readily."

"Exactly. We could save lives." He resumed his seat. "The reason I haven't started already is that I was thinking of casting the protection over the houses, which is no good if an infected person goes inside. But what you did downstairs—your way is much more effective."

"At Balsam's House, they cast a protective barrier in the doorways," Luskell said. "But those wear out and have to be refreshed all the time. Not that bad when several healers share the work, but it would be hard to keep up on more than one house."

"Yes. Better to protect the people."

"This is exactly the kind of work my mother loves."

"Of course, Ketty would be ideal," Bardin said. "But I was watching downstairs. Without wasting a moment or a motion, you cast a protective charm over seven or eight individuals at once. That's no easy task, and you did it perfectly. I'm impressed."

She warmed under his praise. "Thank you. I'm not much of a healer, but I've been doing that charm a lot lately."

"It was a sensible and caring use of your power. So what do you say?"

"I'm … interested. May I have a moment to think about it?" Luskell closed her eyes briefly while she sought out Dadad's mind and shared a quick summary of the project. He was nearby, so it took little power. She opened her eyes again. "I want to help. You should talk to my father first."

"Perhaps he'll join us. Crane would be an excellent addition to our team."

Luskell nodded and laughed in agreement. "He loves this kind of thing."

"Do you want to talk it over tonight and bring back his answer in the morning?" Bardin asked.

"No need." Luskell stood. "He's waiting downstairs." She pretended not to see Bardin's look of surprise. "So if I do this, does that make me your apprentice?"

"It makes you my temporary assistant, and you should be grateful for that much."

She bit back an argument. Yes, it was unfair that Fandek, with no training or experience, had the chance to be a wizard and she didn't, because of body parts. But at least this was something different. It was still related to healing, but it was outdoors and on a bigger scale. That alone was progress.

CHAPTER NINE

Bardin opened the workroom door and gestured for Luskell to precede him. In the passage, she came face to face with a stout wizard she'd seen around but didn't know, a man of about her father's age. He was taller than Bardin, not as tall as Luskell, with thinning dark hair and a long nose.

He frowned at Luskell. "Bardin, what is the meaning of this? You can't bring your girls here."

"His *girls*?" Luskell exploded. "Who do you think—?"

Bardin stepped between Luskell and the other wizard. "You don't know what you're talking about, Raddys. This is Crane's daughter, Luskell."

Raddys took a step back, flustered. "I beg your pardon, Luskell. My apologies."

Luskell nodded once, too mortified and furious to speak. Now she understood what Bardin had meant by *appearances*. Life was so unfair.

"She has exactly the skills I need for my wobbles project," Bardin continued. "We're on our way to talk to Crane about it now."

"Ah, well, good luck to you," Raddys stammered. "Good to meet you, Luskell." He hurried past them to another workroom.

"Raddys is a good fellow," Bardin said before Luskell could comment otherwise. "Particularly when it comes to taking a boy of ten or eleven and turning him into a competent wizard." They took a few more steps toward the stairs before he paused again. "That said, I wouldn't let him get you alone—wandering hands, I hear. And he seems to believe we're all the same that way."

By the time Luskell and Bardin arrived downstairs, Dadad was warming himself by the fire with Dalmer and Fandek. He towered over them, and with his graying beard and tall staff, looked like the definition of *wizardly*. They listened, Fandek open-mouthed and rapt, Dalmer with explosions of laughter, as he related some story. Luskell heard the word *skunk*, so she was reasonably sure she knew which one. Memories of the comic episode from his youth relieved her vexation with Raddys.

Luskell joined them and Dadad draped an arm around her shoulders. "So, Bardin, I hear you've involved my daughter in one of your schemes."

Fandek stared at them. "He's your—?" At a look from Bardin, he shut his mouth.

Bardin turned his attention back to Dadad. "And you, too, I hope. If it works, I'll put together more teams and cover the whole city."

"I'm happy to help. If you like, I can take these two on my team." He smiled at the two apprentices. "It'll keep them out of trouble while their masters recover."

Bardin glanced at the boys. "Take Dalmer, by all means. I'm not sure how much help Fandek will be. He hasn't even begun his training."

"Then he'll begin it now. Nothing like practical experience to make the theory come alive."

"Will Luskell be with us, too?" Fandek asked.

Bardin raised a bushy eyebrow. "Luskell's with me on this. No distractions."

Fandek deflated. Dalmer smacked him lightly on the back of the head. "You can flirt with girls anytime! Do not say no to the opportunity to work with the greatest wizard in Eukard."

Dadad rolled his eyes. "That's never been proven."

Bardin stood in front of the map of the city. "I'd say here and here to begin." He indicated a neighborhood near the wharves and another in the center of the city. The Garden District.

Dadad nodded. "I lived there once. Lots of rooming houses."

"That's where I used to live," Fandek volunteered.

"Breeding grounds for pestilence," Bardin said. "So, you'll take that one, Crane?"

"No, we'll take the waterfront. Luskell, you know that area pretty well. You could look in at the Osprey, maybe check on Dokral."

Luskell beamed at the thought. "Good, I'd like that. If it's all right?" She turned to Bardin. She had to remember who was in charge of this expedition.

Bardin frowned more than usual. "I don't know—isn't that where they found the most recent strangling victim?"

"The neighborhood's crawling with Guards," Dadad replied. "It's probably the safest place in the city."

Luskell wondered how he knew that, but this wasn't the time to ask.

"In that case, it sounds like an excellent plan," Bardin said. "But it's no good if the charm fades as soon as we leave. Can it be made to last?"

Dadad glanced at Luskell. "I believe Luskell can answer that."

She considered. "It's like a concealment spell, isn't it? You thread extra power in at the end and then cut it off. The extra sustains it after the practitioner leaves."

Surprise and approval mingled in Bardin's expression. It was hard for Luskell not to look smug.

"How much extra?" Fandek asked. His voice shook a little. Waves of excitement and nervousness washed off him, to the point where Luskell had to shield herself or be swept away. She had eagerness enough of her own. She didn't need his.

Dadad smiled. "My father once made an enchantment last eighteen years. I imagine that took most of the power he had available. But we're looking at what? A few days?"

Bardin nodded. "That seems reasonable. Then we can go back and see if it's helping."

It was too late in the day to do any more. They made plans to meet the next morning, and Luskell left the Wizards' Hall with her father.

"So are they going to make you a wizard?" he asked.

"No. But Bardin asked me to be on this project. That feels good."

"I hate to say I told you so, but I'll admit I'm relieved. You don't need to go looking for trouble. This project will be useful and keep you busy."

They crossed the square in companionable silence. The chilly dusk brightened with lamplight that gleamed from windows above the street.

"It's still your birthday—shall we stop at the Otter for supper?" Dadad asked. "That way, neither of us has to cook."

Luskell glanced at the tavern with its welcoming lamplight and inviting aroma. "As long as there's no knife fight."

Dadad guffawed. "I'd stop it before it began." He smiled down at her. "Unless you stopped it first."

"Mamam's the Peacebringer, not me."

They entered the tavern. The place was nearly deserted. True, it was early, but Luskell had expected more of a crowd than the two old men drinking at opposite ends of the long communal table.

"Where is everybody?" she murmured.

"Afraid of the wobbles, or already too sick to go out, I'd guess," Dadad replied. "But it's early. Business will pick up later."

Dadad went to the bar to order food and drink, and chat with Berdona, the tavern-keeper. She was a good source of news in the neighborhood. Luskell secured one of the private tables. She hadn't been to The Otter in a while— not since the supper they gave Jagryn for his eighteenth birthday, about two weeks after his arrival on Long Day.

Luskell had hurried home early that day to surprise him. The summer evening was cool after an earlier hard rain, the air sweet and clean. The sky was bright now that the clouds had cleared, and it wouldn't be truly dark until late.

She found her family getting ready to go down to intercept Jagryn. Dadad carried little Crett, and the four of them went downstairs together. Luskell reached the door as Jagryn stepped out.

His face fell. "I was coming to meet you at Balsam's House. Now we can't ... walk home together." He blushed.

"We're taking you out to The Otter for your birthday, so we can have the whole evening together," Luskell explained. "Come on, I'll race you!"

She took off running. She hoped getting there well ahead of the family would grant an opportunity to give him a birthday kiss. Jagryn laughed and leaped after her. He had the wind to keep up, but her legs were longer. Even running in a dress and avoiding puddles, she arrived at The Otter a few steps ahead. And ran headlong into Laki, who whooped and lifted her off her feet. He was taller even than Dadad, and at twenty, strong and energetic.

Luskell hugged him tight. "What are you doing here?"

"Your mother invited me for Jagryn's birthday, but I was not sure whether I could come." Laki spoke Eukardian fluently, but with the formality and precision of a second language. He set Luskell down and greeted Jagryn in traditional Aklaka fashion, both hands held out palm upward. "Jagryn, my friend. Is it really two years since we saved the world?"

"It wasn't the whole world." Jagryn set his hands on top, palms down; then they switched. "But you're right, it doesn't seem that long." He smiled, but Luskell detected a hint of something that tainted his happiness.

Luskell wrapped an arm around each of them. "Can you believe Laki's been in the city most of the summer, and this is the first time I've seen him?"

Jagryn relaxed a hair. "The Government District isn't so far away, is it?"

"Just far enough to be inconvenient for a quick visit," Laki said. "Especially when our time is not our own."

Luskell's family strolled up. Mamam looked over Luskell and her friends with an approving smile. "I thought this would be a nice reunion for you three. I'm sure it was hard to break up the team just as you were learning to work together."

Luskell took Jagryn and Laki by the hand and led them into the tavern. She seated Jagryn at the head of the communal table, took the place to his right, and had Laki sit across from her. Crett strained in Dadad's arms to go to Luskell, so he passed the baby across the table to her and sat next to Laki.

Mamam sat across from Dadad, next to Luskell. "In case Crett gets fussy," she explained.

Crett stared at Laki with huge green eyes. Laki smiled at him, but the baby hid his face against Luskell's shoulder. "He's shy when he first meets someone," she explained.

"He's still shy with me, and I see him almost every day!" Jagryn said. "You'd hardly know he was the same baby from a year ago."

Mamam stroked Crett's hand. "It's the age. A tiny newborn is very different from a one-year-old."

Crett peeped around at Jagryn, who covered his eyes with his hands. When he uncovered them, the baby giggled, and the game was on.

"He's a good-looking fellow," Laki said. "Well, how could he not be, with Luskell's coloring and Aketnan's eyes? And that hair ..." His foot brushed Luskell's ankle under the table. She moved her foot to give him room and that was the end of it, but she enjoyed the memory of that fleeting touch more than she would have admitted to anyone who asked.

Luskell ruffled Crett's fine, red-gold curls. "He was born bald, but we all sort of hoped he'd get the red hair. It's lighter than Ketwyn's, but—"

Mamam flinched. Although Luskell thought of her brother as a lighthearted young man who sometimes visited her dreams, to her mother, Ketwyn would always be the newborn son who didn't live through his first day. Mamam managed a smile. "I'm glad someone got my eyes."

Jagryn finished his game with Crett and dropped his hands into his lap. His right hand found Luskell's left under the table and gave it a squeeze. She glanced at him with a half-smile. His touch was different from Laki's, but as welcome. Although he had kissed her a number of times by now, he rarely touched her when people were around. He smiled back and released her hand.

"Happy birthday, Jagryn," Laki said. "You are eighteen, yes?"

Jagryn nodded.

"You are a man now?"

"I guess so. I don't feel any different."

Laki grinned. "But you'll be a wizard soon! Even better."

Then the food came and changed the subject for everyone. Supper was a whole roasted fish with fresh peas and new potatoes, with a bowl of sweet cherries for dessert. Mugs of good ale further mellowed Jagryn's mood. Laki had a few sips to be polite, then set his mug aside. Like most of his people, he had a low tolerance for strong drink, but didn't need it to be sociable. By the end of the evening, Jagryn and Laki were chatting happily about magic and everything they'd been doing for two years.

"Will you stay in the city now?" Laki asked.

Jagryn sighed and shook his head. "No, I promised I'd go back to Deep River after the summer; see how I like being a country wizard."

Dadad smiled. "That was supposed to be my job." Luskell thought he gave off a wisp of regret, but it was gone before she could be sure.

"Deep River's too small for you," Jagryn said. "It might suit me, though." He turned back to Laki. "What's next for you?"

"We should be finished here in a few days. Then we will meet our band on the Dry Side for the rest of the summer." He winked at Luskell. "Mamam hopes to find me a wife."

Jagryn frowned and Luskell flustered. She tried to hide it behind a bright smile. "Good luck. Maybe you'll have someone to warm you this winter."

Laki shook his head. "Next winter, at the earliest. At Fall Balance, I start my half-year in Knot's Valley."

Dadad joined the conversation. "It's a beautiful spot. Not a place I'd want to spend the winter, but my father was there for twenty-five of them."

"I will not give my life to it," Laki replied. "But after a season of diplomacy, it will be nice to be alone."

After supper, Laki had to go straight back to his father's apartment at Embassy House, in the opposite direction from the rest of the group. Luskell, remembering the one kiss he'd given her, longed to kiss him good night. But not in front of everybody, so she settled for another hug.

The sun had finally set, but the summer twilight lingered. Mamam and Dadad hurried home to put Crett to bed, while Luskell and Jagryn lagged behind.

"Nice to see Laki again," Jagryn allowed. "I'd forgotten he was so—"

"Tall?" Luskell giggled. She'd finished Laki's ale as well as her own.

Jagryn frowned. "Confident. Like a grown-up."

"He's been a grown-up for a few years, remember? And he was raised that way, to be a leader. But now you're a man, too."

Jagryn nodded. "He makes me feel like a little boy. How can I compete?"

"Compete for what?" Luskell shook her head. "You'll be a wizard, he'll be Uklak. How many people get to be either?"

He didn't offer an answer, but she didn't expect one. She slipped her hand into his and they walked the rest of the way in silence. At the bottom of the stairs, he gave her a long kiss. She enjoyed it. But she still half-wished she could have kissed Laki. Not instead. Too.

CHAPTER TEN

"They have roast pork tonight," Dadad announced when he joined Luskell at their table. "You like parsnips, don't you? And I thought mulled wine would be nice on a chilly night."

Luskell pulled herself back from her summer memories to the present winter evening. "It all sounds better than anything I'd throw together."

"You do fine. But your birthday deserves a treat. Too bad Jagryn and Laki couldn't be here."

Luskell wondered if he'd taken a peek at her thoughts, but she couldn't ask without revealing she'd been thinking about them. A dark-haired boy a few years younger than Luskell brought two plates of pork and parsnips, followed by mugs of hot spiced wine.

Dadad smiled at the boy. "Thank you, Druner."

Druner gave him a bashful grin. "I should thank you, sir. If not for you, I'd probably still be picking pockets and trying to care for myself. As it is, I've got a home and honest work." With a small bow, he returned to the kitchen.

Luskell had to smile about that. Dadad had a knack for finding people who needed help and doing what he could for them, even when it didn't require magic.

Father and daughter spent a few moments in quiet appreciation of the good food and drink.

"Oh, I almost forgot. This came for you." Dadad handed Luskell a sealed letter.

Luskell set down her fork, broke the seal and read silently.

Dear Luskell,

Maybe I won't be a wizard, after all. My quest is supposed to be about visiting the dead, but so far, no luck. I want to talk to my great-grandmother, Elika. You made it sound so easy! Help?

Jagryn

Her heart warmed, though the letter was short and impersonal. It was the first word from her friend in a long time.

"What does Jagryn have to say?"

She scowled and shielded her mind. "Don't read my thoughts!"

Dadad patted her hand. "I wouldn't. He wrote his name on the outside."

"Oh. Well, his plan to visit the Other Side isn't going very well and he asks my advice. Am I allowed to give it?"

"You can share your technique. I don't know anyone else who can do what you do, so it might not work for him. Then again, it might give him the direction he needs."

They finished supper and walked home. It wasn't all that late, but dark already on this longest night of the year. The streets were quiet, and Luskell wondered about Dadad's prediction that the tavern would fill up later.

As soon as they got home, Luskell lit a lamp and sat in the rocking chair to reach out to Jagryn. She knew he couldn't reply from this distance and wasn't sure how much he would receive, but it seemed important to let him know right away that she wanted to help. She sought him in Deep River and found him easily. His mind was familiar, though not exactly as she remembered it. That made sense. They were both older and learning all kinds of new things.

> *Jagryn! I got your letter about your quest. I want to help if I can. It's too much to send this way, so I'll write a letter. If you manage it before my letter comes, Knot always warns me not to stay too long. I don't know why, but be careful.*

She moved to the table to write her reply. Over the summer, she and Jagryn had amused themselves by trying to write in the polished, overly tactful manner of the city's politicians and diplomats. She began that way out of habit:

> My dear friend,
>   I hope this letter finds you well. It is my great pleasure to offer advice on your daring quest. I will try to elucidate my method ...

The tone seemed wrong for this letter. She took a fresh sheet and began again:

> Dear Jagryn,

Dadad says I may offer advice, so here it is. I hope it helps. I have never gone to the Other Side except in dreams, so I guess you need to be asleep. It is easiest when the dead visit me; I don't have to do anything! But you can't control or predict that. To go to them, I think about the person I want to see in as much detail as I can before I fall sleep. It helps to imagine a warm, bright meadow where you can't see the sun. If you want to visit Elika, you might use her house, if it's available. You'll have to sleep there, but I know you're not afraid of ghosts. (Yes, I know it was never really haunted. It was a joke.) If you get to the Other Side, don't stay too long.

I finished my contract with Balsam today. Tomorrow I start something new. I'll tell you about it when there's something to tell.
Love,
Luskell

Luskell blotted the ink and sealed the letter. "There. I hope it helps."

"I'm sure Jagryn will be glad to hear from you, regardless." Dadad stretched his legs toward the stove. "What about a tune before bed?"

"I'm out of practice," Luskell warned, but went to get her fiddle from the shelf. She kept it in the front room where it was warmer.

"I won't criticize," Dadad promised. "I like to hear you play, no matter what."

Luskell tuned the instrument. She had hardly played at all this winter and doubted she could do justice to the quick dance numbers that made up most of her repertoire. She chose an old ballad, the first tune she'd ever learned to play. It went at a gentle walking tempo, with a simple, poignant melody. Even without its verses of love and loss, the tune alone could bring a listener to tears.

Luskell felt only a deep joy in the music. Although vexed at off notes, she refused to let it ruin her delight in hearing her fiddle's voice again, in drawing music out of wood, horsehair, and sheep-gut. There was as much magic there as in wizardry, and she promised herself to play every day.

Dadad blinked and wiped his eyes. "Cheerful selection for your birthday."

"Klamamam sings it." As with her parents, Luskell had always called her paternal grandmother by the Aklaka term. She returned the fiddle and bow to their shelf. "Anyway, I need to get my speed back before I try anything else."

"It was lovely. Dokral would be proud."

Luskell kissed Dadad good night and went to her freezing room, where she undressed quickly and shivered under the covers. She lay awake a long time. She was used to falling asleep to healers' conversations and voices from the streets. Tonight, it was too quiet. People were afraid to go out. But somewhere, some woman had to go out for whatever reason. And the strangler was out there, waiting for her.

Luskell shook herself and snuggled deeper under the covers. The strangler probably wouldn't strike tonight. He never took more than one victim at a time, and then dropped out of sight for days or weeks. But there was something worse out there—the wobbles. Hundreds or even thousands were down with it, and many of them died every day.

That was no way to get to sleep. It didn't help that Bardin's project excited her more than she'd let on, even if he wouldn't make her a wizard. She had an idea of someone who might, but she needed to sleep in order to talk to him.

As her bed grew warmer, Luskell relaxed. She quieted her mind and focused her thoughts on a tall, dark man with long, curly white hair, a bushy beard, and deep blue eyes like hers. When she was ready, she allowed herself to drift toward sleep and soon found herself on the Other Side.

Luskell was alone in the broad, rolling green meadow. A steep slope dropped away behind her. In the distance, a low hill rose and blocked her view of whatever lay beyond. She had never been past this spot, nor seen more than four or five people together. Now a tall figure approached from the crest of the hill. He moved faster as he neared her, and then he was there. He gripped a fire-blackened staff.

"Kladadad," she whispered, using the Aklaka child's term for grandfather. He wrapped her in his almost insubstantial embrace. "I held your staff."

"You found it for me."

"Maybe I'll have my own one day."

"I believe you will. But why have you come?"

Luskell stepped back from Knot. "Aren't you glad to see me?"

"Always. But you don't belong here."

He'd said that before, or something like it, but was it true? She could come to the Other Side so easily, and it was always pleasant and comfortable. It was a place to meet people she loved.

"Is this place real?" she asked.

Knot patted his beard as he looked around. "You're dreaming and I'm dead, so who knows? It's as real as anything, I guess."

"How can it be so empty?" Luskell gestured at the broad meadow. "You'd think it'd be crowded, with everyone who's ever died."

Knot glanced around. "This is only the entryway, where people cross over. But the rest is big enough for who's here. It's not everybody."

"What do you mean?"

"As long as a person is remembered by someone living, their spirit abides here. Once they're really forgotten, they fade away."

"That's terrible!"

"Not really. We watch over our loved ones. When there's no one left to remember, there's no one left to watch, and nothing left to do."

"But what if I'm the last one to remember you?" Luskell asked. "Do you mean to say when I die, you won't be here anymore?"

"That'll be a long time, I'm sure. Maybe you won't need me so much. Anyway, those with stories about them seem to last the longest. King Braffin is still around, after centuries. Of course, he has all of Eukard to watch over."

"Klamamam still tells those old Yrae stories sometimes." Luskell wondered if it was too late to make up stories about her brother Ketwyn. Hardly anyone had known him, so how could they remember him?

Knot rested his hand on her shoulder. "It was good to see you, but you've lingered long enough."

"Just a little longer," she begged. "You say I don't belong here, but maybe I don't belong anywhere! I don't have much talent for healing, but I can't find a master to make me a wizard."

Knot smiled gently. "You'll find one. Be patient."

"Maybe I already have." She grinned. "You could teach me!"

He grew solemn. "You know I can't."

"Oh, right. The family thing." Luskell nodded. "What about your master? If he's here, he could do it! You could introduce me, and I'd have a chance to look around, and—"

Knot shook his head. "Ordahn is still here, but no, Luskell. The dead can't teach the living."

Luskell frowned. "You bring us messages."

"Yes, brief things you might not even remember when you wake. So how would you practice magic in your sleep? How could we possibly make your staff?"

Luskell glanced at the staff in his hand. Knot followed her gaze.

"It has no power anymore. It's just a ... souvenir." He squeezed her shoulder. "If I have a message for you, I'll bring it, I promise. Now go." He kissed the top of her head.

The dream faded and shifted into something she couldn't remember when she woke. And she still had no master.

CHAPTER ELEVEN

The stove rattled and clanked in the next room. Luskell wanted to stay under the covers and go back to sleep. Her window was dark, but the sound of her father building the fire signaled morning. The other room would soon be warm, and eagerness for Bardin's project overcame most of her sleepiness.

The window showed a clear, starry sky, but thick fog rose with the sun. The light went gray as Luskell ate breakfast with Dadad.

"We should carry lunch with us," he said. "This project of Bardin's could take all day."

Luskell wrapped up bread, cheese, and dried apples for each of them, and tucked her parcel into an inner pocket of her cloak. They went out into fog that flowed through the streets like a river. Other people passed like shadows.

Bardin, Dalmer, and Fandek waited for them in the warm common room. Dadad let Luskell explain how to cast the protective charm over multiple individuals. They practiced until even Fandek could perform it perfectly.

Dadad bestowed an approving smile on the young man. "You show great promise."

Fandek beamed at Luskell. All her tiredness left her and she was filled with such charitable feelings, she forgot she didn't like Fandek and didn't want to encourage him. Before she could stop herself, she smiled back. She quickly turned to Dalmer with a trivial comment on technique.

Nobody wanted to leave the snug Hall, but when they'd finished their practice, Dadad took the boys and headed toward the wharves. Luskell lost sight of them before they were even across the square. She and Bardin headed for the Garden District, about an hour's walk south. At least, an hour's walk at Luskell's usual pace. Although spry for his age, Bardin was an old man with short legs who leaned on his staff and walked more slowly. In the oppressive fog, it felt like they weren't moving at all. More than once Luskell found herself a few steps ahead.

"Sorry. I'm used to walking with my father. When I was a child, I had to run to keep up."

"I have no trouble believing that," Bardin said. "The man has a long stride and walks with purpose."

Luskell tried to match his pace but soon found herself half a block ahead again. While she waited for him him to catch up, someone touched her shoulder.

"Hello, my dear," a vaguely familiar voice purred. "Lost in the fog?"

Luskell hadn't even heard the man approach. She jabbed an elbow into his soft midsection and ducked away. He stumbled back with a sharp "Oof!" and sat down in the street. His hood fell away from his face.

Luskell peered at the revealed face. "Hey, I know you! From the Wizards' Hall."

He stared up at her. "Oh, of course. You're Crane's daughter, aren't you?" He pressed a hand to his middle. "What was that for?"

"I … don't like to be touched without warning."

"Sounds like the voice of experience." The wizard massaged his ribs, then clambered to his feet. "I'm sorry I didn't recognize you in the fog. What a morning, eh?"

Bardin caught up then. "What a morning, indeed. Hello, Raddys. Are you meeting your new apprentice today?"

"I'm on my way now. Good day to you both."

Luskell watched Raddys disappear into the fog, then turned and walked on with Bardin. She wasn't usually jumpy, but Raddys had given her a scare. It must have been all that talk of a strangler. Raddys's reputation didn't help, though his hands seemed too small. Not that he couldn't use a rope or something. But would the strangler strike during daylight?

Luskell soon wearied of the slow pace. "We'd get there faster if we flew. We're not carrying much."

Bardin stared at her, and his perpetual frown deepened. "I … you … "

Luskell smiled and changed into a pigeon.

Transformation to birds or animals was a useful skill, with a few drawbacks. You couldn't perform other spells at the same time, it took a lot of physical energy, and you had to travel light. But Luskell had eaten a good breakfast and carried lunch in her pocket.

She had to fly higher than she'd hoped to get out of the fog, but the sunshine was worth it. Below her, the thick mist flowed and swirled., hiding the streets and landmarks that would have guided her. She circled, uncertain, her brilliant idea seeming more like a mistake. How would she find her way? Another bird flapped hard to catch up. It had a twig in its beak—Bardin and his staff.

Bardin's presence calmed Luskell's worry. Either he trusted her or he was willing to help if she needed it. Luskell couldn't see the streets or houses, so she paid attention to what she could see. Things looked different, but the city itself hadn't changed. It was only hidden. The highest hills made islands in the fog. Luskell oriented on their familiar shapes and used them to navigate to the right place. She came down through the fog and fluttered to a landing in front of the tall green house where Dokral had his instrument shop. She changed back and sat on the front step to catch her breath.

Bardin reappeared beside her. He wheezed several times before he could speak. "A long time since I've done that."

"Me, too." Luskell finger-combed her hair and did her best to braid it. "Six months, at least."

He raised an eyebrow. "How long have you been able to transform?"

"Two years? No, two and a half. My friend Laki taught me." She pulled the food packet from her cloak.

"You speak of it so casually, as if it were a game or a common task. Yet I know wizards three times your age who never mastered transformation. You're lucky I was able to keep up." Bardin stared into the fog, then glanced at her sidelong with a grudging smile. "You are a most unusual girl."

"Thank you." Luskell grinned and ate part of her lunch. After a moment, she offered some bread and cheese to Bardin.

He accepted it gratefully, and they munched in silence for a time.

"My father does the same thing you do with his staff," Luskell commented. "How does that work? I've never been able to carry anything that wasn't in my pockets."

"A wizard's staff is not merely a thing. It's a part of him." Bardin accepted a dried apple and chewed thoughtfully. "Why did you choose to be a pigeon?"

"It's a common city bird, so it blends in. Excellent eyesight, good sense of direction—"

Bardin nodded. "Good reasons, I suppose. But a pigeon is prey. What if a falcon comes along?"

The blood drained out of Luskell's head and she was glad to be sitting down already. If a falcon dived at her, would she know about it in time to get out of the way? And if she did, what could she do about it? Changing back in midair wasn't any better than being clobbered by a diving falcon. "I ... never thought about it. Is it likely a falcon would be hunting in this fog?"

"I have no more idea than you do. That kind of rashness can get you killed." Bardin's features softened into a smile. "I know it's difficult not to use such a talent. Just be careful."

Luskell remembered Dadad's comment about raw talent being responsible for his scarred hand. "I'll try. Thanks for risking it with me."

"I wasn't going to let you have all the fun. And you were right; we saved significant time."

It was only mid-morning, but between them, they finished all of Luskell's lunch. She scattered the crumbs for some real pigeons and stood up. "While we're here, let's say hello to Dokral and make sure he's well."

"Who is this Dokral?" Bardin asked. "A fellow magic user?"

"A family friend. And my fiddle teacher."

"Music, too? The surprises never cease."

A bell jingled as Luskell opened the door. The shop smelled of cut wood and varnish. Racks of stringed instruments lined the walls, but the shop appeared empty. "Hello?"

A man appeared from a back room. "May I help you? Oh, Luskell!" He clasped both her hands in his and swung her around in a jaunty dance step. He released her and grabbed a fiddle off a rack. "I've just finished this one—try it out." Luskell took the instrument and fussed with the tuning. Dokral picked up another and plucked a few notes. "'Blacksmith's Courtship,' what do you say?"

He launched into the rollicking dance tune, and Luskell tried to keep up. "I'm out of practice. Can we take it slower?"

Dokral laughed and started again at a tempo that was still lively, but playable. He played lead while Luskell took the second part, and this time she was able to finish.

"Not bad. Think how you'd sound if you practiced." Dokral nodded toward Bardin. "Who's your friend?"

"This is Wizard Bardin. You haven't met? I thought you knew everyone."

"Heard the name, but no, we haven't been introduced. How d'you do?" Dokral stuck out his hand.

Bardin shook it. "Very well, thank you." He looked around at the racks of instruments. "So this is your place?"

"It is, but not much business these days, with the concert halls closed and the dances canceled." Dokral shot a pointed look at Luskell. "And the parents too afraid to send their children out for lessons."

"It's not that." Luskell returned the fiddle to its rack. "I've been working. I'm working now, in fact. We're trying to do something about the winter wobbles. Is it bad down here?"

"Is it ever! I had a mild case early on, so I've been able to help some, but there's a lot of folks I'm worried about, especially with Rasana gone."

"And Rasana is ...?" Bardin asked.

"Was," Dokral corrected him. "Local midwife, strangled the other night down by the Garden. Terrible loss to the neighborhood. Not a lot of magic, but she took good care of everyone, not only the mothers and babies." He glanced at Luskell. "I'm glad you're not down here alone."

"I hope we're safe enough in daylight. How are they at the Osprey?" Luskell asked.

"Better than most. Ambug never catches anything, and Ellys had the same kind of mild case I did. So she's been feeding everybody, taking them soup and what have you."

Luskell nodded. "That makes me feel better. Most people will recover with rest, as long as they're warm and well fed."

Dokral explained to them where the illness seemed to be worst and where it hadn't spread yet. Luskell and Bardin thanked him and went out to the neighborhood to put their idea into action. They stopped outside a two-story brick rooming house across the street from Dokral's. Rags stuffed the gap in a broken upstairs window.

Bardin pointed it out. "Good luck staying warm in there."

Luskell closed her eyes and tried to sense the health of the inhabitants. To diagnose a specific disease, she would have to be near the patient, but it was relatively simple to detect the general presence of illness. To the healer's senses, it was like a smell—one whiff and you knew. Luskell's sense was sharp from her recent experience at Balsam's House.

"Good, no infections here." Luskell cast the protective charm over the twelve people she sensed within, adding a push of power to make the protection last. The charm itself was easy to work and required only a little power to cast on one person, but multiplied and enhanced, it was another story. The warmth inside her increased to a blaze, and the tingle in her hands sharpened to an exquisite ache. When she finished, she leaned against the wall of the house to rest.

"Are you all right?" Bardin asked.

"I'll be fine; healing just takes a lot out of me. You want to do the next one?"

They moved on, house by house, sharing the work so each had a chance to recover. In the first several houses, everyone was either uninfected or had already recovered, and Luskell began to think they'd have an easy day. Then it was her turn again and she recoiled at a strong stink of illness.

"Phew! I think there's a whole family down with it."

It took Bardin longer to sense it; then his nose wrinkled. "I see what you mean. Well, we'd better protect the rest of them."

"And then we should go inside."

"I thought you didn't like healing," Bardin said.

"*Like* has nothing to do with it. It's what my mother would do. It's what my father most likely is doing, and he's no better at healing than I am. But we might be able to help these people."

Bardin's frown deepened. "We're here to protect the well. We don't have time to cure the sick."

"I wish I had the power to cure them!" Luskell exclaimed. "I just want to make sure they're not dying. Go on ahead; I'll catch up."

"Oh, no. We're a team, and you've a tendency for rashness. I'm coming with you." He renewed the protection on himself.

Luskell cast protection over herself and the ten healthy people within. Together, they entered the house and followed the stink of sickness to its source. She knocked on a door.

"Coming," a feeble voice answered. A baby cried. A young woman opened the door. Her face was pale and drawn, and her unbound hair hung in stringy clumps around her face. She held a fussing infant. "Yes?"

Luskell wasn't sure how to explain her project. "We're ... checking on people in the neighborhood who are down with the wobbles. Do you have someone to look after you?"

The woman shook her head. "I'm getting better, so I do the looking after. My husband and my mother are both sicker than I was." She stroked the baby's head. "Rasana was going to bring something for the little one's fever. I don't know what's keeping her."

Luskell closed her eyes a moment. So much bad news. "Rasana can't make it today, but maybe I can help." She laid her hand on the baby's burning head. Fever could be helpful, but this was dangerous. She used a fever charm to bring it down, as well as a pain charm to soothe the aches.

The baby stopped crying and rooted against his mother. She sat down to feed him. Luskell checked on the other two members of the family. Both were sick but out of danger as long as they stayed warm and well fed.

"I'll send someone with fresh food for you," Luskell promised the young mother.

When they left that house, it was past noon and the fog had thinned to reveal the sun's pale disc. Luskell's stomach rumbled, and she thought longingly of the lunch she had eaten earlier. She let Bardin take care of the next house. It wasn't far to the Osprey.

The tavern was smaller than the Otter, comfortably crowded with hams and onions hanging from the beams.

Ellys the tavern-keeper, a plump little woman with graying hair, looked up from the bar when Luskell and Bardin entered. She smiled a welcome and came around the bar to hug Luskell. "What brings you down here?" Ellys was another old family friend, and Luskell had often stayed with her and her son Ambug when her parents had business that didn't include young children.

"Wizard Bardin and I are trying to protect people from the wobbles, and help out those who are already sick," Luskell explained. She mentioned the family nearby. "I hear you're feeding people, and I think they could use some help."

"By all means. Ambug!" Ellys called.

A solid block of a young man with thick, pale hair appeared from a back room. "Yes'm?" When he saw Luskell, he grinned all over. "I almost didn't recognize you, little girl!"

Luskell stepped up to him. "Who's little?" She was a shade taller, but he was almost twice as wide.

"Bug, I need you to take a pot of that soup to some sick folks. See if their neighbors will look in on them." Ellys gave him the directions and with another smile at Luskell, he disappeared into the kitchen and reappeared with a steaming pot that he carried outside.

"Do you two have time for lunch?" Ellys asked.

Luskell glanced at Bardin, who nodded. "I'll say. We can't do much good when we're starving."

After the restorative meal, they continued their rounds of the neighborhood.

"Just how many sweethearts do you have?" Bardin asked when they were out of earshot of the tavern.

Luskell glanced at him. "None. Why?"

"That young man didn't seem to think so."

"Ambug? He's an old friend. His mother used to watch me sometimes when I was little. Ambug gave me horsey rides and took me to Braffin's Garden to play. I've hardly seen them at all since I've been back in town."

Bardin snorted in a manner wholly unpersuaded and Luskell didn't bother to argue. Her friends were none of his business.

Again, when they found someone ill, they cast the protective charm on everyone, then went inside to see what could be done for the sick person. Usually it was a matter of easing aches or fever to make the person comfortable enough to rest. Luskell's mother was capable of effecting a complete cure if she caught it early enough, though in Grandpa's case, the damage had been done before she got there. Neither Luskell nor Bardin had that kind of power available if they wanted to help more than a few people. The best they could do with the sickest was refer them to Balsam's House for care.

They kept it up until late afternoon, house by house and street by street. It was a long, tiring day, eased by the satisfaction of helping people who really needed it. Towards sunset, they came alongside Braffin's Garden. As Dadad had predicted, there was a heavy Guard presence. Luskell wondered again how he knew, but took comfort in the many tall plumed hats and dark red tunics. As she passed the entrance to the garden, she halted with a sharp intake of breath.

"What is it?" Bardin asked.

"This is where Rasana was murdered. Right here."

Bardin glanced up and down the street. There was no visible difference between this spot and any other nearby. "How can you tell?"

"Violence leaves an emotional trace. I'm sensitive."

"Can you tell who did it?" Bardin lost his weariness and grew alert, more interested in Luskell's abilities than he'd been since she transformed.

"No. I feel the victim's terror. And ..." Luskell shuddered. "Ugh. The killer's satisfaction—a job well done, I guess. Let's get out of here."

"It's time we were getting back, anyway," Bardin said. "It'll be dark soon. But let's walk this time."

"All right." Luskell was secretly relieved. Flying was faster, but it took a lot of power and she had next to nothing left.

"At my pace. I want to talk to you."

Luskell couldn't think what she might have done to upset him. She waited for him to catch up. "Whatever it is, I'm sorry."

His frown lifted into a slight smile. "You have nothing to be sorry for. But I can see why you won't be a healer."

"You can?" She wasn't sure whether to be insulted or not.

"You have good instincts and the right knowledge and training. You're generous—I might say heedless—with your power. But you're right when you say you lack natural aptitude. And you're restless, impatient, and a little too selfish. Well, maybe that's the age. But ..."

"But what?"

"I shouldn't even think this! What would Ordahn say?"

Luskell stopped in the street. "You knew Ordahn?"

"He was my master. Why, how do you know of him?"

"He was my grandfather's master!"

"Your grandfather? Who was he? Maybe I knew him, too."

Luskell hesitated over which name to give. "He was called Knot at the end. But Ordahn knew him as the Crane."

Bardin considered this, and smiled. "You know, now that I think of it, he sometimes spoke of his former apprentice. The Crane was a tough act to follow. But now I know why your father's name seemed familiar. And why you are what you are."

"What am I?"

"You have the power and the temperament of ... a wizard."

"And yet you won't recommend a master for me."

"No. I couldn't do that." They walked on a few steps. "But if you will allow me to change my mind ..." He stopped and turned toward her. " ... I want you to be my apprentice."

Luskell threw her arms around the old man. "Of course I will! How do we start?"

"First, you let me go. This is not appropriate." He backed away a few steps and straightened his cloak. "We'll start with a test of what you've learned. I warn you, you'll have to do some tasks with other apprentices. They may not be so easily persuaded."

"I'm not afraid of boys."

"I didn't suppose you would be. But I suspect you'll have to be twice as good to earn half the credit."

She crossed her arms. "I can't wait."

He raised an eyebrow and a corner of his mouth with it. "Yes, well ... being in a rush isn't always a good trait in a wizard. I may ask you to slow down, if only for my sake."

When they returned to the Wizards' Hall, Dadad was standing by the door.

"You didn't have to wait for me," Luskell said.

"I haven't been here long. The boys just went home, or in Fandek's case, to the kitchen. And it'll be dark soon." Dadad turned to Bardin. "How are you after a day with Luskell?"

"Worn out." Bardin turned to Luskell. "In fact, I've changed my mind. Do you want to tell him or should I?"

"Uh oh; what did she do?"

Luskell scowled. Why did he assume it was something bad?

"Elbowed Raddys off his feet, then turned into a pigeon without first checking that I could keep up."

"I apologize; I know she's headstrong, but—"

"No apology needed. With your permission, I'd like to take Luskell as my apprentice."

Dadad smiled, one eyebrow raised. "Does she need my permission?"

"I wouldn't want to be on your bad side."

Luskell had only seen a glimpse of anything like Dadad's bad side. Thankfully, directed at someone else. She didn't want to be on it, either.

Dadad grinned. "This should be interesting. I hope neither of you regrets it. When will you start?"

"Tomorrow?" Luskell asked with a hopeful glance at Bardin.

"Always in a hurry. Yes, all right. I'll meet you here tomorrow morning."

As she walked home with Dadad, the long day caught up with Luskell. She half-listened as he told about his day with Dalmer and Fandek. "... hasn't had much in the way of real training yet, but he has a lot of natural ability. You saw how he picked up the protective charm right away. And he's drawn to distress."

"No, you are and he followed you."

"I don't think so. He was right more often than he was wrong. How did it go for you?"

"Same as for Bardin—I'm tired out." Something he'd said came back to her. "Speaking of people drawn to distress, we passed the spot where that midwife was killed, and I picked up traces of emotion. The strangler was pleased with his work. Disgusting."

"Hm." He considered longer than seemed necessary for such a minor anecdote, then shook himself. "I'm sorry you had to go through that. Maybe I should have taken the Garden District."

"It's all right. But I wish Mamam were here to help us. She would have done more good with less effort."

"True. Your grandpa needs her more, though, and you proved yourself more than capable. You obviously impressed Bardin. Do you think you'll like working with him?"

"He's not you, but he's better than Raddys or Larem. I'll be a wizard in no time."

CHAPTER TWELVE

If Luskell dreamed that night, she didn't remember. She woke from a solid, restoring sleep, ready for Bardin to make her a wizard.

Her father joined her as she prepared to go out. "Just a moment; I'll go with you." He lifted his cloak off the peg and put it on.

"I don't need an escort, you know."

Dadad smiled. "It's no trouble. I have business in the neighborhood. If you prefer, I won't see you all the way to the door. I'm still not sure I approve, but I know you want to do this yourself."

"Thank you." When they met up the evening before, she'd been too exhausted to think much about what lay ahead, but now ideas bubbled up. "For my staff, do you think maple would be better, or chestnut? Or maybe cedar?"

Dadad nudged her shoulder with the top of his own walnut staff. "No one could accuse you of a lack of confidence, but don't get ahead of yourself. It's only your first day."

"The apprenticeship might be more of a formality. I know everything Jagryn knows and I have more raw power. I should be able to skip right to the quest."

Dadad stopped in front of the Otter. "That's not for me to decide. Go see what your master has to say about it."

Luskell gave him a quick hug and hurried across the square to the Wizards' Hall. This time, she walked in without knocking. Bardin was waiting for her in the common room.

"Good morning, Luskell. You're early—I like that."

She grinned. "Let's get started!"

It was all she could do not to run up the stairs, but she let Bardin lead the way. He showed her into a workroom; not the same one as before, but they were all basically alike. A number of objects lay on the table—stones, wooden blocks, kitchen implements, candle stubs. He sat and gestured for her to take the other seat.

Luskell sighed. "Door open?"

"Door open. And from now on, you will address me as Master, Master Bardin, or Sir."

"What?" Luskell had never been that formal with anyone in her life. "Yesterday we were practically partners!"

"And today you're my apprentice. So unless you'd like to cancel that arrangement, you will abide by my rules. Agreed?"

"All right ... I mean, yes, sir." Luskell took her seat and tried not to sulk. "What do you want me to do first?"

"I've already seen some of what you can do. We'll start with what you know. Did Crane teach you the theory, or only the spells?"

Luskell crossed her arms and sat back. "He taught me everything he taught Jagryn. Test me. Sir."

"Very well. List the rules of magic."

"What, all of them?" Luskell shuffled through her memory of these so-called rules. Some were simple and obvious, while others seemed too idealistic to have ever been strictly observed. "Magic is a gift. Use it for good," she recited. "Magic is a tool, not a toy. Use it wisely. Respect all forms and users of the Gift, no matter how small. Do not look down upon those without the Gift. Treat them kindly."

Bardin gave her a rare smile. "These are Ordahn's words."

"My father taught us from a little book that his father made when he studied with Ordahn."

"I made one, also. See, I have it with me." Bardin produced it, and flicked through a few pages.

"The same words," Luskell said. "But Knot's was illustrated. He drew the pictures himself."

"There are all kinds of gifts," Bardin allowed. "So, go on."

Luskell recited more rules and theories about magical power. "Our magic is fueled by our physical strength, so when we're sick or injured, our magical ability is weakened, too."

"Or merely fatigued, as we saw yesterday," Bardin added. "So it's important to stay healthy and fit, don't do more than you can safely recover from, and try to avoid injury if you can."

"Well, that's good sense, anyway, isn't it?" Luskell asked. "But, Bardin—Master—if magic is tied to physical strength, why isn't the bigger person always the stronger in magic? You know my mother. She's tiny, but I suspect she has more power than anyone. Dadad thinks so, too."

Bardin nodded. "I'm not so big myself, and Ordahn was smaller. Maybe it has to do with how big you are on the inside." He let her think about that a moment, then got back to business. "What can you tell me about responsible use of power?"

"Obviously, don't hurt anyone if you can avoid it." But was it obvious? Trenn had cursed a knife and used it for no reason other than chaos and distraction. Luskell had wanted to kill him, and might have, had Dadad not intervened. "What if someone uses their magic to do harm? Or kill?"

"Ah. You mean not by accident, or in self-defense. If he's caught, he'd be temporarily stripped of his power and tried by a panel of wizards. If he's found guilty of murder or other serious crime, the loss of power is made permanent and he's turned over to civil authorities."

Luskell's stomach lurched. That sounded like a more formal version of what had happened to Trenn, except he'd chosen to take his own life rather than go to prison. And if she had succeeded in killing him herself?

She swallowed and nodded. "Good to know. So, responsible use of power. You can use magic to stop someone from doing harm, but not to make them do something against their nature or will." Luskell frowned. "What about love spells, then? Or is that not real magic?"

Bardin chuckled. "We may never know. You shouldn't use a love spell for yourself, or on someone who wouldn't be susceptible, anyway; but if they were susceptible, how would you know the spell did anything?"

"I wonder how much anyone doing that kind of magic follows the rule," Luskell said.

"They tend not to be wizards. They might not even know there is such a rule."

"I don't plan to go into that line of work, anyway. Now what?" When Bardin didn't immediately respond, except with a raised eyebrow, Luskell tried again. "Now what, sir?"

"I think we could both use a practical demonstration. How are you at illusions?"

In answer, Luskell produced a stem of lupine that changed into a cloud of blue butterflies. Her lupine had no scent, and she had never achieved the kind of choreography that Jagryn was capable of, but as her signature, the butterflies exploded in fireworks at the end.

"Pretty," Bardin said without much expression. "Finding?"

"It's in the box."

"I beg your pardon?"

"It's in the box, sir?"

Bardin closed his eyes. It was obvious he was trying not to laugh. "No, I mean what's in what box?"

"The handkerchief is in this box." Luskell reached for what appeared to be a solid wooden block and lifted off the top. A folded handkerchief lay inside.

Bardin's expression settled back to his customary frown. "Did I ask you to find a handkerchief?"

"Not in words, no. But you were thinking it."

Bardin's frown disappeared. "As I suspected; she reads thoughts, too. I'll remember that. Concealment?"

Luskell spoke, and the objects on the table vanished. Bardin, being a wizard, would still be able to see them through the spell if he tried, but Luskell was sure anyone without magic would be fooled.

"Good. Can you conceal yourself?"

"Really conceal, or just deflect attention?"

"Really conceal."

Luskell nodded. It was more work, but she knew what to do. She cast the concealment charm over herself. Bardin's satisfied smile told her she'd done well, but she waited to drop concealment until he'd had a chance to voice his approval.

"Not bad. Can you maintain concealment while moving?"

That was more of a challenge. Still invisible, she took a moment to breathe, then slowly rose from her seat. She crept around the end of the table, careful not to make a noise and reveal her position. By the time she reached Bardin's side, she was sweating as if the concealment were a heavy blanket. She held it a moment longer to prove she could, then dropped it. "How was that, sir?"

He jumped. "Not bad. Clearly, you've worked at it."

"Dadad—my father, I mean—made us practice that one a lot. He must have had some close calls."

"Let's see how you do with levitation."

Luskell returned to her place and dropped into the chair. "I can tell you now, sir, it won't be very good."

"Don't tell me. Show me."

She concentrated, and with effort, managed to raise a small stone a finger's width off the table.

"Good. Now a block."

She raised a block, but the stone dropped back to the table. When Bardin instructed her to move the block, it remained stubbornly in place. She released the breath she'd been holding and sank back in her chair. "That's all I can do," she gasped.

"Fine. What about weatherwork?"

"You don't want me to try anything indoors." After a moment, she added, "Or out. I don't have an aptitude for it, but I have enough power to be dangerous."

"It's good to know that early. I'll at least make sure you have a solid grasp of the theory. For now, we'll do some fire work, instead."

This should have been better, but Luskell feared it might be worse even than levitation. Fire was the first magic she'd ever done. Unlike her father, she didn't set any part of herself on fire—only the spell book she was working from. She'd gained more control since then, but fire still made her nervous.

Bardin set a candle stub into a holder and slid it across the table. Luskell studied the candle, took several deep breaths, and spat out the fire spell. They both jumped back as fire consumed the entire candle.

"Sorry! That doesn't usually happen anymore!"

Bardin extinguished the last flames and waved the smoke away. "Well, you've got no shortage of power, and we can work on control. You could probably learn to do it without speaking the words aloud, too." He studied her. "You said you're sensitive to emotions. What am I feeling?"

Luskell reached out. "You're ... uneasy? Nervous. Me, too. Sir. Excited ... proud? Of me?"

This is an experiment I want to succeed. Not everyone who hears about it will feel that way, but I do.

Although startled to hear his voice in her mind, Luskell didn't hesitate to answer. *I do, too, Master.*

Bardin laughed out loud and slapped the table. "Mind-talking, too? And you're spectacular at transformation. Weak in healing, but your training and experience make up for it. You'll need to work on control and finesse, but I think we can make a wizard of you."

"I could have told you that. Sir." Luskell limited her display of triumph to a quick smirk.

Bardin rested his face against his hand and studied her. "The question is, what kind?"

"How many kinds are there?"

"More than you might think. You asked me what makes a wizard. My question for you is this: what is a wizard for?"

"You mean what's our purpose? We ... find what's lost and fix what's broken."

"Your father does, to be sure. Always by magic?"

"I guess not. The finding, usually; not always the fixing. Because it's not always that kind of broken."

"Tell me more."

Luskell paused to think of a good example. "Do you know Druner? He works for Berdona at the Otter. A few years ago, he was an orphan on the streets and he tried to pick my father's pocket. Rather than punish him or turn him over to the Guards, Dadad gave him a note for Berdona and she gave him honest work. When he comes across boys with some power, he sends them here for training before they get into trouble."

"And he is able to do that because he has learned to pay attention. Magic demands attention, and so do people. A wizard has the time and the training to observe and notice what is happening. In an urgent situation, he might take action in the moment. Fix the problem with magic. But if no one's in danger, he might instead guide people to their own solution."

"I wonder if I'd have the patience for that."

"You're young. Patience will come if you let it. But tell me, why do you want to be a wizard?"

Luskell considered. The question sounded simple enough, but this was the first time someone had come out and asked. She hadn't yet put it that way even to herself. "I'm not sure it's a matter of *want*. I think I have to. It's what I am."

Bardin gave her a half smile. "What, you think you have some grand destiny?"

"I don't know how grand it is. But what else am I supposed to do?"

"I'm sure you could find plenty to do that wouldn't require the name of wizard."

"Would you say that to a boy?" Luskell snapped.

Bardin kept his voice calm. "No need for that. Not every apprentice becomes a wizard."

"But would you say that to a boy with this much power?"

Bardin opened his mouth, then shut it again. He nodded. "To be honest, I'm not sure I've met one. But you make a fair point. Still, it's as much your decision as mine. Why is it important to you to be called by that name?"

"Because ... the name is magic!"

Bardin raised an eyebrow. "The power is, not the name."

"No, Master, the name is, too. I wasn't sure at first why it mattered, but I'm beginning to understand. I've seen it—women with power don't get the same respect as men, even if they have the same abilities. But the name and the staff—they do get respect, even if the person isn't impressive."

Bardin fought a smile. "And you think you'll get respect if you call yourself *wizard* and carry a stick?"

"Not if *I* call myself a wizard. If *you* do."

"Well, you may be right. Once people get used to the idea, which could take awhile. But that's a reason from the outside. What's your reason from the inside?" Bardin tapped himself on the chest.

Luskell sighed. "It seems like a waste to do anything less. It's in my blood." She returned Bardin's gaze. "Did you come from a magical family, Master?"

"No, I was the first in several generations. Why do you ask?"

"Try to imagine what it's like to grow up in a household where magic is in daily use, to light lamps, to heal wounds, to communicate over distance, to travel. I—well, how old were you when you discovered your ability?"

"Ten? No, eleven—I'd just had my birthday." Bardin smiled at the memory.

"I think that's about how old my mother was, if not younger. Dadad was twelve, Knot was ten. Children, all of them." Luskell got out of her chair and walked the length of the room as she talked. It occurred to her only after she'd started to pace that it might seem disrespectful, but Bardin didn't say anything. "So, when I was seven or eight, I tried to heal a skinned knee with words I'd heard my whole life. Nothing happened. I tried to extinguish a fire. Nothing. I tried to flick a rock at a tree trunk. Nothing. I thought it meant I wasn't going to have power."

As Luskell came near the door in her pacing, she paused. Although she couldn't see or hear anyone, she was certain someone, or more than one, stood outside, listening.

We have an eavesdropper. May I please close the door?

Take care of it, but leave the door open.

Take care of it. Was that part of the test? She did what she could, and turned to pace back the other way. Behind her, a skunk waddled into the passage—family tradition called for that animal when using illusion as a diversion. Luskell could never get the smell, but figured it wouldn't be necessary. A muffled squawk and retreating footsteps told Luskell her privacy had been restored. Bardin hid a smile.

She continued her story as if there had been no interruption. "I pretended to be glad. I could do something else—be an innkeeper, or a farmer's wife, or a musician. But I couldn't picture that other life." She stopped pacing and faced Bardin across the table. "No matter how hard I tried, it never seemed real."

"When did your power finally arrive?"

Luskell rested both hands on the table and leaned forward. "When I was almost fifteen. When I started dreaming dead people."

CHAPTER THIRTEEN

Bardin sat back. He cleared his throat. "It's common to dream of lost loved ones. How did you know those dreams marked the onset of your power?"

"I didn't. Not at first. But I dreamed of people I'd never met—my brother, my grandfather, Jagryn's great-grandmother—and they told me things I couldn't have known. I didn't recognize it for what it was until later. I found out I had power when I tried to help Jagryn, and ... set a spellbook on fire." With an apologetic smile, Luskell resumed her seat.

Bardin laughed. "You wouldn't be the first. At least it wasn't your hand."

"He told you that story?"

"I consider your father a friend. He's a private person, but forthcoming about some things—particularly his mistakes. I respect that." Bardin gathered the objects on the table into a bag. "So, given you want to use your power to its full extent, have you considered what specific kind of work you'd like to do?"

"No, not really." Luskell hadn't considered anything beyond earning the staff and calling herself a wizard. "I could do what Dadad does, going around and helping people who need it."

"That's honorable work. It generally involves a lot of healing."

"That's all right, as long as it's not the only thing. And not always indoors." Luskell glanced around the low-ceilinged room and tried not to shudder. She appreciated more than ever her father's choice to train her and Jagryn outside whenever possible.

"You seem to have the right instincts for it. It must be a family trait. Was your grandfather Knot the helpful sort, too?"

Luskell's face warmed and she looked down at the table. "He ... did a lot of good in his way, but also a lot of unintended harm. And he deliberately refrained from helping on more than one occasion. That haunted him later."

Bardin waited in silence before speaking. "There's something you're not telling me."

Luskell glanced up. She hadn't exactly lied about Knot's identity, but she hadn't been completely open, either. If Bardin was willing to work with her, he deserved the truth. "He went by another name for most of his life. He created such a bad reputation for himself, a lot of people don't believe he was real. Most of the stories weren't true, but he had plenty to regret."

"You're stalling."

"He called himself Yrae, the Mad Wizard."

Bardin sucked in a breath, then released it as a low whistle. He'd gone pale but did an admirable job of maintaining composure. "I can see why you might keep that to yourself."

"They say I'm like him."

"In power, perhaps. But you're not a monster. Is that why you want to help people? To atone for Yrae's wrongs?"

Luskell hesitated. "I'm not sure, sir. Maybe that's what Dadad wanted to do, and that's what I've seen all my life."

"Understandable, especially in a young man. But you're a young woman. An unsettled life might not be the best choice."

"I can protect myself, if that's what you're worried about."

Bardin held his hands out in a placating gesture. "I know you can. The fog wasn't so thick—I saw what you did to Raddys. And I'm sure he had it coming. What I mean is, a girl your age would be thinking of marriage and a family."

"Well, I'm not. Not yet, anyway." Luskell decided not to point out the obvious, that Dadad was married and had a family. He now confined his wandering to the area around wherever the family lived, but he still did it. "But say I was—what might be a good choice then?"

"When I have a better idea of your strengths, we'll visit the library. You might get some ideas from the Registry."

"What's that?"

"The *Registry of Practitioners*, a record of magic users and their special skills." Bardin stroked his chin. "Hm, the library. I assume you read and write; you could be a scholar, right here in the city. There's all kinds of old material in the library, and we're not close to extracting all the magical information from it. The government employs a few wizards as advisers. You're young for that yet, and I'm not sure they'd want a woman, but with Klanya in office, who knows?" Bardin pondered. "Your ... physical abilities, combined with your thought-reading and sense of emotion, would make you a good bodyguard."

Luskell laughed and nodded in agreement. "I'm not sure someone with a family should be in that position, but as long as I'm unmarried ..."

"With your concealment and transformation abilities, you could be a spy."

"That seems so sneaky."

"Sneakiness defines the job. Transformation would also be useful in exploration and mapping. You could go places and see things that are otherwise impossible to reach."

Luskell grinned. Transformation was one of her greatest skills, but she'd never thought how it could be useful to anyone but her. "Interesting. What else?"

"How far can you mind-talk?"

"At least to Misty Pass. I can send a short message as far as Deep River, but I'm not sure how well they get through."

Bardin whistled. "Hardly anyone could answer at that distance. But you might find work sending messages, as long as there was another practitioner to receive. Have you definitely ruled out weather?"

"It always goes wrong. I'd rather stay away from that kind of work."

"Very well. You don't have to decide now. If you have an idea, it might help you devise a good independent learning exercise for your quest. What did your father do for his?"

Luskell couldn't give the full answer, but she could boil it down. "He broke the curse on his village, and for that, he had to find Yrae. That's how he first met his father."

Bardin's eyes widened. "I never knew. That's quite a quest."

"He doesn't talk about it much around here, but he's a big hero back home. He claims it wasn't a curse and he didn't actually break it; it lifted according to its own schedule. But he did find Yrae, all on his own, and persuaded him to be the man I know as Knot."

Bardin smiled. "You don't have to choose anything that dramatic. I have to say, Crane hasn't left me much to teach you." He seemed both amused and vexed. "You lack discipline, but I expect that will come with time. You're what, seventeen? You're already ahead of most boys your age."

Luskell laughed at that. She'd seen it for herself already. Not in Jagryn, though. He always used great care and thought. What would he say, when he learned she was getting formal training? What would Laki say?

"Go downstairs and get something to eat," Bardin said. "This afternoon, you'll do group work with some other apprentices."

"I haven't heard of that before. Is this a school now?"

"No, or anyway, not yet. It's something new we're trying. My idea, so I'm eager to see how it works out. Meet out front after lunch."

The Wizards' Hall had a kitchen and employed cooks and other staff. Food was always available to any wizard or apprentice who needed it, which was a great convenience to those who lived alone or commuted from a distance. Those who were able paid regular dues to offset the expense, and those not able to pay accepted charity until such time as they could.

Luskell had never taken a meal at the Wizards' Hall. She considered going home for lunch, but she'd have to come back afterward. She was hungry, too, and it smelled good downstairs. The food was laid out buffet-style, so she helped herself to a plate. Some at the table looked askance as she approached.

Fandek smiled and moved over. "You're back! Here, sit by me."

It was too late to avoid him, but it looked like he was almost finished. She sat on the bench next to him. "Thank you. How's the food?"

"Good, and there's always lots of it. I wish you'd come earlier, though. As soon as I'm done eating, I have to go do chores."

"Do all the apprentices have chores?"

Fandek nodded. "I have extra, in exchange for a place to sleep in the kitchen."

That explained Dadad's comment the night before. Fandek had told her about leaving home, but she'd never asked where he was staying. Now it seemed obvious he wasn't paying dues. "Have you started your training yet?"

"In a way. Breet's still sick, but your father offered to substitute until he comes back." Fandek grinned.

"Oh, that's ... good." Fandek didn't react to her lack of enthusiasm. Maybe he had no sense of emotions. "It's hard to picture him teaching in one of the work-rooms here."

Fandek laughed. "He didn't. We walked around Old Town and talked about theory all morning."

"That's more what I expected," Luskell said. "He didn't come to lunch?"

"He had something else to do."

Luskell recalled what Dadad had said about having business in the neighborhood. Another mysterious errand.

"I'm in some kind of group exercise this afternoon," Fandek said. "I don't know what we're doing."

"Maybe something new." Luskell hoped so after her lengthy review with Bardin.

"It's all new to me!" Fandek got up from the table. "Maybe I'll see you later?"

Luskell forced a smile. "I think you can count on it."

CHAPTER FOURTEEN

Luskell met her group in front of the Hall. The ice was long gone from the square, but a raw wind blew. She pulled her cloak around her and watched the others. There were five in all. Bardin had said she'd be with other apprentices, but never mentioned they'd be children. No one else in the group looked older than twelve. Except for Fandek. She wasn't sure which was worse.

Fandek hurried over to her. "I didn't know you'd be here! Are you teaching us that protective charm?"

"I'm here for the same reason you are. I'm Bardin's apprentice."

He chuckled. "Very funny. Since when?"

"Since this morning. I hope that's not a problem for you."

"No, it's ... I mean ... no, of course not! But why didn't you tell me?"

Luskell stood tall and answered in the haughtiest tone she could manage. "Because I didn't think it was any of your concern."

Fandek considered this. "Can't argue with that. I'm glad you're here, but why are we in the baby group?"

"You, because you're a beginner," Luskell replied. "Me, because there's been some mistake."

She looked around for the masters, just as Bardin, Raddys, and two other wizards came outside. Dadad followed a few paces behind. He gave Luskell an encouraging smile. She acknowledged it with a quick nod, then marched up to Bardin.

"Master, you've seen what I can do. Why am I in a group of beginners?"

"I'm sorry, Luskell, but I don't see any other way to do it. You are a new apprentice, in spite of your previous training and skill. And I'm afraid if I put you with boys your own age, you'd be a dangerous distraction. They'd all want to impress you, which would lead to reckless competition."

"That's their fault, not mine!"

"That may be, but it would still be too much of a risk."

She gestured with her head toward Fandek. "What about him, then?"

"Nothing I can do. He's more of a beginner here than anyone. I'm sorry, but this is the best arrangement. You're lucky to be here at all."

"But—"

"No more arguments. Join your group, or go home."

"Yes, Master." Luskell stomped back to the cluster of apprentices. Why should she be penalized for the potential behavior of people she didn't even know and couldn't influence? Meanwhile, those same people got to do ... whatever they got to do, without any penalty. They didn't even know how they were infringing on Luskell by their mere existence. She scowled sidelong at Fandek, the only representative of this group.

"Why do we have a girl in our group?" one of the boys complained in a loud voice.

Luskell started toward him. "I'll show you why, you little—"

Fandek caught her wrist. "Don't waste your time."

"Don't touch me!" She yanked her arm away. He was right, which only made Luskell angrier. And something about his fingers on her skin reminded her of her mother. No, not exactly, but it gave her that same sense of well-being and comfort, enough that she could almost forget her anger. She took several deep breaths to calm herself the rest of the way.

"My apprentice is right," a tall, broad wizard said. He had iron gray hair, worn long like Dadad's. "What kind of farce is this, Bardin?"

"Oh, I don't know, Ysag," Raddys drawled. "I think it's admirable that she wants to try. Besides, nothing's more ..." He fluttered his fingers as he chose his next words. "... charming than a confused young woman."

Dadad and Bardin exchanged a glance. "How do you feel about an irate and powerful young woman?" Dadad asked.

Luskell glared at Raddys and brushed her fingers across the point of her elbow. He lost his smile and clasped his hands over his belly. "You know I mean no offense, Crane."

"I'm sure. Just ... reserve judgment. That's all."

Bardin joined the group of apprentices. "Form a circle," he instructed. He carried a wooden ball into the middle of their ring. When he let go, it floated there. "In this exercise, you'll send the ball to another member of the group. When it comes to you, deflect it to someone else. We're watching for accuracy and quickness as well as power. Call out the name of the boy—pardon me, the apprentice—you're aiming for. Have you introduced yourselves? No? Well, what are you waiting for? Do it now."

"Everybody calls me Lucky," the smallest boy said. Luskell guessed he was about ten. He had dark brown hair and a wide smile. "I could always make the dice go the way I wanted."

The next boy had red hair, like Ketwyn, but with freckles. He might have been twelve. "Gorin," he said, and crossed his arms. His voice cracked on the one word.

The remaining boy, the one who had objected to Luskell's presence, had tousled blond hair and stood a little shorter than Gorin, but with a heavier build. "I'm Thorn," he announced, and gave no clue as to whether this was his real name or a nickname. "And I don't play with girls."

Luskell scowled at him. "I'm Luskell, and I'm not playing."

Fandek smiled around the group and raised a hand. "And I'm Fandek. Nice to meet all of you." His deeper voice came as an unexpected relief after the harsh shrilling of the boys.

The exercise began, and it was harder than it sounded. Lucky shouted out, "Gorin!" but the ball wobbled over to Fandek. He tried to send it to Luskell but had trouble getting it to move at all. When it did move, it went to Thorn, who succeeded in pushing it to Gorin. Gorin sent it to the middle of the circle, where it stopped.

Luskell expected some direction from the masters, but they were talking among themselves. Were they even paying attention?

"I guess it's up to me." Before she could cast a spell, Thorn hopped into the center and pushed the ball with his hand. "Hey! You're not supposed to touch it!" Luskell objected.

"Who says? I don't have to listen to you."

"A little respect," Fandek said.

"Nice, coming from you," Luskell muttered.

During this exchange, the ball drifted to Lucky, who sent it to Gorin, who deflected it to Fandek. Fandek had better luck this time, at least in terms of momentum, but his accuracy was unimproved. The ball floated to Lucky, who sent it in Luskell's direction. Finally! She was beginning to think she'd never get a turn.

"Need help, wizard girl?" Thorn sneered.

"Think fast, Thorn!" Luskell repelled the ball with a flick of her hand.

It shot straight at him and hit him in the face. He sat down hard and clapped a hand over his nose. Blood oozed between his fingers. "You broge by dose!"

Luskell hurried over to him. He squealed and tried to scuttle away. "Hold still!" Luskell pressed her hand to his head to get a sense of the injury. "It's not broken, it's only bloody." She drew on her power—more than she'd used for the repelling charm—to stop the bleeding and ease the pain. Thorn watched her in stunned silence, his eyes wide. After a moment, he felt his nose gingerly, then stared at the blood on his hand. His face went pale.

"Really? Tough boy gets squeamish about blood?" Although Luskell didn't consider herself a healer, blood had never been a problem. But Thorn didn't seem so tough now. The anger drained out of her. She pulled out her handkerchief, spat on it, and wiped his face and hand for him as if he were a much younger child. "Sorry. I didn't mean to hit you."

The other boys crowded around. "How ... how did you do that?" Gorin asked. His freckles stood out in a pale face and he gave off a mix of fear and respect.

Luskell glanced up at him and smiled. "It was a basic repelling charm. Sometimes I don't know my own strength."

"No, not that. His nose. How do you stop bleeding like that?"

"It's one of the first things a healer learns."

Thorn wrinkled his nose, and flinched. It would be tender for a while. "Girl magic," he sneered.

Luskell wanted to smack him. "If that's your attitude, maybe I did mean to hit you. Get up. Everyone's waiting." She held out her hand, but Thorn ignored the offer of help and got up on his own. He moved off as far from her as he could.

The wizards stood back and watched without interfering. Dadad and Bardin exchanged a look and nodded. All five conferred, a quiet but impassioned argument. Luskell couldn't hear what they said, but they kept glancing at her. Finally, they reached some kind of agreement.

Bardin stepped toward the apprentices. "It's clear that Luskell already knows how to repel effectively. The rest of you could use more practice. Luskell, be so good as to instruct the rest of the group."

Dadad gave her a stern look. "Don't hurt anyone." He glanced at Thorn. "Anyone else, I mean."

She scowled at him and mind-talked. *He asked for it.*

And so did you. If you want to be taken seriously as a wizard, you'll have to show greater maturity than the other apprentices.

That was close to what Bardin had told her. Apparently it wasn't enough to display more power and skill. She also had to be the adult in this crowd of children. It wasn't fair!

Luskell took several deep breaths and unclenched her fists. She turned to Bardin. "May I use an assistant, Master?"

"Of course. Who do you choose?"

Luskell gazed at each of the apprentices in turn. Thorn averted his eyes. "Fandek."

His grin was far too pleased as he stepped closer to her. "What do I have to do?"

"Just stand there. We've done this before." His brows drew together in a puzzled expression; she sent him a mental image of their first meeting, when she made him fall. His mouth dropped open as he understood. He shook his head and laughed. At least he was a good sport. This time, she spoke the spell aloud so all could hear it. She used only enough power to drive him back, not to make him fall. When he'd recovered, she did it again, then let him try it on her. It took a few tries and all Luskell's patience, but Fandek finally got it right. Dadad gave Luskell the slightest nod of approval.

After the demonstration, the younger boys took turns with each other. When they could do the charm consistently, they worked with the wooden ball again. By the end of the exercise, everyone's accuracy had improved, and no one else got hurt.

"You've got the makings of a good teacher," Bardin commented. "Maybe you'll have your own apprentice someday."

Luskell gave him a surprised smile. "Thank you, Master. But do you think I'd have the patience?"

"If you work on it. And if you can control your temper."

CHAPTER FIFTEEN

For the sixth day in a row, Luskell approached the Wizards' Hall alone. She'd wanted to do this on her own, but, at that particular moment, a little of Dadad's encouragement would have gone a long way. She took a deep breath and pushed open the front door.

It should have been easier as Bardin's apprentice, but every day was harder. Only the day before, Thorn and Gorin had pestered her unmercifully with newly-learned illusions of snakes and spiders. It didn't matter that she wasn't afraid of snakes or spiders, and certainly not of their unconvincing illusions. In the end, she'd lost all patience and fought back with a bear. Not an illusion of a bear. She transformed into a bear and snarled at them. She didn't hurt anyone, but as soon as she was herself again, Luskell was the one who got the stern lecture, not the troublemaking little instigators. However, they did have to go home and change their trousers.

Luskell didn't mind Thorn and Gorin so much; they were children, after all. Lucky had attached himself to her like a lost puppy. Fandek did everything in his power to get her attention, and if possible, impress her. She wasn't sure which was more annoying. The more advanced apprentices didn't speak to her unless they had to. Dalmer and Terulo tolerated her presence. The rest of them—and their masters—were openly hostile.

Luskell hoped to find Bardin alone so they could start work before she had to deal with anyone else. She enjoyed her lessons with him, even if they did usually take place in a cramped workroom, with the door open and at least one eavesdropper. Bardin's focused attention on areas of weakness could be frustrating, even embarrassing, but they'd seen glimmers of improvement. Already she could light a candle without speaking the spell aloud—and without burning the house down. But it seemed unlikely he'd hand over a wizard's staff anytime soon.

Bardin wasn't in the common room, but Terulo stood with his back to the fire, chatting with a young man who leaned on a wizard's staff. Luskell had seen the young wizard before, probably on some visit with Jagryn or Dadad, but she couldn't recall his name. He stood a bit shorter than Luskell, with a sturdy build. Thick light-brown hair lay in waves over his head. He didn't have much of a beard yet, but an elegant mustache adorned his lip.

Terulo trailed off in the middle of what he was saying. The young wizard's lips formed a tight line as he stared at Luskell. That was the usual way—discomfort, open hostility, or pointed refusal to recognize her existence. At least Raddys wasn't there with his ogling eyes. Before Luskell had decided whether it was worth the effort to speak to these two, Bardin crossed from the dining room.

"Ah, good! You're here. I just saw your father and Fandek down in the kitchen. They're going to find Dalmer and head to the wharves again. We should go back to the Garden District and see how our work is holding up."

Luskell made no effort to hide her relief. "I'm ready when you are, sir."

The young wizard stepped forward. "Good morning, Master."

"Why, Virosh, my lad! I thought you'd already left town. No trouble, I hope."

"No, just family delays. I'll start down the coast today or tomorrow, but I wanted to see you first." Virosh glanced up at Luskell. "Unless you're too ... busy."

Bardin followed his gaze. "Virosh, have you met my new apprentice? This is Luskell."

Luskell could almost hear the words "Crane's daughter" in the silence that followed. But no. He would let her stand on her own.

"We hadn't been introduced. How do you do?" Virosh took Luskell's hand, but no warmth entered his voice or expression.

Luskell gave him a polite nod. "Very well, thank you." Would Bardin abandon her for the day in favor of his former apprentice?

"Come along, Luskell. We have work to do. Virosh, will you meet me here this evening? We can have supper together before you go."

Virosh smiled slightly. "I can delay my departure that long. I'll see you tonight."

Luskell and Bardin gathered portable food from the buffet and left the Wizards' Hall, headed toward the Garden District.

"I don't think your old apprentice likes me much, sir."

Bardin shook his head. "He doesn't even know you. We should walk this time."

"All right." Luskell was as glad not to dwell on Virosh.

Walking was slower than flying, but at least they could see where they were going this time. Luskell blew on her fingers. The low sun wouldn't brighten these streets until near midday, and didn't have much heat to add. She wanted to walk fast and warm up, but made an effort to match Bardin's pace.

"Given the choice, I think Dadad would walk everywhere. Is that just the wizard way?"

"There's all kinds of wizards, but I'd say it is, among those who care about helping folks. There's a place for carriages, or even transformation, when time is of the essence. But you miss the details when you fly; even riding a horse raises you above the common folk. And a carriage shuts you off. Walking puts you down among the people. You can see and hear and sense what they need."

"And save our power?"

"Exactly. And our money. Walking costs nothing, and it allows time to ponder." Bardin gave Luskell a wink. "Not only that, we can save our lunch for lunchtime."

They stayed open for signs of illness along the way, but reserved most of their power for the Garden District. When they reached it, they carefully retraced their steps to check every building they'd visited before. Luskell wasn't sure what to expect, but her confidence grew as they discovered few new infections. Neighbor cared for sick neighbor without fear. The protective magic held.

Luskell and Bardin shared the work of refreshing the protection, an easier task than creating it in the first place. They finished by midday, ate their lunch and made their way back to Old Town. As they passed Braffin's Garden, Luskell sensed the lingering emotional traces of the strangler's attack there. They were weak, diluted by time and buried under more recent events, a whisper of the strangler's satisfaction. She felt queasy in spite of her strong shield.

"What happens after this, Master?" Luskell hoped questions would divert her attention. "It looks like your idea was sound, but do we need to keep coming back here every few days? What about the rest of the city?"

Bardin glanced at Luskell with an approving nod. "I've been thinking about that myself. Your father took Dalmer and Fandek back to the wharves today, but that's still only two neighborhoods and five practitioners, and none of us great healers. I'd like to involve Balsam now."

"That's a relief!" Luskell allowed herself a wry chuckle at her own expense. "I'm glad I could help, but I didn't want to be responsible for the whole city."

"Nor I. I'll talk to her today."

Upon their return to Old Town, they went directly to Balsam's House, pausing on the porch to cast the protective charm over themselves. Bardin reached to ring the bell, but Luskell opened the door and walked in out of old habit. Hanny was crossing the corridor with an armload of clean bedding. Luskell took this to mean she'd found someone else to trade shifts with.

Hanny grinned at Luskell. "That didn't take long! I knew you'd be back. I was just ..." She trailed off as Bardin joined Luskell. "Wizard Bardin—welcome! What can we do for you?"

"My apprentice and I would like to speak with Balsam. Would you be so kind?"

"Your—?" Hanny glanced at Luskell, her eyes and mouth equally round as understanding dawned. "Yes, of course. One moment." She hurried away, but couldn't resist another glance back.

While they waited, Luskell reflected on the polite way Bardin had asked to speak to Balsam. It reminded her of Dadad, though he would have been less formal. Although she'd only spoken to the wizard Larem once, she was sure he would have been brusque and superior. She didn't even like to consider how Raddys would have behaved, especially with someone as pretty as Hanny. But wizards like Larem and Raddys probably wouldn't enter a place like Balsam's House.

Balsam sailed down the corridor toward them, brisk yet dignified. "Bardin, my friend! To what do I owe the pleasure?"

Bardin took both her hands and kissed the fingers. "A professional matter, I'm afraid. To do with the epidemic."

Balsam grew serious. "You're giving us more work?"

"In the short term, perhaps, but I think you'll want to hear this."

"In that case, let us speak in private. Thank you, Luskell; you may go about your duties."

"Um ... duties?" Luskell looked to Bardin, unsure how to proceed.

Bardin smiled at Balsam. "Luskell is working with me now, and she's part of what I have to tell you. Lead on."

Balsam shook her head. "I'm sorry, Luskell. I forgot. I'm getting too old and working too hard. This way."

They followed her up a broad stairway to the upper level, where she had her own apartment. Balsam ushered her guests into the room nearest the entrance, her private office. The furnishings were spare but comfortable. A large window looked out on the bare branches of the maple grove. In summer, the room would be in deep shade, but on this winter day, it was light and pleasant.

Balsam sat behind a large desk. Bardin and Luskell took their seats in two armchairs facing her.

"So, what's this about?"

"Thanks to your good training, Luskell has helped me confirm the practicality of protecting people from the wobbles."

"Has she?" Balsam looked at Luskell. "I thought you weren't going to be a healer."

"I'm not, but Master Bardin is right. I showed him and a few others how to cast protection over multiple people at the same time, and how to make it last. We tried it out in the Garden District, and we think we've slowed the spread of the disease."

Balsam gazed at Luskell and nodded. Then she frowned. "*Master* Bardin?"

"Luskell is my apprentice. I think—we both think—she has the makings of a wizard."

"And yet you have her doing healing work."

"No. Well, yes, at first. She had the right training and experience, so I had her test my idea. But that's why I wanted to speak to you, Balsam. Even with Crane's help, we can't cover the whole city. We're not the best people to do it, anyway. I'd like to create more teams, involve more healers. And you know everyone with the right skills."

"Teams of ...?"

"Wizards and healers, of course."

Balsam smiled and leaned back in her chair. "No, I don't think so. Sorry, but no wizards."

Bardin frowned. "Why not?"

"No offense, my friend, but Luskell's father and your good self aside, wizards in this town do not have a favorable history with my healers. They're just such ... men."

"She's right, Master. I've seen it, too."

Bardin waved off Luskell's comment and focused on Balsam. "Then what do you suggest?"

Luskell both heard and felt the slight chill that touched Bardin's words. She glanced at him uneasily.

Balsam either ignored or did not sense the change in tone. "Tell me your method, and leave it to us. I have contacts in nearly every neighborhood, so we should be able to handle it."

"I'm not comfortable with that."

"You're as bad as Larem!" Luskell sputtered. Bardin turned to her, not exactly glaring, but clearly not pleased. Belatedly, she added, "Sir," and dropped her gaze to her lap. She didn't mean to make him angry. If she had. The downside of being sensitive to emotion was she couldn't always tell other people's feelings from her own.

"We will talk about this later." Bardin maintained a calm tone, but his voice shook.

By contrast, Balsam's voice had a hint of laughter. "I, for one, would like to hear more. Go on, Luskell. What did you mean?"

Luskell glanced up and took courage from Balsam's calm, smiling face. She pressed her hands against the arms of her chair and took a steadying breath. "Larem doesn't make any secret that he doesn't want me around. He doesn't believe I can be a wizard. He doesn't think I should even try."

"Women scare him," Bardin muttered.

"Women with power scare most men." Balsam watched Bardin closely.

"Is that what it is?" Luskell sat up straighter. "As if we were some kind of threat? That's stupid."

Bardin's scowl deepened. "Mind how you speak, Luskell. Is that how you think I'm like Larem—that I'm stupid?"

"No, Master Bardin, of course not." Luskell made an effort to be polite. "But isn't it strange that you don't want to turn over a healing project to healers? Because they're women?"

"No, because it's my project."

"*Our* project." Luskell slapped her chair arm and leaned toward him.

"My idea." Bardin brought his face close to hers, his brow furrowed.

Luskell didn't look away. "Your idea that I showed you how to make real."

Balsam cackled. "My friend, you'll have your hands full with this one as apprentice. Are you sure you want to hold onto this project, too?" Her affection for Bardin washed over Luskell like a warm breeze. They really were old friends.

Bardin blinked and turned toward Balsam. "I had planned to direct the operation myself. But ..."

She smiled. "If it makes you feel better, I'll consult with you from time to time, let you know how it's going."

"If it were anyone but you ..." Bardin sighed and sagged back in his chair. "Here's what we've done so far." He described their methods and outlined the neighborhoods already covered, while Balsam took notes. At the end, they shook hands. "Thank you, Balsam. Make sure your healers go in groups of at least two. We can't afford to lose any more to the strangler."

Balsam closed her eyes. "No. We can't."

CHAPTER SIXTEEN

Bardin and Luskell left Balsam's house and crossed the square. "No group work today, Luskell. You may go home if you wish."

It was already later in the day than such activities usually began, but Luskell suspected that wasn't the real reason. "Are you angry, Master?"

"I was *nearly* angry before. Not now. I thought, after yesterday, you could all use a break from each other."

"I apologized," Luskell muttered. Not that anyone had apologized to her.

"I know you did." Bardin's lips curved into a smile. "And it was an impressive bear. Just try to set a better example, all right?"

"I'll try."

"Good. You've done enough for one day. Go on home."

"I'll wait at the Hall for Dadad. He'll be along soon."

"I'll see you in the morning, then. I'm going to get some rest before I meet Virosh. Stay safe." Bardin raised a hand, then walked off toward home, wherever that was. Luskell imagined he lived somewhere nearby, but she didn't actually know that much about her master.

She went inside the Wizards' Hall to stay warm while she waited for her father. Virosh and Terulo were loitering by the fire again.

Virosh leaned on his staff. He raised his other hand in mock astonishment. "She's back—the girl who wants to play wizard!"

"Actually, I worked at it all morning. Doesn't look like you two have moved at all."

Terulo drew himself up. "We did! We've only been back a short time."

"Well, share the fire. It's cold out there!"

Terulo moved to one of the arm chairs. Virosh remained in front of the fire, but shifted over half a step. Luskell crowded in next to him. "Thanks."

Virosh glanced at her sidelong. "So, Luskell ..." He gave her name an exaggerated pronunciation that dripped disdain. "How did you persuade Master Bardin to make you his apprentice?"

"What's that supposed to mean?" Luskell immediately regretted her defensive reaction. She tried to look knowing, though it was probably too late.

"Nothing, only Master Bardin may be eccentric about some things, but he knows magic better than anyone. You must have shown him something ... impressive." Virosh twitched his eyebrows.

Luskell nearly became a bear again, if only to wipe away that awful leering expression. No. She was supposed to set a good example. She replied as innocently and casually as she could. "I guess I did. I mind-talked, read his thoughts, turned into a pigeon—"

Terulo jumped up from the chair. "You do transformation already? That's what Virosh did for his quest!"

Luskell turned to Virosh with a pinch more respect. "Really? You didn't have Bardin teach you?"

Virosh shook his head. "He suggested it as a good thing to learn on my own. I read about it in a book, then went and lived in the country so I could get to know more animals. It took a long time, but I did it."

"How long?" Luskell asked.

"From Fall Balance till just before Short Day."

"That's ... not bad. Some people take years to work it out, and others never get it." Luskell remembered what Dadad had said about talent versus hard work. She chose to be mature and not brag that she hadn't worked at transformation at all.

"Well, aren't you the little expert on wizardry!"

Luskell made a point of looking down at him. "Maybe I am. What wood did you use for your staff?"

"Ash, from a tree I used to climb. It blew down last winter." Virosh lost his sneer and spoke with genuine enthusiasm.

"I love climbing trees. May I?" Luskell asked.

He held it out and she took it. It was uncomfortable to hold, though less dizzying than Dadad's. The magic in it vibrated faster, but with less power. She held it a moment, then flung it away. It clattered to the floor.

"Hey! What did you do that for?"

Luskell looked straight into Virosh's eyes. "First lesson: never give your staff to another wizard."

He shook his head. "Funny. You're hardly a wizard."

She smiled. "And I still took your staff away. You should be more careful."

"Fine, you've made your point. You know a few things and you're Bardin's apprentice. You can end this farce now and go back to being a healer or whatever." He retrieved his staff and held it in the hand farthest from Luskell.

"Why would I do that? I'll earn my staff and be a wizard, same as you."

Virosh rolled his eyes and smirked. "Please. Everyone knows women aren't built for it."

"No, they don't! What does that even mean?"

"A woman with a staff is just *wrong*."

"Why? It's only a tall stick."

Virosh ignored her. "Maybe you could have a bag or something ..."

Luskell imagined filling a bag with bricks and swinging it into Virosh's smug face. Satisfying, but not the symbol of wizardry. "You just don't want to admit I might get there."

"I don't have to admit anything, because I know you won't. How to put this delicately? Sorry, I can't. Women bleed every month. Obviously, that drains their power."

Luskell put her hands on her hips and spun to face Virosh. "Obviously, you don't know what you're talking about." She didn't want to discuss anything so personal, but her own power tended to surge in rhythm with her monthly cycle. She'd learned to be careful with the fire spell on those days. "Do you even know any women?"

Virosh met her gaze unmoved. "As a matter of fact, I do. My mother is still living, though I'm thankful to say not with me anymore. And I have a lover who has some power." He spoke the word *lover* with relish. "She told my landlady I'm her brother so she can spend the night without raising suspicions." Virosh grabbed Terulo's shoulder and turned him so they were both looking at Luskell. "Terulo, get a girl under you with a little magic in her and you'll be a new man!"

Terulo reddened and dropped his gaze to the floor. Luskell felt as embarrassed, but she picked up enough of his emotions to recognize his reason was different from hers. He wasn't looking for a girl with magic in her, but he lived for a word from Virosh. Hopeless. Then something Virosh had said caught up with Luskell.

"She calls you her brother? You're Hanny's fellow!"

"You know Hanny?"

"I used to work at Balsam's House. I traded shifts with her the day you got back. You should thank me."

"Oh, I do."

"Does she know you're leaving tomorrow?"

"I'll tell her tonight. It's not like I'll be gone forever." Virosh frowned. "Why are you here, anyway? You're not waiting for Bardin now."

"No, my father. I thought he'd be back by now. We usually walk home together."

"Who's your father?"

"Crane." Luskell watched and sensed for his reaction. He managed not to look impressed, but he felt it.

"Oh. Is that so? I ... I didn't know wizards could have children."

"Most don't, and I'm beginning to see why."

Virosh nodded and smiled as if he were in on the joke, not the butt of it. "I'd be happy to escort you. Can't be too careful with this strangler on the loose."

"You'd protect me from the strangler?" Luskell simpered and batted her eyelashes. She wasn't as good at it as Hanny, but she figured Virosh wouldn't know the difference. "Who's going to protect me from you?"

"I ... what?"

"You're not even shielding. It's like you're speaking your thoughts aloud for everyone to hear, including what you you'd like to try if you can get me alone."

"Just because I think it doesn't mean I'd do it."

Luskell snorted. "That's reassuring, I guess. I don't know whether to punch you in the face or go tell Hanny."

Virosh's mouth dropped open. "Don't tell Hanny."

Terulo grinned at the floor. "Careful—I heard she broke little Thorn's nose."

"That was an accident, and it wasn't broken." Luskell turned back to Virosh. "I'm leaving now. You're not coming with me." She turned and strode out of the Wizards' Hall, with a special effort to slam the door on her way out.

Once outside, Luskell stamped up and down in front of the Wizards' Hall. What was wrong with these people? What was it to any of these men or boys whether she became a wizard or not? Why should they care? But even Bardin had trouble turning his project over to women, and Dadad wanted to keep Luskell safe. No one seemed to recognize that she was a person with power—like any of them—who wanted to use it to its full extent.

The short winter day was already giving way to blue twilight. Luskell paused in her pacing and fuming. It was too cold to wait outside, but she was not going back in.

She reached for Dadad's mind. He was getting closer, but still far enough away that it would be a long wait. *Dadad? I'm heading home now.* She stepped out into the square and listened for his response as she walked.

Are you sure? I don't want you walking alone.

I'll be fine. It's better than waiting at the Hall.

What happened?

Nothing, they're just ... tiresome.

Luskell broke the connection. The gloom deepened as she left the open square for the street that led home. The streetlamps had been lit; deep shadows pooled between them. She kept alert for anything unusual. It seemed unlikely she'd meet the strangler. By all reports, this wasn't his neighborhood. But there were other misfortunes that could befall a lone pedestrian.

A man crossed the street ahead of her, then stopped and watched her walk by. The man's general shape and way of moving seemed familiar, but she couldn't see his face well enough to tell if he was someone she knew. Luskell sensed for thoughts or emotions; the mind she touched was completely unknown. Something about it made her recoil, though she hadn't sensed anything precisely wrong. She was almost home, though, and walked faster.

Footsteps sounded behind Luskell, keeping pace. Of course, the one time she decided to walk home alone ... It was too late to deflect attention when she'd already been seen. The footsteps quickened. It would have been better to become an owl or something as soon as she left the Hall, but that had seemed frivolous at the time. Should she change now? But she didn't like to do it without warning in front of non-magical folk. Maybe better to turn around and hit him with a repelling charm. But what if he was someone harmless who only happened to be going the same way?

"Excuse me," a soft voice said. "Should you be walking alone?"

When Luskell felt a hand on her shoulder, she didn't bother to read thoughts. She changed into a small black cat and streaked under the steps of the nearest building.

"What the—? Huh."

Luskell couldn't see much from her hiding place, but her sharp ears picked up the sound of someone walking away on a cross street. A different set of footsteps ran toward her, and a second set followed at a fast walk.

"That was Luskell, wasn't it? Where'd she go?" It sounded like Fandek.

"She won't be far." Dadad paused to catch his breath. "Did you see where he went?"

"That way, I think, but it was too dark to see what he looked like."

Luskell emerged from under the step and took her own shape again. "Sorry."

Dadad smiled. "I'm glad you're all right. What did he want?"

"I didn't wait to find out."

"I don't blame you. Ready to go home?"Luskell nodded, and glared at Fandek. "What's he doing here?"

Dadad glanced between them. "When I told him you were walking home alone, he ran ahead to keep you safe."

Fandek bounced on the balls of his feet and grinned at her, but didn't say anything.

"I don't need your help." It came out harsher than Luskell intended. She tried to soften the effect. "Thanks, anyway. You must be a pretty good runner."

"I grew up in a bad part of town. I didn't know anyone who could outrun me."

I bet I could. Luskell didn't speak this thought aloud. She didn't feel like running races in the street after dark. There was no reason to add to the list of things she had in common with Fandek.

CHAPTER SEVENTEEN

Luskell crossed the empty square in front of the library. The bright summer day was so warm she didn't even need clothes. "Luskell," a man's voice whispered; a familiar voice, but she couldn't place it. Before she could turn, he touched her bare elbow. Her belly warmed and her limbs tingled as if she'd drawn up all her power at once. She swooned in a wave of ecstasy. When she came to herself, she was in a bed in a place like Balsam's House but different, giving birth. She was surrounded by every midwife she'd ever known—including Elika, who had died long before Luskell was born. Labor didn't hurt nearly as much as she would have expected. Only a little backache ...

She woke, and knew without even looking. Bloody sheets, and by her calculation, three days early. Her nightdress was twisted around her waist, so at least it had been spared, but still ... On mornings like this, Luskell wished she had been born a man.

Luskell got up and dug out one of the strips of fabric she kept for this time of month. Folded into a pad and secured with a complicated apparatus of straps and buckles, it would allow her to go out and not further scandalize the men and boys she had to work with. She washed and dressed, then used a small amount of power to draw the blood off the straw mattress and into the bedsheet. It took too much power to clean it all by magic, though. She gathered up the bedding to be washed and carried the load downstairs. Keela answered her knock.

"Morning, Luskell. What do you need?"

"May I borrow the washtub to soak these sheets?"

Keela grimaced. "You, too? Here, throw them in with mine." She indicated the tub of muslin and pinkish water.

"Thanks, Keela. I owe you. I'm already late for a lesson."

"Well, better late for that than, you know ... late." Keela raised her eyebrows.

Luskell smiled. "Good point." At least her dream wasn't true. She wished she had seen the dream man's face, though. She'd let him touch her elbow any time. "I'll see you later and teach you a good laundry charm." She hurried back upstairs and grabbed a bite of breakfast. Dadad was already gone. Luskell ran all the way to the Wizards' Hall and arrived out of breath. Bardin waited for her in the common room. She didn't see any other apprentices.

"You're late, Luskell. The others have already started their lessons."

"Sorry, Master Bardin. I had to ... take care of something."

"No excuses. I'm risking my reputation on the chance that you have what it takes to be a wizard. I expect you to respect my time more than this."

"I've never been late before," she grumbled. "Not in half a month."

"And you won't be again, or this experiment is finished."

"What? That's not fair!"

"Very little in life is. Now, unless you have something else to *take care of*, let's get started while we still have some morning to work with."

Bardin turned without waiting for Luskell's answer and headed up the stairs. She hesitated, then followed. It really wasn't fair, but she doubted he would understand about bloody sheets first thing in the morning. He'd say it was another reason women were unfit for wizardry. Well, she'd show him who was fit for what.

When she reached the workroom, Bardin was already seated at the table. His face wore its usual calm, slightly frowning but kindly expression. "Please take your seat. Today we'll work on levitation."

Luskell gripped the back of her chair and remained standing. She sputtered something incoherent, unable to find the right words.

Bardin's brows came together in a concerned frown. "I said no excuses. However, if you wish to explain?"

Where to begin? Her back hurt. She wanted to go back to bed. She wanted to cry. She wanted her mother. But how could she explain that to an elderly, unmarried wizard? Especially with the door open? "You wouldn't understand, sir." She slumped into her seat.

Bardin touched his fingertips together. "I grew up with five older sisters. I think I know something about girls' mood swings."

"*Girls'* mood swings? Master, a moment ago, you were yelling at me for being late, and now you're all calm like it never happened. How do I know where I stand?"

He sat back in his chair. "First of all, I don't believe I raised my voice. Second, I'm calm now because I thought we'd settled the matter. If I hurt your feelings, I'm sorry."

Luskell slapped her hands against the tabletop. "You didn't hurt my feelings. You threatened to ... to fire me! About something over which I have no control. You think I didn't know I was late? I ran all the way here."

Bardin nodded. "All right, I can't fault you for trying. But you must keep in mind—something you can't control can sometimes control you. Might that affect your fitness to be a wizard?"

"I knew you'd say that!"

"I'm only asking you to keep it in mind. You can't deny you have a temper. The amount of power you have, if you let your moods and emotions control you, you're dangerous."

Luskell knew that already. She wondered if Dadad had mentioned her weather mishaps to Bardin. She hadn't told him the details herself, and didn't plan to unless he asked. "I'll try to remember that. But boys do stupid things, too."

Bardin chuckled. "I never said they didn't. They're probably worse, the way they compete and escalate things. That's one reason I'm taking a chance on you, Luskell. You have as much power as I've ever seen in a young person, but you're different—maybe because you're a girl, maybe because you're you. I want to make you a wizard. But you have to take it seriously."

"I do, sir. I promise." Luskell still felt raw from his scolding, as well as tired and sore, but not angry anymore.

"Then let's get on with this lesson. This is an area where you're still weak."

Luskell sighed. "I know. I've tried to learn levitation for years. Never succeeded."

Bardin smiled. "Then maybe today is your day. What objects have you worked with before?"

"Sticks and rocks, mostly. But I stopped practicing after I hit Jagryn in the head and knocked him out."

"We'll start with something light." Bardin laid a handkerchief on the table and demonstrated the spell. The little white square lifted into the air and floated where he directed it until he returned it to the tabletop. "Now you try."

Luskell scowled at the handkerchief and said the spell. It floated sluggishly just above the tabletop. She directed more power at it and it shot up to the ceiling. When she tried to direct its movement, it darted erratically for a while, then dropped to the table as if exhausted. Luskell knew how it felt. Her back ached.

"Not ... bad," Bardin said. "As usual, the problem is not power, but control."

He had her work with a variety of objects. She could levitate and hold an object, or make it move, but not both. Something was missing; she didn't know what it was and Bardin didn't seem eager to tell her.

The lunch break came as a huge relief. Luskell went home to eat. She needed to change, and wanted to be alone. She wished she could stay home for the afternoon, but she had to go back for group work. She wouldn't give Bardin an excuse to end her lessons.

So Luskell ran back to the Wizards' Hall. Running wasn't considered dignified in a woman, but she'd always loved to run, and her back felt better. She arrived on time and joined the other apprentices around a heap of building stones in the garden out back. Dadad stood in front of them to lead the day's exercise.

"I understand you've all been working on levitation. I'll continue that lesson on a larger scale." With a casual wave of his hand, Dadad raised one of the large stones, and held it steady while he spoke. "Like all magic, levitation requires physical strength. Not as much as lifting with your muscles, but it's still an important consideration. If you throw too much energy into lifting an object, you won't be able to hold it long. If the object is heavy, losing control could be dangerous to yourself or others." The stone settled gently back onto the pile.

Dadad didn't look directly at Luskell, but she suspected he was talking to her. She wasn't sure what to do differently, but she was determined not to fail in front of Thorn or Fandek.

"Your task is to stack these stones into a wall," Dadad said. "Lay down the first level without magic, then use levitation to finish."

Gorin grinned at Thorn. "Is it a race?"

"No. Work together to form a good, solid construction. Help each other. Begin now."

"Lucky and Luskell can work together," Thorn muttered. "I don't need any help."

The five apprentices began hefting stones into place. Luskell's first stone didn't feel too heavy. She was tall, and stronger than most girls. She grew up running races, climbing trees and wrestling with her childhood playmates, mostly boys a year or two older. She was always running to keep up ... until she began to outrun the boys. Still, she couldn't match Fandek for arm and shoulder strength. But neither could Thorn and Gorin, who were racing to move stones in spite of Dadad's instruction. They were puffing and out of breath after two or three.

In her time at Balsam's House, Luskell had learned a lot about making the most of the strength she had to turn or lift patients who were heavier than she was. She relied on her legs rather than her back or arms to do most of the work. She moved her stones carefully and methodically. She felt the weight of the later ones, but she wasn't exhausted.

Lucky struggled gamely and didn't complain, but he was the youngest and smallest of the apprentices. He dragged a stone into place, let out the breath he'd been holding, and headed back for a second. Luskell joined him as he bent to lift it.

"Keep your back straight," she said.

"No, I've got it." Lucky glanced past her, and she followed his gaze to see where he was looking. Thorn was still trying to move stones as quickly as possible. He didn't appear at all concerned with Lucky.

Boys and their odd code of honor—Lucky probably figured he'd lose face if he accepted help from a girl. "Trust me, I'm not trying to make you look weak. I have more experience with things like this, that's all."

"I don't know ..."

"Besides, *Master Crane* said we're supposed to work together. Whose opinion do you care about more, Thorn's, or that of the greatest living wizard in Eukard?"

Lucky blinked, and let his gaze move to Dadad. "He is, isn't he? All right, what should I do? Because these are really heavy."

"Good decision. You don't want to hurt yourself before you get to the magic." Luskell put her hand on Lucky's back to improve his posture. "Keep your back straight, use your legs, and don't forget to breathe." She coached him in proper lifting technique, and he soon had two more stones in place.

"All right, that's a good first stage," Dadad said. "Now begin levitating stones into place. Luskell, please don't smash any skulls."

She did her best to ignore that comment, but he was right to worry. Even without the possibility of hurting someone, she didn't look forward to this part of the exercise. *Like all magic, levitation requires physical strength,* he'd said. That didn't mean a stronger person would necessarily be better at it, but a person without natural aptitude would almost certainly be worse. He'd also said it should take less strength than hefting stones by hand, but Luskell wasn't sure about that in her case.

"Should we do the same thing with levitation that we did with the lifting?" Lucky asked. "Keep our backs straight and all?"

She stared at him. Was that the answer? "Let's try it. Especially the breathing."

She filled her lungs and let the air out slowly while she said the spell. A stone rose from the pile. She used her hand to direct it into place, but imagined the strength in her legs and hips holding it. She controlled her breath and didn't release the stone until it was resting on the stones below.

Luskell glanced at Lucky. He was doing the same thing, shakily but with obvious success. He settled the stone into place and wiped his brow. Luskell smiled at him and started on a second stone. Fandek struggled with his first, and Thorn and Gorin had to be separated to keep them from crashing their stones into each other. Luskell offered advice to all three. Fandek was the only one to accept.

It wasn't much of a wall. It stood less than waist-high on Luskell and stretched from near the back of the Hall to the far side of the garden. It wasn't quite straight and gaps showed in places. It wouldn't keep anything in or out. But it was solid enough to pass inspection. The exercise was over. All five apprentices were tired and sore, almost as if they'd built the little wall by hand.

"I can't believe I did that," Fandek said with a satisfied smile. "This morning, I didn't even know the spell!"

For once, Thorn had no comment. He was too tired to talk.

CHAPTER EIGHTEEN

The day after the levitation exercise, the apprentices were granted a day off from group work.

"I thought you might appreciate something quieter this afternoon," Bardin explained.

Luskell rubbed her back. "I still ache from yesterday." She suspected they'd been given this break because the others didn't want to work with her, but maybe everyone was sore. "I can tell you now, sir, I won't be building walls by magic."

"It's still useful to be able to move something heavy—a fallen tree, a boulder, a body. Today we'll exercise your mind. Have you been inside the library?"

"Yes, years ago." Luskell chose not to mention her trip to the roof the previous summer.

They crossed the square and climbed the marble steps to the arched entrance. Inside was hushed, rustling and whispers somehow quieter than total silence. Daylight shone through tall windows onto wood-paneled walls and the tables in the reading room, where a group of students in immaculate blue and white tunics sat reading. High overhead, the domed skylight let in more wintry sunshine.

Bardin directed her attention to the bookshelves surrounding the reading room. "On this level are volumes on history, politics, commerce, lives of great men, and so on." He pointed to the railed mezzanine one floor above the reading room. "But what we want is up there."

"I remember. Is there something books can teach me I couldn't learn from you or my parents?"

"Possibly." Bardin showed her where to hang her cloak, then stepped up to the vacant librarian's desk, just inside the entrance. At that moment a tall, thin old man emerged from between two of the shelves. His brown clothing blended so well with the wood, he might have emerged from the shelves themselves.

"Good day, Bardin. How may I help you?"

"Brolitt, this is Luskell. I'd like her to have access to the collection, particularly the Practitioners Registry."

Brolitt seemed at least as old as Bardin. He looked down his long nose at Luskell for what felt like hours, then nodded solemnly. "Very well. Would you like to look at it now?"

"Yes, please. That's why I'm here." Luskell did her best to look responsible and trustworthy.

"Don't set anything on fire." Bardin winked, but Brolitt looked appalled and Luskell couldn't breathe. "Sorry. Wizard humor. Of course she wouldn't do anything of the kind."

Thank you, Master Bardin. Please don't scare me like that.

He glanced at her and the corner of his mouth twitched up. *I beg your pardon. But you'll have to be extra careful.*

Oh, I will. I promise.

"If you'll follow me, I'll show you where the Registry is kept."

The librarian was as tall as Dadad and even thinner. Straight white hair fell to his shoulders. He walked at a stately pace between the reading tables, Bardin and Luskell following. The young men there seemed too old for Academy students. Luskell guessed they were from the College, where sons of the wealthy and powerful prepared for careers in government and business. They whispered among themselves as she passed.

"Who's she? Not one of our set."

"One of Balsam's girls?"

"Those witches can't read. Not what I'd ask her to do, anyway."

"She's too young."

"No such thing."

"Quiet!" Brolitt said in a sharp whisper.

These spoiled rich boys were worse than apprentice wizards! They not only thought she couldn't read, they seemed to think she couldn't hear. At least wizards came from all walks of life, experience that might give them a better sense of people.

At the top of the stairs, Brolitt paused before a long shelf of volumes.

"We have quite a collection of magical lore—spellbooks, history and lives of magic users, as well as folktales." He took down a book and offered it to Luskell.

It was a collection of tales, block printed with illustrations. They were all familiar, the kind of thing Klamamam told by the fire: stories of wizardly adventure, humorous animal yarns, and cautionary tales about such characters as Fire Child and Old Mother Bones. The volume did not include any Yrae stories, as far as she could tell. They were probably too recent.

She took down a spellbook, a bound collection of handwritten documents, not all in the same writing. On first glance, the text looked like nonsense syllables. They soon rearranged themselves and their meaning became plain. This wouldn't happen for a person with no magical ability.

"It's the ink that does it." Bardin's voice recalled Luskell to the library. "I'll show you how to make it later on. Now let's see the Registry."

Brolitt drew back a set of curtains, allowing daylight into an alcove where a massive book lay open on a stand to a page that was half blank.

"This is the *Registry of Practitioners*. Since the founding of the city, every magic user has been registered, with their specialty and level of attainment."

"Not *every* magic user," Luskell objected. "I'm not in there yet."

"Adult magic users," Brolitt amended. "Wizards and apprentices are registered when they come of age or earn a staff, whichever comes first; non-wizards when they come of age at eighteen. Do you need anything else?"

"No, thank you, Brolitt. We won't keep you any longer," Bardin said. Brolitt made a slight bow and departed.

Luskell stared at the huge tome. "What is this for? And why is it here?"

"It is a book, and this is a library."

"But why not in the Wizards' Hall?"

"The library is older. And it has to be available to everyone. If you need someone with a particular skill and don't know who to ask, you might find a name here."

"What, page through till you find what you're looking for?"

"Ordinary folk look through the most recent pages. If you have a little magic, the book might behave differently."

What could she learn from this massive list of names? She wasn't looking for a particular skill. And how did a book *behave*?

"Remember when we talked about specialties?" Bardin asked. "A careful look through the Registry might give you some good ideas. If you'll be all right on your own, I'll leave you to it. We can meet at the Wizards' Hall when you're finished."

"Yes, sir, that's fine."

"Be sure to close the curtains before you leave. Too much light bothers the book."

Luskell looked at the half-filled page before her. Each dated entry included a name, a gender symbol, an attainment, and spaces for up to four specialties. She recognized a few names of healers who had recently joined Balsam's House. Their specialties included midwifery, fractures, and general healing. Above them was the name Virosh, Bardin's previous apprentice. His attainment was listed as *Wizard*, and his specialty, *weatherwork*. Of course; that explained his comment about working his way down the coast. He must have been going out on a fishing boat or cargo ship.

"Interesting," Luskell muttered. "But how do I find anything? I wish it could show me what I'm looking for."

The pages rustled, though she hadn't touched them.

"Is that it? I ask? Fine—show me Bardin."

The pages moved on their own, flipping back through years of entries to stop on a page where Bardin's name glittered. His specialties were listed as pedagogy, experimentation and collaboration.

Luskell gasped. Could it be that easy? She didn't know what pedagogy was, but the other two made clear why he was willing to work with her. She took a few deep breaths to calm her racing heart.

"Show me Ketty."

The book flipped ahead several pages to about a year before Luskell was born. There was her mother's name. The attainment *healer* had been crossed out and replaced, boldly, with *witch*. Her specialties: *healing, advanced midwifery, transformation, mind-talking.*

"Show me Balsam."

It flipped back again. Balsam had originally listed herself as witch, but later changed it to healer. She listed no specialty besides healing.

"Show me Crane."

Instead of flipping to a page, light streamed from the book, ribbons marking two places. After a moment's hesitation, Luskell turned to the more recent page, close to where she'd found her mother's name. And there was her father, a wizard whose specialties were listed as fire, finding, transformation, and general. He was so much more than that! She remembered in time not to shout in the library, but really! She followed the other ribbon to a page farther back.

The Crane; Wizard; transformation, healing, concealment

Another hand—Dadad's, she was sure—had added the notation *deceased* but not his many aliases.

"Show me Yrae." Nothing. "Show me Knot." Still nothing. He probably hadn't visited the city under either name.

"Show me Trenn."

Again, nothing. She knew he hadn't earned a staff. He must have left formal training before he came of age, and had obviously avoided registering under his alias, the New Yrae. It fit with his gift for concealment.

"Show me ... witches."

The book sprouted hundreds of glittering ribbons, but mostly in the early pages. Only a handful emerged from the part of the book where living practitioners were listed.

"Show me healers."

As Luskell expected, ribbons glittered from every part of the book. She glanced at a number of entries. Men and women were represented, but mostly women; scattered entries lacked any gender symbol, but Luskell didn't know what that meant. Few listed a specialty unrelated to healing. A similar festoon of ribbons appeared when she asked for wizards. She looked at several random entries from all parts of the book. All men.

"Show me ... Transformation?"

To her delight, the book responded to requests for specialties just as it had for attainments. It made sense; that's what it was for. Transformation was rarer than concealment, which was rarer than finding. There was no way to know whether an ability was actually rare, or simply not listed as a specialty by everyone who had it. She found only a few entries of pedagogy, once she'd guessed the correct pronunciation. One was Bardin's master Ordahn, who probably influenced his student to include it. If she had to choose, what would she list? She considered her own strengths. Not healing, she knew, nor levitation. Transformation, yes; conceal-ment, yes. Mind-talking, probably. Weatherwork, de-finitely not.

"Show me—" What had Balsam called it? "Show me ... crossing over."

A single sparkling ribbon marked a page in the earliest part of the book. So it really was as rare as everyone said; or anyway, no one else had claimed it. With shaking hands, Luskell turned to the page. Three hundred years in the past. The writing was old-fashioned script, but Luskell could make it out.

Serana; Witch; general healing, crossing over

Nothing on the page proved this was the same as her ability, but Luskell knew in her heart; in her guts. Across centuries, she had found a sister. Whether she would list it as her specialty when the time came, she didn't know. But she wasn't the only one.

"Show me Virosh." The pages rustled ahead. She left the alcove and closed the curtains.

Luskell paused at the top of the stairs. She was in no mood to deal with those students and their snobbish attitudes.

Best not to be seen; no mere deflection of notice but full concealment. She drew on her power, then descended the stairs as quietly as possible while holding the concealment steady. She was trembling and sweating by the time she reached the tables. She concentrated on placing her feet, not bumping anyone, keeping her breathing quiet.

A floorboard creaked underfoot. Luskell froze.

One of the students jerked around. "What was that?" It was the one who had said there was no such thing as too young. Blond and blue-eyed, he was probably regarded as handsome by some. Luskell almost lost her focus at the look of horror on his chalk-white face.

The librarian shushed him but didn't leave his desk. The young man's friends stifled laughter.

"Didn't you know?" one of them whispered. "This place is haunted."

Luskell caught herself before she laughed. She retreated to the entrance as quickly as she could without dropping concealment. At the last moment, she grabbed her cloak off the hook. The young man screamed.

The librarian shushed him.

Luskell slipped out the door and ran across to the Wizards' Hall to ask Bardin what pedagogy meant.

CHAPTER NINETEEN

When the group exercises resumed, Luskell often ended up instructing the others on matters of technique. She didn't volunteer; the effort to get Thorn and Gorin to listen was more aggravation than she needed. But if Bardin was present, he would make some innocent comment—"Nicely done, Luskell. How did you do that?"—that invariably led to a demonstration. Was he trying to irritate her enough that she'd quit? Nothing else he did gave that impression. Perhaps it was because she'd asked him what pedagogy meant (*The method of teaching a particular subject*) and he thought she was interested. He pushed and challenged her at every turn ... and seemed to believe she was up to it. She had to admit, there was nothing like teaching someone else to sharpen her own understanding. When the other apprentices paid attention, her instruction was effective. Maybe she would list pedagogy as a specialty.

She wasn't the only one with unsuspected skills. Although Fandek had started out behind the others, he quickly caught up. Dadad had been right. Fandek had natural ability and worked hard to gain skill. Like Jagryn.

She drove that thought away. He was nothing like Jagryn.

Their group spent one raw afternoon mulching the vegetable and herb garden behind the Wizards' Hall. Luskell's muscles ached as she shoveled and raked the composted manure, but at least she wasn't expected to teach anyone. They were scattered all over the large garden. She worked at the back, farthest from the Hall. Across the way, Fandek filled a barrow from the main pile of mulch. It steamed when he dug into it.

Luskell leaned on her shovel and wiped her brow, in spite of the chill. She hadn't done this much physical work since leaving Balsam's House, where most of the herbs would end up. By some quirk of geography, the Wizards' Hall had a large plot with southern exposure, while Balsam's House was mostly in shade.

She turned at the squeak of a wheel.

"Need any help?" Fandek asked.

"I'm almost out of mulch."

"I noticed." He rolled the barrow up and dumped its contents on Luskell's depleted pile. "How is this wizards' training?"

"Do you eat at the Hall?"

"Most meals."

"A lot of the vegetables and cooking herbs came from this garden," Luskell explained. "Next summer, there'll be even more. So you're helping keep yourself and others fed. It's also important to know the names and uses of herbs. They go into potions and medicines, and sometimes you burn them as part of a spell. And you can use magic to extract essences or distill what you need from a plant."

"We're shoveling mulch. Where's the magic in that?"

She snorted a laugh in agreement. "It's also important to know how to grow them. This is about all we can do in winter." She pointed out a few evergreen shrubs. "That's lavender—good for burns, and it can help you sleep. That one's rosemary. Good for a sore throat."

"But we don't mulch them—did I remember that right?"

"Good, you were listening. They don't like their soil too rich." Luskell shrugged. "I know most of this already, from being around healers so much."

"There's not much you don't know." He worked in silence for a time. "Your mother's a healer, isn't she? And your father's a great wizard. I can't even imagine it."

"It's hard to imagine anyone else's life." Luskell pitched a shovelful of mulch onto a bed. "Mamam—she takes good care of my brother and me, and she's a powerful healer, but she can be overwhelming. She has something more than magic."

"What do you mean?"

"She can tell what I'm feeling. It's ... eerie. And annoying." Luskell didn't admit she could do the same thing. "And she has a power that comes from somewhere else." Luskell wasn't sure how else to explain Aketnan, the legendary spirit that sometimes inhabited her mother. "She has influence. But even just as a healer, she's very thorough. I grew up running and climbing and falling down, and I don't have a single scar to show for it."

"Not anywhere?" Fandek thought about this too long for Luskell's comfort. He cleared his throat. "That must be ... challenging. At least you have a mother."

She nodded. "I shouldn't complain. I don't really know anything about your family, except you have a younger brother, and your father passed away."

"'Passed away.' That's good. He came home drunk and fell down the cellar stairs, is what happened. And I'm the one who left the door open."

Luskell flinched at the bitterness in his tone. "I'm sorry."

"I'm not."

He'd said that before, but she had to wonder. "And your mother? Is she ... gone, too?"

All the muscles in Fandek's face clenched. "I was five."

Luskell wasn't actively reading his thoughts, but they were intense enough to pick up without trying. She took an involuntary step back. "Your father killed her?"

Fandek tried and failed to hide his surprise. "I ... I don't know. That's how I remember it, but I was pretty young." He poked at the mulch with his shovel. "That must have been when my older brother left home. Kerf wouldn't have been more than twelve, but I haven't seen him since."

"Do you miss him?" Luskell thought of how much she wished she could see Ketwyn in the light of day instead of only in dreams.

"I was afraid of him, to tell the truth. He was so much bigger, and played rough. Pop used to hit him, but before he left, Kerf was starting to hit back."

Luskell swallowed. "What about you?"

"It's strange. Pop beat on everyone else, but I don't think he ever hit me. Almost like he couldn't see me."

That sounded like Luskell's own habit of deflecting attention when she didn't want to be bothered. "Your power was already protecting you."

"I don't know. Maybe." Fandek shook himself and gave Luskell a quick smile. "I'd rather talk about your family. A healer and a wizard ..." He looked away and cleared his throat. "I heard something. That if two people of power ... lie together ... it increases their power. Is that true?"

"How would I know?" she snapped. This was uncomfortably similar to Virosh's comment about Hanny.

"Just, you know, you've been around magic folk more than I have. At Balsam's House, and in your family ..." He trailed off, his face scarlet.

"Well, I don't know." The heat rose in her face, too.

"Maybe sometime we could ... test the theory." He laughed to let on he was only joking.

Luskell laughed, too, to let on she understood he was joking, though she knew he wasn't. The image in his mind was too detailed, and flattering, if not entirely accurate. "You really think I look like that?"

He went even redder, if that was possible. "You're not supposed to read my thoughts."

"I wasn't trying to."

He started to say something more, then turned abruptly and rolled the barrow away.

Luskell laid down her shovel and picked up a rake. As she smoothed mulch over a bed, she considered Fandek's suggestion. If he'd said such a thing to her when they first met, she'd have knocked him down. Well, he sort of had and she definitely did. But this was different. He wasn't posturing now.

She felt more ready than ever for the experience. She didn't plan to marry anytime soon, and she didn't want to wait. But with whom? Wyllik, for all his teasing, probably wouldn't say no. Bardin thought Ambug was interested. And they weren't the only ones, but a casual tumble wasn't what she was after. But with a man of power ... Only, not Fandek.

Maybe Jagryn, if he weren't so far away and hadn't lost interest. But he was so careful and controlled about everything. Hesitant, even. She craved something ... wilder. She'd had a tiny taste the one time she'd kissed Laki.

But he was far away, too.

"What's on your mind?" Dadad asked as they walked home that evening. Usually they shared stories of the day, but Luskell couldn't imagine putting her thoughts into words. They were halfway home and she hadn't said anything.

"Nothing. Too tired."

He wrapped an arm around her shoulders. "Wizard training harder than you expected?"

"We mulched the garden today. Anyone would be worn out." She considered a moment. "You should teach Fandek to shield his thoughts."

"We'll get to it soon. Why the hurry?"

"I don't need to know what he's thinking."

CHAPTER TWENTY

One month into Luskell's apprenticeship, Bardin spent a morning quizzing her on theory and having her demonstrate spells, much as he had the first day. She was doing well, but for some reason, her master was on edge. She couldn't imagine what she might have done to anger him, and she didn't have a hope of reading his thoughts this time. His shield was impervious.

Luskell completed a demonstration in which she levitated and manipulated three objects at once with good control and even, for her, a measure of grace. Bardin nodded, but didn't say anything.

Luskell sank into her seat, shaking from the effort of working the spell. "What's wrong, Master?"

He blinked. "Only that I must let you go."

"But why? I've been serious, I haven't been late, I've done everything you asked—"

He held up his hand to cut her off. "You have been an excellent apprentice, and a good influence on the younger boys. It's even possible you've earned the grudging respect of a few of their masters. Not that I have to care what they think."

"So ...?"

"So, you've proved your abilities," Bardin replied. "All that's left to earn your staff is the quest."

"Oh. Oh! Really?" Luskell had begun to assume this day would never come, and now it was here too soon. "I thought I was in trouble again."

Bardin shook his head and allowed the corners of his mouth to lift. "No, not this time. I've been looking for excuses to keep you longer, but I can't pretend there's much more I could teach you."

"If you think I'm ready, then I'm ready. What should I do for my quest?"

"I can't decide for you. You have to find something you can't already do and learn it on your own or from someone other than me or your parents. And it might be best if you do something away from the city."

"Right. Because of those masters and apprentices whose respect I haven't earned?"

"I didn't want to say it, but it might take the pressure off both of us."

Luskell had been considering and discarding quest ideas from the start. "All right. I want a quest that has nothing to do with healing, protective charms, death or the afterlife. Or weatherworking. Or books. I have one idea I like, but I don't know if it qualifies."

"Let me decide. What is it?"

"Aklaka Listening."

Bardin tilted his head and studied Luskell. "I didn't know the Mountain Folk did magic."

"Most of them don't trust it."

Bardin rubbed his eyes. "Then how is Aklaka Listening an appropriate choice, if it isn't magic?"

"I didn't say it wasn't. They don't think of it that way, but it comes from the same place." Luskell's mother had been the first to understand the relationship, but it would seem boastful to mention it. "Listening is a method of gleaning wisdom from the natural world. I don't know how it works, but the Listener is an important adviser to the band's leader, the Uklak. It must help to have a non-human perspective."

"You're not Aklaka, though. What makes you think you can learn this ... method?"

"With training, a Listener can do our kind of magic, so it should follow that we can learn theirs. My father can Listen, a little. He didn't feel qualified to teach me, and I probably didn't have the patience then, anyway."

Bardin smiled. "Because you have so much patience now. It sounds like a challenging choice. Won't language be a barrier?"

Luskell grinned. "Aklaka was my first language. And the Listener at Aku's Lap is an old friend of my father. I've spent a lot of time there over the years."

Bardin watched her in silence with a small frown on his face. "You have all the answers, don't you? Are you sure this isn't something you already know?"

"I've seen it done all my life, but no one ever tried to teach me. I don't know whether I'll have any talent for it, but I want to try."

Bardin's expression cleared. "Then I have no objections. Go with my blessing and come back when you've achieved your goal."

Luskell wanted to jump up and down and squeal with joy. She forced herself to stand and smile like an adult, shook Bardin's hand, and left the room. In the hallway, she allowed herself a quiet little happy dance. Just then, the door to another workroom opened and Fandek emerged with his master, Breet. The wizard had been back on his feet for about a week. Luskell did her best to look dignified.

"Somebody got good news," Fandek said.

Although embarrassed that he'd seen her celebration, Luskell couldn't stop grinning. "I'm about to start my quest."

"Good for you!" Fandek glanced at Breet. "It'll be awhile for me."

"Even longer if you don't stop flirting," Breet growled. He gave Luskell a wink that Fandek couldn't see.

"What are you doing for it?" Fandek asked.

"I'm going to the Aklaka."

Fandek's eyes widened. "In winter? But they're in the mountains!"

Breet sighed and shook his head. "Some of us want lunch. Excuse me, please." He moved past Luskell and headed down the stairs.

"The mountains, in winter—is that safe?" Fandek persisted.

Luskell smiled. "It is for me."

Fandek met her gaze and held it. His eyes were similar in color to Dadad's, but not really the same. Smaller, but kind of beautiful in their own way. "So, you're going soon?"

Luskell shook herself and glanced away. "Probably. I need to tell my father."

"Will I see you again?"

She raised an eyebrow. "That depends on how good a wizard you turn out to be."

Fandek accepted that with a bow and turned to follow Breet. At the top of the stairs, he spun on his heel and strode back to Luskell. He laid one hand on her shoulder and gave her a quick kiss on the lips. Then he backed away as fast as he could go, grinning and flustered, his hands in front of him as if he expected her to hit him. At the steps, he turned and disappeared without a word.

Luskell stared after him, at a loss for words or action. How dare he? He'd kissed her, without permission or encouragement. She wanted to be angry at him, but she wasn't. The kiss was too unexpected ... and not that bad. It wasn't sloppy and awkward like Wyllik's. It wasn't eager and curious like Jagryn's nor did it have Laki's wild energy. It was honest and ardent, and over too soon. Luskell was more relieved than ever that she would soon leave town, or she might do something she'd regret.

She descended the stairs slowly, lost in thought about her quest, about Jagryn, about Laki, about Fandek ... No. Not about Fandek.

"Hey. Luskell."

She found Thorn and Gorin blocking her path. She knew from experience that she could sweep them aside with little effort, but that seemed mean on such a happy day. "What?"

Thorn smirked up at her. "We hear you get to go on your quest. Is that true?"

"Yes, it is. What of it?"

Gorin turned red and looked at his feet. "Some of the older apprentices thought you must've ... earned special treatment. You know. To get through so quickly."

Luskell huffed impatiently. "You know what I can do. What do you think?"

He glanced up at her with a crooked smile. "That you probably earned it fair and square."

Thorn stuck out his hand. "I wasn't sure at first, but now I think you'll make a good wizard. Congrat-ulations."

Luskell laughed aloud and shook his hand. "Thank you, Thorn. You know how much I value your opinion."

Lucky left the lunch table and joined them. "You're really going? Who'll help me now?"

"I guess you'll have to help yourself. With a name like yours, you'll be all right." She leaned down and whispered to him. "But don't take your master's advice about women. He has odd notions."

Lucky nodded. "I've heard that. Are you at least staying for lunch?"

Luskell glanced toward the buffet table, where Fandek was filling a plate. He studiously did not look around. "No, I should drop in at Balsam's House to say goodbye. I'll eat there."

She grabbed her cloak and left the Wizards' Hall, her mind full of plans as she crossed the square. The dining room at Balsam's House was about half full—typical for the midday meal. But instead of the usual chatter, the place buzzed with whispers and stifled exclamations. Pervasive fear smacked Luskell as she passed through the door. She brought up a shield against this storm of emotion and took a seat across from her old friend Cedar and another healer she didn't know, a young woman of eighteen or nineteen. Her light brown hair was drawn back in a neat bun.

"Hello, stranger!" Cedar reached across the table and clasped Luskell's hand in hers. "It's good to see you, even under the circumstances."

The other healer watched Luskell with a guarded look in her dark eyes. "Who's this?"

"Right, you haven't met." Cedar put her arm around the young woman, who leaned into the embrace. "Shura, this is my old school friend Luskell. She used to work here, too."

Even through her shield, Luskell felt Shura's suspicion and jealousy evaporate. "Nice to meet you, Shura."

Shura reached across the table to shake Luskell's offered hand. "Balsam speaks well of you."

"What's going on?" Luskell asked. "Everyone seems so upset."

Shura glanced up and down the table. "You know Hanny?"

Luskell nodded. "My last shift here, I traded with her so she could spend time with her 'brother.' What's she done now?"

"It's not what she's done, but what's been done to her." Cedar took up the story. "She was out with that so-called brother last night. They must have had a fight or something, because she decided to come back here by herself in the middle of the night. Two streets over, she met the strangler."

Luskell's appetite deserted her and her mouth went dry. "He killed her?"

"No, she got lucky. A Guard patrol happened along, and the strangler dropped her and ran."

Luskell could breathe again. "That's a relief. So they caught him?"

Shura shook her head. "They lost him, but at least Hanny's safe. I'm worried about her, though. This morning, Balsam sent for some wizard. He's interrogating Hanny now."

"What wizard?"

Shura held out her hands helplessly. "I'm new here—I don't know a lot of names. Tall fellow, dark, something wrong with his hand. Apparently he's someone important?"

Luskell offered a comforting smile. "Don't worry, then. Hanny couldn't be safer. But why him?"

Neither Shura nor Cedar attempted an answer. They returned to their meal and ate in silence. Eventually, Shura spoke again. "If you're a healer, why don't you work here anymore?"

"It's not my greatest talent. When I fulfilled my contract, I decided to try something different."

Shura gave her a puzzled look. "Something different? What else is there?"

"I'm going to be a wizard."

Cedar grinned. "Listen to you!"

Shura glanced between them. "I've never met a woman wizard."

"Well, someone has to be first. I'm about to begin my quest. Once that's complete, I'll earn my staff."

The door at the far end of the dining room opened and Dadad came in. He sat on the bench next to Luskell.

"What brings you here, Luskell?"

"Lunch, but I could ask the same of you."

"Later. Cedar I know, but who's your other friend?"

"This is Shura, a new healer here," Luskell said. "Shura, this my father, Crane."

Shura's eyes widened and she covered her mouth. She recovered herself enough to remember her manners and held out a hand. "Pleased to meet you, sir. I've heard of you, of course, but I didn't realize a wizard like you would come to a place like this."

He smiled and pressed her hand between both of his. "There aren't many places like this, and I think you'll find there aren't many wizards like me." He glanced at Luskell. "Except maybe this one." He stood and rapped on the table with a knife handle. The buzz of conversation quieted. "Excuse me, friends. Your attention, please. You'll be glad to know Hanny is resting comfortably and Balsam expects her to make a complete recovery. However, as it appears the strangler has moved into your neighborhood, it would be prudent if you didn't go out alone, especially at night."

"Did she get a good look at him?" Cedar called out, loud enough for everyone to hear.

"It was dark and she was frightened, but it seems the culprit is taller than average, with a slender build and dark blond or light brown hair, clean-shaven." Dadad spread his hands apologetically. "I know that isn't much, but it's more than we had before."

Luskell wondered about that *we,* but didn't say anything. She and Dadad left Balsam's House together after the meal. Neither spoke as they crossed the square. Hanny's misfortune overshadowed Luskell's good news. It didn't seem right to feel excited about anything.

Dadad broke the silence at last. "I hope you've had a better day than Hanny."

"Bardin gave me permission to start my quest," she said. "I want to do Aklaka Listening."

"Chamokat will be a good teacher." They walked on a few steps without speaking. Although Dadad was calm on the surface, gusts of his worry buffeted Luskell. "I was going to suggest you leave town, anyway. This latest attack—"

Luskell shuddered. "I know. Poor Hanny." She thought about his description of the strangler. It seemed familiar, but she didn't like to consider that. "I can leave anytime. We could go to Misty Pass together and see Mamam and Crett first, and then I'll go on from there by myself."

"That's a good plan. I'll have to catch up with you later, though."

She glanced up at him. His brows pinched together the way they did when he was troubled. "Why? Fandek has Breet back now. I thought you were done."

"There's still Dalmer. I agreed to keep supervising him until Slake's back on his feet."

"And you're looking for the strangler, aren't you?"

Dadad waited a moment too long before answering. "What makes you say that?"

Luskell stopped walking and turned to face him. "Why else would Balsam send for you, when she had Guards right there?"

"She didn't want them to question a traumatized girl, for one thing." Even standing still, Dadad wasn't still. His eyes darted after every pedestrian who passed them, and he appeared to listen for something beyond hearing. "And I could see into Hanny's memory clearer than Hanny herself." He rubbed his hand over his face as if to wipe away what he'd seen. "As best I can tell, he stepped out of the alley, grabbed her, and started to strangle her immediately. But before she blacked out, I think he ... apologized. Or rather, he said, 'I have to do this. It's not personal.'"

Luskell swallowed hard and willed her lunch to stay down. What could be more personal than killing someone with your bare hands? "Was it ... someone she knew?"

"I don't think so. Why?"

"She was with her fellow and they had a fight. If he's not the one who attacked her, then someone should let him know."

Dadad smiled. "Ah, Virosh. He was sitting with her when I left."

Luskell's opinion of Virosh crept up a few notches. "You are looking for the strangler, though, aren't you?" She took her father's arm and they walked on. "That's what you mean when you say you have to check on something."

Dadad glanced at her. "I'm helping the Guards, yes. Don't tell your mother."

"Since when do you have secrets from each other?"

"It's not a secret, exactly. But her opinion was that I should stay out of it. Mine was that I might be of help."

"Does she think you'll be in danger from him?"

"Not me, no." He didn't say any more, as if the conversation were now finished.

"If she asks me, she'll know if I'm lying," Luskell said.

"I'm not asking you to lie. Just don't worry her."

Luskell had to laugh about that. Worry was what mothers did. And with a murderer on the loose in their neighborhood, they all had something to worry about. But a more specific worry had needled Luskell ever since they left Balsam's House. Dadad's description of the strangler was fairly generic—a tallish, beardless man with light hair and a slender build. That could be practically anyone—Virosh, that student who was afraid of ghosts, even the librarian, if the light was bad. But who it sounded like ... was Fandek.

CHAPTER TWENTY-ONE

Luskell and her father went to the coach office the next morning and bought one seat on the morning coach. They weren't the only ones—Keela was there with her whole family.

Luskell joined her to wait while the horses were harnessed. "You're not just picking up the mail."

Keela jerked away, then peered up at Luskell's face. "I didn't recognize you. Why are you dressed like a boy?"

Luskell wore her usual travel outfit of shirt and trousers with a warm tunic and sturdy boots. "This is what I wear for travel, especially in winter."

Keela brightened. "You're traveling, too?"

"To Misty Pass."

"I'm going to Deep River to stay with Grandma and Grandpa for a while." Keela frowned. "Mama and Papa are worried about these attacks."

Luskell wrapped an arm around her friend. "Look on the bright side—you can start training with Brynnit. And we can keep each other company for half the trip."

"That's good news," Keela's father Wyll said. "I wasn't too happy, sending her off alone, but we can't all leave town now."

Dadad smiled. "I feel the same way." He called up to the driver. "How are the roads?"

"Clear on this side. They're having trouble keeping them open east of the mountains. We'll get to Misty Pass all right, but it's always a question whether I'll be able to go on."

Luskell squeezed her father's hand. "Are you sure you'll be all right?"

He ruffled her hair. "Who's the parent here? Don't worry about me."

"I don't want you to be lonely again."

"If it makes you feel any better, I might ask Fandek to come and stay."

Luskell curled her lip. "Why? He has his master back now."

"Because I'll appreciate the company, and it's time he moved out of the kitchen at the Wizards' Hall. Maybe he can keep our rooms for us after I come join you." Dadad winked. "Besides, don't you think he could benefit from my good example?" He spoke in a teasing tone, but there was something behind it that Luskell couldn't quite get at. He was shielding his thoughts.

"He could benefit from anyone's example. Don't let him sleep in my room." Luskell shuddered.

Dadad smiled and hugged her. "Let me know when you get there."

"I will, I promise. See you soon, I hope." She gave him a pointed look. "Be careful."

Keela climbed up into the coach, and Luskell followed. The seat facing forward was occupied by one sleeping passenger and a large hamper, so they shared the one facing back.

"Is that a man or a woman?" Keela whispered.

The other passenger was bundled in so many coats and scarves, Luskell couldn't tell for sure. "Man, I think," Luskell whispered back. "Look at the boots." She held out one of her own feet, large for a girl's. "Then again ..."

The coach rolled away from the office. Luskell looked out the window and waved to Dadad. He smiled and raised his hand, and stayed there until the coach turned a corner and hid him from view. He didn't want her to go. Luskell had sensed that when he hugged her goodbye, and supposed he had all kinds of good reasons. He was also proud of her, and he trusted her to go alone and earn her wizard's staff. It was cold in the coach, but nothing warmed her like her father's pride and trust. Although she was younger than he'd been when he first left home, she had a lot more skill and training. She was ready.

"I need quiet while I mind-talk to Mamam."

Keela's dark eyes widened. "All the way to Misty Pass? Isn't that hard?"

"A long distance takes more power than a short one, but I've done it before. I can't talk long, but I can get a message through."

"Could I do that?"

"Maybe. I'll try to teach you."

Luskell settled back and closed her eyes. *Mamam? I'm on my way to Misty Pass now.*

Her mother's response sounded surprised and worried in her mind. *Has something happened?*

A good something. I'll tell you all about it when I get there this afternoon.

Luskell broke the connection. Mamam didn't need to know about this latest attack until Luskell could tell her in person. She opened her eyes to look out the window again. The coach sped down a broad, tree-lined boulevard, then turned onto the main road that connected Eukard City with the Dry Side. It was a bright, clear morning in the city, but thick clouds gathered over the mountains. Luskell would be snug in Misty Pass with her family by the time the snow fell. And she was at the beginning of something new. She always relished that moment, before the page was written.

To pass the time, Luskell tried to teach Keela to mind talk. It was frustrating for both of them. They soon gave it up, and Luskell switched to the repelling charm. Keela had more success with that one, though they didn't have much room to try it out. She didn't have a lot of power behind it, but Luskell could feel a pressure.

"You'll probably get better with practice," Luskell assured her. "Or maybe your strength will all be in healing, like Auntie Brynnit. She can't do most of these other things, but she's more than capable with matters of the body."

The coach made a few stops to pick up mail, but no passengers seemed interested in making the trip. Around midday, they pulled away from a stop about halfway to Misty Pass. The other passenger finally woke up and stared at Luskell and Keela.

Luskell smiled. "Good day, friend."

"Good day, young fellow," a deep voice replied. The passenger loosened a scarf to reveal a glossy black beard and mustache. "I thought I had this coach to myself. I don't mind company, though. Is this your wife? No, too young—must be your sister."

Luskell was about to correct him when she saw how he looked at Keela, like something for sale or a tasty treat. She didn't want him to look at her that way.

Play along.

Keela twitched. Receiving was easier than sending, so chances were good she'd heard. Luskell adjusted her posture, knees spread and elbows out. She'd spent enough time around boys to know how they sat and moved. Her cloak covered the parts of her body that might give her away, including her long braid.

"Good guess." Luskell lowered the pitch of her voice and hoped for the best. "I'm ... Kell, and this is my little sister, Willi."

"Nice to meet you." The bearded man was still watching Keela, but Luskell didn't sense any emotion as strong as lust. Maybe he liked to look at a pretty face and nothing more. "I'm on my way to Oxbow, if the road's open."

"Oh? What's there?" Keela asked.

"Business interests. I hope you'll be with me that far."

Keela opened her mouth to reply, but Luskell jumped in ahead of her. "We're only going as far as Misty Pass."

"If the road's closed and I have to stay in Misty Pass overnight, I'd welcome your company." He winked.

Luskell struggled to maintain calm. "You'd have to ask our mother."

The man smiled and settled back in his seat. He continued to glance at Keela for the rest of the trip, but didn't speak much. He stroked his beard as if it were a lapdog or pet cat. It reminded Luskell of a character in a play she'd seen at the theater, a smug, proud ruler who kept stroking his mustache and smoothing his beard.

Luskell and Keela ate the food they'd brought along, and the other passenger made himself some lunch from the hamper at his side. Luskell tried to read his thoughts, but soon gave up. In her experience, women often thought along several channels at once, while men tended to focus on one thing, or nothing at all. This man was thinking fast and along several lines, but his thoughts weren't organized in any way Luskell could follow. It seemed clear he had little interest in a girl with family ties; he seemed almost relieved. And Keela wouldn't be left alone with him. That was good enough.

They arrived in Misty Pass late in the afternoon and rolled to a stop in front of the Fogbank, Luskell's grandparents' inn. Things looked different since Luskell's last visit. Across the road, work had begun on a new meeting hall. Massive logs were stacked, ready for the project.

Luskell and Keela got out of the coach, and Luskell made a point of carrying both their bags, in case the other passenger was watching.

"What am I going to do?" Keela whispered. "I'm supposed to go to Deep River tonight!"

"You'll go tomorrow. Let me talk to the driver."

He was on his way inside to refresh himself while the horses were changed. Luskell stopped him at the door.

"Excuse me," she said. "Will you be going on?"

"Guards say the road's clear, so we should get to Oxbow tonight."

Keela looked relieved, and Luskell shared the feeling. The bearded man of business wouldn't be staying at the Fogbank. "My friend isn't feeling well, so she wants to stay here tonight and go down to Oxbow tomorrow. Is that all right?"

The driver nodded. "Let me write out a ticket for you." He dug into his pocket and came out with a handful of paper slips and a stick of charcoal. He made some marks on one of the slips and handed it to Keela. "Show this to the driver tomorrow."

"We should send a note so her people know to meet her tomorrow," Luskell said. "Keela, who was supposed to meet you?"

"Uncle Jagree, I think. But how will a note get to Deep River in time?"

"It won't, but it'll be waiting at the coach office, so he won't worry."

"I hate for him to make that drive twice."

Luskell smiled. "I'll see what I can do." She wrote the note and gave it to the driver. After he went inside, she leaned against the stout log wall and closed her eyes. She calmed and focused her mind, then reached out for the only mind in Deep River that could hear her call—Jagryn. He wouldn't be able to reply from that distance, so it was good to have the written note as backup.

Jagryn? It's Luskell. I know you can't answer, but please take a message to Jagree. Keela is staying in Misty Pass tonight and will come down to Oxbow on tomorrow's coach. I hope he hasn't left yet.

Luskell opened her eyes. "There. That's done. Let's go in and get you a room."

CHAPTER TWENTY-TWO

When Luskell opened the door, Grandma Nari looked up from her cooking with welcome in her eyes, the way she would for any new arrival. For Luskell, her face lit with a big smile. She called down to something near her feet. "She's here! Luskell's here!"

With a delighted screech, Crett pushed himself to his feet and pattered over to Luskell as fast as his chubby little legs would take him.

"Wuwu! Wuwu!" He raised his arms and she scooped him up. He nestled against her shoulder.

"Aw, Crett! I missed you."

"Miss you."

She kissed his cheek, the same shade of brown as hers but baby-round. She pretended to stagger under his weight. "You've gotten so big!"

"Big, big, big!" he giggled.

A door opened and their mother came out of the bedroom behind it. Her joy hit Luskell and left her dizzy.

The strong feeling cut off abruptly as Mamam shielded her emotions. Luskell did the same. It was not about hiding anything. They were both sensitive to emotions and being close together created over-whelming echoes. Especially under these circum-stances, when they'd been apart so long.

Luskell shifted Crett onto her hip and hurried into Mamam's embrace. The top of her head barely reached Luskell's collarbone. Her short coppery hair was shot through with silver. Nothing about her appearance revealed the depth of her power.

Crett whimpered and squirmed around to climb onto his mother. She took him, laughing. "Which one of us don't you want to share?" He cooed and snuggled against her. "I didn't expect you, Keela. How are you?"

"Fine, I guess. The strangler attacked someone in our neighborhood, so I'm going to Deep River to stay with my grandparents until the Guards catch him."

Mamam frowned. "Oh, dear. I wish you had a better reason."

"She does—studying with Auntie Brynnit," Luskell said. "Keela has some power."

This news brought a smile to Mamam's face. "I see it now—like moonlight on running water. Congrat-ulations."

Luskell did not share her mother's ability to see power in others, but enjoyed her descriptions. Knot had been like a raging bonfire, and Dadad shone like the sun. Laki could do it, too. Before Luskell knew she had power, he'd called her the moon—not the moon's sparkling reflection, but the shining moon itself.

"How's Grandpa?" Luskell asked.

"Better." Mamam's lips tightened into a thin line. "He tried to work when he was still sick, and the infection settled in his lungs. We almost lost him because he's so stubborn."

"And we don't know anyone else like that," Grand-ma Nari put in. "Luskell, Keela, are you hungry?"

Luskell turned to her, relieved at this happier topic. "Am I! It's a long time since lunch."

They sat at the table with the coach driver, and Grandma served them an early supper. The other passenger didn't come inside, but he had that hamper. Crett fed himself bread and stew, carefully separating and eating the meat and potato chunks while leaving all the carrots. Most of the gravy ended up on his face, hands and shirt, but Grandma was there with a damp cloth before he could spread the mess around.

"So, Luskell, what brings you here now?" Mamam asked. "I thought you planned to wait and come with your father. Or are you worried about the strangler, too?"

"I think we all are. Remember Hanny?"

Mamam nodded. "Talented healer, when she puts her mind to it." Her eyes widened. "She's not—?"

"No, but it was close. At least now they have a description. But I would have come anyway. Bardin gave me leave to start my quest. And Dadad wanted to come, but he agreed to supervise Dalmer while his master recovers from the wobbles." She was glad she could give a valid reason that didn't involve his search for the strangler.

Mamam stared at her. "Your quest, already? That didn't take long."

"It seemed like forever, some days. But there wasn't much left for Bardin to teach me, thanks to you and Dadad."

"So you'll earn a staff and be a wizard?"

"If I succeed with this last step."

"And then what?"

"What do you mean?"

"Once you're a wizard, what do you plan to do?"

Luskell hesitated. "I don't know," she admitted. "Wizard things. Maybe like what Dadad does, helping people."

"You could have done that as a healer."

"That's your life, not mine."

Mamam's cheeks reddened and her green eyes flashed. She drew a deep breath through her nose. "You're right, of course. I just thought—"

"If I had your talent, I'm sure I'd be a healer," Luskell said. "Not having it means I get to think about doing something else. It's nothing against you."

Mamam allowed herself a smile. "I know. So what do you plan to do next?"

"I'm going to Aku's Lap and learn to Listen."

Mamam smiled, and Luskell felt her relief even through the shield. "That should be reasonably safe, anyway. And Chamokat will be a good teacher."

"Mm." Luskell kept her expression bland. She had already decided to ask Laki to teach her, but it hurt nothing to let her parents believe it would be Laki's uncle.

After the meal, Nari helped Keela get settled in a room. Luskell put on her cloak and Mamam wrapped up Crett. Luskell held him while Mamam put on her own cloak. Crett wouldn't go back to his mother, so Mamam carried Luskell's bag and Luskell carried the baby. They walked up the road and a short way into the woods to a small cabin with a green door.

Although the family had never lived there for long at a stretch, it was the only home that belonged to them alone. The single room was crowded when all four were there, but arranged for maximum efficiency. Her parents' big bed filled one corner. Crett's trundle bed fit under it, to be pulled out only at night or naptime. Luskell's bed was in the opposite corner. A small table and four chairs sat in the middle of the room, with cupboards for food and medicine around the walls. A fire burned low in the grate, warming the small space.

Mamam set down Luskell's bag, hung up her cloak, and stirred the fire. Luskell lit the lamps by pointing at them. A warm glow gleamed off the whitewashed log walls.

"You've gotten better at that," Mamam said with approval. "No words, even."

"Bardin had me work on subtlety and control."

"Hm." Mamam didn't say any more, but Luskell heard, "You'll need them."

Mamam sank into the rocker in front of the fire. She seemed tired, as if she'd been working heavy magic. Crett whimpered and struggled in Luskell's arms. She set him down and he toddled over to his mother. She lifted him onto her lap.

"Are you all right?" Luskell asked.

"I'm fine. Papa still takes a lot of healing, and then there's everyone else."

"Everyone else?"

"I took a page from your book. Whenever a coach arrives, I throw a protective spell over everyone."

"At the inn?"

"In Misty Pass."

Luskell whistled low. "By yourself?"

"I could have used one of your teams. But cases of wobbles are way down, so it's worth it." The baby fretted, and she opened her bodice to nurse him.

"I thought he was almost weaned," Luskell observed.

"He was, but the upset of coming here ... it's not surprising he wants to be a baby awhile longer."

"No' a baby," Crett murmured with his mouth full, and then went back to nursing.

Mamam smiled. "He missed you. He misses his father. I do, too."

In the relaxation of nursing the child, Mamam's shield slipped. Luskell felt a hint of … desire. She wanted to escape the embarrassing familiarity of it, but there was nowhere to go. It wasn't as if she didn't know where babies came from. In Crett's case, she knew quite literally, having assisted with his delivery. But she had deliberately not thought too much about the act that put him there, and her, too. She knew what married people did together; she wanted to do it herself. But these were her *parents*.

"You haven't told me about your trip." Mamam's voice was soft and drowsy, but she really wanted to know.

"Nothing much to tell."

"Why didn't Keela stay on the coach, if she's going to Deep River?"

"There was one other passenger who took us for brother and sister, I guess because of my clothes," Luskell explained. "So we played along. It didn't make sense for Keela to go on without me. And I don't think she wanted to travel alone with him."

"Did he say something? Or touch her?" Mamam's voice grew sharp, all drowsiness fled.

"No. He just … watched her. I mind-talked to Jagryn, so they should know in Deep River not to expect her till tomorrow."

"That was good thinking."

"I try."

Mamam and Crett both dozed off in the rocking chair. Luskell pulled out the trundle bed, then lifted the sleeping child and tucked him under the covers. She sat on the hearthrug, warm in the fire's glow, closed her eyes and quieted her mind. She reached out to her father.

Dadad? I'm in Misty Pass. He couldn't answer from that distance, so she tried to anticipate his questions. *The trip was quiet.* He didn't need the details. *Mamam and Crett miss you. We'll see you soon, I hope.*

She broke the connection, then reached for another mind. A thrill ran through her. Aku's Lap was not as far as Eukard City. Laki would be able to answer.

Except she couldn't find him. Not there? Where would he be? It was winter, and Aku's Lap was the winter camp. She ended her search and took a moment to calm her frustrated mind again. She reached out for a different mind.

Chamokat? Can you answer me?

Yes, Luskell! Where are you?

Misty Pass. I wanted to talk to Laki, but I can't find him.

He's not in Aku's Lap. He's doing his half-year in Knot's Valley.

Now Luskell remembered Laki saying something about this. She sat up straighter, proud they'd named their sacred valley for her grandfather. A skilled practitioner in the valley could prevent destructive volcanic eruptions. Knot had played the role for decades. But the volcano, Aku, had become jealously attached to Knot. After his death, the Aklaka had decided to take turns in the valley so the mountain wouldn't become attached to one person again. But they named it for him.

I forgot he planned to do that, she said.

He's probably the most capable young man for the job. He had to take his turn in winter so it wouldn't interfere with his embassy duties.

That was why Luskell had rarely seen Laki over the summer. And now he was sequestered in a remote valley. She was tempted to ask Chamokat to teach her. It would be simpler than finding the valley, which she hadn't visited before. Then again, Laki might enjoy some company.

Thank you, Chamokat. I'll see if I can reach him there.

Luskell checked that her mother was still napping. She wasn't doing anything wrong, but she didn't feel like answering questions. She closed her eyes again, redirected her search, and reached for her friend's mind. She had only a vague notion where Knot's Valley was and had to make several tries. Frustrated and tired, she almost gave up, then made one more attempt. This time her search touched the familiar mind of her old friend.

Luskell—that must be you.

Chamokat told me where you are. How is it?

Peaceful. She could almost hear the chuckle in his mental voice. *I like it. This is my second time, and I'll come back again if they need me to. I'm glad it's not for life, though.*

I think Knot would agree with you. Laki, I need to ask you something. Will you teach me to Listen?

I'd love to! I thought you'd never ask.

Really? Do you think I have the patience for it?

That's not for me to say. But we'll talk about it when we meet face to face. I'll be finished here in two more months. I look forward to your visit.

Luskell shared the sentiment. She wanted to touch more than his mind. She broke the connection and opened her eyes.

Mamam was awake and watching her. "Who were you talking to?"

Luskell frowned. "I wish you wouldn't do that."

"Then don't wear it right out on your face. Your lips move!"

"I let Dadad know I was here, and then I talked to Chamokat."

Mamam's lips twitched. "Not Laki?"

"He wasn't there."

"Oh, that's too bad. Where was he?"

"He's doing his half-year in Knot's Valley. I forgot."

"Yes, he told us about that, didn't he? Harsh place in winter." Mamam gazed up at the rafters, her face relaxed in the firelight. "It was earlier in the season when your father and I were there. When we rescued Knot."

Luskell knew this story but kept quiet and let her mother tell it.

"He should never have gone back there. If he had only stayed with Stell! But then your father and I wouldn't have reunited, and there would have been no you." Mamam caressed the top of Luskell's head. "This was when Naliskat started his rogue band with the intention of clearing the 'abomination' — Knot — out of the valley. He got his Listener to feed Aku lies; she was jealous already, so it wasn't difficult. They wouldn't call it magic, but they used some kind of power to have the mountain hold Knot, as if he'd been turned to stone. Your father freed him but then Aku started to quake. Crane had to calm her, and then we had to get Knot down to the valley. Have you learned levitation yet?"

"I'm not naturally good at it, but I can use it if I have to."

Mamam nodded. "I'd never had to use it on a living body, or over such distance. Crane helped, but I did most of it. None of us were worth much by the time that was over. And then Aketnan ... took me over."

"And you made peace between the two groups of Aklaka?"

"That's right. It was so cold, but we cast spell tents and your father held the weather clear until everyone was ready to move out the next morning. And then ... we changed history."

"You did, you mean."

"Aketnan did. Kala did. Naliskat, too. Governor Dillet. Not really me." Mamam yawned and rose from her chair. "I'm ready to sleep. How about you?"

"More than ready." And more than happy her mother had changed the subject before Luskell had to lie.

CHAPTER TWENTY-THREE

Luskell stood up and discovered she was as tired as she'd pretended to be. It took a lot of power to mind-talk over long distances, and she hadn't rested between her conversations. She undressed and crawled into bed. It was a struggle not to fall asleep immediately, but she put it off long enough to imagine Knot, standing in the warm, bright meadow of the Other Side. Luskell held the image in her mind until it was as clear and detailed as she could make it. Then she welcomed sleep.

It no longer surprised her to open her eyes in the land of the dead. As always, it was bright and pleasant and quiet. There never seemed to be much activity, but this time Knot was already there, waiting for her. He held out his hand and she grasped it.

"I need to ask you something. How do I get to your valley from Misty Pass?"

Knot studied her with furrowed brow, and she was sure he would refuse to tell her. At last, he spoke. "On foot or on the wing?"

Luskell smiled. "On the wing, so I can go soon."

He shook his head and smiled. "You never did like to wait. Well, neither did I." He told her where the valley lay on the Mountain, with landmarks to watch for along the way. "There's a lake, frozen this time of year. The trail down from the ridge crosses a waterfall by a stone bridge. It was concealed in my day, but there's no need for that anymore. I don't suppose there's anything left of my cabin now." He gripped his fire-blackened staff, and Luskell felt a wisp of sadness—a ghost of the grief he'd felt over the loss of his home.

"Thank you, Kladadad. I'll find it."

"Who's there now?"

"A ... friend." Luskell swallowed. "Nalaklak. The Uklak's son. He's a Listener."

Knot nodded. "I know who you mean. His father tried to kill me once."

"Yes, that's the one," Luskell replied uncomfort-ably. "Is it all right that he's in your valley?"

"I have no say in the matter. I forgave the father, and your friend has a gift with Aku, so I'm happy he can use it."

"He's going to teach me."

"I hope you'll be a good student. But be careful. Some things are clearer in the high places, but it's easy to lose your way. Now go. You've been here long enough."

"Can't I stay a little longer? I missed you."

"You never knew me, Luskell. And this is no place for the living."

"But why not, when it's so easy to cross over? I could see you every day."

He gave her a pained smile. "I admit you have a gift. But it's not a healthy habit. You leave a part of yourself whenever you visit. There's no danger in a brief chat once in a great while, but if you come too often or stay too long, you could significantly shorten your life—or die while you're here and never get back at all."

"I didn't know." Luskell shivered. On her few visits, they had always sent her back before she was ready, but this was the first time anyone had explained why. She would have to make sure Jagryn knew about the danger. She embraced Knot and closed her eyes. For an instant, she felt his weightless kiss on her forehead. Then her arms were empty and her dreams turned to nonsense. But she knew where to go.

When Luskell woke, something warm and heavy weighed down her covers. Crett had left his bed for hers sometime in the night. He could barely walk but was already a climber, like his sister. He had even dragged his own blanket along. She tucked it around him.

Crett's eyes popped open. "Bre'fas'?"

So much for going back to sleep. Luskell kissed his nose. "All right. Let's see what there is."

A forgotten dream nagged at her, a job she was supposed to do or a message she had to share. But with whom? Maybe it was only a dream for once. The mundane tasks of the morning chased away any details, but the feeling lingered. This was why she couldn't learn magic from a dead teacher. Luskell changed and dressed Crett for the day, then started the breakfast porridge. She tried to keep him quiet so Mamam could sleep, but he was a talkative child, even if most of what he said was nonsense. When she remembered, Luskell spoke to him in Aklaka so he could learn the language as she had, without really trying.

Mamam sat up in bed. "I dreamed I was in Aku's Lap. Now I know why." She smiled. "This is a nice surprise, though."

Luskell gave the porridge a stir. "It's almost ready."

"I could get used to this."

"Don't. I won't be here long."

They ate together, then went up to the Fogbank to see Grandpa Eslo. He was awake and cheerful, chatting with Keela while he ate breakfast in bed.

"There you are!" Keela said when Luskell came in. "He's been asking for you."

Crett reached out to the old man. Luskell set the child on his lap.

"Your friend has been filling me in on all the news and gossip from the city," Grandpa Eslo said. He pretended not to notice when Crett grabbed a piece of toast from his plate.

Luskell had never seen her grandfather's face so thin. "You're ... looking well."

"No, I'm not, and you know it. But I'm better than I was." He held out his hand. Luskell took it and gave it a tentative squeeze. He returned the squeeze, which encouraged her.

Mamam checked him over. "Yes, much better, as long as you don't overexert yourself. Let's not crowd him. Luskell, keep your visit brief."

Mamam left the room. Keela scooped up Crett and followed her.

Grandpa Eslo gazed at Luskell. "So is what I hear true? You're going to be a wizard?"

"That's my plan." She waited anxiously for his response. A long time ago, Grandpa Eslo had objected to wizards in general because of the action, or inaction, of one. He believed his young wife, Lukett—Luskell's grandmother—had died because the wizard Yrae refused to come to the inn and heal her. But he had warmed to wizards and magic after he met Luskell's father. "What do you think?"

"Someone has to be first," he said with a grin.

Luskell laughed. "That's what I said!"

He sobered. "Just ... don't go bad. Not like Yrae."

"He didn't mean any harm."

Grandpa Eslo frowned. "How could you possibly know anything about it?"

"Because I know him. He speaks to me in dreams."

Grandpa shuddered. "Why would Yrae do that?"

She looked at him with a puzzled frown. "You know why. Because he's my other grandfather."

Grandpa Eslo drew breath to answer and convulsed with harsh, painful coughs. Before Luskell could say anything, her mother burst in.

"All right, that's a long enough visit."

Luskell stood. "I'm sorry! I didn't mean to hurt him!"

"Not your fault—he shouldn't talk that much. Bring me a mug of hot water, and then maybe you can help Grandma."

Luskell hurried to do as she was told, sure it was her fault. She brought back the hot water. Grandpa Eslo continued to cough and struggle for breath. Mamam added some herbal mixture to the water and gave it to him to drink. The coughing subsided. He lay back and closed his eyes. Mamam watched a moment, then led Luskell out and closed the door.

She turned to Luskell with a serious expression. "What happened?"

"I ... told him Knot was Yrae. I forgot he didn't know! Will he be all right?"

Mamam ran her fingers through her short hair and sighed. "I think so. And he probably should know. Now wasn't the best time."

"I didn't think about it until the words were already out."

Mamam smiled. "Maybe your quest should be thinking before you act."

Crett was with Keela in the kitchen, playing with kindling from the wood-box while Grandma Nari cooked. She turned to Luskell and her mother with a welcoming smile. "So you're going to be a wizard like your father and grandfather! Has a girl done that before?"

"Someone has to be first," Luskell replied miser-ably.

"It surprises me your mother didn't try it." Grandma Nari grew serious. "Keela's been telling me about the strangler. They haven't caught him yet?"

"Not that I've heard." Luskell welcomed the change of subject, though she wouldn't have chosen this one. "That's why Keela's going to Deep River."

"And why your father didn't come with you." Mamam narrowed her eyes and studied Luskell's face. "Crane's looking for the strangler, isn't he?"

Luskell shrugged. "He's trying to help the Guards, but he hasn't had much luck."

"Not surprising, if the strangler isn't using magic," Mamam said. "You'd have to be in the right place by coincidence, or listen to the thoughts of everyone in the city until you found the right one."

"Dadad said something similar. He's good at finding hidden things, though," Luskell pointed out.

Mamam nodded. "That's what I'm afraid of."

"Surely Dadad wouldn't be in any danger!"

"No, but ... he likes to find broken people and try to fix them. Knot, Trenn ... but this strangler doesn't deserve that chance."

"It sounds like there's not much hope, anyway." Luskell chewed her lip thoughtfully. "What if you went by emotion instead of thought? Would one of us be able to find him? Look for the anger or hate that would drive someone to do a thing like that?"

"You'd still be looking for one in thousands. And I wouldn't want you getting close enough." Mamam frowned. "It might not work, anyway. Someone who could do this kind of thing might be ... cold. Or he might not feel what you'd expect."

Luskell remembered that strange trace of satisfaction at the scene of the attack on Rasana. She couldn't understand how a person could kill without feeling something stronger. When Trenn had threatened her, he was awash in fear and anger and self-loathing. When she'd thought of killing him, she was fueled by pure, molten hatred. But when he died, she could only feel sorry for him. What kind of person felt nothing?

That seemed familiar, though. The man in the coach. She hadn't detected much in the way of emotion at all. But the strangler was supposed to be wiry and clean-shaven. Even so, Luskell was glad Keela had agreed to stay the night in Misty Pass rather than go on to Oxbow.

CHAPTER TWENTY-FOUR

Crett's howl distracted everyone from thoughts of the strangler. Mamam scooped him up, but he didn't stop crying.

"Show me what hurts."

He held out his hand. A long splinter stuck out of his palm.

"Oh, you poor baby! Here, I'll make it better."

Crett pulled back, whimpering. "Hurts."

"I know it does. Luskell? Hold him on your lap, please."

Luskell sat and took Crett from Mamam. He con-tinued to sob, leaning into her with his hand tucked against his chest. Luskell gently pried it away and held it out so Mamam could remove the splinter. At the first tug, he howled again, as loud as when it went in. He tried to pull his hand back. Luskell was still stronger.

"Nasty old splinter is all gone," Luskell comforted him.

"Hurts!"

"Not for long, love." Mamam stroked his hair. "Keela, pay attention and I'll teach you a pain charm." She touched Crett's hand and spoke the words aloud for Keela's benefit. Once his shrieks subsided, she gently cleaned the wound, then healed it as if it had never been. "And a kiss to make it all better." She smooched his palm and buzzed her lips to make him giggle.

"All better!" he crowed.

"You girls want to make yourselves useful?" Grand-ma Nari asked. "Maybe you could entertain this little one, keep him out from underfoot."

"All right. Come on, Crett. What do you want to do?" Luskell asked.

Crett slid off her lap and hopped in place, his injury forgotten. "Watch 'em build!" He grabbed Luskell by the finger and towed her to the front door.

"Let's get your coat first."

The three of them bundled up and went out, where it became plain what Crett wanted. Across the road, workers were building the new meeting hall from logs as thick as Crett was tall and notched at the ends to fit snugly together. They used long poles to push a log up slanted skids. Crett grunted with them and raised his arms, then cheered as the log settled into position. It reminded Luskell of levitating stones with Lucky, though these builders made a neater job of it.

"I build," Crett announced.

He gathered twigs and started to stack them. Keela helped gather more twigs. Luskell summoned a stick into her hand. Crett laughed and hopped up and down in his excitement at the trick. Emboldened by this success, Luskell turned to summon another twig.

A builder shouted. Instead of settling into place, the log wobbled and started to roll back down the skids. They tried to hold it with the poles, but they weren't fast enough. Luskell called on her power and spoke the levitation spell, using her breath, her legs, her arms—everything she had. The log fought her, heavier and more unwieldy than the building stones she had struggled with behind the Wizards' Hall. She strained against its downward roll. It slowed, then paused long enough for the builders to get their poles in place and push it back up. This time, it settled and was still. The builders laughed and slapped each other on the back.

Crett whooped and tossed his sticks into the air. He didn't know what Luskell had done, any more than the builders did. Luskell plopped onto the ground next to him. Levitation still took more out of her than most other magic.

Keela stared at her. "I was about to call your mo-ther. I was sure someone would be hurt or killed. But you ... I didn't know you could ... something so big ..." She puffed out a breath.

"I wasn't sure I could, either." Luskell shuddered. She had used her power to prevent disaster, this time. What if she had made things worse?

Late that afternoon, Luskell and her family ate an early supper with Keela, then saw her onto the coach. The sun had already set and fog gathered in the twilight.

Keela hesitated at the open coach door. "I don't like traveling alone at night," she confided to Luskell. "But I'm more nervous about traveling with strangers."

A woman about Mamam's age leaned out. "Then let's be friends."

It turned out the woman and her daughter had the same idea of escaping the strangler. They were going to stay with a cousin in Sweetwater, about halfway bet-ween Misty Pass and Oxbow. Keela stepped up into the coach with renewed confidence.

Mamam waved as the coach rolled away. "I suppose you'll fly away soon, too."

Luskell took a squirmy Crett from her. "I'll take tomorrow to prepare, probably go the day after."

They headed back inside the inn to help Grandma Nari serve supper to the other guests. "Leave in the middle of the day, when it's warmer. It'll be easier to fly."

"Thank you. I'll do that." Luskell accepted this as good, practical advice from one who knew. She also recognized that her mother wanted her to stay as long as she could. They had often been at odds in recent years, but maybe those times were past.

"Have you ever flown to Aku's Lap?" Mamam asked.

"Dadad took me once, remember? When we lived here after Crett was born." Luskell didn't reveal that she wasn't going to Aku's Lap. Going alone to Knot's Valley, a place she'd never been, was asking a lot when Mamam already felt protective.

"I still don't like it. I could have Nari watch Crett so I could go with you."

"You can't!" Luskell tried to wipe the panicked look off her face. "This is my independent quest. You're not supposed to help me." She was stretching Bardin's injunction, but she had to quash Mamam's idea imme-diately. "Besides, it wouldn't be fair to Crett, both of us leaving at once. And what about Grandpa?"

Mamam nodded slowly. "You're right. He still needs me, if only to keep him from doing anything rash."

After the supper crowd thinned out, they returned to their house in the woods. Luskell unpacked her fiddle, tuned up, and played all the songs she knew. She'd been practicing regularly since her birthday and had most of her speed back. The really quick tunes were ragged, but she didn't care. It felt too good to make music for her family.

Crett stomped and spun and fell over. Mamam scooped him up and swung him around until they were all laughing too hard to continue.

Luskell put the fiddle away. "Come here and I'll tell you a story."

She sat in the rocker and Crett climbed onto her lap. She told him one of Klamamam Stell's humorous yarns, then sang an Aklaka story. She wasn't as good at it as a trained Aklaka Singer would be, but she knew it well. She'd first heard it when she was no older than Crett. She finished with Aku's Lullaby.

Luskell tucked the drowsy Crett into his bed. She was sleepy too, from the long day, and the lullaby. It didn't affect a singer who was alert, but one who was already tired had to use care. She shook herself to alertness. She needed to know how much she could take with her using only the pockets in her cloak, and didn't want to leave it until time to go.

"I hope I can bring my fiddle. Laki's never heard me play."

"I think they'd all like to hear it," Mamam said. "Bring some food to share, too."

That was Aklaka hospitality: a guest never arrived empty-handed. Luskell laid out her cloak on her bed. The fiddle and bow fit snugly into the largest pocket. The next largest held spare socks, underclothes, and a clean shirt. The remaining pockets would hold several bread rolls and a few small apples, enough food to get her where she was going, plus jerky and dried fruit to add to Laki's rations. There was no way to take anything more if she planned to fly.

"I'm going to bed—this bird needs her rest."

Luskell spent the morning with Grandpa Eslo and Grandma Nari. Grandpa didn't mention what she'd said about Knot, and she didn't bring it up. Instead, she played her fiddle for him. It seemed to do him good, and she liked having a chance to play for someone new. She ate a big lunch at the Fogbank before going home to change into her travel clothes. Mamam filled the pockets of Luskell's tunic with rolls of bandages and packets of dried herbs, in case she got sick or injured on the way.

"Do you have your cloths?"

"I shouldn't need them."

Mamam frowned. "You don't know how long this quest might take. I guess Kala could help you if—"

"No, you're right. I should bring them." Better to over-prepare than have to improvise from Laki's supplies. Luskell got the folded fabric and securing belt from her satchel. She hoped they would fit in with the fiddle, but it was too tight. With regret, she removed the instrument and stuffed in the cloths. "This would never happen to a boy."

Mamam hugged her. "There'll be another chance to play for Laki and everyone. I'll put the fiddle up where Crett can't break it." She glanced at where he napped on the trundle bed.

Luskell slung a water flask over her shoulder and pulled on her cloak, heavy and lumpy with her supplies. She was tempted to rouse Crett so he wouldn't wake later to find her gone. But did a goodbye and promise to return mean anything to a child not yet two? What if he cried? That might be worse. She kissed his warm little cheek and stepped outside.

Mamam joined her. "Remember to stop frequently for food and rest. Five times, at least."

"I know all that," Luskell assured her. "And it's not that far—Dadad rested only three times."

"You don't have anyone to watch out for you. Stop more often than you think you need to."

Although she'd never been to Knot's Valley, Luskell suspected it was farther—and more remote—than Aku's Lap. Mamam's advice made sense, and Luskell vowed to herself that she would take six breaks on the way.

"This day's not getting any warmer. I should go before I need to eat again." She gave her mother a quick hug, then focused her mind and body on the transformation. In addition to power, the spell required an intuitive understanding of the animal whose form she would take. She chose a raven, a strong bird with good senses that wouldn't stand out in the forest, if anyone happened to see her. When she was ready, she spoke the words that completed the change and flapped away over the treetops.

It was a beautiful day for flying, clear and windless. The sunlight on Luskell's black feathers warmed her. Transformation required too much power to indulge in often or frivolously, but for a short time, she gave herself over to the joy of flight. The forest was thick with tall firs, cedars and hemlocks. Luskell was above them all, a dizzying, thrilling prospect. The Mountain loomed white over the green forest, apparently close enough to touch. She doubted she would ever tire of soaring above the rest of the world, traveling almost effortlessly from here to there, as the raven flies.

After she'd had her fun, Luskell lighted on a towering hemlock's drooping top to get her bearings. She picked out Knot's first landmark—a rock spur at the top of a ridge—and took off again. When she arrived, it seemed too soon to rest, but she had promised. She landed on the ridge and changed back to human form.

The wind whipped her hair into her face; it was blustery on the exposed ridge, and colder than in Misty Pass. Luskell stumbled into the shelter of the protruding rock and sank to the ground. Her stomach rumbled as if she hadn't eaten all day. She pulled out an apple and devoured it, even the core. There was no point doing anything about her hair when she'd be transforming several more times.

Luskell drew her cloak around her and looked down on the forested slopes below. Misty Pass was beyond view, and she saw no other sign of human habitation. She shivered from cold, and at an unnerving thought. Nobody with any sense would come here alone. She knew where she was going and how to get there, but she didn't know where she was. No one did—except maybe the dead, who supposedly watched over their loved ones. They wouldn't be any help if things went wrong.

"It's a good thing I'm a wizard, then. Or nearly."

Luskell stood up and transformed again for the next leg of the journey.

By careful stages, she approached her destination. The forest below grew more sparse, revealing patches of snow. The size and variety of trees dwindled. At her sixth rest, above the timberline, she ate the last chunk of bread. The setting sun tinted Aku's icy peak with a rosy glow. But if Knot's directions were good, she had to be close. Luskell forced herself to rest even as the sky darkened to twilight. Then she changed once more—an owl now—and flew on.

She soared over the last ridge and spied a frozen lake. A faint trail traversed the hillside and crossed a waterfall by a stone bridge. Luskell followed the trail to its end near a low mound. She transformed and immediately felt the chill. A thin layer of snow crunched underfoot.

"This had better be the place," she muttered.

The fading light revealed a thread of smoke rising from the mound, which had the shape of a typical Aklaka winter lodge. It was a roughly circular space hollowed out of the ground, covered with a dome of branches and turf. She found the hidden entrance under a camouflaged deer hide, and stepped carefully down into the concealed living space.

"Laki?"

No answer, and she was too spent to mind-talk. Strange that he should be out after dark, but he couldn't be far if the fire still glowed. She stirred it up and fed it. Off to the side, a pot steamed—something fragrant of smoke and fish. Luskell was tempted to try a bite, but Aklaka manners were second nature to her. It was impolite to take food before it was offered. By the fire's light, she found the water jug and drank deeply—that was allowed. Another search turned up a pot into which she could relieve herself; preferable to going back outside on a winter night. With those needs taken care of, she tidied her hair and looked around for a comfortable place to wait. Furs lay heaped over a bed of springy branches. Luskell sat, then gave in to exhaustion and lay down. She drew the furs around her and closed her eyes. As she drifted, she relived hazy memories of being put to bed in a lodge like this one, when she was no bigger than Crett. And Laki was there, a big boy of six, promising to teach her everything he knew.

That's what she'd come for. He would teach her to Listen, yes. But they weren't children now. There were many things they could learn together. Luskell was ready— almost. She devoted a little power to preparation, no longer regretting the time she had spent among midwives and healers. Then she slept.

CHAPTER TWENTY-FIVE

"Who's there?"

Laki's familiar voice roused Luskell. "It's me." She emerged from her furry cocoon.

"Luskell? What are you doing here?" He moved into the firelight and pushed back his fur-lined hood. The light gleamed off the planes of his lean, dark face.

"You said you'd teach me to Listen." Luskell shrugged off the furs and climbed to her feet.

"I should have guessed it was you." Laki picked up her cloak, gave her a pointed look, and hung it on a peg near the door. He laughed and walked around the firepit to hug her. "But I meant in the spring, when I was done up here."

"Should I go?" Luskell held him close, more aware than she'd ever been of his body's warmth and strength. And height; she liked looking up for a change.

Laki stepped back, his hands on her shoulders. "No, don't go. It might make the sleeping arrangements awkward, but ..." He shook his head and smiled. "Well, you're here. We'll figure something out. You must have flown, so you'll be hungry."

"Later." She held his head and stood on tiptoes to kiss him. Same as the first time, kissing Laki was like flying and falling and left her dizzy. She drew back and looked into his startled eyes. "The sleeping arrangements don't have to be awkward. I want to … I want you to …" She wasn't sure how to ask, so she sent him a mental image.

His eyebrows shot up and a smile slowly grew. "If that's what you want, say it in words."

"I don't know how to say it in Aklaka." An excuse, but true. She'd learned the language as a child, and adults didn't speak of such things in front of young children.

"When we're not being vulgar, we speak of 'doing love.'"

Luskell laughed. "In Eukardian, we say 'making,' but it's almost the same." She gave him a mischievous grin. "What do you say when you are being vulgar?"

"Luskell! I'm not going to tell you that."

"Please?" She made big, begging eyes at him.

Laki glanced away and snorted a laugh. "Fine. We say—" He barked a single harsh syllable.

"*That's* what it means? I've heard it before, in insults. Hilarious, impossible insults, now that I know what it means."

"It's the impossibility that makes them funny. And keeps fights from breaking out. But you see? It's not a word you'll need to use."

"Maybe not today." Luskell closed her eyes. Her voice shook. "Laki, I want to … do love. With you."

He drew her close and whispered into her hair. "You love me, then?"

"How can you ask that? I've always loved you."

"Why now?"

Luskell pulled back enough to look into Laki's eyes. "Because in your world, I'm an adult now. Because I'm ready. Because I want to. Don't you?"

He gazed at her. "I do—have for a while now. But if you're serious, you'd better eat first."

This was really happening. The thought turned her knees to jelly and she sank down beside the fire. He dished up a single bowl of the food that was making her mouth water. Luskell's stomach growled—she was hungrier than she wanted to admit. "Aren't you eating?"

He sat next to her with the bowl. "When two Aklaka are ... interested in each other, they show it first this way." He dipped his fingers into the dish and brought them to her mouth. She opened her lips and he fed her a stew of smoked fish and some kind of root. It was delicious, and she licked his fingers clean.

"Now me," Laki instructed.

Luskell fed him a bite. The sensation of his tongue on her fingers was as dizzying in its own way as his kiss. She had often seen Aklaka feed each other, when she was too young to understand. Now it dawned on her why so many of them went off in pairs after the meal. She and Laki fed each other until the bowl was empty. Luskell was no longer hungry, but not yet satisfied. When Laki leaned over and licked a stray morsel from her lips, she kissed him again.

"Now?" she asked.

"There's no rush."

He undid the ties of her tunic and lifted it over her head, followed by her shirt, and woolen undershirt, and the camisole under that. Luskell wanted him to get on with it, but he stopped and stared at her chest.

"What?"

"You have breasts!"

She smacked him on the side of the head. "What did you expect? I'm not a child, you know." She covered them with her hands.

Laki moved her hands away. "No, I see that. They're beautiful."

Luskell hadn't given them much thought. They were on the small side, but in proportion to her slender build. Laki couldn't get enough of looking at them, and when he kissed them, Luskell was happy they were hers.

Gradually, they helped each other out of the remaining layers of clothing, right down to their socks. Now it was Luskell's turn to stare. Laki's lean, muscular body was even more beautiful than she'd imagined. She'd seen naked males before, but they were always either very young or very sick. This was different—a strong, healthy young man as interested in her as she was in him. "It'll never fit."

"It will, but it might hurt," he said. "So if you'd rather not ..."

"No, I don't care. Waiting hurts more."

He touched and kissed her in the expected places, and some unexpected ones. Every touch was a revelation and every kiss, incandescent.

"You've done this before," she said.

"Some. Not what you want—that'll be a first for me, too."

"I don't believe you. I didn't know what it was about at the time, but I've seen you share food with girls. And boys?"

He smiled. "If someone is genuinely interested, it's impolite not to at least accept the food. But you don't have to do ... everything. Or anything more than talk, if you're not interested. When we're coming of age, we get together and ... play. So we know what we like, and how to please a partner."

"How often does that turn into the boy forcing himself on the girl?"

"That's what would happen in your culture. You're still learning to respect women. But in mine? Punishment would be swift and severe. So it doesn't happen."

Luskell didn't like hearing her culture criticized, but she had to allow he might be right. She considered how much she'd gone through to get this far in her wizard training; and that was nothing compared to Rasana and the other victims of the strangler. Maybe she'd be better off to live among the Aklaka. Except they didn't have wizards. Laki's attentions drew her back to the moment.

She trailed a finger over his muscular shoulders. "You never played with me before."

"You were too young. And your people are ... diff-erent about such things."

Luskell guessed that must be true, or she wouldn't be getting such an education now. "So you're saying your people never do love until they have a permanent partner? I don't believe that, either."

"No, most seem to get plenty of experience before they settle down. But for me ... it's different."

"Were you waiting for me?"

"Maybe. So, how about less talk, more play?"

"Playing" was a joy, but what followed was a new ecstasy altogether. Afterward, they lay together in an exhausted heap on the bed of furs.

"You have made me the happiest man in the world," Laki declared. "How about you? Is that what you came here for?"

Luskell sighed contentedly, then giggled. "Even better than I expected," she said when she could find the words. "I'm tempted to marry you just for that."

"It's one good reason."

Luskell kissed him and got out of the bed.

"Where are you going?"

"I have to—" Luskell also didn't know the adult Aklaka word for *urinate* and she refused to say the equivalent of *wee-wee*. "I'll be right back. Don't go anywhere."

"I won't. We're not finished yet."

When she returned, he was sitting up, with a basin of water and a cloth. "This is ... your people would call it a wedding night ritual. Something special the first time."

With the wet cloth and more than a few kisses, he bathed her all over. The water was warm and soothing, and then invigorating as it cooled on her skin. There was a smear of blood on the cloth. She'd known to expect it, though it had been too dark to see when she used the pot. Seeing it now made the whole experience more *real*.

When Laki was finished, Luskell took the cloth and washed him in the same way, which led directly to doing love again.

They held each other afterward, drowsy and happy. "Mamam will be surprised, but pleased, I think," Laki murmured. "She always liked you."

"You'd tell her?" Luskell wasn't sure she wanted to share this with anyone. It was personal.

Laki laughed. "Why would I keep my wife a secret?"

Luskell shot upright, all drowsiness fled. "Your *wife*? Oh, no. You didn't think—"

She closed her eyes and held her head. Luskell knew how Aklaka relationships were organized: any two adults could pair up and live together. If they had a child, the bond became permanent, with social and legal ramifications. She hadn't considered that it might affect her. But that was why he'd waited. Not only for her to be ready, but because of his position as the future Uklak. His partner would be more than a companion and lover. She'd be an adviser, someone whose aptitudes complemented his. And she could be the mother of the next Uklak. He wouldn't choose that person by accident.

"You aren't going to stay with me?"

Luskell met Laki's disappointed gaze. Stay. To an Aklaka, it meant marry. If two people shared a lodge and a bed, they were recognized as a couple. In this place, there was nowhere else for Luskell to sleep. She couldn't go home afterward. "No. But ... I wanted you to be first."

"First. Not only."

She couldn't lie to him. "Well, no. Probably not. How should I know? But I'm glad it was you first, not someone in the city that I hardly know."

He frowned. "Is there someone in the city?"

"No! But ... maybe there would have been."

"Why not Jagryn?"

"Because I chose you. Laki, you taught me to talk! And to climb trees, and to swim." She reached for his hand and held it tight. "You said I was the moon. You taught me to fly."

"And you say you love me?" Laki's intense gaze held hers.

"I don't just say it." She smiled in an attempt to lighten the mood. "You're my friend. I trust you more than anyone."

"But you won't stay with me."

"I'll stay awhile." She spoke Eukardian. He knew the language as well as she knew Aklaka; she hoped the switch would make her meaning clear. "We can enjoy this time together."

He sighed. "I can't hope for more?"

"If you'd asked me when I was six, I would've said yes."

He gave her a lopsided grin. "That's not fair—I wasn't interested in girls yet."

"If it makes you feel any better, I might not marry anyone. I'm only now beginning to see what I might do with my life, with my power. Maybe I'll do like my mentor Balsam. They say she had a lover in every town she visited."

"I wouldn't stop you from using your power. I'd help you."

"It's not that simple. I'm ... going to be a wizard."

"What do you mean, going to be? You aren't already?"

She leaned over and kissed him. "Thank you. You're the first who didn't say, 'But you're a girl!'"

"I think we've established you're a woman. What does that have to do with being a wizard?"

"That's what I'm trying to find out. So far, it's not an obstacle except in some people's minds. But power alone isn't enough. You need a mature wizard to say you've got power, skill, and wisdom enough to be trusted." She lay back and drew a fur over both of them.

Laki grunted. "Oh, well, if you need wisdom ..."

"Hush. I'm working on it. And now I'm on the last step to earn my staff—the quest. That's why I want to learn to Listen."

"I'm happy to help, but I still don't understand why you won't stay with me. I know wizards can marry if they want to."

"It's rarer than you might think. They're—we're—difficult to live with. Anyway, I don't see how I can be a wizard and also the Uklak's wife."

"I won't be Uklak for a long time."

"You don't know that. But if I'm a wizard, my path won't always be the same as yours. And not all your people would approve."

"It wouldn't be simple, but—" Laki broke off with a sigh. "What if you have my child?"

"Don't worry about that. Mamam and Auntie Brynnit taught me a technique to prevent conception. It's like a basic protective charm, but on the inside. I can—"

"But what if?" Laki interrupted.

"Then I'd have it, of course."

"And if it were a girl?"

Luskell closed her eyes. Laki's mother Kala was Uklak— leader—of their band of Aklaka. Her son would inherit the role, for which he had trained all his life. If he had a daughter, she would inherit the role from him, and someday pass it to her son. "Then ... I don't know. But it won't happen. I'll be careful."

CHAPTER TWENTY-SIX

Luskell had a convoluted dream that kept starting over. It concerned a complicated ritual or bureaucratic pro-cedure, required to allow her to do love with Laki again. She was about to understand it well enough to complete it when she woke to sunlight shining through the entry. She rolled away from the glare and groaned. She was so sore she could barely move. They'd had a busy night, sleeping and waking and doing love. It hadn't seemed so bad at the time.

Laki let the flap fall behind him, shutting out the light. "Are you finally waking up?"

"What do you mean finally?" Luskell grumbled.

"It's almost noon."

"Well, you wore me out."

"*I* wore *you* out?" He grinned. "I haven't been awake long myself, but it's a beautiful day out there." He emptied two pails of water into the jug.

Luskell found her clothes and put them on again. She walked with care to the fire and eased down beside it. Laki served her a bowl of leftover fish stew with dried berries and flatbread. She was hungry and accepted it gratefully. "Has anyone done love here before us?"

Laki sat beside her with his own breakfast. He swallowed a bite and looked thoughtful. "I don't know. I think it's safe to say Knot didn't. Maybe your parents?"

Luskell considered. "I doubt it. The one time they were both here was when they rescued Knot, so there wouldn't have been much opportunity. And I'm not sure they were even a couple yet."

"My parents were both here then, too. They'd already had me, but perhaps were less of a couple than yours. But that's when they reconciled, so maybe." He smiled and gazed into the distance. He shook his head and glanced at Luskell. "Since then, though … it seems unlikely. Aku's keeper doesn't receive many visitors, and never only one at a time."

"Why not? Is it a rule or something?"

He leaned over to kiss her. "No. But the location is remote, and most of my friends can't fly. I hiked up with the supply party in the fall. We all spent a few days with my predecessor, then he hiked back out with the others. Midway through my term, a party brought fresh supplies, and in the spring, they'll bring up my successor. We're either alone or with a crowd."

"So we're special."

"Luskell, you've always been special." The lightness had left his voice, and his eyes had that intense look again.

Luskell looked away. "Do you know who your successor will be?"

Laki frowned. "Oh, probably Kiraknat. Remember him?"

"I think so. You don't seem pleased."

He shook his head. "I don't believe he's ready. Yes, he's older than I am, but his Listening skill is still ... rudimentary. He keeps putting his name in, so I have a feeling Mamam and the elders will choose him simply to make him stop."

"Kala won't choose him if he's really unqualified," Luskell said. "I was surprised when I didn't find you home last night. Why were you out after dark?"

"I ended up having a long chat with Aku. It took longer than I expected to settle her down."

"But she's all right now? Not about to blow?"

Laki smiled. "I don't think so. After we eat, I'll take you up and introduce you."

"Can't you do that from here? We're as much on the mountain here as anywhere."

"There's a special place, a ... thin place. It's easiest to Listen to Aku there, and to make her hear. I don't know why. Knot might."

"Is it wise to introduce me so soon? Doesn't she get jealous?"

"Not as much anymore. And she'll want to know you. Because of who you are. Who you come from."

Luskell nodded, and thought it over while she ate. Aku had loved Knot ... and nearly killed him. So would the Mountain love Luskell, or hate her? "Do we have to go today?"

"Did you come here to work or to play?" Laki countered.

"Both, I guess. But I can barely walk."

"You did ask for it."

"I know. I'm not blaming you. The fact remains, I am too sore for hiking."

"You asked me to teach you to Listen. It's easier to hear big things, Aku's the biggest around, and the weather is

clear today. We might not get a better chance. Use some of
your healing magic, and let's go."

He obviously didn't understand how much power
healing required from her, and how little would be left for
Listening. Then her pocket rustled. She silently thanked
her mother and took out the packet of willow bark. She
wouldn't have to use a lot of power to ease her pain.

"Is there hot water?" Luskell asked.

"Here." Laki filled a cup for her from a big pot over the
fire and set it in front of her. He added dried venison and
vegetables to the simmering pot, covered it, and moved it
back from the fire where it would stay hot but not boil dry.
"That'll be something to look forward to when we get back.
Now for trail food." He filled a bag with dried berries and a
few strips of the jerky, and dipped their water flasks into
the jug.

Luskell crumbled willow bark into the cup and let it
steep while she finished her breakfast. After she ate, she
used a charm to ease her aches; the willow bark would do
most of the work. It was bitter and hard to swallow, but by
the time they were ready to leave, she could walk almost
normally.

Even so, the hike felt long. Luskell wished she already
had her staff, if only to lean on. But it was a beautiful day,
clear and cold and still in the protected valley. At first, they
hiked through sparse woods, but soon reached the
timberline. The air was bitterly cold, the direct sunlight
surprisingly warm. An icy breeze struck Luskell's face. She
wrapped her scarf over her mouth and nose. Snow lay thick
in places, but it hadn't snowed in a few days. Laki's coming
and going had made a path through the deep parts.

On an open talus slope, the wind had cleared the snow
away and left the rocks bare. As Luskell followed Laki

across the slope, she stopped and shivered, but not from cold.. "Knot made this trail."

Laki turned to look back at her. "I thought you hadn't been here before."

"I haven't, but I feel him everywhere. He stacked these rocks by magic." She smiled with a sad sort of happiness. "Part of him is still here."

"This is a good sign," Laki said. "If you're sensitive to traces of magic worked before you were born, you shouldn't have any trouble Listening to what Aku says today."

He turned and continued hiking at a quick pace. Luskell followed, glad now of all the times she'd had to keep up with her father. It wasn't too difficult on this part of the trail, which ran fairly level. Farther on, it grew narrow and rough as it dipped down into a snow-choked creek bed. Luskell picked her way down the rocky slope. Ahead of her, Laki took a careful step onto the snow field. He laughed and charged across the surface. It had a dusting of fresh snow over a thick crust. Luskell followed, but she didn't laugh. On the other side, the trail climbed a steep slope that made her ache just to look at it.

Laki waited for her to catch up. "Come on, not much farther now."

The trail took the form of rough stairs, suitable for long Aklaka legs. Luskell was tall, but even she had to stretch to make each step. On one stretch, she heard her trouser seam pop.

"I can't picture Mamam climbing this, with her little legs."

Laki glanced down at her. "They must have flown."

Luskell chose not to voice the obvious question: *Then why didn't we?* She knew the answer. He wanted her to save her power for Listening. How much would it require?

At the top, the trail disappeared on a broad, windswept ledge. A rough cliff face loomed overhead. Laki paused and leaned against it. Luskell joined him and they ate from the bag of trail food while they rested. This place had an eerie familiarity, from family stories and half-remembered dreams. Luskell crossed the ledge and looked over. The world fell away into a deep canyon, with a wild river far away at the bottom.

"Careful," Laki warned.

"I won't fall." Luskell took a step back, though she wanted to stand right at the edge. "Imagine what it must have been like, to stand out here for months on end. Poor Kladadad."

Laki joined her and wrapped his arm around her shoulders. "I'll never forget the dream he sent me. I didn't really understand it—I just knew someone was cold and needed help."

Luskell leaned against him, taking comfort in his warm, solid presence. "I guess we'd better do this, before that describes me. How do I Listen to Aku?"

"Come over here." He led her to the cliff face. "Press your hands against the rock. Close your eyes. Quiet your mind. Reach out with all your senses, into the Mountain."

Quieting her mind was nothing new. She had to do that before she mind-talked or controlled a dream. But she wasn't comfortably positioned in a warm room now. The thin air left her lightheaded, and the cold worked its way under all her warm layers.

She wrenched her attention back. The rock. The Mountain. She tried to Listen. Nothing. She pulled her mittens off and laid her bare hands on the rock. She pressed her face against the stone. Her cheekbone ached with cold. Stonesmell filled her nostrils so much she could taste it. But she heard nothing but wind. And then ... not quite nothing. Luskell sensed the faintest vibration in the rock, deep and distant, but steady. Almost like breathing.

She focused on that, followed it down, and touched a vast, alien mind. Images rode the vibration. Snow. Wind. Rain. Sun. Glaciers, advancing and retreating. Forests growing, flourishing, dying. Rivers flowing, eroding rock, carving channels. And through it all, voices. Human voices, singing a song Luskell knew well. She knew some of the voices, too.

She opened her eyes and stepped back from the cliff face. "She's dreaming. She's dreaming of Knot."

Laki smiled. "Among other things. That's mostly how it is when she's calm."

"That was easier than I thought it would be." She pulled mittens back over numb fingers.

"Then again, the subject is hard to miss. Now we'll try something trickier."

"Play first?"

Laki raised an eyebrow. "You haven't even worked yet."

They had another snack, then hiked back down below the timberline. Luskell was hopeful that Laki had changed his mind and they were going back to the lodge, but he stopped in the middle of the woods.

"This is a good spot. Try Listening to the trees."

Luskell looked around. "Any one in particular?"

"Any tree. Or all of them, if that's easier."

In a way, it was easier than Listening to the Mountain. The trees had smaller voices, but there were more of them, and they seemed to be talking to each other. There was a constant murmur that she couldn't quite understand. It traveled up and down the trunks as well as between the branches.

"I hear them," Luskell said. "I don't know what they're saying." She relaxed her concentration and the murmur faded but did not disappear. She turned to Laki with wonder. "I still hear them!"

He grinned. "You're attuned to them now."

"And I'm worn out. That took more power than I expected."

"It will get easier, with practice. Let's have something to eat."

"And then ... play?"

"You were a good student today. You'll have your reward."

They returned to the warm lodge, where heat and time had transformed water and dry morsels into a satisfying soup. Luskell slurped it happily. "Remember that awful soup I made for us in Misty Pass?"

Laki laughed. "It wasn't that bad—it just needed more time." He finished his bowl, then rooted around in one of the supply baskets. He brought out a folded skin and a bag that rattled. Unfolded, the skin revealed itself to be a one-hundred-square Baktat board. Laki carefully set up the stones.

Luskell looked on in disbelief. "That's not what I meant by play!"

"It's good for your focus. Besides, I haven't played against a decent opponent since summer. Indulge me."

"You know I'm not a decent opponent!"

"Beat me, and we'll do whatever you want."

That promise focused her mind, though there wasn't much chance of her winning. Laki was a genius at Baktat, perhaps even better than his father, a strategic master. But Luskell assumed when Laki won and they did whatever he wanted, it would be the same as what she wanted. Luskell stayed in the game right to the end.

"I think that's the best you've ever played," Laki said. "Have you been practicing?"

"Dadad and I play sometimes. We're equally bad at it, so it's fair." She yawned and leaned against Laki. "So, what do you want to do now?"

"Get into bed. I'll be right there."

Luskell undressed down to her underclothes. It was too cold away from the fire to go farther than that. She got under the covers and waited. Laki joined her and held her close.

"What do you want me to do?" she whispered.

"Sleep."

Warm and drowsy, Luskell fought sleep for a time. She thought she wanted to do love more than she wanted to sleep, in spite of her soreness. But it felt nice to be held. And she was so tired. Using power the way she had in recent days took a lot out of a person. Then Laki murmured Aku's Lullaby into Luskell's ear. She had no defense against that. She slept.

Luskell stood at the edge of the cliff. She wouldn't have hiked here at night, but she didn't remember flying. Aku's peak gleamed above her in the twilight. The canyon below should have been lost in darkness, but she could see clearly a teeming city at the bottom.

"Am I dreaming? I was just here."

"I saw. You met my Aku today." Knot stood beside Luskell, on the spot where he once spent months as Aku's prisoner.

A painful lump rose in Luskell's throat. She turned toward him. "I was afraid I wouldn't see you anymore."

He smiled down at her. Because it was a dream, she could see his eyes even in the dark, his eyes that were her eyes, the same dark blue as the twilight sky. "So. Nalaklak is the man you choose?"

"He's teaching me to Listen."

"And much else besides."

Luskell looked away. "That's my business."

"True. I'm the last to judge on such matters. Just ... make it his business, too."

"I won't run away in the night, if that's what you mean."

Knot flinched. "But you will leave."

"Laki knows that. It's no secret."

"All right, as long as you're sure. I'll let you get back to him. Before I do, though, I've learned something you should know."

"You sound so serious. Is it something bad?"

"It could be. This is all rumor and hearsay—the dead are worse gossips even than the living!—but I think it's true. It confirms my belief about the danger in visiting us on the Other Side. It isn't only that the place itself saps your life-force, though that would be enough to encourage caution." He paused, gazing at her.

"I know, I should be careful and not stay too long. What else?"

"You'll be drained more quickly if you have contact with souls of the dead. The touch of a living soul is like a drug to them."

Luskell shuddered. "You mean I can't hug you and Ketwyn? That you'd hurt me?"

"With someone who cares about you, there's less harm; we give as well as take. But someone who doesn't know or love you—"

"And when you visit my dreams?"

"That's different. We're on your territory. No one can directly harm you; but don't let anyone persuade you to do something stupid."

Knot took Luskell in his arms. She clasped him tight. His touch lacked the weight and warmth of a living person, but felt more real than other spirits she'd touched in dreams. She pressed her face to his shoulder.

"Aku dreams of you," she whispered.

"She's welcome to. She shared a chunk of my life." He stepped back. "But I don't visit her dreams."

CHAPTER TWENTY-SEVEN

A full night of unbroken sleep was exactly what Luskell needed. Her pains had vanished, her magic was re-stored, and her body felt strong and rested. But Knot's warning concerned her. Jagryn was trying to cross over, but he didn't know the danger. While Laki slept beside her, Luskell reached out for Jagryn's mind.

If you get to the Other Side, don't stay too long and don't let anyone touch you who doesn't care about you. I wish you could answer! Send me a letter in Misty Pass. Be safe.

"Who are you mind-talking to?"

Laki's voice broke Luskell's concentration. "Not that it's your business, but I needed to tell Jagryn some-thing important. About his quest."

Laki frowned. She leaned in to kiss him. Why should Laki be jealous of Jagryn when Luskell was with him here? "Let's stay in today," she whispered.

Laki held her close and whispered in her ear. "Is the sun out?"

"I don't know."

"Then go check."

Luskell could not believe his self-control. His body clearly wanted what hers did, but he refused to go any further until she left the bed and peeked out the door-way. Muted morning light revealed large flakes drifting down. "It's snowing."

"Really snowing, or a little flurry?"

"It's coming down pretty steadily."

"Wind?"

"None."

Laki sprang out of bed. "Then let's make a plan for the day."

"But ... but what about—?"

He grinned. "Later. Don't worry. You won't be sorry."

While Laki fetched water from the spring, Luskell foraged around in the supplies and put together some breakfast. He came in with pails of water and ice chunks. White flakes clung to his hood, and he wore a delighted grin.

"This is perfect! You can Listen to snow!"

"You think so? I couldn't understand the trees."

"You will. It just takes practice."

After the meal, she layered on all her warm clothes and they went outside. At least they didn't have to hike anywhere—snow fell everywhere.

"You're lucky there's no wind today," Laki said. "It's much easier to hear snow when it's not blowing all over the place."

"So do I Listen to all of it at once, or just one flake at a time?"

"Each snowflake carries its own message."

"How do I choose?"

"You don't. Let them choose you."

Luskell closed her eyes and lifted her face to the falling snow. It tickled her eyelashes and melted in cold, wet kisses on her cheeks. And as the flakes melted, they released their words: *Love. Fear. Power. Danger. Choices.*

Luskell lowered her face and stared at Laki. He watched her with a satisfied smile. "Well?"

"I heard them," she said. "No, I *felt* them. They're much clearer than the trees."

"If you know how to Listen, it's hard to miss the meaning of something that touches your skin."

"Were they talking to me? About me?"

"We ... hear what we need."

"But why do they care about us at all?"

He smiled. "They don't. Listening is about being still, focusing on something else so you can see what's right in front of you; what you already know but don't know you know. When things that aren't human seem to talk to you, it's really you talking to you."

Luskell didn't completely understand, but it gave her confidence. "I want to try the trees again."

She didn't wait for permission, but headed straight into the woods. The trees here were mostly all the same kind, a compact, slow-growing fir that thrived at high elevations. In this sheltered spot, they were symmet-rical cone shapes. The lowest branches spread out bare-ly a hand's breadth above the ground. The trees had narrow crowns and grew too sparsely to form any kind of canopy overhead. Nearly as much snow reached the ground as in the open.

Already, Luskell could sense their whispers. She shook snow from a convenient branch, then pulled off her mitten and rested her fingers on the upward-curving blue-green needles. They tickled her skin; they weren't sharp enough to hurt. She closed her eyes, quieted her mind and Listened. At first, all she heard was an unintelligible murmur. She applied more power. She could almost understand, but her hand ached with cold. When she withdrew it, the voices of the trees grew muffled and faint.

Luskell breathed on her fingers to warm them, then put her mitten back on.

"Are you quitting so soon?" Laki asked.

Luskell jumped. She hadn't heard him approach. "I don't want to, but I couldn't feel my fingers. Why can't I do this?"

"You can. I'm sure you were close."

"I've seen you Listen without touching anything."

He smiled. "I've been practicing since I was three. This is your second day."

Luskell nodded and tried to calm her thoughts. He'd said it was hard to miss the meaning of something that touched your skin. She should be able to do this. She pulled off the mitten and touched the branch again.

She still couldn't understand, but she pushed more power into the effort and began to perceive a pattern— repetition, call-and-response, themes and variations. It wasn't that each tree had its own part. Each tree contributed its own version of three or four parts.

Luskell focused on the tree she touched, and the undifferentiated murmur began to untangle into distinct lines, like the voices in a part song. She focused further on what she thought of as the bass part: the roots. As she Listened, the meaning emerged. The roots spoke continuously of water, rock, soil conditions. They spoke to their own tree and to all the other roots.

And to Luskell. She dropped the branch and squealed. "I hear them!" She threw her arms around Laki and gave him an exuberant kiss. "I understand them! It's like harmony, with lines and chords and everything! I have to tell Dokral! No wonder they make fiddles out of trees!"

Laki laughed and hugged her. "I wouldn't have described it that way, but you're the musician. You're just beginning, though. What else can you hear?"

Luskell returned to her tree and took a moment to regain her calm focus. Now she concentrated on the trunk and its concerns with growth, insects, wood-peckers, disease. The branches were almost entirely devoted to cones and the sun, with snow a lesser topic. Luskell broadened her focus to take in the rest of the grove, and heard more of the same, varying from tree to tree. And something else.

She turned to Laki as she drew on her mitten. "They mostly speak of what you'd expect from trees—water and sun and cones and so forth. But they also seem to pass gossip, like people! I kept hearing about a 'power-ful stranger.' What does that mean?"

Laki raised one eyebrow and smiled. "Don't you know? That's probably you."

"No, it isn't! Is it?"

"Let's go warm up and have something to eat. Then we'll see how powerful you really are."

Luskell hoped he was making a veiled reference to doing love, but after lunch, he put his outdoor gear back on.

"Are you sure you want to go out so soon?" She tried for a seductive tone, but it mostly made her voice sound strained.

Laki's expression was difficult to read, and Luskell knew better than to read his thoughts. He'd be able to tell. "For this lesson, I need you to be a little on edge. Let's go."

He took her back to the woods. His trodden path was already half filled with snow. It reached almost to the tops of Luskell's boots. Off the path, it was deeper still.

"It feels colder," Luskell said.

Laki nodded. "We don't have to go farther than this. What does the snow say now?"

She lifted her face to the falling flakes. They were smaller now, falling more thickly, with an icy wind behind them. Their touch was a sting, not a kiss. They bore a variety of messages, but one repeated again and again.

"Blizzard?"

"We won't come out tomorrow," Laki confirmed. "So, while you have the chance, Listen to the trees without touching them. Once you've got that, we'll try something new."

Luskell closed her eyes and reached out with her senses to the tree nearest her, and by extension, to the whole forest. As she expected, it took more power than when she touched a branch. The voices were quieter, so she had to Listen harder, but it didn't take long to pick up meaning again. The roots were still muttering away about water and soil. The trunks and branches had all their previous concerns, as well as the coming storm. There was also a hint of some other danger, somewhere, a rumor repeated so many times it lost most of its meaning. For all Luskell knew, it had to do with last summer's fire season.

She opened her eyes and reported to Laki all she'd heard.

"You see? You're very good at this." He grinned. "Try it again." He moved several steps away from her.

Luskell stamped her feet to keep the blood flowing, then closed her eyes to Listen. As she reached out to the forest again, Laki began a loud, apparently pointless conversation. He took both parts himself, half in a comical, high-pitched voice.

Luskell laughed and opened one eye. "Will you be quiet, please? What are you doing?"

"It's easy to Listen when you have no distractions besides the cold. I'm going to try to break your concentration. Don't let me."

Luskell exerted more power to Listen while at the same time blocking out Laki's nonsense. It took more focus than Luskell knew she had, but soon, she was back in the middle of the forest's multi-voiced con-versation. She wasn't sure when Laki stopped talking, but by the time she noticed, he had started something even more distracting.

How's it going? Is it working?

Mind-talking? That's not fair!

I'm doing my job. You do yours.

Luskell had worked hard learning how to hear mind-talking. She'd never thought about how to block it. Maybe it could be blocked like emotions. She put up a shield like the one she used with her mother, and Laki's nattering was reduced to a whisper. This required more power than merely ignoring his spoken voice, but she thought she could maintain it for the duration of the test.

She took a deep breath, quieted her mind again, and devoted herself to Listening to the forest. It was always the same basic themes, but the longer she Listened, the more new information she picked up. The rumor of danger seemed to come from the direction of Misty Pass. That got Luskell's attention, but if she understood correctly, the danger—whatever it was—had already passed. Probably something to do with all the timber that was felled for the new meeting hall.

Luskell was deep in Listening when Laki deployed his last tool of distraction. In all the new snow, she didn't hear him approach, but suddenly he stood behind her, his hands on her shoulders.

"I can't concentrate if you're going to sneak up that way."

"I didn't sneak. I thought you might be cold after so much time."

"So much—" How long had it been? It was hard to tell the time with the thick clouds and falling snow, but it might have been darkening toward evening. Her stomach growled loudly. "I guess I got caught up in Listening."

"You're doing well, but I'm cold and hungry. Let's get out of this snow."

"I'm ready, too." Earlier she would have welcomed this suggestion as an invitation to do love. Now she wanted warmth and supper more. But even so, she was sorry to leave the forest in the middle of the story.

CHAPTER TWENTY-EIGHT

Luskell flew over the ocean at night, all alone with nowhere to land. She flew blind. Waves roared in the dark. She cried out; the tumult swallowed her voice.

Calling for help ended the dream, but something still roared. Luskell sat up with the covers around her for protection from a blast of cold air. She blinked around the fire-lit lodge. Laki fastened the flap over the doorway, muffling the sound and shutting out the wind.

Luskell squinted at him and rubbed her eyes. "Is it morning?"

He dumped a pail of something white into a pot. "It must be. We won't see the sun today." He returned to the doorway and opened the flap enough for the pail to fit through. Snow swirled in on a sharp wind and the noise rose to a howl before he fastened the flap again. "Stay in bed if you want. We can't go out in this weather." He dumped another pail of snow into the pot.

Luskell gave him a mischievous grin. "Only if you get back in with me."

Laki glanced at her sidelong and shook his head. He cleared his throat. "Can't. Have to make sure the smoke hole stays open." He took a long branch and poked it through the hole. A flurry of snow sifted in.

Luskell shivered into her clothes. The lodge's underground construction in the sheltered part of the valley kept out most of the wind, but icy drafts slipped around the door flap and down the smoke hole.

Laki looked up from preparing breakfast. "The good news is we have plenty of food, and all the water we can scoop right outside the door. No need to risk getting lost on the way to the spring." He used the branch to brush out the smoke hole again. "The bad news is, the snow keeps drifting over the hole. We might have to sleep in shifts tonight, or risk suffocating."

Luskell frowned. This problem reminded her of something. "What did you do when you were alone, not sleep at all?"

"There used to be a small snow shed over the smoke hole; it must have blown off in the last big storm."

Luskell tried to grasp the elusive memory. Some-thing to do with smoke, and shelter, and safety. Then it came to her—camping out with Mamam and Dadad, the warmth of a campfire enclosed in an invisible bubble. She stood close to the firepit and gauged the size of the smoke hole with her hands. She worked a spell with her voice and fingers. No more snow got in, but the smoke wasn't trapped.

"What did you do?" Laki asked.

"It's a spell tent—something Dadad taught me and his father taught him. This is a tiny one, just big enough to cover the smoke hole. The snow will slide off it instead of piling up. It holds heat in, too, but lets smoke and bad air out."

He smiled and shook his head. "You even think like a wizard. How long will it last?"

"They're good for about half a day before they have to be refreshed. Why?"

"These blizzards usually last two or three days."

Luskell sat by the fire and accepted breakfast. Two or three days wasn't a problem. The spell tent was so small, it wouldn't require much power to refresh. But it was a long time to be stuck inside.

They shared cleanup chores after breakfast, then played a long game of Baktat that lasted through lunch. Laki won, as Luskell predicted, but he praised her improvement.

"I wish I had my fiddle with me. I'm better at music than games."

"I wouldn't mind singing with you. It will pass the time."

Even without the fiddle, music was a pleasure. They sang songs they both knew, and Luskell taught Laki a few new ones. Neither had more than modest talent as a singer and their voices didn't really blend, but they weren't trying to perform for anyone but themselves. When they ran out of songs, they moved on to stories. They both knew some Aklaka stories, which were best sung. When their voices tired, Luskell taught Laki how to cast a spell tent, and tried to Listen to the storm, which made her almost as dizzy as kissing Laki.

After supper, they mended clothes. Luskell sat near the fire in her long woolen underwear and stitched up the seam she'd split in her trousers on the first day's hike. A week ago, it would have been hard to imagine sitting around so casually with any man, even Laki, in this state of undress; not that her winter underwear was at all revealing.

She smiled across the fire at Laki. "Why so far away? I won't bite."

He gave her a half smile and gazed in silence a moment. "If I sit over here, I get to look at you." His smile grew. "I remember the first time I saw you. I had just turned five—I remember there was a big party. Afterward, Mamam told me Aketnan and Crane were coming and they had a surprise for me."

It always startled Luskell to hear her mother called by the name of the legendary spirit she hosted. Aketnan the Peacebringer was an important figure to the Aklaka, and they treated Mamam with respect and awe.

"I remembered them," Laki continued. "Even though I was so young and hadn't seen them in almost two years. But my uncle Chamokat spoke often of his old friend Crane, and Aketnan saved my life once."

"I've heard about that all my life." Luskell's mother shared the story both as a warning against using power soon after transformation, and to illustrate the kind of situation that made the risk acceptable. "Do you really remember, or only what you've been told?"

Laki's brow furrowed in a thoughtful frown. "I re-member fragments. I remember watching the big people from high in a tree. I remember how excited and on edge they were about the stranger who'd come. He was smaller than my uncle, but ... bigger on the inside. I didn't know his name yet, but I wanted him to look at me." He gazed off beyond Luskell.

Her heart fluttered. What came next was terrible, but he was talking about her own father, before he was her father. Laki, at three, had seen the truth—bigger on the inside.

"The next thing I remember is a loud crack, and then I was on the ground, looking up at another stranger."

"Not the fall?"

Laki shook his head. "You'd think, but no. I guess it happened too fast. There is a strange bit in between, where I'm climbing a grassy hillside and it's bright and warm. But that must be from another time because it was cold when I fell."

Luskell shivered. Aklaka didn't speak of *the Other Side*. At the end of life, they *Climbed out of the Valley*. It sounded like they ended up in the same place. She knew her mother had power. She hadn't understood till now how much. "No, you just weren't ... there very long."

Laki opened his mouth as if to ask a question, then shook his head and went on with his story. "I remember a quiet voice I couldn't understand, but I had to listen. And green eyes. I'd never seen green eyes before. I couldn't look away. Then everything hurt and I cried, but Mamam was there and it was all right again. Better than all right. No wonder I was excited to see them again." He grinned. "And about the surprise."

Luskell blinked away tears. She'd almost lost him before she knew him. "So this visit isn't the first time I've surprised you?" She forced herself to match his grin and found it wasn't forced. She hadn't lost him, and that was something to celebrate.

He laughed. "Far from it. I never knew when you were coming to visit. The grown-ups might have known, but to me, you seemed to always appear unannounced. You were with us often enough to feel like one of us, and yet still exciting."

Luskell squawked and fell over backward. She pounded the floor in her mirth. "Me! Exciting!" She sat back up and wiped streaming eyes. Laughter was a better reason for tears. "So go on—tell about the first time you saw me."

"Your parents hiked into Aku's Lap, and Crane had something in a pack on his back. Aketnan took it out to show me—a baby, not quite a year old, with round, blue eyes and fluffy, curly hair." Laki stared across at Luskell. "You could barely walk, and you were just starting to talk. I couldn't understand a word, but you were—" He hesitated.

Luskell tried to be patient as she waited for him to finish. What was she? Beautiful? Mysterious? Magical?

"You were the loudest baby I'd ever met."

"What?" she protested, laughing.

"You were! Your mother said, 'Laki, this is Luskell,' and you grabbed my nose and shrieked. You didn't cry much, but when you did, it was like a lightning strike or an avalanche." He grinned. "I had to respect that. I pro-mised to teach you everything."

Luskell's mouth dropped open. "I remember that!"

"You can't! You were only a baby."

"I do, though. Like you said, it's a fragment—I'm in bed in a lodge at Aku's Lap, and you're there, promising exactly that. And now you're fulfilling your promise."

Laki bit off a thread and neatly folded the garments he'd been mending. "What else do you remember about me?"

Luskell gazed into the fire and considered. "This was later. I must have been going on six, and we joined you for part of the summer. That's when you taught me to swim."

He nodded. "That was probably the last time I saw you naked."

"Every child in the swimming hole was naked. No-body cared."

"True. I didn't know then it would ever be something special." A warm flush rose up Luskell's neck and face, not of embarrassment or modesty. Laki swallowed visibly. "Do you remember foraging with the other children? I can still hear you, loud as ever, 'Dig here! Pick there!'"

Luskell shook her head. "I can't believe I was so bossy!"

"Wherever you said to dig, we found roots. Where you pointed, we found mushrooms or berries. You were already your father's daughter."

Luskell couldn't answer. She'd heard all her life about her father's sense for hidden things. Spells of finding came easily to her once she began her training, but she'd been blissfully unaware of any ability earlier.

"You could run, too," Laki added. "Faster than a lot of us."

Luskell giggled. "That's what comes of having older boys for playmates. Didn't matter where I was—Eukard City with Wyllik and Ambug, Deep River with Jagryn and his brother, Aku's Lap with you and your friends—there was always some big boy I had to keep up with."

Laki scowled. "And now you know too many young men."

"You're jealous! Even though it's your bed I'm sharing."

"For now." He'd lost his grumpy frown but Luskell would have heard the regret in his voice even if she couldn't feel it.

"If now was all I had, I'd spend it right here with you. I can't promise more than that."

Laki nodded, accepting or resigned. "It's early yet," he said, though it wasn't clear how he could tell. It had been dark all day. "I'll heat some water and brew us a drink before bed."

Luskell would have been happy to go straight to bed, but didn't stop him as he busied himself with this activity.

The hot drink warmed her from the inside, making it easier to leave the fireside and climb into bed when the time came. Laki did love with passion and enthusiasm, so he must have gotten over his low mood. Maybe he enjoyed it more if he felt like he'd waited. Luskell enjoyed it no matter what. She used the protective charm faithfully, there was no one to interrupt them ... and little else to do. If now were all she had, life would have been perfect.

CHAPTER TWENTY-NINE

Luskell woke in the night. The blizzard still howled, its voice muffled. The lodge must have been buried in a deep drift. In the banked fire's dim glow, she could barely see Laki where he sat up next to her, alert and anxious.

"Laki, what is it?" She touched his shoulder. The muscles were tense.

"Listen," he whispered.

"To what? I can't hear anything over the storm."

"Not over it—under it. Listen to Aku."

Luskell doubted her skills were up to the task. She had only Listened to the Mountain in a special place, with her skin touching the rock. And that was in calm weather. Then again, they were on the Mountain right here, sleeping in Aku's pocket. It couldn't hurt to try.

Luskell closed her eyes and quieted her mind. She couldn't do anything about the raging blizzard, but took Laki's direction and Listened under it. She reached with her senses into the ground, out among the tree roots, up to

Aku's ice-cloaked peak, down into her fiery heart. Once again, Luskell entered Aku's dream. Many of the images and voices were familiar, but the Mountain's sleep was restless. Fretful. Anger bubbled up, and peaceful images turned violent. Mudslides buried landscapes, raging torrents overwhelmed river valleys, hot breath flattened forests.

Luskell yelped and jerked the covers over herself. "What's happening?" The images dimmed, lurking at the edges of awareness. "Is it because I'm here? Is she jealous, like with Knot?"

"No, I don't think so. But Mother Aku is waking," Laki said, his voice calm but quivering with tension. "And she never wakes happy."

"But that's why you're here, right? To calm her."

"In the middle of a blizzard? If I tried to reach the place where we touch, I'd get lost and freeze to death, if I didn't fall over a cliff first." He massaged his brow with one hand.

Luskell found his other hand and squeezed it. "Do you have to go there to calm her?"

"It's the best place. The easiest."

"But not the only place. Dadad says Knot once calmed her from Deep River."

Laki stared at her. "He was a mature wizard who had done nothing but deal with Aku for eighteen years. And it nearly killed him."

"All right, then, think how much better off you are! You're not nearly that far away. You can Listen to Aku from here—why couldn't Aku hear you?"

Laki Listened in silence. A tremor jolted the ground beneath them.

Laki gasped. "This is bad. She's not supposed to wake up this fast, with no warning." He made an audible effort to slow his breathing. "Calming Aku takes a lot of power, even in the best place. I might not have enough."

"Use mine," Luskell replied without thinking.

"What? How?"

Now that she'd offered, she couldn't back out. "We'll do it together. I already know the song."

"You do?"

"Laki, I've known it my whole life. I used it on Trenn, remember? I sing it to Crett when he's fussy. And I've got loads of power just going to waste here. It'll be like Bardin's teamwork exercises."

"Only it's not practice, and if we fail, people will die. Including us."

Luskell shivered. She'd never heard Laki sound so grim. "Then we won't fail."

They got out of bed and Laki stirred and fed the fire. They pulled on all their cold-weather gear. Out-side, the storm shrieked.

"I can try it alone first," Laki offered. "It's my job, not yours."

"I can't sit here and do nothing. We'll do it to-gether."

Laki opened the flap. Wind and snow rushed in. "Keep one hand on the lodge," he instructed. "Hold onto me with the other. Don't let go."

He climbed through and Luskell followed into a dark, swirling blur. The wind came from all directions at once and dealt Luskell a stinging, snow-filled slap in the face. Although she gripped Laki's hand, she couldn't see him. She pressed her other hand against the lodge, just above the opening. She couldn't hear anything but the storm.

She closed her eyes and ducked her head against the wind as she Listened again to Aku. She was glad Laki had forced her to practice Listening through dis-tractions; the blizzard was more distracting than any-thing he could dream up. Even so, as soon as she began, Luskell wanted to withdraw and hide. The peaceful images had almost all disappeared, replaced by increasingly frantic images of destruction. The soothing voices had been silenced.

Stay with me, Laki whispered in her mind.

Luskell squeezed his hand and steeled herself. Aku's mind was vast and alien, her anger overwhelming ... but not so strange, after all. The Mountain was ... growing. She was scared and in pain. She was having a tantrum. Frightening, but familiar. Luskell imagined holding Aku the way she would Crett.

Both hands grew numb with cold in spite of thick mittens. Luskell had to take it on faith that she still held Laki's hand. It was almost a relief to touch Aku's raging thoughts; at least some of them were warm. She knew when Laki began to sing, though she couldn't hear him. Luskell added her voice and her power. She couldn't hear herself, either—the wind carried her voice away like ashes. One verse was usually enough to put a child to sleep, and have any adult in range yawning. Though she was prepared, after all five verses, even Luskell felt groggy. Aku still roiled with barely con-tained fury. They kept singing, and their combined power carried the lullaby directly into Aku's heart. At last, the Mountain began to listen.

Luskell didn't detect any immediate change in the turmoil ... except that Aku's attention was now on them. It reminded Luskell of a time she had picked up Crett during a tantrum and he'd popped her in the nose with a small, flailing fist. The surprise of it more than the pain had brought her to tears, which in turn stopped the tantrum cold. Crett kissed the owie better and allowed Luskell to hug him.

She continued to sing and push power through Laki into the Mountain. She added all the affection she could find—her love for Crett and her parents, for Laki and all her friends, and the love she knew Knot had borne Aku.

The ground jolted under Luskell's feet. She stumbled against the lodge and lost her grip on Laki's hand. She'd lost her connection with Aku, too, though she could still faintly sense the Mountain under the storm. The rage was gone.

"Laki?" The storm whirled Luskell's call away. Her first instinct was to search for him, but she didn't dare take her hand off the lodge. Then they'd both be lost. She fumbled over the surface of the lodge until she found the doorway. Something lay almost in the opening—Laki, inert. Luskell climbed through and pulled him in after her, glad it was down, not up. Her power was spent, but she still had muscles and training in how to move a person larger than herself. Laki flopped to the floor and lay still. Luskell wanted more than anything to join him. She fastened the flap over the doorway first to shut out the wind. Snow had already drifted over the floor.

Laki rolled over with a groan. "Luskell."

"I'm here." She knelt beside him and gripped his hands between hers.

"We did it ... didn't we?"

She collapsed next to him. "I hope so, because I've got nothing left."

He trembled and made a strange huffing noise.

"Are you cold?"

He nodded, then shook his head, and continued to shake and huff, laughing and shuddering at the same time. "G-good thing you had so much to give. If you've ever got a h-half-year to spare, we could use your t-talents up here."

She laughed weakly. "They'd let a girl?"

"I d-don't know. One h-hasn't volunteered before."

"I'll think about it. Maybe in summer, though."

"S-smart. You might have to f-fight K-k-kiraknat." Laki trembled harder. "I th-think I might be a l-little ch-ch-chilled."

It was too much effort to answer. Luskell draped an arm over him and held him close. She sensed Aku through the ground, rage spent, dreaming. She frowned. "Why didn't we calm Aku from in here? Why did we go outside?"

Laki groaned. "Because we're fools. Aku's probably laughing at us."

They lay there for what felt like a long time. Luskell roused herself enough to say, "We'd be warmer in bed."

"Mm," Laki replied.

They continued to lie on the floor. Luskell watched snow sift through the smoke hole. It meant ... something. She had forgotten to refresh the spell tent, and now it had failed. Next to calming Aku, that hardly seemed important.

She poked Laki to get him moving. They crawled across the lodge and climbed into bed, stopping only long enough to pull off their boots. Luskell held Laki under the pile of blankets and furs, and watched the smoke hole, though she couldn't remember what she was watching for. For the snow to ... stop. It did. Good.

No, bad. Her exhausted mind pulled itself together enough to remember. If the snow wasn't getting in, that meant the hole was blocked. If the hole was blocked, smoke from the fire couldn't get out. The lodge would slowly fill with smoke and poisoned air. Laki and Luskell would fall asleep and not wake up.

Was that so terrible? Sleeping forever sounded like the best idea she'd had in years. She could go to the Other Side and ... never come back. Not good. She drag-ged herself out of bed and found the branch Laki used to clear the smoke hole. Her arms trembled so hard, it took three tries to push it through. She dropped the branch and nearly fell beside it. She tried to cast a new spell tent. Nothing happened. The only alternative was to put out the fire.

She hated to do it. On the contrary, she preferred to build it up. Her hands were only now getting feeling back, and even in all her clothes, she felt chilly around the edges. But it was too great a risk. With regret, she spoke the extinguishing spell—the second spell she'd learned, right after the fire spell. It was simple but powerful magic. With only a few days' experience, Luskell had once helped Laki and Jagryn put out a wildfire and save a farm. But for the first time since then, nothing happened. Her power was spent.

Luskell emptied the water jug over the glowing embers. She swept the pile of snow off the floor and into the firepit. Then she stumbled through the darkness and shivered into bed.

CHAPTER THIRTY

Luskell woke only when the cold penetrated all the furs and blankets. Laki shivered beside her and peeked over the edge of the covers.

"The fire's out," he muttered. "Why?"

"I didn't want us to die," Luskell replied. "I think I can manage a spell tent if you can get a fire going."

Laki huddled under the covers a moment, then sprang to the fire pit. He cleared the smoke hole, then piled up kindling, lit it with a flint, added a log, and dived back into bed. Luskell blinked. He hadn't used magic, but accomplished the job almost as quickly as if he had. Still feeble, she found enough power to cast a tiny spell tent over the smoke hole.

They both spent the day recovering in bed, Listening to Aku under the continuing blizzard. They had huge appetites but no inclination to cook. They ate the dried rations Luskell had brought and snuggled together under the covers. When they eventually re-gained enough strength to do love, it was less about desire and more about gratitude for being alive.

By the day after that, the storm had ended. After breakfast, Laki cleared the doorway and a path through a drift past his waist.

"Hoo! Beautiful day! We should go out!"

The blast of air made Luskell's face ache. "In that cold?"

"Fresh air!" He took two pairs of snowshoes from where they hung from the roof. "Let's go!"

Luskell rolled her eyes, but knew better than to argue. She bundled up in all the clothes she'd brought with her. Laki smeared a pale ointment onto his face, and she had to laugh—he looked like a clown. "What's that for?"

"It may be cold, but it's so bright even my skin will burn, and so will yours."

He passed her the pot of ointment, and she coated her face. Then she strapped on the spare snowshoes, and followed him into a glittering white world.

"Why not fly?" she asked.

"You need your power for Listening. Besides, doesn't it feel good to move around?"

It did. Their one physical outlet had helped, but it wasn't the same as getting out and really stretching their muscles. They snowshoed out of the valley, down into a deep canyon where it was marginally warmer. The effort warmed them more. At the bottom of the canyon, a river ran too fast to freeze.

"We call this the Bright," he said.

"Does it turn into Deep River?" she asked.

"No, that one we call the White. It flows east, to the Great River. The Bright flows west and empties into Eukard Sound."

"I suppose you want me to Listen to it." Luskell hated to stop moving, but she quieted her mind and reached out to the rushing stream. At least she didn't have to touch it! The river spoke in a rapid chatter, many voices all talking at once and clamoring to be heard. Luskell picked up a word here and there, many the same she'd heard from the snowflakes. That made sense—where did snow end up, after it melted? But the river didn't just shout out single words. It spoke fluently in long, articulate sentences, telling a tale with no beginning and no end.

Luskell opened her eyes and smiled at Laki. "Now I know why Klamamam is so happy living by a river. They're both storytellers." She shivered. "Can we go back now?"

He laughed. "Soon, I promise. While we're here, see if you can Listen to rocks."

She'd heard about this from her father, who claimed rocks took a week to say one word. Luskell was sure he must have exaggerated, but as she Listened, it became clear that not only was he telling the truth, he was overly generous in his estimate. She listened to the deep, slow voice for as long as she could bear, which was not long enough for meaning to emerge.

"Who has patience for that?"

Laki raised an eyebrow. "Not me, even in summer. Thank you for trying."

"So am I a Listener now, or is there more for me to learn?"

"All you need is practice."

By the time they snowshoed back up to the lodge, they were both too exhausted to do anything but eat cold food and sleep. But as she drifted off, Luskell felt triumphant. She had learned to Listen. She would be a wizard.

Luskell woke in the night. All was quiet, and she was warm in Laki's arms. It was dark, but she could see.

Jagryn stood beside the bed, watching them in silence and shivering. Luskell lifted the covers and Jagryn climbed in beside her.

"Did you get my message about not letting them touch you?" she whispered.

"Yes. I'll be careful."

Laki awoke. "Hello, Jagryn. When did you get here?"

Luskell didn't sense jealousy. In fact, he didn't seem surprised.

"Just now. I'll be gone in the morning."

"It's no trouble if you want to stay," Laki replied. "Did you bring food to share?"

Jagryn dug into one pocket and pulled out rocks, leaves, and a stick. "It's my staff." From the other he triumphantly produced one slice of bread.

Laki was unusually withdrawn in the morning. Luskell guessed he was Listening to Aku, though she couldn't understand why he wouldn't tell her about it. At last, he looked up from his breakfast. "You should think about leaving soon."

"But I have all these new skills to practice." She winked and smiled.

He remained sober. "You can practice anywhere. Deep River, even."

Luskell's breath caught. She remembered her dream about Jagryn. They hadn't done anything, but he had been in bed next to her. In the dream, Laki hadn't been jealous, but that wasn't real. Had he read her thoughts and misunderstood? Or maybe she'd spoken Jagryn's name aloud.

"I expect a supply party soon," Laki continued. "It would be awkward, if they found you here. They'll make assumptions. Raise expectations. So unless you plan to stay with me ..."

"You know I don't. But I can still learn from you." Luskell was sure the supply party wasn't due for weeks yet. He was trying to get rid of her, but she didn't have the heart to call him on his fib. He had reminded her there were other people in the world, something she had almost forgotten.

"Luskell, I can't teach you any more."

She was willing to take it as a compliment. Then it hit her. He had spoken Eukardian, with an odd catch in his voice. "Do you mean, there's no more you can teach me, or you can't teach me ... after this?"

"Both. You need to leave. Today, if you can." He turned away.

"What's wrong?"

"Don't you know?"

She wanted to claim ignorance, but she'd felt his regret before. It was hard to miss the meaning of something that touched your skin. He'd touched all of hers. "Laki, I'm—"

Laki continued before she could finish her apology. "It's not your fault. You never promised to stay. I thought I could accept that, but ... I can't. This whole thing was a mistake. I'm sorry."

"It wasn't a mistake," Luskell said. "If things were different, I would stay with you in a heartbeat!"

"If things were that different, you wouldn't even be here."

"Maybe not. I know there's more I have to learn and do. But I won't regret this time, and I don't want you to, either. Your wife, whoever she is, will be a very lucky woman."

He laughed at that. "I don't regret doing love with you. How could I? It hurts me that it has to end. That it's all we have."

Luskell gave him a playful shove. "It isn't *all* we have. But until either of us finds someone else, I would be happy to do this again, whenever you like."

"And if one of us does find someone else?"

"Then we'll always be friends. That's a promise."

He smiled. "Like my mother and your father."

She furrowed her brow and shook her head. "Not quite like, I don't think."

"I would say exactly like."

"They were ... lovers? When?" Luskell had thought herself open-minded about such things, but it was shocking to imagine her father with anyone but her mother.

"Long ago, when they were young. Before she was Uklak. Before he went to Babiya Island."

"How do you know about this? No one's ever said a thing to me!"

"Well, why would they? But Uncle Chamokat once mentioned in passing what he called their fling. I asked far too many questions and got him to tell me what he knew or guessed. I gather it was brief and passionate, and then Crane was gone. By the time he came back, everything was different—Mamam was Uklak, she'd asked Naliskat to stay with her, she had me—and Crane had found Aketnan."

"I have to be glad about that," Luskell said. "But I wonder why he didn't stay."

"I suspect because he was a wizard. He would have to give up too much to live among people who didn't trust that kind of power." Laki laid one hand against Luskell's face. "That's your reason, too."

She nodded and swallowed. "If it was just you, just your family ... but there's still a lot of distrust. And I can't hide what I am." She thought about Dadad and Kala, Laki's mother. "But they were able to be friends. We can be like that, too. Is that so bad?"

"No. It still hurts."

"I'm ... not sorry, but I didn't mean to cause you pain. I'll get my things and leave you in peace." She gave him a lingering kiss. "Thank you. For everything."

"I should thank you, too."

"Well, why don't you?"

She led him to the bed and they did love one last time. It was less playful this time, more tender. After that, she washed and dressed and loaded her pockets again. She mind-talked to Mamam to let her know she was on her way back to Misty Pass, but not where from.

Laki put on his warm things and walked outside with her.

"So, this is goodbye, then." His jaw muscles were tight.

Luskell gripped both his hands in hers. "For now. Never doubt how much I care for you, Laki. But don't wait for me. You're free."

Laki looked down at their hands and back at her, one eyebrow raised. She lifted his mittened fingers to her lips and kissed them. She forced herself to let go, turn around, and fly away. They were both free.

CHAPTER THIRTY-ONE

Luskell flew hard on her return. She was halfway to Misty Pass before she remembered she was supposed to rest often. She glided to the ground, transformed and collapsed in a boneless heap, her hair unbound and tangled. She didn't even try to move. She couldn't help remembering.

"Not my fault."

She sat up, drank water, ate bread, jerky and dried berries to fuel the rest of her flight to Misty Pass. It was a risk to take it without a break, but as long as she was flying, she wasn't thinking about Laki. She'd always cared for him, and now she found him attractive and exciting. But he loved her more. The hurt in his eyes when he'd asked her to leave, the intensity of his farewell. What had it cost him, telling her to go when he wanted her to stay?

It *was* her fault, at least in part. There was nothing to be done now except follow her chosen path. Be the best wizard she could be, and hope her friend found someone better suited to being the Uklak's wife.

In the afternoon, she arrived home and trans-formed on the doorstep. With shaking hands, she pushed the green door open and stumbled inside.

Mamam dozed in her rocker by the fire, Crett asleep in her arms. She roused and blinked at Luskell, then jerked alert. "I didn't expect you so early." Mamam smiled and stood up with effort. Crett drooped against her shoulder. "You must be hungry."

"Famished," Luskell replied. "Thirsty. Tired." She shrugged off her cloak and dropped into a chair at the table.

Mamam laid Crett in his bed, then set a water jug and bread, cheese and apples on the table. "Tea water's nearly hot. Oh, and there's a letter for you, from Deep River."

"From Jagryn?"

"No, Keela." Mamam retrieved the letter from the mantel. "Why, were you expecting something from Jagryn?"

"No, I forgot—I heard from him, mind-talking. It's fine." Luskell poured herself a mug of water and drained it in two large gulps. Too hungry to bother with the knife, she tore off a hunk of bread and took a big bite as she skimmed Keela's letter. She'd gotten to Oxbow without any trouble, and Jagree was there to meet her; mind-talking to Jagryn must have worked.

Mamam patted Luskell's shoulder as she passed, and sucked in her breath. She pulled out the chair across the table and sank into it. "You've ... been with a man."

Luskell sputtered and nearly choked. "Don't do that! You promised."

Mamam reached across and held Luskell's hand. "I didn't do anything. I would have guessed it if we were meeting for the first time. But you're my daughter—I couldn't miss it." She sighed. "There were things I wanted to tell you first."

Luskell scowled. "I was careful, if that's what you mean."

"It's one of the things, and I'm glad to hear it. It's too early to be sure, but you don't seem to be pregnant, at any rate." Mamam got up and took the steaming tea kettle off the fire. She poured water into the teapot and brought it to the table. "Whose idea was it?"

"Mine." Luskell devoted herself to slicing cheese and choosing an apple from the bowl.

"And this fellow—did he treat you right?"

"Mamam! It was Laki. Of course he did."

Her mother visibly relaxed. "That's a relief." She smiled. "I always wondered if you two might get together. I imagine it'll be a disappointment for Jagryn, though."

"I don't think he's interested anymore." When she had dreamed about letting Jagryn into her bed, they hadn't done anything but talk. "I guess I wouldn't turn him down if he wanted to, but I don't know."

Mamam's eyebrows twitched up. "I see. So this—with Laki—isn't permanent?"

Luskell looked away. "No. But I wanted him to be first." She gave her mother a sharp, defiant glance. "And I don't regret it."

Mamam held up her hands in a mock-defensive gesture. "I'm glad. A trusted friend is a good choice for your first time." She paused and studied Luskell. "I ... did the same thing when I was about your age."

That caught Luskell by surprise. She smiled at the thought. "You did? Who was your trusted friend?"

Her practical, no-nonsense mother gazed off over Luskell's head, a dreamy expression on her face. "A beautiful young wizard who grew up to be your father."

Luskell couldn't hide her confusion. "But ... but then ... what about Ketwyn? Why did you have Walgyn's baby if you were with—?"

"I wasn't." Mamam sighed. "Not then. Your father and I had known each other only a short time, and we were both awfully young. But it was his birthday, and after what he'd been through ... And he was so ..." She closed her eyes and smiled. "I wanted to give him something. Before I went back home."

"You *left* him?" Luskell's anger flared over this long-ago injustice to her beloved father. Even though she had just left her own first lover. It wasn't the same.

Mamam's lips curled into an ironic smile, but she spoke in soothing tones. "We parted on friendly terms. We had our own paths to follow."

Luskell remembered what Laki had told her. "Do you think he waited for you?"

"I know he didn't. We didn't make any promises, other than to find each other again someday."

"So you know about Kala, and you're all friends?"

Mamam's eyes widened and she snorted a laugh. "I knew before she and I were introduced. But I wonder how you found out." She nodded. "Because somehow Laki knows. Not much of a secret, is it? So we might as well be friends. And I couldn't say anything; I didn't wait for him, either. When your father and I met again years later, it was a better time for us to be together. And you sealed the bargain."

"I don't think I'll marry Laki," Luskell said.

"You don't have to decide now." Mamam tilted her head as she watched Luskell. "It may be too late, but will you hear the rest of my advice?"

Usually advice was the last thing Luskell wanted. But her mother had been talking to her like an adult, not a child. Not judging, but sharing. "All right."

"Making love can be wonderful, but we have to be careful about more than having babies. Try not to break any hearts."

Luskell kept her face impassive. Was Laki heartbroken? He'd agreed to try things her way of his own free will. He knew it might not work out. He'd been asking for heartbreak. Luskell still didn't like being responsible for it.

"Don't do it in anger, or to make someone jealous. Don't use people, or let them use you. Don't do it to fill an empty place, or only to feel something again."

"Who would do that?"

Mamam gazed at her. "Do it out of affection and joy. And be careful."

"I will. I promise."

A tiny grunt and a patter of footsteps signaled the end of Crett's nap. He toddled up to Luskell's side and slapped his hands against her leg. "Wuwu back! Where go?"

She lifted him onto her lap. "I went to see Laki. Remember him?"

Crett raised both arms and screeched. Luskell wondered if she'd been that loud as a baby. "Go city?"

"No, Laki's not in the city now. He's way up the Mountain."

Mamam shook her head. "Aku's Lap is not exactly 'way up the Mountain.'"

Luskell swallowed. "I never said I went to Aku's Lap. I've been to Knot's Valley."

Mamam stared at her. She was shielding her emotions, but Luskell saw her deliberately calm herself. She swallowed, took a deep breath, and forced a shaky smile.

"That's right, you told me Laki was there. It ... must be beautiful this time of year."

"In between blizzards," Luskell agreed. "But cold."

"You didn't tumble into Laki's bed by accident. You had this planned."

Luskell nodded. She didn't think Mamam was really angry, but it was better not to push it.

Mamam let out a long breath. "It's probably better that way. And we haven't had an eruption yet, so Aku must like you. All the same, I'm glad you got home be-fore your father. I'm not sure how he'd take it."

"You could remind him that you were the same—" Luskell gasped. "What do you mean, I got home before him? He's here?"

"Didn't I tell you? He's on his way—should be here before supper."

That explained the good mood and the dreamy looks. And the sympathy.

Luskell finished her food and stood up. "That's good. He must have finished ... what he was doing." She didn't want to speak of the strangler in front of Crett.

"He didn't say. I'll be glad to have the family back together."

Luskell went into the curtained corner of the house that served as a closet. "Maybe we can all go to Deep River now."

Mamam snorted. "You don't have to be in a rush to give Jagryn his chance, either."

"I'm not. Dadad needs to go there because Jagryn's close to earning his staff."

She stripped out of her travel clothes, which she had worn almost constantly for a week. They would need a wash, and she knew she could use a bath. As for her hair, she wasn't sure whether to wash it or chop it all off. She made do with a rough braid that at least got it out of her face.

When Dadad walked through the door a short time later, Luskell was mostly prepared for the rush of emotion flooding off her parents. They were more than her parents. They were lovers of long standing who hadn't seen each other in weeks. Mamam flew into Dadad's arms, and he lifted her off the floor and spun her around. He gave Luskell and Crett a quick hug and kiss, but his attention was mostly for Mamam.

Luskell picked up her cloak from the floor and emptied the pockets, then put it on. She lifted her brother. "Come on, Crett, let's go see Grandma and Grandpa. Maybe we can have a bath at the Fogbank."

Mamam gave her a grateful smile. "Wait for us there. We'll be over for supper."

CHAPTER THIRTY-TWO

It had snowed in Misty Pass, though not as heavily as in Knot's Valley. The road through town had been cleared, the snow heaped up on either side. Crett wanted to climb the frozen mounds, but every attempt ended with him lying on his back or sitting in the snow. Luskell finally lifted him to the top, where he crowed in triumph.

"I flied!"

Luskell laughed. "Maybe someday, Crett. Come on, let's go. I'm cold."

She carried him the rest of the way to the Fogbank. The common room was empty, but warm. Grandma Nari poked her head out of the kitchen.

"Luskell! I didn't know you were back. Did you see your father?"

Luskell set Crett on his feet. He trotted over and hugged Grandma's knees. "He just got home. That's why we're here. They seemed to want a moment alone."

Grandma arched a brow. "Thoughtful of you. Will you stay for supper?"

Luskell smiled. "We'll all be eating here. Before that, could we bother you for some bathwater?"

"Of course. You know where the tub is, don't you?"

Luskell stepped out the kitchen door and lifted the washtub down from where it hung on the outside wall. Something flickered in her awareness, a nagging sense of being watched, or of something trying not to be seen. She peered into the trees beyond the yard, but it was already too dark to see far into the forest. She shook her head— probably nothing but a twilight predator on the hunt.

Luskell brought the tub into the kitchen and set it in front of the cookstove. She helped fill it with water from the big cask. Grandma Nari added boiling water from the kettle until the bath water was warm enough for Crett. He dabbled his hands in and gave his ap-proval by splashing and squealing.

While Luskell undressed Crett, Grandma pulled a curtain across to screen the kitchen from the common room. The kitchen window was already shuttered. She set out soap and a washrag. "And here's a towel for each of you. Do you need anything else?"

"Keep us company?" Luskell bathed Crett and told her grandmother about learning to Listen. She left out that she and Laki had been alone the entire time.

"So, they talk to you? Trees and rocks and so forth?"

"Not *to* me, exactly. Trees talk to each other; Aku talks to herself. With the rocks, it's more like eavesdropping. Snowflakes, though ..." Luskell paused to consider. "Snowflakes just *say*, and if you know how to Listen, you hear something true."

Grandma Nari smiled and shook her head. "Well, I can't say I understand it, but it sounds like a great adventure. I'm proud of you. Not every girl gets to do such a thing."

Luskell glanced up at Grandma Nari's strong, lined face, still full of life and good humor. "They didn't have your example." Luskell had never known her as any-thing except an innkeeper, but according to family stories, she'd lived an independent life of travel and some risk before she settled down with Grandpa Eslo. She was equally at home in an apron or on horseback.

As Luskell was about to lift Crett out of the tub, he splashed water everywhere. "Look what you did! You got both towels wet!" She picked him up and buzzed her lips against his belly. She used the driest of the towels to rub him down. He squirmed away from her and ran, naked and giggling, into the common room.

Grandma Nari chuckled. "Get into the tub while it's still warm. I'll catch the little fish, and bring you a dry towel." She followed Crett and made sure the curtain was pulled all the way across.

Luskell undressed and settled into the tub. A big pot of stew simmered on top of the stove, the savory aroma adding to Luskell's pleasure. She smiled as she listened to Crett's squeals and Grandma Nari's calm voice. She couldn't make out all the words; the familiar voices were a comfort, especially when Grandpa's deeper tones joined them. That meant he was out of bed, great progress since Luskell had last seen him. She hummed contentedly as she scrubbed herself, then unbraided her hair. It felt rough and flat, but washing transformed it into a tangle of soft, springy curls.

Grandma Nari came in with the towel and Luskell stood up to take it from her. "Just look at you."

"Did I miss a spot?" Luskell looked herself over quickly for smudges, scrapes or bruises.

Grandma smiled. "No, but when did you turn into a woman? Fellows are going to start noticing."

"Oh, they've been noticing."

"Nothing wrong in that. But don't be in a rush—be sure you choose the best one."

Luskell's heart thumped hard. Had she chosen the best one, and let him go? Or was the best one still waiting for her? "How do I know who that is?"

Grandma glanced back toward Grandpa Eslo. "The one you choose."

Luskell finished drying herself and dressed again. She pushed back the curtain and joined Crett and Grandpa Eslo in the common room. They sat together in a big chair by the fire, busy with a toe rhyme.

"Glad to see you out of bed. You must be doing better." Luskell wrapped an arm around her grand-father's shoulders and kissed his whiskery cheek.

Grandpa coughed and looked up from Crett's foot. "So. Are you a wizard now?"

"Almost. I need to demonstrate to Bardin that I accomplished my task, and then he'll give me a staff." Luskell settled into the other arm chair and began to comb her damp curls. She basked in the fire's heat. She hadn't felt truly warm since the blizzard, but she was getting there.

Grandpa eyed her a moment, then turned back to Crett. "Seems like you'd be in a hurry to get back to the city, then." His voice sounded thick, probably a result of his long illness.

"I just got here! Do you want me to leave already?"

"Don't go, Wuwu!" Crett shouted.

Grandpa tickled Crett's foot and made him giggle. "Crett's right. I see you little enough as it is. Just ... don't change, all right?"

Luskell leaned forward and placed her hand on his knee. "Grandpa, I can't help that. But I'll always be your Luskell."

He glanced around with a quick smile. "I know. I can't imagine you'll hang around here long, though. You'll want to go claim your stick."

She laughed gently. "I need to practice Listening. And I'd like to go to Deep River first. It's been a while."

"What happened to your rush to be first?" Grandpa asked.

He was right—when she'd started this project, she'd been in a hurry to be a wizard as soon as possible. She'd thought she already was one, in all but name. But Bardin had talked a lot about patience, and thoroughness, and care. About wisdom and maturity. She wasn't there yet. Not even close.

"It's not a race," she said at last. "I don't even have an opponent. And there are more important things."

A few other guests arrived for supper, including Mamam and Dadad. Grandma had the family sit at the end of the long table nearest the fire so Grandpa Eslo wouldn't have to leave his armchair. She brought him a bowl of stew there. He ate a little, but mostly stirred food around. Mamam watched him with a worried look. As usual, Crett seemed to get more supper on his face and hands than into his mouth.

Luskell looked at him and laughed. "I don't know why I gave you a bath!"

"A boy needs a fresh start every now and then." Grandma wiped him off and he squirmed down from Dadad's lap. He pattered over to Grandpa and scram-bled into the chair.

"Eat you food, Gampa."

"You first, Crett."

The old man and the little boy fed each other bits from the bowl. It wasn't tidy, but they both ended up eating more than they had on their own. Grandpa set the empty bowl aside and they both dozed off in the chair.

Meanwhile, Mamam and Dadad shared private glances and smiles throughout the meal. Luskell suspected they were holding hands under the table. It would have been embarrassing if they hadn't looked so happy.

Dadad related his uneventful journey from the city, and Luskell shared a little about learning to Listen. Dadad, at least, could understand.

"Sounds like it came to you easily," he said. "Must have been dull." His eyes twinkled in the lamplight.

Luskell smiled. "It was more work than some things, less than others. But not dull—except for the rocks."

Dadad guffawed. "I don't imagine you had the patience for that."

"Who would? But I got to help calm Aku — *that* wasn't dull!"

"I should say not! But how did you get all the way to Knot's Valley?"

"Flew, of course."

Dadad scowled and leaned forward. "Not a very wise use of your power. I'd expect better sense from Chamokat."

"It was my idea. And I was with Laki." Luskell grew warm all over at the memory of all the ways she'd been with him.

Dadad watched her. "There's something you're not telling me."

Mamam touched his arm and shook her head.

"It was during a blizzard," Luskell continued before Dadad could ask awkward questions. "We couldn't even get to the easy place; we had to do it from the lodge."

"At that distance, it would be easier with two." Dadad smiled approvingly. "It must have taken a lot of power."

"Neither of us was good for much the whole next day." Luskell felt safe to change the subject. "So, did you catch the—?"

He glanced at the other guests and answered in an undertone. "Not here."

They spoke of trivial things for the rest of the meal, then collected the sleepy Crett for the walk home. Luskell carried him so her parents could hold hands. They walked without speaking. The night was cold and still, the dark sky bright with stars above tall treetops. Luskell wondered if Laki was looking at the stars.

Back at their house, Luskell played a few tunes on her fiddle. Crett was already half asleep in Mamam's arms, so she left out the dance numbers and stuck to ballads and lullabies. Her chest tightened as she bowed the long notes of a sweet love song. She wasn't sure whether it was missing Laki, regret over her decision, or just the music. It felt too good to be warm and rested for her to be really glum.

Luskell put the fiddle away and helped get Crett ready for bed. He never really woke up, so it seemed safe to ask. "What about the strangler, Dadad?"

"I didn't catch him. There haven't been any more murders since you left, though. It's possible he's in jail for something else, but I have a hunch he left the city."

Dadad's hunches had proven on many occasions to be more than guesses. Luskell grinned. "That's good, isn't it?"

"Not if he takes his crimes to some other town. I volunteered to talk to people out this way, see if anyone noticed anything unusual."

"What makes you think he came this way?" Mamam asked.

He glanced at her but didn't answer right away. He cleared his throat. "Luskell, your friend Fandek—"

"He's not my friend."

"Fine. Your fellow apprentice Fandek disappeared the same day you left town. I think he might have tried to follow you."

"What does that have to do with the strangler?"

"Fandek used to live near the site of at least one murder. And he fits Hanny's description of the man who attacked her."

Luskell crossed her arms. She'd thought the same, but it felt off. "So do a lot of people. Fandek is not a killer."

"I hope not. But you don't know that."

Luskell considered. How much did she really know about Fandek? That he'd come into his power relatively late in life, but had talent. That he found her attractive. That he wasn't bad-looking himself. That his father beat his sons ... She pressed her lips together and bit the inside of her cheek until she was sure she could control her voice. "What are you saying?"

Dadad squeezed her shoulder. "Only that I'm wor-ried you might be a target."

"I think I can protect myself against Fandek."

Dadad nodded. "You're probably right. But I'll feel better when we're all in Deep River."

Luskell frowned. "What are we going to do, curse it to keep strangers away?"

His hurt look told her she'd gone too far, but he answered in a calm voice. "It's off the main road far enough that I don't think he'd go there. Anyway, can't I want to go home?"

"Sorry, I didn't think of that," she said. "I'm ready to go anytime."

Mamam gave Luskell a sharp look. "You may be, but I'm not quite ready to leave your grandpa yet."

"Your mother's right as usual, Luskell. And much as I want to check up on Jagryn, I did promise to talk to people here, especially back in the woods. That could take awhile."

"Have you heard anything from Jagryn?" Luskell asked.

Dadad frowned. "No. I'm worried he might have given up."

"What if I were to go on ahead of you? I could find out how far he's gotten and let you know."

"I don't want you traveling alone."

Luskell waved off his concern. "In my travel clothes I look like a boy. I'll be fine."

Mamam's brows pinched together, but Dadad gazed at Luskell, considering. "Fandek wouldn't be fooled. He knows your face."

"And I know his. If I see him, I can disappear." She allowed herself a sly smile. "And let you know where he is."

Dadad arched a brow. "Lure him out? It could work."

"Oh, no," Mamam said, her tone sharp. "Crane, you are not using our daughter as bait for a murderer." Her cheeks were pink and her eyes had a dangerous gleam.

Dadad stroked her hand. "I wouldn't have suggested it, but she might be onto something. Fandek has some talent, but nowhere near Luskell's power or skill. She has your uncanny senses. I doubt he could get close enough to hurt her."

Luskell nodded vigorously. "Fandek isn't good at shielding yet. I'd feel him coming even if I didn't see him. And I can do the repelling charm without even thinking about it."

"As long as you don't try to pick him up in a whirlwind." Dadad gave Luskell an encouraging smile, and turned to Mamam. "If he's following her, this could be the way to bring him into the open, before anyone else gets hurt."

"And what if this Fandek isn't the killer?" Mamam asked.

"Then at least we'll know where Fandek is, which would be a load off my mind," Dadad said. "And in that case, Luskell's disguise should keep her safe—the killer wouldn't even know she's a girl."

Luskell undressed behind the curtain and slipped into her nightdress. She climbed into bed and snuggled under the covers. Though she missed the warmth of another body next to hers, it felt good to lie in her own familiar bed, wearing something clean and loose. She closed her eyes and drifted, half listening while her parents continued the discussion. She was eager to use her power for good, either by catching the strangler or rescuing Fandek from his own foolishness. She had planted the seed in Dadad's mind, and now relied on him to bring Mamam around to what felt like another part of her quest.

CHAPTER THIRTY-THREE

Luskell held Crett on her lap, making sure he ate more breakfast than he dropped on the floor. A meal with her family, nothing special, yet the first breakfast they'd all eaten together since before her birthday over a month earlier. Mamam hummed a cheerful melody as she brought a plate of toasted bread to the table. Dadad grinned, hooked his arm around her waist and pulled her onto his lap. She squealed but didn't make much effort to get away.

Luskell smiled and shook her head. They'd always been like that, but she'd never considered what it meant.

Crett banged his hands on the table. "Mam-amamamam!"

Mamam slapped Dadad lightly on the shoulder. "Stop it, Crane. We're embarrassing the children."

Luskell laughed out loud. "No, it's all right—much better than fighting, right, Crett?" She spread jam on a slice of toast and offered it to him.

Mamam smiled and leaned her head against Dadad. "Luskell, do you still want to go to Deep River by yourself?"

"Yes, if you'll let me. What changed your mind?"

"I reminded her the morning coach starts running again this week. You wouldn't be traveling at night," Dadad said. "I'll send a letter to your grandmother this morning, so she'll know to expect you soon."

"Why not send me instead?" Luskell grinned, eager to go now it was decided.

"We have to do your washing first," Mamam re-minded her. "You can go in two or three days. If you mind-talk with Jagryn when you leave here, and again when you're close to Oxbow, he can have someone there to meet you."

"He must have heard when I let him know about Keela's delay, so that should work."

Dadad wrote to Klamamam and took the letter to the Fogbank to go out on the morning coach. Luskell helped Mamam wash her travel clothes. It was too damp to hang the wet clothes outside. She strung them near the fire, but they wouldn't be dry enough to wear for at least two days. That wasn't so bad. Luskell hadn't known she missed her family until she had them back. It also gave her a chance to play her fiddle, the only other thing she'd missed while she was with Laki.

She practiced Listening in the forest behind the cabin. The trees here were bigger and more varied than in Knot's Valley, but their conversations were comfortingly familiar. The different varieties spoke to each other as if they were all family. The evergreen cedars and firs reminded her of grandmothers, sharing food with the dormant, leafless maples. The trees nearest the cabin seemed to recognize her, the way they might remember birds and squirrels returning to the same nests year after year. So, Laki was right; she could practice anywhere. It wasn't as nice without him, but she could do it. Perhaps she would list it as a specialty in the *Registry of Practitioners*.

She picked up a hint about danger, as she had in Knot's Valley. Perhaps that wasn't the trees, but something she knew but couldn't see. Like the strangler following her. If he had. She would have to keep alert.

Finally, the day came when Luskell could go. She packed a satchel with her fiddle, nightdress, two changes of clothes, the ever-present cloths, and a pair of shoes. She wore her usual travel outfit of boots, trousers, shirt, and tunic over woolen underwear. That would disguise her appearance and keep her warm in the drafty coach.

Her family waited with her for the coach. "I'm not convinced this is a good idea," Mamam fretted. "Luskell, promise me you won't look for trouble."

"Why would I do that?"

"Because you're seventeen and you have power. Don't go out of your way to attract this killer, whoever he is."

"I won't, I promise."

"Let us know when you get to Deep River," Dadad said. "We'll join you as soon as we can."

When the coach was ready to go, Luskell hugged her parents and brother. Crett clung to her and whim-pered.

"Go, too!"

Luskell freed herself from his little arms and kissed his hands. "You'll get to ride in the coach soon. But today, you have to help Mamam take care of Grandpa. Can you do that?"

"I help."

Luskell climbed into the coach. A family of three— father, mother, and little girl—joined her after a quick breakfast at the inn. She guessed they had been traveling since before dawn. They all looked sleepy, but they were in good spirits.

The father turned to Luskell as the coach pulled away. "Well, young man, where are you headed this fine day?"

She answered in a deliberately low voice. "Deep River, to help my grandmother."

"Good lad. We're headed to Bitter Springs, to see my wife's people."

Luskell smiled. He hadn't said they were getting away from the strangler, though it seemed likely. She had other matters to think about. She leaned back in the seat as if going to sleep, and reached for Jagryn's mind. He couldn't answer from this distance, but she would know when he heard her. Strange—she couldn't find him. It was a long way, but she had reached him from farther. Maybe he was still asleep, though it seemed late for that.

She tried again after they'd passed the town of Sweetwater, with no better success. She stamped her heel against the floor of the coach, then smiled apolo-getically at her startled fellow passengers. Luskell had counted on Jagryn to send someone to meet her, as he had for Keela. No one else in Deep River had any skill with mind-talking, but if she couldn't find him, neither his skill nor hers was any good.

Luskell got off the coach in Oxbow and tried again. Still nothing. She sat on the bench in front of the coach office to think the problem through. It couldn't be the distance. This close, Jagryn might even be able to reply, if he heard her. But he didn't seem to be there at all. What a day for him to go traveling! Luskell couldn't imagine where he'd go, but he was an apprentice wizard. Although his quest didn't require a journey, maybe he'd felt the need to get out of town.

So. Luskell was in Oxbow, but nobody knew it. She didn't have the funds to go back to Misty Pass, which would be a waste, anyway. She'd have to get herself to Deep River.

She gazed at her satchel for a long time, then stepped inside the small log building.

"Excuse me. Do you have a place where I could change clothes?"

The attendant looked up from his desk. She recognized him from previous trips. He smiled. "I know you, don't I?" He gazed at the ceiling and bit his lip. "You were trying to get to Eukard City but you were short of funds. Your Giant friend wanted to trade me his knife."

"Aklaka," Luskell corrected him. "But you're right. That was years ago. I'm surprised you remember."

"It was a beautiful knife. I kind of regret not trading." He shook his head. "And not many girls dress like you. Did you get where you were going that time?"

She gave him a wry smile. "We saved the day. So, changing clothes?"

He gestured toward a door to her right. "There's a room there you can use. Ladies often do, after a day's travel."

Luskell nodded politely, went into the little room and closed the door. She slipped off her tunic and opened her satchel. Two dresses, a nightdress, underclothes, stockings, shoes, and her cloths. She somehow had to wear it all.

The nightdress was loose enough to fit over the trousers and shirt. She topped it with a petticoat, followed by both dresses. The tunic barely fit over everything. She stuffed the shoes, cloths, and remaining undergarments into the inside pockets of her cloak. She hoped this outer garment would disguise her obviously padded figure. And that she didn't look as ridiculous as the man she and Keela had ridden with, in his layers of coats and scarves. She gazed with regret at her fiddle, the only thing left in the bag. Once again, she didn't have a pocket available.

Luskell stepped out of the changing room. "Thank you. My ride is late. May I leave my satchel here until someone can pick it up?"

The attendant handed her a piece of chalk. "Put your name on it. I'll hold it here for seven days."

"Keep it safe."

"You keep yourself safe. One of our local girls went missing three days ago. It's better not to be out alone."

This advice was chillingly familiar. "I'm heading down to the inn for lunch. I'll keep my eyes open for anything strange."

Luskell had eaten a packed lunch on the way, but she bought another lunch at the inn. As she began to eat, she overheard a conversation that confirmed the town's wariness: a woman's body had been found near the lake. Strangled.

Luskell forced herself to finish her food. She would need it. After the meal, she considered letting Mamam know she'd made it to Oxbow. But Mamam could answer, which meant she could ask questions. Questions whose answers would worry her. Instead, Luskell mind-talked to Dadad. It was too far for him to answer.

I'm in Oxbow. The strangler has been here ahead of me, but I'm safe. I promise I'll be careful and let you know when I get to Deep River.

She didn't like to leave the modest bustle of the town, but she didn't want an audience for her transformation. She used a little power to deflect attention, and walked into the countryside. She sensed someone following and turned to look. There was no one visible, but she couldn't shake an uneasiness; whenever she Listened, she heard, "Danger!" It would cost more power, but she put on full concealment and crept onward until she was unlikely to be seen. To be sure, she crouched in a patch of tall grass. It was time to put on wings.

Luskell had been eagles, owls, pigeons and ravens. She remembered Bardin's advice, and chose to be a goose—fast, untiring, and big enough that it was unlikely to be attacked in the air. She held the image in her mind, concentrated, and performed the spell. She beat her wings and launched out of the grass.

Luskell honked in alarm at a startled cry. She didn't know whether this person was already there or had followed her, and didn't get a good look, beyond a quick impression of long black hair. Whoever it was, they were soon left far behind.

CHAPTER THIRTY-FOUR

Luskell flew straight to Deep River without stopping. There would be food and rest at the end. She reached the Blue Heron late in the afternoon. As soon as she changed back, she leaned against the wall to catch her breath before she went inside.

Rakkyn was arranging the common room for sup-per. A small, well built man in his early twenties, he had become Luskell's grandmother's business partner around the time of Luskell's last visit. He turned with a smile when Luskell opened the door. "Luskell! Good to see you. Like old times, eh?"

"I promise not to spill on you," she said.

Klamamam was standing in the kitchen with Auntie Brynnit—Jagryn's aunt, not Luskell's, but like family.

"Luskell! With your hair fluffed out, you look like Knot!" Her grandmother met her in the kitchen door-way with a hug and a kiss.

"It comes undone whenever I transform." She tugged at the tangled mess. "I'm ready to cut it off."

"Oh, don't do that!" Klamamam patted Luskell's head. "I wasn't sure when to expect you. Did you let anyone know?"

"I tried. Do you know where Jagryn is?"

"I haven't seen him yet today. Hungry?"

"I flew here from Oxbow, so yes, I'm famished!" She threw her cloak over the back of a chair and sank into it. Klamamam brought her bread and cheese, and they allowed her to eat in peace.

"Jagryn was over yesterday to help me mix medicines," Auntie Brynnit said. "He hadn't shown much interest in healing before, but he asked a lot of questions and was very helpful. Maybe he'll develop those skills, after all."

Luskell chewed and swallowed. "So he is in town?"

"He was yesterday morning, but I don't think I've seen him today, either." Auntie Brynnit glanced over at Klamamam. "Could be out at Huvro's place."

Klamamam turned to Luskell. "When should I expect the rest of the family?"

"They'll be along in a few days, probably. Grandpa Eslo's been sick, and Mamam wants to make sure he's well enough before she leaves."

Klamamam nodded. "Wobbles is hard on older folks. Your father mentioned a lot of people were leaving the city to get away from the epidemic."

That told Luskell he hadn't mentioned the strangler. "It's bad there. So it hasn't spread here?"

"We don't get too many visitors in winter, and we don't travel much. They canceled the winter dance in Bitter Springs to be safe, though."

"On top of Grandpa being sick, Dadad had some other business to finish. I offered to check on Jagryn's progress and let Dadad know how he's coming along." Luskell fanned herself. The cozy kitchen had grown steadily hotter since she came in.

"Are you all right?" Auntie Brynnit stared at her, thinking *Wobbles*. "Your face is sweating."

Luskell wiped her forehead. "I'm fine, but I'm wearing all my clothes! I guess I should shed some layers before I roast."

"You can have Crane's room," Klamamam said.

Luskell had to think about which room she meant. "You mean Uncle Jelf's room?"

"It was your father's before that." Klamamam and Auntie Brynnit both looked sad. Old Uncle Jelf had lived at the Blue Heron for almost sixteen years, with Klamamam to keep him fed and sheltered and Brynnit next door to keep him as healthy as possible. He had died a little over a year ago, at the advanced age of eighty-two. Klamamam blinked and smiled. "Go on in, it's all ready for you."

Luskell picked up her cloak and went through the common room, past the stairs and into Dadad's old bedroom. The back of the brick oven projected into the room, warming it. Luskell was warm enough on her own. She bolted the door and peeled down to camisole and drawers. She lay back on the bed and took a moment to mind-talk to Mamam while she cooled down.

I'm in Deep River. I had to leave my satchel and fiddle in Oxbow, so pick it up for me when you get there. Mamam would know what that meant, and Luskell braced for an argument that didn't come.

We'll do it, Mamam replied. *But what happened?*

Tell you when you get here.

Luskell put on only one dress with fewer layers underneath. She couldn't bear the heavy woolen underwear yet. She extracted shoes and stockings from her cloak pockets and put them on, then wrapped her much-lightened cloak around her and returned to the kitchen.

"Leaving again so soon?" Klamamam asked.

"I'm going to see if Jagryn's home. I'll be back for supper."

Luskell left the inn and walked up to Jagryn's pa-rents' house behind the school. Old, dirty snow lined the road. She avoided the worst of the mud puddles, but couldn't do much about the chilly breeze blowing under her skirt. Boots and trousers began to seem like a better idea.

A group of children burst from the schoolhouse and ran, laughing and shouting, down the middle of the road. A few older girls followed at a more restrained pace. Uncle Elic emerged after them. He smiled at Luskell as he came down the steps.

"Luskell! I heard you might pay us a visit. Are your folks with you?" Uncle Elic was her father's oldest friend. His brown hair was shot through with at least as much gray as Dadad's, and he had deep lines around his eyes, but he still had the widest grin of anyone Luskell knew ... except Jagryn, who had inherited his father's smile.

"They'll be along in a few days. Is Jagryn around?"

"I don't know; I missed him at lunch, but he might be home now. Let's go see."

He showed Luskell into the house, where Aunt Sunnea greeted her with a warm hug. "You've grown into quite a young woman. How are you? How's the family?"

"We're all fine, thanks."

Aunt Sunnea stepped back from the door. "Come in and sit down."

"I don't think she's here to see us, Mama." Her daughter sat in the rocker by the stove, a dark-haired baby on her lap. "Hello, Luskell. Looking for Jagryn?"

"Hello, Sulika." Luskell smiled at the young woman. "And this must be little Myluki!" Luskell had always liked Jagryn's older sister for her direct manner and frank good humor. And she felt indirectly responsible for bringing Sulika together with her husband, Myn. "Is Jagryn here?"

Aunt Sunnea shook her head. "I haven't seen him today."

"You might find him at Elika's old house," Sulika said. "You know it, don't you?"

"Sure. Has he moved there?"

"No, but he's been spending a lot of time working on it and doing private, wizard things," Uncle Elic said. He and Aunt Sunnea shared a fond, proud glance. "He often sleeps there two or three nights in a row."

Luskell guessed he had taken her advice, but it didn't explain why she couldn't reach his mind. Unless he'd left town completely, or was deliberately blocking her. "Thank you. I'll check there."

It was cold out and the sun was low. Luskell hurried to Elika's old house at the other end of town. She knocked but got no answer. No light shone through the windows, but all the shutters were closed, so it was hard to tell for sure. She pushed against the door. Inside, the latch clanked but held.

The only door in Deep River that locked was at the Village Hall. Most doors were held closed by a heavy wooden latch that could be lifted by means of a string hanging out through a hole. This one sounded like iron, which made sense—Jagryn's uncle and brother were blacksmiths.

Luskell felt for the latch-string and found the hole. The string had been pulled in, a simple and effective way of securing the door. So someone was inside. Luskell tried to sense another mind. At first, she didn't pick up any thoughts. She was about to give up when she sensed something, incoherent and barely there at all, but familiar.

She focused power into a small levitation spell to lift the latch, and pushed the door open. It closed behind her and the latch fell back into place. Luskell looked around. The fire was out and no lamp was lit.

"Jagryn?" No answer.

Even in the gloom, Luskell knew where things ought to be. This was where she had first practiced magic with Jagryn and Laki, and where Dadad had taught her and Jagryn when the weather was bad. She was responsible for at least three scorch marks on the floor. She felt for the table and found a lamp there. She lit it and shone it around. One chair stood at the table, the other next to a low bed in the back corner. A man-sized lump lay on the bed.

"Jagryn? What are you doing, sleeping during the day? Wake up!" When he didn't respond, Luskell hurried to her friend's side. He slept with no blanket over him. His arm drooped over the side of the bed. She picked up his hand and held it. "Jagryn?" He didn't respond. Luskell felt a prickle of fear. She couldn't see him breathing.

Luskell forced herself to think calmly. His skin was cool, but not dead-cold. She found a weak pulse. His breathing was slow and shallow, but he was alive. She laid a blanket over him, then kindled a fire. How could anyone sleep in such a cold room? She returned to the bedside and tucked the covers more snugly around him. Her foot bumped a mug beside the bed. She picked it up. It was empty, but had recently held some-thing that smelled of mint ... and something else.

Heart pounding, Luskell looked around and soon found a tiny vial, also empty, and sniffed it. She recognized the scent of the powerful sedative that healers called "drops." Luskell was familiar with its use to treat severe pain or to calm stubborn coughs, though she preferred her sleep charm as a safer option.

"How much did you take?" She smoothed the dark, tousled hair back from Jagryn's brow. For a moment, he looked as young as Crett. Then he frowned in his sleep and looked as old as the world.

His eyelids fluttered and she thought he was about to wake. She tried again to read his thoughts. Again she detected something not quite coherent. "Dreaming? Well, maybe I can help that way."

Luskell stretched out beside him and laid her head on his chest. She closed her eyes. His heartbeat thumped in her ear, which would have been more reassuring if it weren't so slow. But touching him, it was easier to pick up his dream-thought. She carefully followed it as it became stronger. She'd never read a person's dreams before. It was harder to follow than a regular thought, but familiar, too. And she recognized where she was.

The meadow. The light. The warmth.

He had crossed over. He was dreaming of the Other Side.

CHAPTER THIRTY-FIVE

Luskell found Jagryn on his knees, facing uphill. What if he'd already stayed too long? She'd shared Knot's warning, and he'd told her he understood. No, that was a dream. He never wrote to her in Misty Pass, either. Luskell knew mind-talking over a long distance wasn't reliable. She should have written to him as soon as she got to Misty Pass.

Taking the blame didn't help anyone. She fought to remain calm and in touch with his dream.

lub-DUB

His heartbeat, slow but steady, reassured her she was not too late. She knelt beside him and rested her hand on his shoulder. "Jagryn."

He turned to look at her. It took him a moment to focus. "Luskell?"

She smiled encouragement at him. "So, you got here. Did you speak to Elika?"

"I ... think so."

lub-DUB

Luskell frowned. "How long have you been here?"

"I don't know. She sent me back, but I keep getting lost, and the others couldn't tell me where to go."

"What others?" Luskell tried to steady her voice.

"I don't know who they were. They said they'd get help, but they haven't come back."

"Did they touch you?"

"Maybe. You said I should let them, but I don't remember."

lub-DUB

"No, I said you *shouldn't* let them. You heard only part of the message. That's why you didn't write to me."

"I did write to you."

"Where?"

"Eukard City, where else?"

"Oh, no; and when I thought you understood, I was dreaming. What a mess." Luskell pushed the worry away. "Well, you're found now. Come on, we shouldn't stay here. I'll show you the way."

She stood and waited. He nodded like he understood, but took a long time to get moving. When at last he stood on his feet, Luskell turned him to face downhill. At the bottom of the slope, their bodies were visible, lying in the little house.

lub-DUB

"It's so far." Jagryn's voice was weak.

"It isn't really. Let's go."

She looked back as a murmur swelled behind them. A crowd of souls flowed down the hill toward them. Luskell grabbed Jagryn's arm and tried to run. Hands reached for them. Luskell swatted them away, but one got a hold on Jagryn. He stumbled and fell. An indistinct soul gripped him. It took on solidity and brightness, a blissful expression on its face.

lub-DUB

lub-DUB

lub-DUB lub-DUB lub-DUB lub-DUB

"Get away from him!"

Luskell dragged the soul off him. Touching it chilled her, but Jagryn's racing heartbeat steadied. She shoved the dead soul into the crowd, yanked Jagryn to his feet and ran.

Always before, she woke after a few steps or moved into other dreams, but this time, she kept going, step after step. Was it because she wasn't asleep, or because they were both in a drugged dream? It didn't help that Jagryn kept stumbling to a halt. At least the dead had stopped following, as if there were some boundary they couldn't cross. Before long, she had Jagryn's arm over her shoulders and supported most of his weight. They were all the way into the room before the dream ended.

Luskell opened her eyes and lifted her head from Jagryn's chest. His face was pale and drawn, with lines where it should have been smooth. Had she really brought him back or had he stayed too long? Was he—?

His eyes blinked open. He stared at her. "What are you doing here?"

"Don't you remember?"

He frowned and shook his head. His eyes widened. "You were in my dream."

"If that's what it was."

He got out of bed and staggered into a shadowed corner to use the chamber pot while Luskell pretended not to hear. "Are you all right?"

"Fine," she said. "Are you?"

"Why wouldn't I be?"

"You don't look so good." She picked up the vial and held it out to him when he returned. "Tell me about this."

Jagryn hesitated, then took it from her. "I shouldn't have to. You know all about these things."

She crossed her arms. "Pretend I don't."

He collapsed back onto the bed. "It's ... a sleeping drug. I got it from Brynnit."

"You mean you stole it."

"It was from an old batch. She asked me to get rid of it, and I helped her make more."

"But you kept it. Why?"

"Because I couldn't sleep when I needed to."

"I don't understand," Luskell said.

"I was trying to think about Elika, everything I know about her, like you said. But if I was alert enough to imagine all those things, I was too alert to sleep. If I was ready to sleep, I'd just drop off. So I thought, what if I could imagine everything I wanted to dream, then take something to make me sleep when I'm ready?"

"That's not a bad plan, in theory," she admitted. "But how much did you take? If this was full—"

"It was only about half-full. Probably less. Maybe four or five drops?"

"One drop would have done it. And you never take this when you're alone."

"I didn't know that."

"Well, you should." She didn't know she could be this angry at a friend, especially amiable Jagryn, but now she wanted to strangle him.

"But it's all right! I did what I needed to, I met Elika, and you helped me back. Now I can be a wizard." Jagryn smiled up at Luskell, but the smile didn't last. "What's wrong?"

She grabbed his shoulders and shook him, half-lifting him off the bed. "I thought you were dead!" She held him tight, crying as she released her anger and worry. Soon her tears turned to laughter.

Jagryn patted her back. "What's so funny?"

"Nothing. But you're not dead, are you? You're alive. I don't know what I would have done ..." She released him and flopped back beside him. "Whew! I think those drops got to me, too. I'm all loopy. I need to close my eyes while they wear off."

"Yeah, I still feel kind of strange." He lay back and closed his eyes.

Luskell drifted in a soft haze. She tried to work out how the drops could have affected her through Jagryn's dream, but she couldn't keep her mind on one thing. It was a nice sensation, though, like floating or soaring. She rolled onto her side as Jagryn did the same. They kissed, and then their clothes vanished and they were wrapped up in each other, doing—no, *making*—love, naturally and easily without any talk or fuss. It was the Lightning Kiss, only better.

Luskell opened her eyes. The lamp had gone out, but a low fire still burned. She was dressed, her clothes disordered, but no more than she would have expected from sleeping in them.

Jagryn sat up and stared at her. "Was that real?"

"I ... don't know." Could two people have the same dream? She'd found her way into his dream earlier. She raised up on her elbows. "It might have been the drops. But if you want to, we could come back here and try it when we're awake."

Jagryn shook his head and leaned his forehead on his knees. "Luskell, you spoil everything."

"I ... what?"

"Never mind. I'm not myself today. But you should go now."

Luskell sat up and leaned toward Jagryn. He folded his arms and hunched his shoulders as if trying to avoid contact, but he didn't move away. "Jagryn, tell me what I've done wrong."

He stared past her at a scorch mark on the floor. "I didn't mean to do that."

"Neither did I. It was a dream. A nice dream that we shared."

Jagryn shook his head. "That must mean I wanted to. But I didn't *mean* to. You come to town like an avalanche and roll over everything in your path. Who can stand in your way?"

"Nice way to talk to a friend! I don't expect you to marry me, Jagryn, or even make love again, if it was so terrible for you."

"Not terrible, no. I thought the first time would be ...different. But that wasn't *your* first time, was it?" The scathing tone was back. "Don't tell me—Laki. Of course."

"If it makes you feel better, I probably won't marry him, either."

"No? What do you plan on?"

"Same as you—I'm going to be a wizard. Now, come on. When was the last time you ate?"

"I don't even know what day it is. But I'm hungry."

"And there's no food in this house. Come back to the Heron with me."

He stared at her. The drug hadn't completely worn off, and he was weak with hunger—not at his best to begin with, and she'd somehow made things worse. Anger rolled off him in hot waves, and desire, and something else. Guilt? Over what? A dream?

At last, Jagryn sighed and nodded. Luskell held out her hand to help him up, but he struggled to his feet on his own. They walked together to the inn, not talking or touching.

CHAPTER THIRTY-SIX

"Oh, good, you found him." Klamamam greeted Luskell and Jagryn from the kitchen, little knowing what the search had entailed. "Hungry?"

"Starving," Jagryn muttered.

"Typical man—he got working on something and lost track of time." Luskell forced herself to smile and make light of it. "Who forgets to eat?"

She settled Jagryn at one of the small tables under the front windows. Fatigue and hunger made him docile. Rakkyn brought them two plates of food. Eating occupied them for a while. She was as glad not to talk.

About halfway through his meal, Jagryn looked at Luskell with a puzzled frown. "What do you mean, you're going to be a wizard?"

"Just what I said. Remember Bardin? I'm his apprentice, and I'm doing my quest to earn a staff."

"I didn't know a girl could ... I mean, of course *you* could, but—"

"Somebody has to be first."

"So what's your quest?"

It felt strange to have an ordinary conversation, but it came as a relief. "I'm learning to Listen. That's why I went to see Laki."

He scowled and steamed with jealousy, but he didn't comment on that. "That would be an unusual specialty to put in the *Registry*."

"If I do. Hey, you were in the city when you turned eighteen, weren't you? Did you register? I didn't think to look you up."

"Of course. Crane took me in the morning while you were still at work. I put transformation and illusions as my specialties. But if I go back, I'll add weatherworking."

"What? When did you learn that?"

Jagryn blushed which made him look younger again. "When you were busy at Balsam's House. Crane thought it was better if we didn't tell you. Are you angry?"

"I should be, but I know why he did that. You've got the temperament for it, and I don't."

He nodded. "It's useful for a country wizard. I could delay storms while they finish harvest, ease drought, keep off lightning—"

The door opened and a fair-haired, pink-cheeked young woman came in. Luskell recognized her, though she had to dig to come up with the name. Ruvhonn, that was it. Luskell and her friends had done their first major work of magic at Ruvhonn's family's farm. Later, Luskell had been in school with her, though they hadn't been close. Ruvhonn was older than Luskell, nearer Jagryn's age. Ruvhonn glared at Luskell, which shed some light on the questions Jagryn wouldn't answer.

Luskell jumped up and went to meet the young woman. "Ruvhonn, hello! Do you remember me? I'm Stell's granddaughter, Luskell. We met the day of the fire out at your place, the summer I was staying here."

"Oh ... yes. It's ... good to see you again." Ruvhonn glanced at Luskell, but her attention was mostly on Jagryn.

A small gold earring glinted on her right earlobe. Luskell recognized it as part of an old courtship ritual that hung on in Deep River long after it had died out elsewhere. This lone earring meant the girl was available for courtship but not yet betrothed. Luskell didn't have to read Ruvhonn's thoughts to know she wanted to be. The way she looked at Jagryn was enough.

Ruvhonn walked over to the table by the window. "Jagryn, did you forget we were supposed to meet in front of the Village Hall today? I waited and waited."

"I'm sorry. I got busy with some work and lost track of time."

"You'll have to get used to that with a wizard," Luskell said. "Are you hungry? I'm finished, so you can have my seat." She held the chair and put on what she hoped was a welcoming smile. Ruvhonn hesitated, then sat. "So you're seeing Jagryn? All I can say is, you couldn't do better and you won't be sorry." Luskell wished she could stop grinning, but her mouth seemed to be stuck. Her jaw ached.

"Luskell, please be quiet," Jagryn said, without heat and without looking at her.

Luskell's face grew hot. She knew she was babbling, but how dare he! She picked up her empty plate. Rakkyn brought supper to Ruvhonn, so at least Luskell didn't have to go back to the table. Jagryn's voice gained a warmth it had recently lacked, and Ruvhonn laughed at something he said. Luskell couldn't even look at them.

"Klamamam, I wish I could stay up for stories, but I'm going to bed now."

Klamamam frowned. "Do you feel all right?"

"I'm tired. I probably shouldn't have flown here in one go." *I shouldn't have come here at all.*

Luskell went to her room and bolted the door. She removed her dress and flung it into the corner, as if it were at fault. She yanked on her nightdress and climbed into bed, too confused and angry to sleep. Everything was all wrong and she didn't know why. Because of a dream? If it was a dream. And such a good one, she wanted to experience it waking.

Not much chance of that now. He had another girl, and Luskell ached with jealousy. How could he, when Luskell had saved his life? Saved him from his own foolishness. She'd been blaming herself, but she wasn't the only one who could have told him not to stay too long.

Luskell closed her eyes and began to form a picture in her mind of someone she'd seen only twice. She knew a lot about the woman, though, and where to find her. She held the image in her mind as she finally relaxed into sleep.

Luskell opened her eyes, once more in the bright warm meadow with no sun. She wasn't alone. A small, sharp-featured woman waited for her. Her long, dark hair hung loose around her shoulders. Elika. She waited for Luskell to speak.

Luskell towered over her. "You! How could you do that to Jagryn?"

Elika regarded her calmly. "I didn't do anything. He came to me on his own. You're the one who taught him how to cross over."

"But you sent him back alone, when he'd taken drops! He got lost, and there wasn't anyone to help him."

Elika tilted her head. "I didn't know that. I can't watch everything my descendants do."

"But what if I hadn't found him? He might have stayed too long."

"We thank you for helping him. I assume he's all right now."

Luskell gripped Elika's not quite substantial shoulders. "He might have died! Why didn't you tell him the danger?"

"I thought he knew. Why didn't you tell him?"

Luskell huffed and stamped her foot. This wasn't getting anywhere, and she had to think about her own time in this place. She forced herself to speak calmly. "Elika, you once asked me to give Sulika a message, that she was marrying the wrong man. Do you have a message for anyone this time?"

Elika looked Luskell straight in the eye. "No. I don't. Now you'd better go. You don't want to stay here too long."

There was no long walk this time. Elika and the meadow and the warmth swirled away into other dreams that scattered on waking. The only thing Luskell could afterward recall was that in all of them, she was alone and lost.

CHAPTER THIRTY-SEVEN

By morning, Luskell's anger had abated, but she still felt lost and sad. Not at all like a powerful near-wizard. She dragged herself out of bed.

"Good morning, Luskell," Klamamam greeted her. She set a bowl of porridge and the cream pitcher on the kitchen table. "Feeling better?"

"Some." Luskell slumped into a chair.

Klamamam paused her cooking and eyed Luskell. "Wouldn't guess it to look at you. If I didn't know better, I'd say you'd lost your best friend."

Luskell sat back in panic. Was it obvious? "No, it's just been a long winter. And I've been working without a break for more than a year."

"So you came here, where I always put you to work." Klamamam's gentle smile couldn't quite mask her skepticism.

"I don't mind that kind of work. Could I have today off, though? I want to … go out."

"Visiting friends?"

"Something like that."

"Perhaps find Jagryn again?"

Luskell's face grew hot and she looked down at her porridge bowl. "Not today."

She finished her breakfast, then put on her outdoor clothes. She did plan to go visiting, but not to people if she could help it. She went out the back door into a cold but sunny morning, and descended the steps cut into the river bank. The water ran fast and dark between ice-fringed banks.

"Hello, friend," Luskell said.

The river answered her. Without trying, she heard its rapid, many-stranded voice. She was already attuned, and she knew why. Years ago, before she was aware of her power, this river had tried to speak to her, and she had almost understood. Now she calmed her mind to Listen. At first, she feared she might drown in the churn of images. The river was far from its source and running full, its story more tangled and complex than what she'd heard from the Bright. She exerted her power to find some sense in it. It spoke of ice and thaw, snow and rain, fish and roe. And ... memories of Knot, distant and faint, but definitely there. Luskell didn't know whether those came from Aku herself, or from the wizard's own long-ago touch that changed the river's course.

Luskell returned to herself with tears in her eyes, and the beginnings of a smile. Her time in Deep River was not turning out the way she'd expected, but she could still use it well. Laki was right. She could practice Listening here as well as anywhere. Maybe better.

She reached out to the big old cottonwood whose bare branches stretched over her head. It didn't have much to say on this winter morning—sleepy thoughts of sap and spring. The tree's voice was as familiar as the river's. Luskell had spent many happy summer days in its branches. Did it remember her?

She paused in her Listening to reach out to the one who had taught her how. It no longer felt too soon, and she owed him her thanks. And an apology.

Laki, I'm Listening in Deep River.

... good? His response was faint and broken, but his mind voice was a comfort.

Very good. Thank you for teaching me. I'm sorry I made such a mess of things.

He didn't reply immediately, and she thought she'd lost the connection. When he answered, it was in fragments, almost like Listening to snow.

... young ... forgive ... don't ... Jagryn ...

Luskell wasn't sure what it meant. Before she could ask, the connection cut off. Laki was finished talking to her. Had she managed to make things worse?

While she stood by the river, clouds covered the sun and snow began to fall. Luskell climbed back up the bank to Listen to the snow without the river interrupting. Not many flakes touched her when she stood in one place, but walking along the road increased the number. They spoke of love and kin, power and danger. So these were things she knew but didn't know she knew. Or didn't always remember. She had a place here, and she didn't always hurt those she loved. She was determined to use her power to help those who needed it. And danger? The strangler was still out there. He needed to be stopped.

Luskell stopped walking. The snow flurry had slackened, and new voices interfered. They were like the trees, but tiny. She looked around, surprised to find herself near the Village Hall. She didn't know she'd gone so far.

Luskell followed the voices toward Myn and Sulika's house, which sat near the Hall but back from the road. A grove of leafless trees grew at the beginning of the path. They were small, twigs no taller than Luskell's waist, with sleepy voices. They seemed familiar, but theirs weren't the voices she'd heard.

The sun beamed through a gap in the clouds onto a new outbuilding in front of the house, a sort of shed made of windows. The glass was fogged, but Luskell saw someone moving inside. She tapped on the door.

Sulika opened it. Her bright blue eyes widened in surprise, but she smiled a welcome. "Luskell! Come in where it's warm. What brings you here?" Dark soil clung to her fingers and stained her apron.

Luskell stepped in and Sulika closed the door behind them. Inside was warm and humid, with shelves full of green things in pots. The tiny voices grew stronger. "I think your plants did. What is this?"

"It's a greenhouse. I got the idea from Brynnit's big window, but I wanted more space than that." Sulika laughed and waved toward the shelves. "Jagree and my brother Crane worked out the design, and then I order-ed the window panes from the city. Mama and I sewed the cover to keep it warm at night. Crane added the little stove for really cold weather, like today."

Luskell couldn't suppress a sigh at the thought of Sulika's handsome brother, her own father's namesake. He was the first man she'd ever really noticed. "How is Crane? I haven't seen him yet this visit."

"Extremely well, I think." Sulika set a tray of seedlings in small pots on a wide work counter. "He moved in with Grammy Sudi last year after Grampa Ohmc died. He's getting married this spring. You remember Bramynna, don't you?"

Luskell laughed. "I pushed him to talk to her at the summer dance two years ago. I'm surprised they waited this long."

Sulika winked. "Unlike me, my brother takes his time. He learned more than smithing from Uncle Jagree. Anyway, after they're married, Grammy's giving them the house and she's moving in with Mama and Papa. But you wanted to know about the greenhouse. I can start seeds early, and grow some vegetables all winter." She snipped off a lettuce leaf and gave it to Luskell.

Luskell tasted the lettuce. It was crisp and flavorful, almost as if it had come from a garden in summer. "Plant magic?"

Sulika glanced up at the light streaming in and smiled. "Maybe a little. Mostly the sun." She perched on a high stool in front of the seedlings. She lifted them carefully from the soil and transplanted them to larger ones. She talked to them in a quiet voice.

Luskell barked a laugh, then covered her mouth. "You talk to them and they answer!" She climbed onto a second stool and leaned in to watch.

Sulika glanced around with a smile. "I would hope so."

"Are those cherry trees out there?" Luskell asked. "One of them grew from the pit you gave Myn, didn't it?"

Sulika nodded. "That's a strong one. I suppose they told you that."

"They seemed ... familiar."

"Mm-hm. I can't believe you came just to talk about plants. Are you looking for Jagryn again?"

Luskell's heart fell. Just when she'd begun to feel better ... "No. I thought I might have seemed rude yes-terday when I didn't stay to visit."

Something squeaked. Sulika leaned down and pulled a blanket back from a basket under the lowest shelf. Her baby fretted in his sleep, then stuck his thumb in his mouth and settled down again.

Sulika watched him a moment, then smiled at Luskell. "And you hadn't even met Myluki before. But you weren't rude. I'm sure we'll see you plenty while you're here, and Jagryn's closer to your age. And you're both wizards, or so I hear."

"Nearly. I'm afraid I might earn my staff first. Jagryn's quest hasn't gone smoothly."

"And you plan to help him?"

"I gave him some advice. I'm not sure it was any good."

"Hm."

Sulika didn't say more, but she didn't ask Luskell to leave. It was pleasant in the warm, plant-scented greenhouse, so Luskell stayed and watched Sulika at her work. The young woman was absorbed in the small plants, treating them like children.

Luskell turned her attention to the baby, Myluki. She figured he was about half a year old. He'd been born the previous fall, soon after Jagryn returned to Deep River. He'd written a long letter about the new nephew, but also about how much he missed seeing Luskell every day. It was the last long letter she'd received from him.

"Sulika, are you happy with Myn?"

Sulika looked around. She pushed a strand of dark hair off her forehead and left a smudge of soil. "Most of the time. Why?"

"Well, I ... I sort of helped bring you together, and I'd feel bad if it didn't work out."

Sulika laughed. "Let's say we're both happier than we would have been had I married Foli. Foli and Rakkyn are happier, too."

"That's good to know. So the town accepts them?"

"It might have been different if two men like them had moved here from somewhere else. But they're ours." Sulika squinted at Luskell. "But what's your real reason for asking about me and Myn?"

Luskell sighed. "I'm seventeen now, and people are starting to hint that I'll be married soon. Or that I should be."

"And have you had any serious offers?"

"One—Laki."

Sulika smiled. "Oh, I liked him! So handsome, and he seemed very ... complete for someone his age."

"He is," Luskell agreed. "But I'm not sure I want to marry him, or anyone. Or whether I should, if I want to be wizard."

"I guess you wouldn't have to, would you? You might not need a husband to support or protect you. So, do you want to? Not a bad position to be in. It might be easier, if you don't have to make space in your life for someone else." Sulika glanced at the sleeping baby. "Or more than one."

Luskell nodded. "I could probably live a long time without a husband or babies, but ... it's not wrong, is it, for people who aren't married to make love? Because I don't want to live without that."

Sulika snorted. "You know how I feel. And most of your family, too. I didn't realize you'd had that experience yet." She studied Luskell, who tried not to look away even with the heat rising in her face. "Oh. That's when Laki asked you." Sulika smiled a knowing smile. "No, I can't say that's wrong. You've loved him a long time."

Luskell nodded.

"He must be disappointed, though," Sulika went on. "Still, better to be honest than string him along."

"I knew you'd understand!" Luskell said, filled with relief. "I don't want to marry, but I don't want to hurt anybody, either. They say Balsam had a lover in every town she visited. That might be nice."

Sulika clapped a hand over her mouth. "Luskell, you shock me!" But she was laughing. "I can't believe I'm hearing this from someone so young."

"I heard it from some of the healers at Balsam's House," Luskell admitted. "I don't know whether any of them were really doing it or only dreaming. But if I'm not thinking of marriage and family, and if I choose trustworthy men like Laki, why not?"

"I can't imagine there are many men like Laki." Sulika chuckled. "I hope you're not scouting for candidates in Deep River. It would cause such a scandal!" The baby began to fuss, and Sulika hopped down from her stool. She lifted the basket. "Come up to the house for tea?"

Luskell followed Sulika out. The house was like most in Deep River, small and solid, built of river cobbles and field stone mortared together. The front room had south-facing windows that kept it light and pleasant even on a winter afternoon. While Sulika washed up and put the kettle on, Luskell changed the baby, then played with him until his mother was ready to feed him.

Sulika took Myluki and settled into the rocking chair. "You're so motherly. I'm not sure why you don't want a baby."

"What I am is sisterly," Luskell corrected her. "And I don't want one *yet*. Maybe someday, but I have things I want to do first."

"Fair enough."

Myluki was still nursing when the kettle boiled, so Luskell made and poured the tea.

"You talked about a scandal," Luskell said. "I hadn't thought of that."

Sulika laughed gently. "You wizards are above such things."

"I don't know if it's wizards or the city or what," Luskell replied. "It never occurred to me. But in Deep River, everything I'm doing probably appears scandalous, including wanting to be a wizard. Maybe especially that!"

"It might have been that way when our fathers were young." Sulika sounded sleepy, the way Mamam got when she was feeding Crett.

"But it isn't scandalous for people to make love when they're not married?"

"I suppose it is to some people. But in a small town, you often look the other way. Some things aren't worth the fuss."

"But what if ... one of the people is thinking of marrying someone else?" Too late, Luskell realized she had described Sulika's former situation. "I don't mean you! But it can turn out all right. It's not always wrong, is it? I mean, they're not even betrothed."

Sulika snapped alert, her eyes wide. "Luskell, are you telling me you and Jagryn ..." She frowned.

"No! At least, I don't think so."

"Wouldn't you know?"

"It's complicated," Luskell sighed. "He's doing his wizard quest and got mixed up in something he didn't understand. It's possible I saved his life. And then ... something happened that might have been a dream, but we both had it. I liked it, and I thought he did, too. But I didn't know." Luskell bit her lip.

"About Ruvhonn." Sulika sighed. "Nothing against you, Luskell, but we all like her. She comes to the school almost every afternoon and helps Papa with the younger children.

And when Jagryn came back from the city, he moped about for weeks, until he started seeing her. She's good for him—kindhearted, steady, a good head on her shoulders."

"You knew I was looking for him. Why didn't you tell me he had a girl?"

"What I'd like to know is, why didn't he?"

That silenced whatever Luskell might have said. It was a good question, but she wasn't sure she wanted to think about the answer.

Sulika watched her without comment for a moment. "Are you going to try to get him back?"

"Back?" Luskell held her head in both hands. "Did I ever have him?"

CHAPTER THIRTY-EIGHT

Luskell wandered back to the Blue Heron in time for lunch. The fresh air and conversation with Sulika had improved her mood. She still didn't know what to do about Jagryn, and she was so out of her usual routine, she barely knew what day it was. How many important tasks had she forgotten? But she was excited about the possibilities for Listening in Deep River.

After lunch, she helped Klamamam by sweeping the guest rooms.

"The best room is free now if you want to move up there," Klamamam offered.

Luskell had been born, and presumably conceived, in the large upstairs room. She had performed her first transformation in one of its windows. It was her favorite room in the inn; it was her father's, too. "Let's save it for Mamam and Dadad when they come. I like having Dadad's old room."

"Will they want to be upstairs, with the baby?"

Luskell laughed. "Crett loves stairs—he'll climb up every chance he gets, anyway."

"Hard to believe he's that big already. But is it safe?"

"From what I've seen, he's as surefooted as Dadad or me. We'll have to watch him, that's all."

Luskell kept busy with chores the rest of the day and tried not to dwell on Jagryn—which meant she thought about little else. She had meant to help with his quest, then blundered into something she couldn't undo. Part of her wanted to see him again, to explain or apologize or something. Another part was afraid of what might happen if she did. It would be better for them to keep apart. Except Luskell wanted to see him.

She was helping serve supper when the whole family walked in: Uncle Elic, Aunt Sunnea, Sulika with Myn and Myluki, Crane and his intended, Bramynna, and Jagryn. Luskell changed her mind. She didn't want to see him. She let Rakkyn serve them. Sulika was Rakkyn's oldest friend, so it didn't seem odd. Luskell stole glances from other parts of the room. They were a laughing, talkative bunch, but Jagryn ate in silence. He was with his family, but alone. Ruvhonn wasn't with him. But he never looked at Luskell.

Most of the guests that night were locals, with a couple of the travelers staying overnight or passing through. A bald man with a big black beard looked familiar, but Luskell couldn't place him until she heard him talking about "business interests." He was the passenger from the coach, back when she'd first left Eukard City. She wondered if Keela knew.

Her question was answered when the old weaver Briato and his wife Keena came in, followed by Keela, their granddaughter. She smiled at Luskell, then paled and beat a hasty retreat back out the door. Briato turned with a puzzled look on his face. "What's wrong with the girl?" He started for the door.

Luskell stopped him. "Have a seat, Briato. I'll have a word with her."

She found Keela huddled on the bench next to the door. "Hey. You all right?"

Keela nodded, then shook her head, but she didn't speak.

Luskell sat next to her. "It was a relief to read your letter in Misty Pass, to know you got here safely. Have you started with Brynnit yet?"

Keela nodded again. "Most afternoons, when the twins are at school." She spoke in a tiny voice and her teeth chattered, but at least she was speaking.

"You'll learn a lot. It's kind of cold to sit outside, though. Come in and eat."

Keela looked up, her eyes wide. "That man ... with the beard. He's the man from the coach, the one who kept ... looking at me."

"I know. I didn't expect to see him again, but he did say he had business interests on the Dry Side." Luskell stood up from the bench. "He's not staying in Deep River, though. I heard him tell Klamamam he has to move on right after supper." She took Keela's arm. "Come in and eat. Rakkyn and I will make sure he doesn't bother you."

Keela still looked nervous, but allowed Luskell to usher her back inside. She sat at the table with her grandparents and kept her eyes fixed on them and the food, away from the bearded stranger. For his part, the stranger watched Keela with curious interest. Toward the end of the meal, he beckoned Luskell over. Close up, she saw he wasn't actually bald. His scalp glittered with closely-shaved stubble. That was one way to deal with wild hair.

"May I bring you something else?" she asked.

"No, I need to be on my way. I wanted to ask, do you by chance have a brother in Misty Pass?"

Luskell remembered in time the fiction they'd enacted in the coach. She smiled. "Why, yes, I do." It wasn't even a lie. "He'll be joining us in a day or so."

"You resemble him. So that girl is your sister?"

Luskell glanced at Keela. "Good guess." She accepted the man's money with a polite smile, and watched to make sure he left without bothering Keela. He was probably harmless, but it did no harm to stay alert.

Myn and Sulika took the baby home after supper, while the rest of Jagryn's family stayed to hear stories by the hearth. Luskell listened, too, from a shadowed corner behind the last row of seats. She loved her grandmother's stories better than almost anything, but tonight, she couldn't concentrate. She needed to talk to Jagryn, even if she didn't know what to say.

Jagryn. Maybe mind-talking would be easier.

Across the room, Jagryn twitched. He lifted his head and finally made eye contact with Luskell. *What?*

She clung to the thrill of his mind-voice in her head. *I … missed you.*

He looked away and didn't answer immediately, but didn't break contact. *I missed you for a while, too. I got over it.*

Luskell's stomach lurched. She'd meant to apologize and assure him she hadn't planned to cause trouble and didn't mean to cause more. Now she wasn't sure that was true.

She broke contact and went to her room. Seeing him didn't help. Not seeing him didn't help. But maybe sleep would. She lay drowsing, drifting toward sleep, deliberately thinking of other things. It was good to see Keela. It seemed like so long since the two of them had left Eukard City in the coach to Misty Pass. How many days? Three in

Misty Pass, she recalled, then seven memorable days with Laki. She smiled to herself at the thought. Then three more in Misty Pass, a day of travel, and a full day in Deep River. Fifteen days; half a month already.

Luskell sprang upright, wide awake. Counting days was usually second nature—Mamam and Auntie Brynnit had taught her early on to track her monthly cycle. She wasn't regular enough for it to be really useful, but it didn't hurt to be familiar with her personal variations, moods, and symptoms. If nothing else, she knew when to be careful with the fire spell. She hadn't thought much about it lately, but if her count was right ... something was wrong.

No. Not possible. She'd been careful. The count must be wrong. She lay back down and ran over the days again, with the same result. She tried to Listen to her body, though she wasn't sure what to Listen for and couldn't hear much of anything over the sudden rush of worry.

Luskell rolled over and tried to sleep. No need to worry until there was something to worry about. She was just ... late. *If* she was. It was probably nothing. In the morning, she'd talk to Auntie Brynnit. She would know.

Although it didn't change anything, that decision was comforting enough to allow for sleep. Luskell's dreams were filled with scenes of childbirth, crying babies, and children in peril—not the most restful night. It was a relief to wake in the morning, alone in a quiet room. Then the worry came back. She was late.

CHAPTER THIRTY-NINE

Luskell had to force herself to eat breakfast. The lack of appetite increased her worry, though she didn't feel sick, exactly. For Klamamam's benefit, she maintained a false cheerfulness while they did their morning chores.

"Well, Luskell, what are your plans today?" Klamamam asked.

"Maybe I'll visit Grynni and Greelit. I didn't get over there yesterday, and I'm interested to know how they're getting along with Kanala." The twin girls were old friends of hers, and she'd helped in the early train-ing of their horse, Kanala. Visiting them was a good cover, though she really wanted to see their mother.

Klamamam smiled and nodded. "They ride that horse most mornings, but you might catch them before they head out."

Luskell tried not to hurry, though she was anxious to talk to Auntie Brynnit. She walked past the stable to the house. Down the road, the two girls rode their sorrel mare, heading west from town. There was a good chance she'd catch Auntie Brynnit alone.

"Good morning, Luskell," Auntie Brynnit greeted her. "You just missed the girls."

"I thought I saw them. Keela's not here, is she?"

"Not till later. You could catch her at Briato's, though."

"No, I ... I wanted to talk to you." Luskell glanced around the front room to make sure there was no one else there, though there weren't any good hiding places for anyone larger than a cat.

Auntie Brynnit studied her soberly. "So serious. Is something wrong?"

"No. At least, I hope not. It's just ... private."

"I understand. Well, sit down and tell me about it."

Luskell sat at the table where her mother and Brynnit had tried to teach her healing. As soon as she was settled, a small black cat floated onto her lap. Luskell stroked its back and scratched its head. "Is this one of Secret's kittens?"

"Grand-kitten, at least," Auntie Brynnit replied. "We call her Magic. She's useful, but only so much." She sat across from Luskell and waited without saying anything more.

Luskell tried to word her question in a way that would get an answer without voicing her real fear. "Is it normal to be late sometimes?"

"Of course it is. Impolite, but normal."

Luskell frowned. "I don't mean for meals or appointments. I keep track of my cycles, like you taught me, but they're not predictable. Is that normal? Am I normal?"

"Luskell, you're taller than my husband, you're go-ing to be a wizard, and you commune with the dead. And you ask about normal?"

"Well?"

Auntie Brynnit smiled. "Of course you are. So, what's going on? How unpredictable are they?"

Luskell considered. "Usually, they're somewhere between twenty-six and twenty-nine days. A couple of times, it was only twenty-four. Once it was thirty-six."

"That doesn't sound like a problem. Irritating, maybe, if you're trying to plan around it. What are we talking about this time?"

"It's been thirty days. No, thirty-one now."

"So a little long for you, but not too far outside your normal range. Unless ... you have reason to be anxious?" The blood rose in Luskell's face. There was no way to tiptoe around her real worry. She nodded and Auntie Brynnit released an audible breath. "All right. Can you tell me when?"

"The first time or the most recent?" Luskell asked.

Auntie Brynnit raised her eyebrows. "Well, start at the beginning, then."

"The first time was almost two weeks ago, when I was with Laki." She couldn't help smiling. She would never tire of that memory. "I was there a week, and we did ... we *made* love almost every day. Sometimes more than once."

Auntie Brynnit blushed for her. "Sounds like a pleasant time. Maybe a honeymoon?"

Luskell remembered the wedding-night ritual and sighed. "It could have been. I told him no."

"Would a baby change that?"

Luskell met Auntie Brynnit's gaze. "I don't know. I guess it changes a lot of things, but ... I don't know."

Auntie Brynnit nodded and gave Luskell a sympathetic smile. "All right. So the most recent time was about a week ago?"

"Ye—" Luskell broke off and began again. "Maybe. It might have been ... day before yesterday."

"But by then, you were here." Auntie Brynnit shook her head. "Jagryn?"

Luskell nodded. "But we're not sure anything actually happened. Did you give him drops to get rid of?"

"Yes, when he came to work with me the other day."

"He thought they'd help with his quest to the Other Side. And they did, but he took too much. I had to bring him back, and they affected me, too. So it might have been only a dream. A vivid dream we both had."

"Drops can do that. I've never heard of two people having exactly the same dream, but I don't know everything." Auntie Brynnit gazed at Luskell and shook her head. "You know about Ruvhonn?"

"I do now."

"Does Ruvhonn know about ... you and Jagryn?"

"I'm don't plan to tell her. I didn't even know about her until after."

"Did you ask?"

"No, why would I?" Luskell said. "But I didn't come to talk about that. I just want to know if I'm pregnant, and if so, who by."

Auntie Brynnit came around the table and lifted the cat off Luskell's lap. "That close together, I doubt I can answer who. You might have to wait until it's born and see who it looks like." She studied Luskell. "Even that might be tricky. You have enough Aklaka heritage that even Jagryn's child would likely be brown. And they both have dark hair and eyes. Blue eyes would point to Jagryn, I guess, but barring that, you might never know for sure." Auntie Brynnit laid her hands on Luskell's abdomen. Her brow furrowed as she concentrated. "Hm. Either you aren't pregnant, or it's too soon to tell. Even if you conceived your first time, two weeks isn't very long. And two days? Maybe Ketty could sense it, but I can't."

Luskell clutched at this bit of hope. "She didn't, when I came back from Knot's Valley. And I was careful."

"Every time?"

"Every time," Luskell affirmed. But had she been, that last time with Laki? Using the protective spell was habit by then, so probably, but she didn't remember clearly. And with Jagryn, she'd been dreaming. She had no memory of whether or not she'd used it. "I haven't been sick or anything. And I remember Mamam was exhausted with Crett. I haven't been tired except from using magic."

"Not everyone gets sick, or not right away," Auntie Brynnit said. She resumed her seat. "But if you were careful, this is probably just a long cycle. Try to be patient, but if after another week nothing's happened, I'll check you again."

"I have to wait a week?" Luskell wailed.

"It's a chance to practice patience," Auntie Brynnit replied and smiled. "But if it's causing you discomfort, there are spells and herbs to move things along. Bring on your bleeding."

"Why didn't you say so?" Luskell felt dizzy with relief for a moment. Then she sobered. "What if I am pregnant, though?"

"This early? You wouldn't be anymore. You'd never know."

"Oh." Luskell pondered this. She was tempted. Everything could go back to normal. But Laki's child? Jagryn's? "I'll wait a few days. It won't hurt anything to wait, will it?" Auntie Brynnit shook her head. "It's a chance to practice patience, like you said. It'll be good for me."

Auntie Brynnit reached across the table and squeezed Luskell's hand. "That's my girl. It's probably nothing, but if it's something, I'm here to help, no matter what you decide.

Either way, it's not the end of the world. But ... I hope you'll talk to your mother about it."

"I hope by the time she gets here, there's nothing to tell."

CHAPTER FORTY

"Thanks for your help, Auntie Brynnit. I should get back now." Luskell half stood.

"Stay awhile," Auntie Brynnit said. "The girls will be back from their ride soon, and I know they want to see you. They were with their cousins all day yesterday, or they would have been at your door already."

Luskell resumed her seat with a brief pang of envy. Cousins. Grynni and Greelit had something like ten, including Jagryn and his siblings. Jagryn's brother had once dubbed Luskell an honorary cousin, but she didn't have any cousins of her own.

"They're are almost fourteen," Luskell said. "Any sign of power in either of them?"

Auntie Brynnit smiled and shook her head. "Nothing obvious. They might have Jagree's way with animals, though."

"That would suit them."

Auntie Brynnit smiled. "Yes, it would. Better than healing. But it's too soon to say. Jagryn's gift didn't appear until he was nearly fifteen."

"Not so different from me."

It was worth the wait for the welcome the twins gave Luskell. They were smaller and had to stretch to hug her, but they clearly were not children anymore.

"How long can you stay?" Grynni asked. She twisted the end of one black braid around her finger. She was the smaller of the two, but already developing a woman's curves.

"I don't know," Luskell replied. "The rest of the family is supposed to join me in a few days. I imagine we'll stay until spring, at least."

Greelit whooped. "Till summer!" Brown curls trailed over her forehead, unwilling to stay in braids. "Did you bring your fiddle?"

"My folks will bring it." Luskell chose not to explain why she'd left her bag in Oxbow. It would have made a funny story, except for Jagryn's part in it. She hoped the bag was still at the coach office when her family arrived there.

Greelit stood on one foot. "I hear you're going to be a wizard. Lucky!"

"I don't have my own horse, though."

Grynni laughed. "But we can't fly!"

"Come to the stable," Greelit ordered. "Kanala wants to see you."

Luskell glanced at Auntie Brynnit with a barely suppressed smile and followed the girls to the stable, where the horse munched her oats. The filly had grown into a strong mare, obviously well cared-for. Luskell stroked the horse's glossy, red-brown neck under the creamy mane. "Look at you, so beautiful! Do you still like to run?"

"Does she!" Grynni sighed. "It's almost as good as flying."

The twins introduced Luskell to Storm and Smoky, their father's big gray draft horses.

"And we keep this stall for Whitefoot," Greelit said, pointing out an empty stall next to Kanala's. "That's Ruvhonn's bay. You know her, right? Jagryn's girl?"

Luskell made herself smile, though she couldn't sustain it long. "Yes, we've met."

She stayed to help groom the horses. She could almost forget her worry in the pleasant, ordinary activity. Jagryn walked past as she left the stable, and it all came back. He didn't see her, but walked down to the house at the edge of town.

Luskell hesitated. It would be easy to go back to the inn, but how easy would it be to avoid Jagryn the whole time she was in Deep River? Especially if it turned out she was carrying his child. She didn't want to be the one to start the conversation, but the longer she waited, the more awkward it would be. This was one of those things magic couldn't fix. She waited, frozen to the spot. With a growl, she stamped her foot and strode off toward Elika's house. No, that was wrong. Toward Jagryn's house.

The latch-string was out, but Luskell didn't have the nerve to barge in. She knocked. The door remained shut and Jagryn didn't answer. For the briefest moment, his mind touched hers. It was a thrill akin to physical touch, something she hadn't appreciated when they were on better terms. It should have provided an easier way to have this conversation, though the previous evening's failure seemed to show otherwise. Jagryn withdrew, and when she reached out, she found his mind firmly shielded.

Luskell knocked again, harder. "Jagryn, I know you're in there."

"And I know you're out there." His voice came from so close by, she jumped. He stood right on the other side of the door. "Go away, Luskell."

"No. I want to talk to you."

"And you always get what you want?"

"Jagryn, that's not fair. Maybe something happened that shouldn't have, but this doesn't help. Please open the door."

"I don't want you in my house."

"Fine. I'll stay out here. But I'm going to talk to you whether you like it or not."

"Like you do everything else."

Luskell's throat ached all the way to her stomach. She sat on the stoop. It was new and well built, not quite a porch but broad and roomy. She pressed her hands against the planks. "I missed you."

"You said."

She pushed ahead. "Well, it's true. And I hardly ever heard from you, so I didn't know you had a girl. I didn't come here to make trouble."

"And yet here we are."

"I only meant to help with your quest. When I couldn't wake you, I should have gone for Brynnit, but I thought I knew what I was doing. Then when what happened ... happened—if it really did or if it was a dream—I remembered last summer. How special that was. And I thought we could pick up where we left off. I didn't know I was too late."

"But you'd just been with Laki. What kind of game do you think this is?"

"I don't think it's any kind of game! And I'm not sorry about Laki. At least he was free. But I am sorry about you." Luskell waited for a response. The latch rattled—he must have been leaning on the door—but beyond that, she heard nothing from him. "If I'd known ... if I could go back ..."

"Don't say that." Again, his soft voice startled her. He sat in the open doorway close behind her. "That was the best dream I'd ever had. I wouldn't change it."

He placed his hand on her shoulder. She laid her hand over his and rested her cheek against both. It was hard to miss the meaning of something touching your skin, but the meaning here was confused. His touch, warm and solid, seemed to say everything would be all right. But how?

"But ... but I thought you were angry with me."

"I was furious," Jagryn said, completely calm. He'd always had better control than Luskell. "With you. With myself. Less so now, but I can't invite you in. I don't trust either of us."

Luskell reached out to his emotions. He was like Aku, about to erupt, but held in check by force of will. Angry, and something more. She shivered, and not just from the cold. "I guess I understand. Are we friends again?"

"Friends. I don't know." Jagryn sighed. "You have no idea what you do to people."

"I don't do anything to people."

"Please. When I was growing up, you'd blow into town without any warning, this amazing creature who was around incredible magic every day, who'd been everywhere, who had no fear. Your enthusiasm was contagious; we were yours to command."

This was so close to what Laki had said, Luskell could almost believe they'd planned it. "I'm not like that!"

"You can't see yourself." Jagryn snorted a sad laugh. "And then I found my power. I could finally do something you couldn't! So of course you had to go and have power, too, more than anybody."

She scowled. "I didn't do it on purpose."

"I know. But I was jealous. I didn't want to share you with Laki. I didn't want to share magic with you. Then you kissed me, and nothing else mattered. You were so thrilled about doing magic, and you had so much power, and .... I wanted us to go on doing magic together forever."

"I wanted that, too," Luskell said. "Last summer, when we were together in the city ... that was the best time."

"Learning magic or kissing me?"

"Both. I wish ..." The lump in her throat ached even more, and her lips tingled.

Jagryn squeezed her shoulder and withdrew his hand. "I suppose you imagined I'd always be waiting for you, to do whatever you wanted."

"I did not!" But Luskell had to admit she'd pictured something very like that.

"That's what I imagined. But then Ruvhonn got her courtship ring and was plainly waiting for me. For me! And she was kind and thoughtful, someone I'd known even longer than I'd known you. And she was *here*."

"Do you love her?"

He sighed. "I thought I did."

"Why didn't you tell me?"

"I don't know. You were far away, not part of any of it. Maybe I didn't want to compare Ruvhonn to you. Maybe ..." He was quiet for a long time and Luskell couldn't think of anything to say. "And now you think you're pregnant?"

Too late, she shielded her thoughts. "It's too soon to tell." She leaned forward and hugged her knees.

"I'll do the right thing, if you want me to."

"I don't even know what that is."

"I'll break off with Ruvhonn and marry you."

Luskell's heart leapt, but then she felt sick. So maybe she really was pregnant. She believed Jagryn's promise, but no happiness underlay it. Love did, but it was faded and strained. "It's probably not even yours."

"Doesn't matter. I'll do whatever you say."

"Thank you. What I say is, don't tell anyone any of this, and don't do anything you'll regret."

"If I stay with Ruvhonn, I have to tell her what happened between us."

"No, you don't. What good would it do? It was a dream!" She couldn't bring herself to say *only*.

"She should know what kind of man I am, so she can make her own decision."

"You're a good man. One dream doesn't change that."

"But given half a chance, I'd make that dream real."

Luskell squeezed her eyes shut and pressed her hands against the edge of the stoop, hard enough to hurt. "What, go inside and see if it's as nice when we're awake? Do you really want to know?"

Jagryn inhaled sharply. "Say you'll marry me."

"I can't promise that."

"Then you should leave."

Luskell pushed herself to her feet and turned to him. "You're right. I should."

He looked at her with reddened eyes, as if he'd been crying, though there was no sign of tears now. His mouth had forgotten how to smile. She wanted to hold him and make it better. Except that would only make it worse.

"I'll see you, then," she said. "I hope we can be friends again."

Jagryn nodded, but said nothing. He stood, went into his house, and closed the door.

CHAPTER FORTY-ONE

Luskell still felt queasy when she returned to the inn, but managed to eat lunch with Klamamam. In fact, food helped.

"I'm sorry I was out so long. Did you need my help?"

"I'm glad you had a good visit with Grynni and Greelit," Klamamam replied. "I can still run this place alone when I have to, especially at slow times."

Rakkyn joined them in the middle of the afternoon and all three sat around the table, chopping vegetables for a stew. Luskell was happy to let Rakkyn do the onions. He had perfected a technique that somehow caused almost no tears.

"Leave the roots attached until the last moment, see?" he said. "Of course, if you need an excuse for a good cry, you can always cut them the other way."

Luskell smiled uneasily and chopped her carrots and potatoes in silence. She half wished she had taken the onions, instead. She did need a good cry ... or a good scream. In Klamamam's words, she'd apparently lost her best friend, and she might be pregnant, maybe with his child. In spite of Auntie Brynnit's comforting words, she was almost sure she was. And a baby would change everything.

Rakkyn scraped the chopped onions into a bowl. "Tell us a story, Stell. Something we haven't heard before."

Klamamam laughed. "I'm sure you've both heard everything I know." She thought a moment. "All right, you might not know this one. I don't think I've told it since before Crane was born."

She told a tale of Yrae the Mad Wizard, an almost unspeakable villain. He used his tremendous power to cause chaos and misery to innocent victims. Luskell imagined the pleasant thrill with which the original listeners heard this story, believing it to be true as they sat warm and safe around the Blue Heron's hearth. But it wasn't true—far from it. This tale, and others like it, had come from the imagination of Yrae himself, into the receptive mind of Stell, the girl he loved and left. It struck Luskell that at the time, her grandmother had been no older than she was herself, unmarried and expecting Luskell's father. She had raised her son alone, and he had turned out fine. Better than fine.

Was that what Luskell wanted to do? She tried to picture it, but she couldn't place herself. Would she have her child in Deep River, or back in the city? She wouldn't have to be alone. Her parents would let her stay with them. But what about being a wizard? She had imagined an itinerant life, finding people who needed her help, maybe even taking an apprentice someday. A child wouldn't preclude such a life, but would surely complicate it. At the very least, Luskell could forget about flying anywhere.

Maybe when the child was old enough, she could give it to its father. She was sure Laki would take it. He would want Luskell, too, but he would accept the child, especially if it was a girl and if he had no other children. His daughter would grow up to be Uklak, a position of responsibility and honor. She wouldn't have a choice in the matter; her future would be fixed.

Or if the child were more likely Jagryn's, Luskell was sure he would accept it, too. He'd said Luskell could ask him to give up Ruvhonn. But maybe it would be better to let Ruvhonn have him, and the baby, too. If she'd take it. Hardly likely; why should she, unless Jagryn could persuade her? And in that case, Luskell would have to give up Deep River, too. Bad enough to lose her friend, but her family's home, too?

Maybe the best thing would be to bolt back to Auntie Brynnit and beg for the charm to bring on her bleeding. It would be simple, and quick, and over. No one else would need to know. But ...

"I love them both," Luskell muttered. Klamamam and Rakkyn stared at her. She'd spoken aloud without meaning to. "Yrae and Knot," she hastened to explain. "Yrae meant well, but he caused himself so much pain for so long. He found love only as Knot, when it was almost too late. I ... feel sorry for him."

Klamamam nodded. "I did, too, even before I knew who he was. But he's at peace now." She gazed at Luskell. "You're like him, and not just around the eyes. You don't always think things through, but you mean well."

Luskell felt dizzy. How much had Klamamam guessed? She scraped the last of the carrots into a bowl and stood up. "I need some air."

She wrapped up and went out again. It was not a beautiful day for a walk. The sky was sullen and gray, the winter afternoon already almost as dim as evening. At least it wasn't snowing yet. Luskell hurried past Jagryn's house without looking to see whether he was still there.

Beyond the town, Luskell found it easier to breathe. She would visit Knot's grave. She could tell him her troubles, and maybe he would visit her dreams later. He was buried near her brother Ketwyn. She hadn't seen him since her birthday.

As she walked toward the graveyard, she tried Listening to the sagebrush that grew on either side of the road. It wasn't so different from Listening to the forest, with the same topics of water, soil, insects, fire. And vague hints of danger.

Luskell returned her attention to the road. A figure approached from the north. A man, based on the way he moved. Before she could discern his face, he plunged off the road and disappeared into the brush. Such behavior was too strange not to investigate. Luskell forgot her plan to visit Knot's grave. She changed into an owl and flew silently over the shrubby prairie.

With owl eyes, it didn't take long to find the stranger by his movement. Something about him seemed familiar. Luskell lighted near him and resumed her own form. She had been in another form such a short time, she barely felt it. Only then did she remember she might be pregnant and shouldn't transform. Nobody knew whether it was actually harmful, but neither did anyone want to be the one to find out.

Luskell pushed the thought away and crept on a course to intercept the stranger. It wasn't difficult to find him. He tried to run, bent low, and crashed through the brush, swearing when clothes or skin encountered sharp branches. He almost collided with Luskell and yelled when she put out her hands to hold him back. He was fair-haired, nearly as tall as Luskell, and met her gaze with a look of terror.

"Fandek? What are you doing here?"

CHAPTER FORTY-TWO

"Luskell, you're safe!" Fandek clasped her in a crushing embrace.

The intensity of it took Luskell by surprise. For a moment, she let him hold her. He'd learned to shield; imperfectly, but enough to muffle any strong emotions or stray thoughts. She drew strength from his strength, warmth from his warmth. Then she remembered herself and pushed free. The whole day had been upsetting and she was not herself. That was the only explanation.

"Why wouldn't I be, except that you tried to squeeze the life out of me?"

"Sorry." Fandek gazed at her. "I thought I saw someone sneaking along, just off the road, like he was following you. I wanted to cut him off, but I lost him."

That sense of danger in the sagebrush ... But Luskell remembered her father's suspicions about Fandek. And her own. "It could have been a coyote or bobcat. The only one I see lurking just off the road is you." She backed away a step. "What are you doing in Deep River?"

"I wanted to be with you."

"You followed me here? How?"

"I begged a few rides, but mostly on foot."

"Impressive. How did you know where to go?"

"The first part was easy—you told me you were going to Misty Pass to join your mother. By the time I got there, you'd already gone somewhere else. I thought I'd lost you, but I remembered what you said about Aklaka Listening. I guessed you'd come back to Misty Pass eventually. I did odd jobs around town to earn my keep until you came back." Fandek grinned. "Lucky break the innkeeper needed a lot of help."

"You were working for Grandma Nari? She never said a word!"

"She's your grandmother? I didn't know that." He bit his lip and gazed back the way he'd come. "I wasn't sure what kind of welcome you'd give me, so I never let on I knew you. I said I was stranded and needed help to get back on the road."

"But you knew when I got back?"

"I was out back chopping wood when you fetched the wash tub."

Luskell remembered that bath in Nari's kitchen, when she'd thought she had privacy. "You spied on me?"

"Not really *spied*. I ... eavesdropped. That's how I knew you were planning to go to Deep River."

"Listening to private conversations is spying."

"Conversations held in public aren't private." Fandek's expression grew wistful. "I saw you with your family. Hard to believe you're related to your mother."

"I know. Sometimes I wish I had her looks." Luskell scowled at him. "I have her temper, though."

"Your looks are fine. I was thinking more her size and her hair."

"My brothers both got the red hair."

Fandek raised an eyebrow. "I didn't know you had more than one."

"My older brother is ... gone."

"Mine, too! Oh. You mean *gone*. Sorry."

Luskell waved off the apology. Technically, she never knew Ketwyn. "Dadad noticed you'd left the city. He thinks you're the strangler."

Fandek's mouth dropped open. "That isn't fair! I'm trying to help you." He glanced around. There was no one else in sight, and they were down in a hollow that hid the town from view. "Besides, we're alone and it's getting dark. Wouldn't I have attacked you by now?"

Luskell crossed her arms and thrust out her jaw. "Try it."

"See? I'd be stupid to try anything with you. We both know it. But I kept having these ...visions, I guess. About some kind of trouble. When I knew where you were going, I started making my way down here."

"All to protect me?" She shook her head. "That was ... kind. But unnecessary."

"When you were in Oxbow, I saw someone following you. But when I caught up, I'd lost him and you were nowhere around."

There had been at least one murder in Oxbow, and Luskell had sensed someone, too. She shuddered. "I was in the air. I can take care of myself."

"Even so, you shouldn't be out alone. Where are you going? I'll come along."

"I was planning to visit my grandfather's grave, but you're right—it's getting dark. I'll have to do that another day." Luskell heard a sound that was so far from ominous, she laughed. "Are you hungry?"

"Breakfast was a long time ago."

"Come on, then. We'll go back to town and find you supper."

Luskell Listened again. The hint of danger was still there, but less distinct. Probably a wild animal, by now on the trail of easier prey. Unless the danger was Fandek, rendered less a threat by Luskell's awareness. She found that difficult to believe. He was harder to read than he should have been with his imperfect shield, but his clumsy hug had felt sincere.

"I dreamed you were in trouble," he said.

Luskell's stomach lurched. He didn't know the half of it. "I will be if I don't get back and help with supper."

She returned to the road, careful to keep Fandek where she could see him. There was no harm in playing it safe.

"So, why did you come to Deep River?" Fandek asked. "It's seems about as out-of-the-way as you could get."

"I was born here. My father was born here. My grandfather is buried here, and my grandmother still lives here. We visit whenever we can."

"But in the middle of winter?"

"My father has an apprentice in Deep River. He's nearly finished with his quest, so I came on ahead to check his progress."

"Why you and not Master Crane?"

The respectful tone improved Luskell's opinion of Fandek a smidgen. "Dadad had other business to finish first. And Jagryn's project is in an area where I have expertise."

Fandek halted in the middle of the road. Luskell had to stop and turn to prevent him from getting behind her. "Jagryn—I thought I'd heard the last of him when Master

Crane passed me back to Master Breet. Just my luck." He started walking again.

Luskell fell in beside him. "What do you have against Jagryn? You've never even met him."

"Nothing, except he was apparently the best apprentice ever."

Luskell chuckled. "You should know, Jagryn was the first formal apprentice Dadad ever had. He's talented and methodical. I'm sure it made him easy to teach. He's more than two years ahead of you, though he's younger. You're not in competition."

"Really? Then you're not his sweetheart?"

Luskell's heart stuttered. "We're old friends. Nothing more."

"Your father implied otherwise."

"He doesn't know everything."

They arrived back at the Blue Heron. The supper crowd had not yet gathered, but the inn was fragrant with the savory aroma of stew simmering. Luskell took Fandek into the kitchen.

"Klamamam, do we have room for another apprentice wizard? This is Fandek, from Eukard City. Fandek, my grandmother, Stell."

Klamamam smiled her familiar smile of welcome and held out her hand. Fandek took it. "Any friend of Luskell's is welcome here. What brings you to Deep River, Fandek?"

"I ... wanted to get out of the city for a while, and I knew Luskell and her father were coming here."

"Dadad filled in for Fandek's master while he was sick," Luskell supplied. She wanted to be clear that Fandek was not her friend, but it felt mean to say it straight out. Making it about her father seemed a reasonable compromise.

Fandek nodded. "He's a great teacher. Luskell's not so bad, herself."

That was all it took for Klamamam to give Fandek a room for the night or as long as he needed it, as well as meals. Luskell ate supper with him, and he helped clean the dishes afterwards. He seemed honest about his intentions. But she made sure to bolt her door before she went to bed.

Luskell was back on the terrace at the Governor's Mansion on a warm summer night. She wasn't surprised Trenn waited for her, but his companion startled her. She threw herself into Knot's arms.

"I wanted to see you so much! I was going to visit your grave today."

"That's probably better than visiting me on the Other Side. But we came to warn you."

"Of what?" She stepped out of Knot's embrace.

"There's a bad man hanging around," Trenn said. "He isn't what he seems."

"What bad man? What does he look like?"

"Tall," Trenn said.

"Short," Knot said at the same time. They exchanged a glance. "Around your height, maybe. Wiry build. Light hair."

Luskell shivered. It was almost the same vague description Dadad had gotten from Hanny. The one that sounded like Fandek. "Are you telling me the strangler is here in Deep River?"

"I'm not sure who he is," Knot replied. "But he's up to no good. So be careful."

"I'll try. Deep River isn't a place where a stranger can hide for long."

338

"He might not need long."

"I can try to sense his presence." Luskell turned to Trenn. "Mamam thought the strangler might not feel. Is that possible? To kill without emotion?"

"I never killed anyone but myself. I felt that."

Then they were gone. Luskell lay on a table with her back exposed. Someone used an obsidian knife, like the one Laki had tried to sell, to remove part of her spine for some ritual purpose. It didn't hurt that much, considering ...

CHAPTER FORTY-THREE

Luskell whooped once in celebration. She had never been so happy to see bloody sheets.

She got up and dressed for the day, then gathered her nightdress and sheet for washing. She slid back the bolt and opened the door. Fandek waited on the other side.

Luskell yelped. "What do you want?"

"Sorry! I heard you shout, and I came to help."

Knot's voice echoed in her mind. *He isn't what he seems.* "I banged my knee, that's all. Excuse me, please." Luskell dodged around him and into the kitchen. "Monthly laundry," she explained to Klamamam, and dumped her load into a washtub. She added cold water. It could soak until after breakfast.

As Luskell moved to her place at the table, she heard Mamam's voice in her mind.

Luskell? We're coming today, on the evening coach. Will you tell Jagree?

Yes, I'll tell him. Remember to pick up my fiddle.

Thanks for reminding me. See you soon.

Luskell beamed ... straight at Fandek, where he stood in the doorway. She sobered and took her seat. He pulled out the chair across from her and sat down, wearing a grin of his own.

Klamamam served them each a bowl of porridge. "Haven't seen a big smile like that since you got here." Her eyes twinkled as she glanced at Fandek.

"I just heard from Mamam. They're coming tonight." Luskell was glad she had a reason to be happy besides her real reason or Klamamam's assumed one. Secrets were too complicated. She blew on a spoonful of porridge. Eating was the best way she knew not to talk.

Fandek didn't take the hint. "You heard from your mother? All the way from Misty Pass?" He somehow managed to look skeptical and impressed at the same time.

Luskell gazed at him. He had a pleasant face. It was hard to be suspicious by daylight. "We have a gift."

"Maybe you can teach me sometime." Fandek grinned. "Or at least show me around after breakfast."

"I have chores to do. Some washing, and—"

"I'll take care of that," Klamamam interrupted. "You can see about getting your folks a ride from Oxbow."

Luskell insisted on washing the breakfast dishes first. Fandek insisted on helping.

"We took care of ourselves, after Mom died," he explained. "No women at our house, so no women's work. Just ... work."

"Well, thank you," Luskell said. "The job goes faster with two."

"Never been to the Dry Side before. Can't wait to see it by daylight."

Luskell couldn't prevent him from tagging along after that. "We won't go far. It's too cold, and there's not much to see."

She fastened her cloak and led the way out. Heavy clouds hung low and flat. A few snowflakes fell, and Luskell Listened to them by habit: *Love. Friendship. Danger.* These were all things she knew. And the danger wasn't vague anymore; it was here, in Deep River. But where? No strangers had stayed at the inn (except Fandek) but that didn't mean the strangler wasn't lurking somewhere. A barn or shed, maybe. A root cellar. But he hadn't killed anyone since Oxbow. What was he waiting for?

At the next house, Uncle Jagree paused on the doorstep to kiss Auntie Brynnit.

"Hello, Luskell," Auntie Brynnit called. "Who's your friend?"

Luskell resisted the urge to correct her. "This is Fandek, from Eukard City. He's an apprentice wizard, too."

Uncle Jagree grinned. "Don't know how many more of those Deep River can stand."

Auntie Brynnit nudged him playfully. "So, Luskell, how are you today?

"Never better."

Auntie Brynnit smiled. "Glad to hear it."

Uncle Jagree glanced between them, but neither Auntie Brynnit nor Luskell gave him any clues. Auntie Brynnit kissed him again and went inside.

Luskell waited for him at the roadside. "Uncle Jagree, I heard from Mamam this morning. They're coming on the evening coach."

For the briefest moment, the solid blacksmith smiled in a way that could only be called dreamy. "Good news. I'll be happy to fetch them. Do you want to ride along?"

"Yes, if there's room. Thank you."

"Is there room for me, too?" Fandek asked.

Uncle Jagree nodded. "Sure, if Luskell doesn't mind. Little Crett takes up hardly any space, and they never bring much luggage."

Luskell turned away with a frown. Did she have to share everything with Fandek? "It's fine with me." It was a good idea to take him along, to keep an eye on him. She couldn't forget Knot's warning. Someone in Deep River wasn't what he seemed, but Uncle Jagree could be trusted to the ends of the earth. And then she'd be with Mamam and Dadad. Nothing bad could happen then.

"Good, I'll stop at the inn after supper, then. See you." Uncle Jagree crossed the road to the forge.

Fandek watched him go. "That man loves your mother."

"Everyone knows that." Luskell was impressed that Fandek, a stranger, could tell. In her experience, men were often oblivious to emotion. She wasn't about to let him know it. "They're old friends. He helped her through a hard time, many years ago."

"More than just friends. But not anymore?"

"There's no 'just' about real friends," Luskell said. "Back then, she wasn't available, and he was younger than either of us. And then Brynnit captured his heart, about the time my parents found each other again. So it all worked out."

"If you say so. Come on, show me around," Fandek urged. He looked eagerly at the quiet village where nothing much ever happened. "I've never been out of the city before."

Luskell laughed at that. "There are people here who've never been farther than the next little town over. You'll fit right in." She shivered. "We can't stay out long, though. It's cold, and I didn't bring my mittens."

Fandek grabbed her hand. "How's that?"

His hand was warm and fit nicely around hers. They both had long, slender fingers, and she had a momentary wild idea about teaching him to play the fiddle. She shook herself, disguising it as another shiver. Long fingers could also fit around a throat. She withdrew her hand from his and tucked it inside her cloak. "You'd be chilled in no time. This way."

She led him further along the road and pointed out the flour mill and the brewery on the river side, and the weaver's and carpenter's shops across the road.

"It's like they've always been here!" Fandek exclaimed. "Like they *grew* here!"

"They were built, like anything in the city," Luskell said. "More recently, too, though they are old. Most of these stone houses were built over a century ago."

"What's that one?" He pointed at Elika's house. Jagryn's house.

Luskell hurried past it. "It was the healer's house a long time ago. No one lives there now." She waved toward the open field beyond the house. "That was going to be a vineyard, but the vines all died in a drought a few years ago. See the stumps?"

Fandek ignored her effort to change the subject. He glanced at her sidelong. "Vacant house? Sounds like a good place for courting couples to go in and warm up."

"I wouldn't know."

Luskell set a fast pace back through town, but Fandek kept up easily. She pointed out the Village Hall, with Myn and Sulika's house behind it, and the school and teacher's house, where Uncle Elic and Aunt Sunnea lived. Where Jagryn still lived, at least some of the time. Luskell resisted the urge to sense for his thoughts, or mind-talk. She didn't want to see him.

When they reached the edge of town, Fandek stood and gazed out over the landscape. "You can see forever! Let's keep going!"

"No, it's too cold. We need to go back." It was one thing to show him around town, but wandering off alone with someone she wasn't sure about seemed like asking for trouble.

Fandek obliged and turned back, but he was so taken with Sulika's greenhouse, Luskell relented and let him have a closer look. Sulika was inside and opened the door for them. The warmth was a welcome relief.

"Hello! Who's this, Luskell?" Sulika asked.

"Sulika, Fandek. Fandek, Sulika. He's another apprentice wizard from the city."

"Welcome, Fandek." Sulika shook his hand. "What brings you to Deep River?"

"I'd rather be Crane's apprentice than Breet's," Fandek replied, and Luskell blessed him for not bringing her name into it. "Looks like I beat him, but he'll be along tonight, I hear."

Sulika beamed. "And the whole family, I expect. I haven't seen Crett since he was practically a newborn."

After more small talk, Luskell extracted Fandek to return to the Heron.

"The people here are so welcoming," Fandek said. "Are they all your relatives? What's Sulika to you?"

She's Jagryn's sister. But that answer wasn't helpful. "My grandmother is the only blood relative still living here. Sulika is the daughter of my father's oldest friend. She and her brothers are like cousins to me." *Or, they were.* "Jagree, who you met before, is their uncle. Brynnit was my mother's apprentice, and we rent rooms from her sister and brother-in-law in Eukard City. I rode with their daughter as far as Misty Pass when she came to stay with her grandparents." And why had Keela come to Deep River? But somebody *here* was up to no good.

"So the whole town is one big family?"

Luskell nodded. "For better or worse. "

"And everybody knows everybody else's business?"

Luskell thought about this before answering. "They think they do. As I understand it, everybody has a secret or two." Too late, she realized she might be making them look vulnerable. "But they look out for each other. You have to work at it to get into any kind of deep trouble."

Fandek smiled. "I'll keep that in mind."

CHAPTER FORTY-FOUR

Luskell and Fandek returned to the Blue Heron. Luskell's toes were numb with cold, and she had to stamp the life back into them. When they rode to Oxbow later, she would wear trousers and boots.

Klamamam called to her from the kitchen. "Luskell, if that's you, you're just in time to hang the washing."

Luskell found her nightdress and sheet heaped in a basket. She lifted out the damp sheet and draped it over the line strung across the warm kitchen. Luskell could reach it from the floor; Klamamam needed to stand on a stool.

"What can I do?" Fandek asked.

Klamamam passed him two pails. "Fill one with potatoes and the other with carrots. Oh, you don't know where the root cellar is. Here, I'll show you."

Luskell looked around the end of the sheet. She did not like leaving Fandek alone with her grandmother. Whoever the strangler was, he targeted independent women, which described Klamamam if it described anyone. Luskell couldn't exactly follow them around without looking suspicious herself. She did the next best thing and followed the trail of their emotions, without leaving the warm kitchen.

Whenever Luskell opened herself to others' emotions, she risked being overwhelmed by powerful or unexpected feelings. She reached out tentatively at first, but found nothing troubling. Klamamam radiated calm contentment, underlaid with a sense of loss, a permanent, bittersweet note since Knot's death. Luskell also sensed a growing seed of affection for Fandek. It moved Luskell toward trusting him. Almost. Not quite.

Fandek was in a good mood, too, with a building sense of anticipation. About the ride to Oxbow? It wasn't much to get excited about. Maybe riding with Luskell, though he'd been with her all morning. Was he looking forward to ... something else?

By the time Luskell had finished hanging the wash, Klamamam was back, and Fandek arrived a short time later with his pails of root vegetables. Luskell felt silly for her suspicions, but couldn't quite shake them. Just because he wouldn't murder a woman in her own place of business with a relative nearby didn't make him innocent.

The three of them finished last night's leftover stew for lunch. When they'd eaten and washed up, Klamamam had Luskell and Fandek scrub and chop the two pails of vegetables in preparation for the evening meal. After that, they were free until supper. Then Uncle Jagree would take them to Oxbow, and all would be right again.

Luskell and Fandek sat close to the fire in the common room. It wasn't quite as snug as the kitchen, but it got them out from under Klamamam and Rakkyn's feet.

"Teach me the mind-talking thing," Fandek said. "That seems like actual useful magic."

"It is when it works. Have you started with it at all?"

He shook his head. "Breet said I wasn't ready. Is it really so advanced?"

"I don't know. I can understand why they might not teach some of the dangerous things to a beginner, but this? Maybe Breet isn't good at it."

Fandek smiled, an expression that lit his face. It was contagious. Luskell fought it, but couldn't help smiling back.

She continued her lesson. "I must have had an aptitude for it, because I got it the first day. Not on the first try, mind you, but after a lot of practice, I had the idea. The next day I sent a message to my mother in Eukard City."

Fandek whistled. "That's something. Did she answer?"

"No. She didn't get the whole message, so she wasn't sure what was happening. But I wonder ... I'll bet she could, if she tried. She has loads of power."

"Tell me what to do. Is there a spell?"

"Not exactly. Mind talking requires intense focus, combined with natural ability. You reach out to another receptive mind, and when you've made contact, you give them the message."

Fandek rolled his eyes. "You make it sound so easy!"

"For me, it is easy. I've been doing it awhile. The trick is, you have to know where the recipient is. Otherwise, the message has nowhere to go."

"And how do I know I've made contact?"

"Trust me, you'll know. It's like the window flies open and you touch, no matter the distance. Here, I'll show you."

Luskell pulled her chair around to face his. She closed her eyes and reached out. She found Fandek's mind almost instantly. Their knees were almost touching, and he definitely had a receptive mind.

Don't try to answer. Remember what it feels like. She opened her eyes. He stared at her, his mouth half open. "Breathe," she said aloud.

Fandek gasped. "That was ... it was like ... whew!" He blinked and shook himself. "Like you put your hand in my mind." He looked away, then back. "You really think I could do that, too?"

"I'm sure of it, now. You had no trouble hearing me, right?"

"You told me not to try to answer, but to remember what it felt like."

"Good, you've got it!" Luskell recalled her own first experience, in which garbled messages proved embarrassing to all concerned. "It's a good idea to shield your thoughts, to keep the message clear. You don't want to send out whatever pops into your head."

"Got it. Intense focus, natural ability, shielded thoughts." Fandek tensed and held his breath.

Luskell laughed. "Not like that! You have to concentrate and relax at the same time. Go ahead and close your eyes, though. It helps."

She watched as he tried again. At first, he appeared calm and relaxed; properly meditative. As he worked, a variety of expressions crossed his face—puzzlement, a frustrated frown, calm forced back into place.

Fandek opened his eyes. "Gah! I can't do this! It's like somebody threw a heavy blanket over my head!"

"It was the same for me," Luskell assured him. "Try again. I'm sure you've almost got it." She wasn't, but it sounded like what an encouraging teacher would say.

He took several deep breaths and closed his eyes again. Frown lines formed between his eyes, but his focus appeared unwavering. Luskell felt the first tentative touch in her mind. It was intimate—shockingly so—but different from Jagryn's familiar touch.

Luskell? I ... think I'm doing it. Do you hear me?

Clear as anything.

She broke contact first, and opened her eyes. "There, you see? You're a natural."

Fandek's eyes shone, and his smile once again lit his face like a summer day."You're a natural teacher. I could kiss you!"

Luskell scooted her chair back. "Please don't." She still felt his touch on her mind. A kiss was the last thing she needed now. It was bad enough to go too far with Jagryn, a trusted friend. Fandek was neither. She needed to keep her head.

All afternoon, the savory aroma of chicken stock filled the inn. For supper, Klamamam and Rakkyn turned it into a hearty soup, thick with chicken, vegetables, and eggy little dumplings. Luskell and Fandek joined them in the kitchen for the first bowls.

"Eat up, and then you can help serve until Jagree comes to fetch you," Klamamam said.

Luskell went to her room to change into her travel clothes first. As she pulled on her warm undershirt, it crackled and her hair stood up. The air was dry and full of little lightning. She wondered what kind of weather they might be in for on this ride, but finished dressing and returned to the kitchen for an apron.

Before she got there, the front door opened to admit the last person she would have expected.

Jagryn's eyes were bloodshot, circled with bruise-like smudges in a pale, drawn face. He gripped her arm. "Luskell? I need your help."

CHAPTER FORTY-FIVE

Luskell stared at Jagryn. "You look terrible. Are you ill?"

He rubbed his eyes. "I haven't slept well since ... the other day. I wake up as soon as I start to dream."

Behind him, snow fell heavily. Luskell wanted to run out and Listen to it, but drew Jagryn inside and closed the door. "What do you want my help with?"

Jagryn swayed on his feet. "Sleep, for one thing."

She steadied him with a hand on his shoulder. "I know a good sleep charm—"

He cut her off. "No magic. No drops. What about that Aklaka lullaby?"

Luskell smiled. "That probably would help. It puts you to sleep quickly, but it's a natural sleep. You'll be able to wake when it's time."

"Good. I heard Master Crane's coming, and I want to complete my quest before he gets here."

"Is that wise, when you're exhausted?" For his benefit, she put on a composed act, though her heart fluttered with worry.

"It might help." He managed a weary smile, a slight lift at the corners of his mouth. "So, will you?"

"Of course." It meant she wouldn't be able to go to Oxbow to meet her parents, but they didn't know she'd planned on it. And Jagryn had asked for her help, as if they were friends again. "Have you eaten?"

The corners of his mouth lifted a little more. "You keep asking me that. No, not much today. No appetite."

"You can't do magic on an empty stomach. And Klamamam made chicken soup."

Jagryn's eyes widened, and he leaned toward the kitchen. "I wouldn't say no to a bowl."

"Good. We'll go to your house after."

Jagryn shook his head. "We'll go to my parents' house. Safer."

"You're right. Klamamam, can we give Jagryn some supper?"

Klamamam came to the door and waved him into the kitchen. "Come in, son. I expect you know Fandek?"

Jagryn stared at Fandek and frowned, though he seemed too tired for strong feelings.

Fandek stood up and offered his hand. He was taller than Jagryn. "You'd already left the city when I started my training. How are you?"

"Been better." Jagryn glanced at Luskell. "Another sweetheart of yours?"

Luskell's face turned hot, but Fandek answered before she could. "I wish! She doesn't even like me." He let his hand drop and resumed his seat.

Jagryn gave another tired smile. "Good." He turned his attention to the soup and demonstrated the return of his appetite. Klamamam refilled the empty bowl.

"Jagryn has some work he wants to finish before Dadad gets here," Luskell said. "He asked me to help, so I won't be able to ride along to Oxbow. Fandek, you can still go if you want to."

Fandek shook his head and waved his hand. "In this weather? No, I'll stay here where it's warm."

Luskell nodded. "Fine. Excuse me, will you?" She got up and returned to the common room, where Rakkyn prepared for the supper crowd. "Rakkyn? I need to ask a favor."

He smiled. "Anything. What can I do for you?"

She glanced back toward the kitchen. "I need to go with Jagryn for a while. Fandek is staying here."

"And you need me to keep your secret? You can count on me." Rakkyn tapped a finger to his lips and gave a sly smile

"It's no secret. Will you make sure Fandek isn't left alone with anyone?"

"There's no trust between sweethearts these days." Rakkyn quirked an eyebrow. "So by 'anyone,' you mean pretty girls? Or is it boys you're worried about?"

Luskell laid her hand over Rakkyn's mouth before he could say any more. "Rakkyn, if you were anyone else, I would slap you silly. I don't know Fandek that well. I didn't invite him here, and he might be dangerous. So don't leave him alone with *anyone*." She glanced toward the kitchen.

Rakkyn sobered and carefully removed Luskell's hand from his mouth. "Why didn't you say so? You can count on me." He nodded at Luskell and returned to the kitchen as Jagryn came out. Klamamam would not be left alone with Fandek.

Jagryn still looked exhausted, but stronger now that he'd eaten. "Ready?"

"Yes, let's go." Luskell put on her cloak and pulled the hood forward. They went out into the darkening evening. She guessed the sun had barely set. The heavy clouds and snow brought night on early.

"So you think the lullaby will work?" he asked.

"I use it on Crett all the time."

"But does it work on adults?"

"Laki used it on me." Luskell caught a whiff of jealousy off Jagryn. "You can stop that right now."

"Stop what?" The studied innocence of Jagryn's tone was almost, but not quite, believable.

"Please, you don't even have the decency to shield your emotions. Every time I say Laki's name, there it is. The jealousy. Just stop it."

"Why did you leave him if you love him so much?"

"Because ... I don't love him more than I love you. You know what I'm talking about."

Jagryn didn't say anything, but attempted to shield. The jealousy lingered, though not as strong.

"Jagryn, you have no more claim on me than I have on you."

"If you're having my baby, I'd say we both have a claim."

Luskell raised her face to the snowflakes. *Love*, they said. *Power. Trust. Danger.* "There is no baby. I was wrong. Nothing to worry about."

"Oh." A mix of relief and disappointment leaked through his shield. He really wanted to be a father ... someday. "My offer holds."

"We are not talking about that tonight. I'll help you sleep so you can do your work and earn your staff. That's all."

They met groups of bundled-up children, heading home from school. Light from the schoolhouse windows spilled across the path to Uncle Elic and Aunt Sunnea's house. Luskell and Jagryn stepped up onto the porch. Luskell raised her hand to knock.

Jagryn pushed past her and opened the door. "I still live here, remember?" Aunt Sunnea turned from the stove with a smile that disappeared when she saw Jagryn's face.

"Baby, do you feel all right?"

"I'm not a baby," he said without heat. It was exactly the kind of thing Crett would say. Luskell wondered if the youngest in a family was ever allowed to really grow up. "I haven't been sleeping well, so Luskell's going to help me. And yes, I have eaten."

Aunt Sunnea glanced at Luskell, her brows drawn together with motherly concern. "What kind of help?"

"I'll sing him to sleep," Luskell said. "I won't stay long."

Jagryn had his own small room at the back of the house. Luskell turned her back while he undressed and got into bed. Then she sat in a chair next to him. "Ready?"

"I need to think about Elika first." He swallowed. "Will you come with me?"

"I'm not supposed to do it for you."

"No, I'll do it myself. But if you could follow me, like you did before, to make sure I'm doing it right ..."

"I can do that much. See you on the Other Side."

When Jagryn was ready, he lay back and closed his eyes. Luskell took his hand in hers and sang the lullaby. By the middle of the second verse, he was snoring gently. Luskell felt for his thoughts. When he began to dream, she followed him to the bright, warm meadow where no sun shone.

Elika waited for them there. "Well, what is it this time?"

Jagryn's mouth stretched in a grin. He no longer appeared exhausted. "When I visited before, I wasn't myself."

"You brought a friend."

He glanced at Luskell. She squeezed his hand and released it. "You don't need my help now. Can you get back on your own?"

Jagryn turned and looked down the slope behind them. Their bodies were visible in the distance. "I won't get lost this time."

"Don't stay too long, and don't let anyone touch you other than Elika. I don't want to come fetch you again."

"I'll make sure he gets back," Elika said.

"Thank you." Luskell hugged Jagryn, then without thinking, kissed him. It was no Lightning Kiss, but maybe just as dangerous. She turned down the slope and didn't look back.

CHAPTER FORTY-SIX

Luskell took two steps down the slope and opened her eyes in Jagryn's room. He slept on, his eyes twitching as he dreamed. She wanted more than anything to stay until he woke, to make sure everything went well. But this was his quest. He needed to do it himself. And she needed to trust him to come back in time.

Besides, it wouldn't do to stay in his room longer than she had to. As far as anyone knew, Ruvhonn was his girl. Maybe that would change. It wasn't Luskell's place to cause a scandal. She'd already done enough damage. Still, her heart warmed as she watched him sleep. She squeezed his hand and reluctantly let go.

"Will he be all right now?" Aunt Sunnea asked as Luskell closed the door behind her.

Luskell exhaled a long breath. "I hope so. He's worn out; he'll sleep a long time. If he doesn't wake at breakfast time, shake him."

"And if that doesn't wake him?"

Luskell closed her eyes a moment, then looked at Aunt Sunnea with a forced smile. "Then send for me. But I doubt you'll have to." She pulled the door open and almost walked into Ruvhonn and Uncle Elic on the porch. Ruvhonn froze with one mitten half off.

Luskell stepped aside to let them in. "Pardon me, I didn't know you were there."

Ruvhonn frowned, and the anger that washed off her drove Luskell back. "I heard Jagryn's voice earlier."

Aunt Sunnea stepped up to play the diplomat. "He's sleeping now."

"Then why is *she* here?"

"I was just leaving," Luskell said. The ghost kiss tingled guiltily on her lips.

"No, I was." Ruvhonn turned and fled up the path.

Elic watched her go, then turned to Luskell, his brows knit in a puzzled frown. "What was that about?"

Luskell sighed. "She thinks there's something between me and Jagryn."

Aunt Sunnea studied her. "And is there?"

"I don't know. There might have been, once. Now ..." Luskell gazed out at the falling snow. The wind had picked up and it felt colder. "She's not walking home, is she?"

Elic shook his head. "She stables her horse at Jagree's. On a night like this, she's smart enough to stay in town." He considered. "With us, usually. But she knows enough to stay at the inn or with Brynnit and Jagree."

"This is my fault," Luskell said. "I'll watch for her, make sure she's safe." She pulled her hood up and left the house. Before she left the shelter of the porch, she felt for Jagryn's thoughts. He was still dreaming, but he was no longer on the Other Side.

She hurried through the blowing snow. It was nothing like the blizzard on Mount Aku—she could see far enough that she was in no danger of getting lost—but it was cold and getting colder. She picked up traces of Ruvhonn's feelings: vexation, jealousy, affection, loss. Luskell didn't raise her face to the snowflakes. They wouldn't tell her anything she didn't already know. She reached for Fandek's mind.

Fandek—did a girl come in, light hair, pink cheeks, kind of angry?

Whoa! This feels so strange. Um, no, it's just me, Rakkyn, your grandmother, and a few old fellows playing dice.

A flash of light revealed a figure working in Sulika's greenhouse. Darkness closed again, broken by a muffled rumble of thunder. That was Sulika, dedicated to her plants, working with them even during a storm. Luskell Listened to their tiny voices. They seemed to be wailing. It was probably past time to pull the cover down; they were cold. So was Luskell. She hurried on. Near the inn, she collided with someone hurrying the other way.

"Who's that? Luskell?"

Luskell knew the voice. "Sulika?" She stepped back, and recognized the bundled figure. She had the baby tucked under her cloak. Luskell felt a chill that had nothing to do with the snowstorm. "Don't go home. There's someone hiding in your greenhouse."

"What? I have to go home. Myn'll be home for supper soon."

"Where are you coming from?"

"Grammy and Crane's."

"Go back there. I'll get Myn to meet you."

"If it's not safe for me, why is it safe for you?"

"Fine, I'll get Young Crane to go with me. But trust me, something isn't right. We're safer in groups."

It was only a few steps back to Aunt Sudi's house. Luskell and Sulika nipped inside and closed the door behind them to shut out the storm. Aunt Sudi, Young Crane and Bramynna sat around a table littered with mugs and plates.

Young Crane grinned at his sister. "Back so soon? Is the storm that bad?"

"No, Luskell made me come back. She says there's someone in my greenhouse."

"Is that Luskell under all that snow? It's good to see you."

Luskell managed a smile for Young Crane. He was as handsome as she remembered, with his dark blond hair, big brown eyes, and blacksmith's build. "It's not safe for anyone to be out alone. There's someone lurking, up to no good. Besides, the storm's getting worse."

Young Crane wrapped an arm around Bramynna. "I guess you'll have to stay here tonight."

She smiled at him. "What a shame."

"Will you come with me to fetch Myn from the Hall?" Luskell asked.

"Of course. Let's go." He wrapped up and lit a lantern. The two of them hurried through the snowy night. "I heard thunder earlier," Young Crane shouted over the wind. "Was that you?"

"No, I don't do weather. That was thunder snow."

"I didn't know that was possible."

"It's rare. I've only heard it once before."

They met Myn as he left the Village Hall and started up the path to his house.

"Come with us," Young Crane said. "Everyone's at my house."

"Why?" Myn squinted through the blowing snow. "Is it a party?"

"Yeah, to celebrate the thunder snow."

"I saw someone hiding in Sulika's greenhouse, and I had a bad feeling," Luskell explained.

"Trust a wizard's intuition," Young Crane advised.

Myn shook him off. "I want to see for myself."

He waded through fallen snow to the greenhouse. The door stood open, and the lantern light showed no one inside. Something dark lay on the floor. Luskell scooped it up.

"What is that?" Myn asked. "An animal?"

The thing was dark and hairy like an animal, but had no substance under the hair. Luskell gasped. "No, it's a false beard! Keela was right! It's not Fandek at all!"

Myn turned to Young Crane. "Do you know what she's talking about?"

He shook his head and showered snow over some of the small plants. "No, but she was right—someone was hiding here, and now he's run off."

While Myn secured the door and tugged the cover into place, Crane searched with the lantern for footprints that might show where the no-longer-bearded stranger had gone. One large print showed clear just outside the door to the greenhouse.

"Not much of a trail, though. We wiped it out when we came up the path." He held up the lantern to better light the way they had come, now a muddle of tracks.

"Wait, look!" Luskell trudged down to the roadside. One of the cherry saplings lay broken, flattened under a large boot print. "Sulika won't be happy about that."

The others joined her and tried to discern a trail, but it disappeared again into the wheel marks and their own tracks in the deserted road. The rest of the town was apparently smart enough to go home and stay indoors. Luskell parted from the men outside the inn. She could hardly wait to get back inside where it was warm, even if she did owe Fandek an apology. Then she remembered Ruvhonn. If she hadn't taken shelter at the inn, she might be trying to ride home in this storm.

"Crane, lend me your lantern. I need to check something in the stable."

"Do you want me to come with you?"

"No, I'll be fine. I'm almost a wizard, remember? Go on home. This'll only take a moment."

He handed her the lantern and joined Myn at the door to his house. Luskell crossed to the stable. From outside, she heard the horses' restless stamping and whickering. She raised the lantern to peer inside. A high-pitched scream carried over the noise of the storm. Ruvhonn burst out, pursued by a taller figure who knocked Luskell to the ground as he passed. She hit him with a repelling charm; he stumbled but didn't fall. Luskell climbed to her feet and followed through snow almost to her knees. The wind and snow made it impossible to run, but she closed the gap enough to see Ruvhonn reach Elika's house and duck inside. Her pursuer got a foot in the door before she could close it and forced his way in.

Luskell reached out to Fandek again. *Bundle up and meet me at that vacant house I showed you. There might be trouble.*

See? I said you were in danger.

Not me, but someone is.

Luskell broke the connection and reached for another mind. Now that she knew precisely where Jagryn was, she found him even though he was sleeping. *Wake up!* She made her mind voice as loud as she could and hoped it would work. *Ruvhonn's in danger. Meet me at Elika's house NOW.*

CHAPTER FORTY-SEVEN

Luskell reached for the latchstring. It was in. She didn't even bother listening for thoughts. She waved her hand, the latch lifted and the door blew inward. Luskell stepped in and cast her light around. The scene it illuminated was exactly what she'd feared: Ruvhonn sprawled across the table as a man, groaning with effort or pleasure, strangled her with his bare hands. Ruvhonn kicked feebly and tugged at his fingers to no avail.

Luskell threw everything she had into levitation and the repelling charm. It lifted the strangler and flung him off Ruvhonn, who fell back with a gurgling cough. Luskell's pulse pounded in her ears. She tried to calm herself enough to remember the binding spell. The strangler climbed to his feet. With a sneering glance over his shoulder, he pushed open the window behind him and jumped out into the snow.

An owl soared in through the open doorway. A moment later, Jagryn held Ruvhonn in his arms. She leaned against him, still coughing weakly.

Jagryn glanced back at Luskell. "What happened?"

"The strangler left the city the same day I did. Bad luck brought him here."

"Maybe his bad luck. Let's stop him."

"You better take Ruvhonn to Brynnit's."

"You're going to face this madman alone?"

"She won't be alone." Fandek stood in the doorway with a lantern. "Which way did he go?"

Luskell pointed. "Out the window. He won't be able to move very fast, but I don't know how well you can see to follow."

"No, it's clear and the moon's shining." Fandek turned and ran outside.

"I thought it might help," Jagryn explained. He scowled after Fandek.

Luskell rested her hand on his head. "Hey. I told you, no jealousy. Fandek came all the way to Deep River to help me, and I'm going to let him. Besides, I just saved your girl for you."

Jagryn sighed and nodded. "Yeah. Thanks." He lifted Ruvhonn and carried her to the door.

Luskell took her lantern and followed them. She made sure the latchstring was out and closed the door behind her. "Here, you'll need this, now you don't have owl eyes." She gave him the lantern.

"What about you?"

"I have my father's sense for hidden things, and thanks to you, moonlight. I'll be fine."

Luskell jumped off the stoop into the soft snow and ran, as best she could, in the direction Fandek had gone. The storm had been divided by a narrow corridor of clear sky. The moon shone down on gleaming snow and Fandek's lantern bobbed ahead.

Do you see him?

Yeah, and I'm gaining on him. I think my legs are longer.

That meant Luskell's legs were longer than either of theirs. She stretched out and tried to move faster. It wasn't easy. This was the former vineyard, full of stumps waiting to trip someone. Luskell avoided them, but saw Fandek go down ahead of her. The strangler was farther ahead, struggling against the wind but also taking advantage of the break in the storm. Luskell hit him with a repelling charm. Again, he stumbled but didn't fall. She wasn't close enough to hit him hard, and couldn't seem to make up the distance. The break in the storm was closing. If she couldn't stop him, he would disappear into the night, find another hiding place, and live to kill again.

She plodded to a halt, a desperate plan forming. The air was still full of lightning. Luskell would have chosen any other weapon, but this was what she had.

Fandek! I'm going to try something risky. Stay back!

She followed the dark figure with her eyes while she gathered the sparking threads. It was more difficult to control without Jagryn's help. But her own power was surging, whether due to the time of month or her anger. A few more ... almost ... not yet ... NOW! He tripped and went sprawling into the snow as a blinding bolt struck with a sizzle and crack where he would have been. Somebody yelped in the dark. At the same time, the whole right side of Luskell's face exploded in sharp, stinging pain. Her ears rang and her right eye was a world of agony all its own. Dazzled by the lightning, she couldn't see out of either eye.

Fandek?

I've got him! He went down, and I put a binding spell on him.

Luskell tried to remain calm. *Fandek, where are you? I can't see.*

No wonder! That lightning strike was close to you.

I'm hurt. Something hit me in the face.

You're not the only one. The lightning must have blown up one of these old stumps. This fellow has a bunch of splinters in his legs. It doesn't look too serious, but I'll bet it hurts.

Can you move him?

Yes, I ... oh.

What?

Nothing. I'm dragging him back your way now.

She soon heard them over the wind and the noise in her ears, Fandek grunting and cursing, the strangler swearing about wizards and yelping in pain. She was in too much pain herself to spare him any sympathy. Vision returned to her left eye, though blurred by tears.

Fandek reached her and stopped to rest. He gave her the lantern. "It'll be easier if you carry this." She took it and he stared at her, then looked away.

"What? Is it bad? Is there a lot of blood?"

Fandek took a shuddering breath. "There's ... some blood. Does it hurt?"

"Yes, a lot."

Luskell held the lantern and faced forward, her hand on Fandek's shoulder. He walked backward and dragged the bound strangler. Storm clouds covered the moon again and snow swirled around them. Luskell could barely see but managed to guide him back to the Blue Heron.

They were nearly there when she felt the touch of her mother's mind in hers. It was so familiar, comforting and strong, she would have cried if she didn't already have tears pouring down her face.

Luskell, we're staying in Oxbow tonight. The weather's too bad.

Yes, here, too. Did Jagree get there?

He did. Let Brynnit know he's staying here.

I will.

Luskell, what's wrong? Your answers are all faint and broken.

I can't explain now. When you come tomorrow, bring a Guard with you.

A Guard? Why?

In spite of pain and trouble, Luskell managed a grim smile. *We caught the strangler.*

CHAPTER FORTY-EIGHT

Luskell and Fandek plodded back to the inn through deepening snow. Luskell wept silently with cold and pain, and wished the ordeal over. Their prisoner's heels left grooves in the snow as Fandek dragged him. He continued to grumble and swear at intervals.

"Hush," Fandek said in a quiet voice backed with power. The man fell silent.

When they reached the Heron, Luskell paused. "I don't want to take him inside. Too risky."

Fandek set the prisoner down in the shelter of the building and hunkered beside him. "Where do we put him, then?"

Luskell crouched, shivering, to consider the problem. There was an old cell under the Village Hall, but she wasn't sure it locked anymore. "Chuck him down the root cellar," she said at last. "He won't freeze down there, and the latch is on the outside."

"Shouldn't he see a healer first?"

Luskell sputtered out a breath. "Here, let me."

Fandek held the lantern over the man's leg. It didn't help much; Luskell's left eye watered and she couldn't keep her right eye open. With blurred vision and her hands, she found a rip in the man's trouser leg and tore it open wider. Mostly by touch, she found and yanked out the splinters. He hissed with pain but had run out of swear words. She rubbed fresh snow over the wounds to clean them, then drew up the remains of her power to perform a rough healing spell. Her whole body ached with the effort, and when she released the magic into the wounds, she felt sick and dizzy. They'd scar, but she didn't have the power for anything more refined. The weatherworking had drained her. And it didn't even do much good.

The man sat silently while she worked. "Thanks. That's much better," he said when she'd finished.

"Don't talk to me. You're a monster!"

He snickered. "Have you seen yourself lately?"

Fandek got between them. "Quiet," he said to the strangler. "Don't make things worse."

Fandek unbound the man's legs and pulled him to his feet, then guided him to the root cellar and helped him down the steps. Fandek came back up alone and closed and latched the door. "I bound him again. Now what?"

After a foggy moment, Luskell answered. "I heard ... from Mamam. They'll be here tomorrow." She shivered. "I told them to bring a Guard."

She remained kneeling in the snow. She knew she should get up and go inside. That was the sensible thing. Fandek said something she couldn't follow. She gazed at him, uncomprehending.

Do you need help to stand?

The touch of his mind on hers roused her. She nodded and he took her hands to help her up. She gripped his hands and leaned against him. Her eyes were still streaming, but the pain had dulled, or she was used to it by now. Fandek guided her indoors.

By their voices, Luskell identified the four blurry forms around a table as Klamamam, Rakkyn, Keela's Grandpa Briato and Jagryn's Grandpa Yshna. Dice rattled, followed by a shout of laughter that died when Luskell entered the room. She wiped her left eye. Briato stared in horror, and she pictured the skin peeled off half her face. It hurt enough.

"Rakkyn, get Brynnit," Klamamam said, her voice calm but firm. "Thank you, Fandek, I'll take her."

"I'm all right," Luskell mumbled, but leaned on her tiny grandmother all the way into her room.

"Of course you are. Now sit here and I'll get you cleaned up."

Luskell sank onto the bed. Klamamam brought the basin and a cloth to wipe blood off Luskell's face. She was clearly avoiding something—Luskell couldn't tell what—but when she bumped it, the pain jolted from Luskell's eye all the way to her toes. She howled, and Klamamam started back. Water slopped onto the floor.

"I'm sorry, dear, I didn't mean to."

"It hurts! What is it?" Luskell sobbed.

"You have splinters in your face. One is stuck in your eye."

"Well, don't touch it!"

Klamamam stroked Luskell's hair, well away from her right eye. "I won't. We'll wait for Brynnit."

"How ... how big is it? It feels like a whole branch."

"Not that big. Big enough, though."

Rakkyn poked his head in the door. "Brynnit says she'll be over as soon as she's finished with Ruvhonn. Poor girl's all bruised around her neck."

"Thank you, Rakkyn. Close the door, please. When Brynnit gets here, show her in."

Luskell clung to Klamamam's calm voice. As long as someone knew what to do, everything would be all right.

Klamamam helped her out of her cloak and boots and had her lie back against the pillow. "Can you tell me what happened out there?"

Luskell had to think about where to even begin. It took her mind off her pain, so she went back to the start of the evening. "Jagryn asked me to help him sleep so he could finish his quest to visit the Other Side in dreams, the way I do." She took a steadying breath. "The whole reason I came here ahead of Dadad was to help Jagryn. And I wanted to make things right with him."

"Were they wrong?" Klamamam's voice was quiet and gentle, not judging.

"I think I made Ruvhonn jealous." Luskell wadded the edge of the quilt with her hands. "I didn't mean to. But she showed up at his house, and she was mad because I was there. She stormed off before anyone could explain. I felt responsible, so I said I'd find her and make sure she was all right. The weather was bad by then."

"I hope she appreciated it. Is she still angry?"

Luskell sighed. "Probably. I hope not. I didn't have a chance to look for her. I saw someone in Sulika's greenhouse and I thought it was Sulika, but then I met her on the road. Something wasn't right and Dadad always says to trust my intuitions. I made Sulika go back to Aunt Sudi's house, and Young Crane and I went to fetch Myn. Myn wanted to look in the greenhouse first, and there wasn't anyone there but we found a false beard and I knew who it was! He had supper here the other night, and he was on the coach with Keela and me!"

Klamamam nodded. "I remember. I thought he went away that night."

"He wanted us to think that, but Fandek saw someone following me last night. I didn't believe him, but he was telling the truth."

"Fandek seems like an honest fellow."

"I know that *now*," Luskell replied, more impatiently than she intended. Her eye hurt. "Then I remembered about Ruvhonn. I knew she wasn't here, so I went to see if her horse was in the stable. Before I got inside, she screamed and ran out with somebody chasing her. They went right to Elika's house. I followed and told Fandek to meet me there."

"But you never came back in ... Oh. You wizards and your mind-talking."

"I'm glad I taught him; he seems to have a gift for it." Luskell still found it hard to credit Fandek with anything. She would have to learn. He'd earned that. "I woke up Jagryn the same way. I went inside and sure enough, that monster was strangling Ruvhonn. I got him off her, but I couldn't remember the binding spell and he jumped out the window. I let Jagryn take care of Ruvhonn. Fandek and I chased the strangler, but he had a head start and the snow was deep. We were gaining on him and then Fandek fell and I couldn't quite catch up and he was getting away! He'd been attacking girls and women in the city and now he was trying to hurt my friend's girl right here in Deep River, and I said, Enough! I called down lightning, but he tripped in the snow and the lightning hit a stump instead and that's where the splinters came from. It didn't even stop him. I spoil everything." She ended on a sob.

Klamamam held Luskell's hand and kissed the top of her head. "That's not true."

"It is! If I hadn't tried to help Jagryn, Ruvhonn would have been safe with him instead of out by herself."

"Then this strangler might have gotten Sulika and the baby, or someone else going about her business." Klamamam paused. "What happened to him? Did he get away?"

"Fandek used the binding spell that I couldn't even remember. We put him in the root cellar, and I told Mamam to bring a Guard when they come."

"You put a murderer in my root cellar?"

"I didn't think you'd want him in the best room."

"So you don't spoil everything. Maybe you get overhasty and let your temper carry you away. You have a lot of your grandfather in you."

The door creaked open. "Busy night," Auntie Brynnit said. "I ... oh." She stepped closer to the bed. "That must hurt." She extended a hand.

"Don't touch it!"

"I won't, yet. I'll give you something for the pain, and then I need you to sleep. Would you rather have the charm or the drops?"

"No drops!"

"You might change your mind tomorrow. We'll use the charm for now."

The pain charm relieved enough agony that Luskell could relax. She sighed. "Thank you."

"Ruvhonn says you saved her life. Maybe not only hers. So Deep River thanks you back."

"Mm." Luskell waved toward her face. "How bad is it?"

Auntie Brynnit studied her. "I'd rather let your mother deal with it, but who knows when they'll get here."

"She ... trusts you," Luskell mumbled. "Oh. Jagree's with them. In Oxbow."

"I guessed as much. Now, are you sure about the drops?"

"Mm-hm. I need my dreams to be clear."

"Fair enough." Auntie Brynnit began to say the sleep charm. Luskell didn't hear the end.

CHAPTER FORTY-NINE

Luskell sat on coarse, tufty grass above the muddy lakeshore. It was warm and bright. So she was ... dead? She'd never seen a lake or mud on the Other Side, and the grass was different. When she glanced up, the sun shone in the sky. So not yet.

"I know this place," she said. "But I've never seen it in summer."

Next to her, Knot leaned back on his elbows and stretched his long legs in front of him. "This is how it was the summer I taught your father to be a wizard."

"It's beautiful." Luskell swatted a fly, but not before it bit her cheek. "Buggy, though."

"So it's a good thing summers are short up here." Knot gave her one of his rare, radiant smiles.

"Why am I here? Do you have something to tell me?"

"I thought it might take your mind off what's happening."

She felt another stinging bite on her face and smacked a mosquito. Her hand came away with a bloody smear. She tried to remember what was happening. "The strangler? We caught him ... didn't we?"

"You and your friend handled that danger very well. But you didn't come through unscathed."

"Oh. I got hurt, didn't I?" Another fly bit her face. She couldn't swat them before they took a nip. "Will I be all right?"

"That's up to you."

"How can it—Ow!" Luskell slapped at a horsefly, once again too late. "That one bit me on the eyeball!"

"We should move inside." Knot stood and took up his fire-blackened staff.

Luskell followed him up the slope. A small cabin stood where she expected an Aklaka lodge. "But this was burned."

"I told you, this is how the valley was the summer I taught your father to be a wizard."

"Did you teach him to be a father, too?"

"That, he had to teach himself. He did well."

Luskell sat on the stoop and gazed back toward the lake. The bugs weren't so bad here, and after all the snow and cold, she wanted to enjoy the sunshine. She wasn't sure what would happen if she went into a house that didn't exist, even if it was a dream. "Do I have to worry about how long I stay here?"

Knot sat beside her, his staff across his knees. "No. I'm visiting your dream, so you're all right however long it lasts. I did influence the setting." He smiled again.

She gazed out over the valley and sighed. It was so peaceful. "Were you happy here?"

"Happy. That's not a word I used much. I was useful. And it could be very beautiful. I was ... content. Until

Crane came and reminded me of what I'd left. But I wouldn't change any of it. No point in regrets. Just move forward and try to make things as right as you can."

Luskell nodded. Her mouth felt too heavy for speech. As the dream faded, the insect bites hurt more.

"Mamam!" Luskell sat upright and clutched at her eye. Half her head was swathed in bandages. The pain was centered in her right eye. The house was quiet and the window dark, but the lamp was lit.

Jagryn sat beside the bed. He jumped at Luskell's shout, then gently pressed her back onto her pillow. "Shh, it's all right. She'll be here as soon as she can." He stared at Luskell, then averted his gaze.

"You can look, unless it's too terrible."

"It's ... better than it was, I guess." He turned to her again, as if forcing himself to look.

"Why are you here?"

"We're all taking turns. Auntie Stell took some persuading before she'd leave you and go to bed."

"But why aren't you with Ruvhonn?"

"She's sleeping now, too. Brynnit didn't think it was a good idea for her to wake and find a man in her room."

Luskell snorted. "But it's all right for me?"

"Nobody tried to strangle you."

There was nothing to say to that.

"Thank you for helping her," he continued.

"It had to stop."

"This doesn't change anything between us."

A weight settled in Luskell's gut. "So we can't be friends?"

"What? No, I mean my offer to marry you still holds."

"But Ruvhonn needs you."

"And you don't? What if no one else will have you because of ..." He waved vaguely toward the right side of his face. "But it doesn't matter to me."

The spurt of anger made her eye hurt more. "So you'd still take me even though my looks are ruined. You're too kind."

Jagryn scowled. "That's not what I meant! Didn't you say you love me? Didn't you kiss me?"

"I did, and I meant it. But I'm not going to marry you."

"But why not? If we love each other—"

"Because listen to us! All we do is argue! And as long as one of us thinks we might have a future together, we'll never be through. So I'm saying it: as of now, we're through." Jagryn cast his eyes downward. He tried to shield his emotions, but he'd never been good at it. He was sad and disappointed, but not as heartbroken as Luskell might have expected. In fact, he was relieved. She tried not to be miffed. This was supposed to be what she wanted. She gave his hand an encouraging squeeze. "Besides, I'm a terrible influence. You said it yourself, I spoil everything. Ruvhonn is much better for you."

He glanced up at her. "Maybe. So you've chosen Laki after all?"

"No." Luskell swallowed. Her throat ached as she made the decision.

"But why not? You said yourself he was free. And he used to say you were the moon."

"So? Maybe I want to shine with my own light. Anyway, I told you, I can't choose one of you over the other. So I won't choose either. Maybe we three can be friends then. Now give me a pain charm before I rip your eyes out."

"My pain charm's pretty weak, but Brynnit left some drops."

"No drops."

"I told her you'd say that." He worked the pain charm. It was weaker than Auntie Brynnit's, but it helped. He followed it with a sleeping charm, which was stronger, and held her hand while she drifted off.

When Luskell woke again, it hardly seemed she'd slept at all. She didn't remember any dreams, and the window was still dark. Jagryn was gone. Now Fandek sat beside her bed.

"Hey," he whispered. "How do you feel?"

"Like somebody poked my eye with a stick." She reached out a hand to him. "Thanks for being there. I'm sorry I didn't trust you before."

He took her hand and held it. "Well. Maybe you still shouldn't."

She liked the soothing feel of his hand in hers. "What's that supposed to mean? You weren't the strangler."

Fandek looked away and dropped Luskell's hand. "I come from a family of bad men." He clasped his hands in his lap and spoke to the floor. "I recognized the strangler. He's ... my brother."

Luskell felt a queasy thrill in her guts. Her heart thumped hard and her eye throbbed. She drew a shaky breath. "I thought your brother was younger than you."

"No, that's my little brother, Deklyn. He's all right. I hope. This is my older brother, remember? Kerf. The one who left home when I was small. I hadn't seen him in all these years, but I knew him."

Luskell lay quietly awhile to think about this. "Don't let him out."

"I won't, I promise. But what if I'm like him?"

"You're not." Luskell had read his unguarded thoughts, felt his unshielded emotions. In spite of the bad first impression, she should have known all along. "You're not," she repeated. "Your first act of magic was to help another. That's what healers do."

"I thought I was a wizard."

"I don't think so. Wizards cause accidents."

A slow smile bloomed on Fandek's face. "You think I might be a healer?"

Her eye throbbed again. "I hope so, because I'm hurting here. Help me out."

"I don't know any healing magic yet. Not even a sleep charm. But Brynnit left some drops."

Luskell sagged. "Fine, give me the drops. Not too much."

He carefully measured the medicine into a cup of cold tea. Luskell drank it down and handed back the cup so she wouldn't drop it. The effect was not as instant as a charm, but it was still fast. She didn't feel pain or much else. Nothing but Fandek's hand in hers.

CHAPTER FIFTY

When Luskell opened her eye again, the window admitted early, wintry light. Her injured eye hurt, but the medicine or Auntie Brynnit's healing magic dulled the pain. She sat up carefully.

Klamamam dozed in the chair at Luskell's bedside. She started awake when Luskell shifted the covers. "Well, good morning, dear. How do you feel?"

"Better, I think. Might be the drops. May I get up?"

"As long as you don't do anything strenuous."

Klamamam helped Luskell out of bed. She was groggy from the drops, and it was surprisingly difficult to navigate with only one eye. She appreciated the support as she relieved herself and cleaned up. She felt better just to wash half her face, but then she was ready to get back into bed.

"I saw Knot last night."

Klamamam paused in combing out Luskell's tangled hair. "Yes. I did, too. He said he was taking care of you. That worried me." She continued her task.

"Why?" Luskell enjoyed the grooming attention, even when the comb pulled.

"I feared he meant you were dead. But your injuries seemed more painful and disfiguring than dangerous."

Luskell shuddered. "Painful. Yes. And I suppose I deserve a few scars."

Klamamam drew Luskell's hair into a single braid down her back. "We should wait until your mother gets here. She'll know." She finished the braid and stroked the top of Luskell's head. "It's early, but if you're hungry, I'll bring you some breakfast."

"I could eat."

Luskell lay back and closed her eye. She wondered how long she would have to have the bandage over the other. It was tiring and disorienting with only one. She dozed off again while waiting for the food, but roused when Klamamam came back with a tray. Luskell's mouth watered at the aroma of fried ham. With a heel of yesterday's bread and a wedge of cheese, it was a feast.

Luskell was still eating when she heard the swish of sled runners. Mamam swept into the room on a wave of worry. Auntie Brynnit hurried to keep up.

"Maybe I should have waited for you," Brynnit was saying. "But we didn't know when you'd get here, and she was in such pain."

"You did right." Mamam stood at the bedside and held Luskell's hand. She didn't say anything more, but Luskell felt the moment when she shielded her emotions, like a door quietly closed.

"I'm glad you're here," Luskell whispered, overcome. She tried to shield her own feelings, but couldn't manage it. Her magic would be weakened until her body recovered.

"I'd have come sooner if I could've." Mamam carefully unwrapped Luskell's bandages. She looked away as the last of it came off. "Did you save the splinter?" Although her voice was composed, Luskell could hear the tension in it, in spite of the shield.

"It's here." Auntie Brynnit gave Mamam a small dish. They kept it out of Luskell's view. "The longest one, there."

"Where did they come from?"

"A stump, in that field next to Elika's old place," Auntie Brynnit explained. "Some years back, Liko and Alill planted grapes there again. They were doing all right until about three years ago. Remember that hot summer?"

Mamam shook her head wearily. "Do I! It was even hot in the city."

Auntie Brynnit nodded. "I doubt there ever would have been enough water, anyway. They cut down the dead vines, but Liko hasn't grubbed out all the stumps yet."

Mamam studied the splinter. Luskell finally got a good look at it and immediately wished she hadn't. It was as long as her little finger and about half the thickness, with a knife-like point at one end. Her eye started to hurt again. She looked away and swallowed hard to keep her breakfast down.

"What could make a stump burst into splinters?" Mamam wondered.

"Lightning," Luskell said without looking up.

"A lightning strike? In winter?"

"Not a natural strike. I called it down. To stop the strangler."

"Stop him? You could have killed him!"

"I know. I meant to. But I missed. He took a few splinters in the leg, but I got the worst of it."

"You certainly did." There was no anger in Mamam's voice. "This is why your father didn't want you playing with weather. You're strong enough to be dangerous, especially at this time of month." She did something to the injured eye and the pain decreased dramatically. She applied a salve and a new dressing. "This eye looks bad, but the good news is, I can prevent scarring on your face."

"I don't care about a few scars. And you can fix the eye, right?"

Mamam took Luskell's face in both hands so she couldn't look away. "You'll be scarred plenty. Luskell ... there's nothing I can do. This eye will never see again."

Luskell stared at her mother. Then she screamed.

Mamam threw her hands up as if to fend off an assault. She had shielded her own emotions, but had to be open to her patient's feelings. She regained her calm more quickly than Luskell would have. "Are you in pain? Do you need drops?" She picked up the vial.

"No, I don't need any more drops!" Luskell swung wildly and knocked the bottle from her hand. It hit the floor but was too light to break. Auntie Brynnit picked it up and placed it in her pocket. "Get out of here! Leave me alone!"

Mamam gave her a long look. "All right. Come on, everyone. Let's give her some time." She herded the other women out of the room and closed the door.

Luskell threw herself down on her left side and wept until her pillow was soaked and her left eye hurt almost as much as her right. She didn't—she couldn't—blame anyone but herself. But to lose her eye? She'd assumed it would slowly get better and one day, she'd have normal vision again. Or it would be damaged but still capable of sight. Not that it was gone forever.

It was all she deserved. She'd been blind to so much: what she was doing to Laki and Jagryn, everything Fandek had done for her. She supposed she should be grateful to have one eye left.

The door squeaked open and she stiffened. A strong, warm hand squeezed her shoulder. Luskell rolled over and flung herself into her father's arms. "I spoil everything!"

"Not everything." Dadad stroked her hair. "I helped the Guards bring the strangler up from the root cellar."

"Are you going to try to fix him?"

He sighed. "I wish someone had gotten to him when he was a lot younger. Something terrible happened, and it twisted him. I'm not sure there's anything left to fix now."

Luskell recalled Fandek's comment that his father used to hit his brother until his brother started hitting back, and the hazy memory of his mother's death. Was that what twisted him? "So that's why he killed women?"

"It wasn't for fun. He tried to flee his compulsion, but there was only one relief."

"Is he gone now?"

"The Guards took him away. He'll go back to the city for trial. But I wanted to compliment you—he had a good binding on him."

"That was Fandek. I couldn't remember it when I needed it."

"Someone took care of the wounds on his leg. Was that Fandek, too?"

"No. He doesn't know any healing yet." Luskell pulled back but didn't let go of her father. "He should, though. He'll be better at it than I am."

He raised an eyebrow. "You've warmed to him."

"We should both have trusted him more."

"Perhaps. I understand he's related to the murderer, though."

"And Fandek still bound him and put him in the cellar."

"Because your lightning showed him where to go, and probably stunned the strangler." He chuckled. "An extravagant spell, but effective. I'm sorry anyone had to get hurt. Especially you."

Luskell clutched him tighter. "But I used magic to try to kill someone! They'll want to strip me of my power!"

"I would argue that even knowing the possible consequences, you chose to use the weapon at hand to defend a community from a known threat." He gazed at her with gentle smile. "You have suffered an injury and a temporary loss of power. 'They,' a group that includes Bardin and me, will likely conclude you've been punished enough. In fact, we might decide to commend you."

Luskell brushed off the idea of commendation. "Jagryn did his quest to the Other Side."

"With your help?"

"I may have hurt him as much as I helped." She shivered as she recalled the souls who wanted to touch him; the lines on his face. "He did it himself in the end, though. You can give him his staff."

"I never doubted him. I'll see him today to talk about it, but I'm sure you're right. He'll have a staff before we leave here. What about you?"

Luskell sighed. "I shouldn't have come here. I made a huge mess."

"You're not the first. And if you hadn't come to Deep River and the strangler had?"

"When you put it like that ... But I still made a mess."

"Did you earn your staff?"

She swallowed hard. "Maybe. I don't want to talk about it. Not yet."

"All right. Maybe later." He kissed her on the uninjured side of her face. "I'm here if you need me. We all are."

She tried to smile, though tears slipped down her face. People loved her ... and she'd let them down. She'd assumed without asking that Laki wanted whatever she wanted, and ended up toying with his wholehearted love. She'd failed to imagine Jagryn finding someone else, someone more suitable, and pictured him always waiting for her to spare him a thought. And Fandek; he'd had some clumsy moments, but he'd never pretended to feel anything but genuine interest and affection. She'd given him distrust in return, until it was almost too late.

Wizardry was simple compared to people.

CHAPTER FIFTY-ONE

Mamam allowed Luskell half a day to wallow in self-pity. At midday, she brought a tray with two bowls of soup to Luskell's room and closed the door behind her. She gave Luskell one bowl and took her own to the chair on Luskell's left. "You must be hungry. Go ahead and eat. We'll talk after."

Luskell accepted the bowl in silence; she didn't trust her voice. She ate a spoonful of Klamamam's soup, then another. It was the most delicious medicine ever, and gone before she knew it. Luskell put her spoon down. "I'm sorry I screamed at you." She spoke to the bowl.

"I'm sorry, too. I should have prepared you."

"Is it even possible, for something like this?"

"I wish I could do ... something."

Luskell looked at her mother. Her face was drawn with worry, and she'd been crying, though her cheeks were dry now. "You brought Laki back from the dead."

"I was there the moment he hit the ground. Maybe if I'd been with you when this happened ... I don't know; eyes are tricky. How do you feel now?"

Luskell considered. "It hurts less than it did. I guess I'm still getting used to the idea that it's not coming back."

"Me, too. Let me take a look." Mamam inspected the wound with the practiced confidence that brought comfort to everyone she treated. She said some magic words and reapplied salve and dressing. "The good news is, there's no infection. Healing should go quickly. And you can eat all you want."

"When will I be able to do magic again? I can't do anything."

"Soon, I suspect. Healing takes a lot of strength, but if you don't let yourself get run down, your power will return."

"So I'm to do nothing except eat and sleep?"

"Sounds like a cat's life." Mamam smiled a little. "But you're not an invalid; you need to rejoin the world."

"Not yet. I need something besides food and rest. Did you bring my fiddle?"

"Yes. I didn't realize it was so urgent."

"I didn't, either. But I think I need music more than people, and just now, I can't sing." Even saying the word, her throat clenched painfully.

"There's people, and there's people." Mamam glanced toward the door. "A certain boy wants to see you."

Luskell sighed. "Which one this time?"

"The one you most want to see." Mamam went to the door, opened it and beckoned.

Quick footsteps pattered across the floorboards. Luskell had to turn her head to see, but she knew who to expect. Mamam lifted Crett onto the bed.

Luskell smiled and blinked back tears. She'd barely thought of her small brother since the day she left Misty Pass, but Mamam was right. At this moment, he was the boy she most wanted to see. "Hey, Baby."

Crett frowned. "Not baby." He patted her bandages. "What this?"

Mamam drew his hand back. "Careful, Crett. Don't hurt her."

"It's all right," Luskell assured them. "I got splinters in my face, Crett."

He cringed, perhaps remembering the splinter they'd pulled from his hand. "I make better." He scrambled over her and kissed her bandaged face.

"That is better. Thank you, Crett." Luskell hugged him. "I'm glad you're here."

He grabbed her hand and tugged. "Up now."

Luskell laughed. "You're right. I should get up now. Lying around in bed is boring."

Mamam picked him up. "I thought I'd take the little one out visiting. Will you be all right here?"

"I'll be fine. See you later."

They left and closed the door. Moving carefully, Luskell got out of bed and made herself ready for the day. Everything looked kind of flat, and she had to turn her head to see to the right, but she could function. Maybe it wouldn't be that bad.

She found Dadad and Fandek at one of the small tables with paper, pen and ink.

"Weren't you going to see Jagryn?"

Dadad smiled at her. "I meant to. I got involved in an interesting talk with Fandek here. But you can help. Sit down." He got up and she took his seat.

"What are you doing?"

"I want to write a letter," Fandek said. "But I haven't had much schooling, so my handwriting is bad and my spelling is worse." He gave her a rueful grin.

"And you're right, I need to find Jagryn," Dadad continued. "So if you could help Fandek ..."

Luskell nodded. She could be useful, without overtaxing herself. "Sure, I'll help." Dadad patted her shoulder and left the inn. Luskell turned her attention to Fandek. "Who are you writing to?"

"Master Breet. I left town without telling anyone, and now I'm not sure when or even if I'll go back. If I do, I want Breet to know what I was thinking."

"What do you have so far?" Luskell reached for the page, thinking she would suggest words and phrasing, and help with the spelling. When she saw the blots and illegible scrawl, it was difficult not to laugh. "That is the worst handwriting I've ever seen."

Fandek shrugged. "I told you. Maybe you could do the writing?"

She took the pen and a fresh sheet. "Go ahead—dictate and I'll take it down. 'Dear Breet,'... "

Fandek frowned. "Do I have to say 'Dear'? We barely know each other."

"Fine, no 'Dear.' I'll put 'Master.'"

"'Sorry I left town without saying.'"

Luskell spoke the line as she wrote it. "'I apologize for leaving Eukard City without giving you notice.'"

"Um ... really? That doesn't sound like me."

"Trust me, in a situation like this, you want to be as polite as possible, in case you ever want him to take you back. It makes it sound like you've thought about it and care what he thinks."

"I guess so. How do you know things like that?"

"I've been around diplomats most of my life. So, after you apologize, what's next?"

"My excuse?"

"No excuses. What about an explanation? What was so important?"

"Explanation. I like that better. 'I had a dream that a loved one was in danger, and—'"

"Loved one?" Luskell interrupted.

Fandek reddened and grinned at the tabletop. "Friend?"

"Better. 'I had a vision of a friend in danger ...'"

"'. . . and I had to make sure nothing bad happened to her.'"

"'. . . whose safety I felt compelled to ensure.'"

Fandek shook his head at Luskell's phrasing but didn't ask her to change it. They worked at the letter line by line, laughing together when the words seemed too ornate. She let him approve each line before she committed it to ink, but mostly he took her suggestions.

"'I have a chance—'"

"Let's say 'opportunity,'" Luskell suggested.

"I like that! 'I have an opportunity to study with a great healer—'"

"You do?" Luskell asked.

Fandek beamed. "Your mother said she ... saw something in me. And you did, too. She said she'd teach me, so I'll see where that leads. She already taught me a basic pain charm, and I got it right away."

Moved by his happiness, Luskell reached across and squeezed his hand. She had forgotten about her injury while they worked, but when she touched him, she felt a rush of well-being that was more than absence of pain. He didn't know yet how to control his healing power; it flowed out toward a need. As Dadad had noted weeks before,

Fandek was drawn to distress. Luskell didn't want to drain him. She smiled and released his hand. The sense of wellness diminished but didn't fade entirely.

They finished the letter and read it over together.

Master Breet,

I apologize for leaving Eukard City without giving you notice. I had a vision of a friend in danger, whose safety I felt compelled to ensure. It turned out to be true in ways that surprised me. We are both safe. Now I have an opportunity to study with a great healer. If this turns out to be where my real talent lies, when I return to the city, I will probably go to work at Balsam's House to hone my skills. I appreciate your mentoring and hope you wish me well in my new vocation.

Your grateful apprentice,

Fandek

Luskell studied him. "You've made your decision."

"I haven't thought about it very long, but it feels right."

Luskell nodded. She'd been wrestling with a decision of her own, but now she realized it had made itself. "I need to write my own letter."

Fandek grinned. "Can I watch?"

"Not much to see."

"Maybe not. I'd watch you do anything."

CHAPTER FIFTY-TWO

Dear Master Bardin, Luskell wrote, I achieved my quest ...

The door opened, and Luskell looked up from her letter. She expected one or both of her parents, not Jagryn. When Dadad went to find him, she'd assumed Jagryn wouldn't come to the inn, and she'd been relieved. And guilty over the relief, because he was her friend. By reflex, she tried to protect herself from his unshielded emotions, but she hadn't recovered enough yet. She recoiled at the wave of strong feeling that washed out from him. Warm affection, and worry, and jealousy ...

"Sorry!" Jagryn muted his feelings with an imperfect shield. He approached their table and spoke to Fandek with surprising politeness. "May I speak to Luskell a moment, please?"

"Of course. We're done here, aren't we?" Fandek took his letter and went to the kitchen to help Klamamam. Jagryn sat in his vacated chair.

"Did Dadad talk to you?" Luskell asked.

"No, I haven't seen him. I was over at Brynnit's, visiting Ruvhonn." He smiled. The shielded affection warmed, and the jealousy faded. "While I was there, Aunt Ketty came and did something that made the bruises practically disappear. She said you were up." He shifted in his seat and placed his palms against the tabletop, then folded his hands in his lap.

Luskell didn't know how to put him at ease, or even if she wanted to. In spite of herself, she was glad to see him. "How is Ruvhonn?"

"Scared. But grateful. Alive, thanks to you. Brynnit and Ketty both say she should recover completely."

"And the strangler's in custody, so all's well."

"How can you say that?" Jagryn's jaw worked. "Ruvhonn hates me, and now you're ... like this."

"Jagryn, I lost an eye. I'll get over it." Her throat tightened and she swallowed hard against a painful lump. Maybe saying it would make it so. "Why does Ruvhonn hate you?"

"Because I told her about ... you know. Us."

"Why? There's no us, Jagryn. We settled that last night."

"So you meant what you said?" Jagryn sighed.

"I did." Luskell shook her head and looked at Jagryn with exasperated affection. "Could you find a worse time to tell her?"

"I know. You bring out the stupid in me. But I thought she should know." He slumped in his seat. "Can you still be a wizard?"

"I don't know why not. They say my power will come back as I recover."

"So what are your plans?"

"To leave here as soon as the weather and my parents allow."

"Oh." He glanced around and stood up. "So, your father's looking for me? I should go meet him."

Luskell didn't try to stop him. After he left, she finished her letter, folded it and put it in her room. She took her cloak down from the peg and put it on.

Klamamam came to the kitchen door. "Are you going out? Do you need anyone to come with you?"

"No. I'm just rejoining the world."

Luskell left the inn. It was a bright afternoon, and the light shocked her eye. No one had shoveled, but there was a path through the snow to Uncle Jagree and Auntie Brynnit's, trodden by comings and goings. When chunks of snow slid into her shoes, Luskell wished she'd put on boots, but it wasn't far. She tapped on the door and entered before anyone could invite her in.

"Luskell, I didn't expect you! Good to see you up!" Auntie Brynnit greeted her with a warm hug. "Were you looking for your mother? She planned to stop in at Sudi's."

"No. I wanted to check on Ruvhonn."

Ruvhonn sat by the stove. The pink was gone from her cheeks, and faint bruises showed around her throat. She glanced at Luskell and Auntie Brynnit, and nodded slightly. Auntie Brynnit pulled another chair around for Luskell. She sat and waited.

Ruvhonn broke the silence. "Thank you," she said in a hoarse whisper. "I heard you got hurt. Are you all right?"

"If I'm not, it's my own fault. I'm shuffling around a day later, so I guess it could be worse. How about you? Going home today?"

"Tomorrow, I think. To be sure." Ruvhonn coughed.

"Don't strain your voice. I came by to find out ... are you really angry with Jagryn?"

Ruvhonn clenched her fists in her lap and made a growly noise. A tear slid down her cheek. "Yes," she whispered. "But I understand. How could he not prefer you? You shoved a grown man off me without even touching him. You called down lightning! You and Jagryn … you're alike."

Luskell squeezed her eye shut and struggled for calm. "We have a long history of doing stupid things together. That creates a bond, but it doesn't mean we're a good match."

"But you made love. Doesn't that mean—"

"It means we shared a vivid dream about something that may or may not have happened." Luskell couldn't help smiling. "And I won't lie—I enjoyed that dream. I didn't want him to tell you, but maybe it's better this way. Secrets don't help."

Ruvhonn frowned. "I don't understand."

Luskell took Ruvhonn's hand. The other girl started and looked directly at her for the first time. "You're right about me. I have a lot of power. Or, anyway, I had a lot and hope to have it again. One of my gifts is to know what other people feel, and I still have that. I can tell you're scared, and jealous, and full of regret. You want … something. Maybe you want Jagryn to come back so you can forgive him. Maybe you want him, period. I don't blame you."

Ruvhonn's mouth dropped open and the pink returned to her cheeks. "You could have guessed those things."

"Yes, anyone could have. I didn't. I felt them. I know them. I also know when Jagryn speaks your name, he … lifts. Everything about him warms. His whole being becomes lighter when he thinks of you. Did you know that he came out of a deep sleep and literally flew to your side?"

"Because you called him."

"Or because I told him you needed him."

Ruvhonn looked at Luskell without speaking. Maybe she had no voice left, or maybe she had no answer.

"Ruvhonn, I won't compete with you. Why would I, when I've already lost? Whatever he feels for me is what a lovesick boy feels. He loves you like a man. Don't push him away, because I won't be here to catch him."

Without waiting for an answer, Luskell got up, nodded to Auntie Brynnit, and left. She almost fell, stepping down from the doorstep. Things weren't where they should be, and she was so tired, she shook. All the writing and talking had worn her out, and now her eye hurt again. She staggered back to the inn and leaned against the kitchen doorframe. Fandek was peeling potatoes and chatting with Klamamam as if he'd known her his whole life. Luskell cleared her throat. "Fandek, do you want to try out that pain charm?"

His face brightened as if she'd offered him a treat. "You bet!" He wiped his hands and came to her. He touched her bandaged face lightly over her eye and spoke the charm. His slow and careful pronunciation was the only thing to reveal he'd learned it only that day. The effect was immediate, and included a touch of the euphoria she'd felt before.

"How's that?" He lifted his hand from her head.

"Perfect. You put something extra on there."

"Not on purpose."

"Well, don't change anything. I feel better than better." She did, too. Standing so close, she wanted to kiss him. But maybe not today. "I'm going to go lie down for a while. If I don't hear Dadad when he comes back, will you send him in?"

"Anything you say."

Luskell went to her room and closed the door. Her pain was gone for now and the euphoria hadn't lifted, but fatigue made her slow and clumsy. She slipped off her shoes and lay down. She fell into a brief, restful slumber. She woke when Dadad came in the front door and considered getting up to meet him, but it felt too good to lie there. Soon, he tapped at the door.

"Luskell?"

"Come in." She rolled onto her side so she could see him. "Did you find Jagryn?"

"We almost missed each other. He came home just before I left. He already has a branch from their cherry tree we can turn into a staff."

Luskell smiled at the news, but couldn't keep a tear from running across her nose. "That's good. He's worked so hard."

Dadad wiped the tear away with a gentle thumb. "And what about you? Are you ready to talk yet?"

She sighed. "I learned to Listen. I might have a talent for it. But I don't think I'm wise enough yet to be a wizard."

"Admitting that means you're probably close."

She reached for the letter on the table beside the bed and handed it to him. "I'm sending this to Bardin. Read it."

Dadad took the letter and read it silently. Luskell remembered every word she'd written.

Dear Master Bardin,

I achieved my quest, but I've decided I want to explore it in more depth before I claim my staff. I will not return to the city before Fall Balance. Thank you for taking a risk on me. I hope when we meet again, I will be worthy of the name Wizard.

Dadad passed the letter back. "What brought on all this maturity?"

"I've been rash and impatient and selfish. I've hurt people."

"You're Yrae's granddaughter, all right."

Luskell swallowed. "I need a place where I can go by myself for a while and be useful and not do any more harm."

Dadad gazed at her. His love and sympathy wrapped her like a blanket. "We both know a place like that. I'll help you if I can."

CHAPTER FIFTY-THREE

As she had promised Jagryn, Luskell returned with her family to Misty Pass as soon as her condition and the weather allowed. In theory, it was spring now, though still cold in the mountains. She hiked with Chakalan and Kiraknat, the two young Aklaka men who made up the supply party. Chakalan was around Laki's age, with the straight black hair typical of most Aklaka, and the faint beginnings of a beard. Kiraknat was a year or two older and had wild, bushy hair like Knot, or Luskell herself. Perhaps he was a distant relation. As children, they had condescended to let Luskell play with them because of her friendship with Laki, though she was much younger. She had never been able to beat them at foot races, but bested them at tree climbing from an early age. They would always be taller, though neither was as tall as Laki. Or as good looking.

The men carried packs, but most of the supplies were lashed to two small sleds they pushed downhill and pulled up. Luskell carried some supplies and her personal items in her cloak pockets, and helped with the sleds where the trail was steep or muddy. At this altitude the trail was mostly covered with compacted, icy snow. This was good for the sleds, but made for treacherous hiking. Luskell mostly hiked between the two men. She was as sure-footed as they, but they knew the trail better—and had two eyes each.

In front, Chakalan kicked steps in the icy snow to help them climb. Luskell lifted her end of the sled and placed her feet precisely in the steps. She tried not to look down the steep slope that dropped off to her left. It wasn't so bad when the trail climbed an open slope, but sheer drops made her nervous. She didn't trust her eye to tell her where the edge was. At least on the left, she knew where it was

As soon as her injuries had healed and her full power returned, she had challenged herself, training her magic and her remaining eye to make up for what she'd lost. Early on, she went out alone to climb Klamamam's old cottonwood that overhung the river. Deep-grooved bark on the trunk made it an easy tree to begin climbing, and she reached the first fork with no difficulty. She climbed higher with increasing confidence ... until she reached for a convenient branch that turned out to be beyond her grasp. As her hand swept through nothing, she lurched and almost lost her footing. She hugged the trunk and closed her good eye against the dizzying prospect of icy water swirling below. When her heart rate returned to something near normal, she considered calling for help or climbing down, then reached again for the branch above her head. By moving her head slightly from side to side, she had more sense of depth. She climbed slowly, taking her time to determine exactly where the handholds were. She climbed until she was higher in that tree than she'd ever been before, breathless, terrified, exhilarated.

If anything, the descent was slower and more harrowing. When she stood on the ground again, she was exhausted and trembling. She told no one about the near-miss, but climbed every day for the rest of her time in Deep River.

At the top of the slope, Luskell set down her end of the sled and climbed back down to help Kiraknat with his sled. This was not required—Chakalan could have done it—but Luskell insisted. She needed the experience and the challenge. When she reached the top again, she was breathing hard and sweating, in spite of the snow and ice. She turned away from the Aklaka and removed her eyepatch to wipe away the sweat before carefully returning it back in position.

When the bandages first came off, her ruined eye admitted a little light, enough to confuse her. She didn't want to force people to look at her scars either. She tied a strip of black cloth over it. It didn't look much better and tended to slip off, but it was better than nothing.

Jagryn mostly kept his distance. When they had to be together, their interactions were cordial but guarded. Luskell told herself it was for the best, though she missed their old ease. It hurt to know they would never have that back, and it was mostly her fault. But a few days before she was to leave Deep River, he sought her out ... and brought a gift.

"I don't like that rag over your eye," he explained. "This has more polish. And it matches your hair,"

It was an eyepatch, made with skill and care from supple, dark brown leather. "You made this?"

"Remember all my failed apprenticeships? I guess I learned enough to cut a pattern and stitch leather. Here, let me." Jagryn lifted away the cloth and tossed it aside. He flinched at the exposed scars, but didn't look away. Luskell tried not to tremble at his touch. He positioned the patch and buckled the strap behind her head, under her braid. The fit was secure and comfortable, and no light leaked through. Jagryn stepped back and surveyed his work. "You look dangerous."

"I am." Luskell managed to keep a straight face for a moment, but soon broke into a genuine grin. "It's the strangest gift I've ever received, and the best. Thank you." She pulled Jagryn into an embrace. The thought crossed her mind that this might be a bad idea, but it was too late to change her mind. They held each other for a long time. Although she had lost an eye, something more precious had been healed.

"So, that's it?" Jagryn asked. "You're going to leave me here?"

"I'm not leaving you. I'm getting out of your way."

She was out of his way now—too far for mind-talking, and a letter wouldn't be delivered here. Not that she'd told him where she was going.

The hiking party took a rest at the base of the last ridge. As she sipped water from her flask, Luskell eyed the long switchback trail above them. They were above the timberline. It was all in plain view, and her companions assured her their destination lay just beyond the top of the ridge.

"It doesn't look steep," she said. "Can you handle the sleds without me? I'd like to fly the rest of the way."

The two exchanged a look. They already knew about her ability and had not seemed to distrust her for it. For a moment she feared she'd misjudged them. Then they smiled.

Chakalan nodded. "I understand. This is a difficult hike if you're not used to it."

Luskell jumped on the excuse. "I admit it, when the trail is narrow and icy, I get nervous."

He waved his arm. "Go, then. Fly. We'll see you on the other side."

Luskell flinched. But Aklaka did not speak of the afterlife in those terms. He meant only the other side of the ridge. She turned away from them, tucked the eyepatch in a pocket, and focused on her favorite form. She transformed into a large eagle. She had to flap hard in the chilly air, but was halfway up the hill before they set foot on the trail.

Luskell had last flown two days before, with her father from Misty Pass to the Aklaka winter camp, Aku's Lap. She would have gone alone, but Dadad wanted to accompany her and visit his friends there. He insisted she follow his lead and take frequent rests, and wouldn't set out until she promised. Perhaps he already suspected what she was about to discover. When she transformed, she had two eyes again.

She already knew bird eyes were good, revealing details and colors even wizards wouldn't notice or couldn't see. And now she had depth again, and the whole panorama.

Without her promise and Dadad's example, Luskell would have been tempted to fly straight through without a break. As it was, it was hard to change back. At the first rest, she sat on a stump to eat and drink, but first she had a long cry.

"Why does the eagle have two eyes when I have only one?"

"The eagle isn't you. You imagine it perfect."

"But what if I imagine myself with two eyes?"

"That's wouldn't be you, either." He showed his scarred hand. "Scars don't let you forget."

It got easier after that. At least she could have two eyes temporarily. It was better than nothing.

The Uklak Takalanatlan—Laki's mother Kala—met them when they arrived in Aku's Lap. Dadad had alerted her by mind-talking. She was a woman about his age, a shade taller, grave and dignified when she needed to be, with a brilliant smile that lifted the lines of her face when she was delighted. This smile greeted their arrival.

"I hope you can stay—the supply party is about to leave for Knot's Valley, so Laki should be back here in a few days."

"No, we can't stay long." Dadad explained the reason for their visit.

Kala glanced at Luskell, and the solemn look erased her smile. "I see." She questioned Luskell until satisfied that they knew what they were asking. "I suppose it is appropriate. I give my permission."

Now here Luskell was, back in Knot's Valley. She glided over the lake, gray with ice. Snow lay deep over much of the valley, but it had lost all its fluff and sparkle. It was compressed and icy and tired. But Knot had shown her what this place looked like during the brief mountain summer. She pictured how the snow would melt every day until the height of summer. Grass would grow, wildflowers would dot the meadows, and the lake might be barely warm enough for swimming. Before summer's end, new snow would fall.

Luskell soared over the lodge and the trees behind it. The short distance to the end of the trail was nothing to eagle's wings. She landed a safe distance from the cliff's edge and transformed, with reluctance, back to a one-eyed girl. It had been a short transformation; she rested on her feet.

A few steps away, Laki stood with his eyes closed, his hands pressed against the cliff face. He was so intent on Listening, he didn't react to Luskell's arrival. Perhaps he hadn't heard it.

She stood and watched him. She hadn't tried to mind-talk with him since receiving his fragmentary reply in Deep River; it had felt like a rebuke. She wasn't sure what to expect from him.

"Laki."

He turned with a start, then squawked and ran to her. He lifted her off her feet and spun her around. "You came back! I'm glad you changed your mind." Laki moved to kiss her. Luskell turned her head. His lips touched her jaw. He stepped back to look at her and gasped, unable to hide his shock. He stared a moment. "What happened?"

Luskell drew out the patch and put it on. Her hood dropped back as she fastened the strap. "As usual, I didn't think something all the way through." She blinked away the tears blurring her vision.

Laki sighed. "Oh, Luskell ... Was anyone else hurt?"

"Only a murderer." She smiled, though her throat ached.

"And your hair?" He patted her short mop of curls.

"I left the braid with my klamamam. If I'm in Knot's Valley, I don't need his hair, too. It's good to see you, Laki. I'm glad you're not angry."

"Angry? You know I'm always happy to see you. Didn't I say I forgive you? You're young enough to be excused a few mistakes. But you could have saved yourself the trouble. I'm about to go back down." He gestured toward the cliff face. "I was just saying my goodbyes. The supply party is due with my relief any time."

"I know. I came up with them. They'll probably reach the lodge about the time you do."

Laki frowned. "I don't understand. Why didn't you wait for me in Aku's Lap?"

Luskell took a deep breath and blew it out. "Because I'm your relief."

"I wasn't serious, you know."

"What, you don't believe a woman can be Aku's keeper?"

"Well, no woman *has*. Trust you to be the first. But why?"

"Because this is where I need to be right now."

"So you'll give up on being a wizard?"

"I'm not giving it up. Maybe when I have my staff, I'll even find another girl to be my apprentice so I won't be the only one. But that can wait. For now, I'll stay with Aku. I can get better at Listening. And maybe she'll help me learn to hear, and to see."

Laki cupped her face in his hand. "Luskell, what happened to you?"

"It's not what happened, it's what I did. I was selfish and I hurt people, when if I'd thought for a moment ..." She broke off, unable to finish.

"So you're going to hide out like Yrae for the rest of your life?"

Luskell managed a smile. "No. I'm like him, and I've learned enough from him to know I can't hide, and I shouldn't try. But for a half year, yes, I will stay here and do Yrae's work. Knot's work. We already know I can. I'm sure I'm better qualified than Kiraknat."

"I have no doubt about that. How did he take it?"

"He wasn't happy, but he accepted Kala's decision with enough grace to join the supply party instead."

Laki nodded. "He's not a great Listener, but he's generally a good sport. Still, this seems extreme. Are you sure?"

"I hope the time alone will make me wiser."

"Alone. May I visit?"

Luskell longed to tell him yes. "You'd better not." Laki started to protest, but she held up her hand for silence. "I wouldn't trade our time together for anything. I'll tell you what I told Jagryn: I love you both too much to choose either of you. So I choose neither. I won't have you waiting for me, or suspending your life for me. We're all three better off as friends, with no one left out."

Laki pursed his lips and nodded. "Maybe you're right. And you've met someone else, haven't you?"

Luskell was about to deny it, then stopped. Fandek had promised to wait for her, and she hadn't told him not to. She wasn't sure how she felt about him, but she wanted to find out.

"Maybe," she admitted. "I'm trying to stop making impulsive decisions, so I don't know yet."

Laki smiled. "All right. I wish it could be me, but as long as you're not always alone ..."

Luskell hugged him tight. "You'd better go meet the supply party. I'll catch up."

She watched him go. He kept turning with a bemused smile, until he disappeared below the lip of the plateau. Luskell walked out to the edge of the cliff, as close as she dared, and Listened. A cold wind swirled down off the glaciers, a reminder that spring was a relative term. But even here, life was returning. She could hear it. It hurt to tell Laki goodbye, as it had to tell Jagryn. But already the hurt was easing. There was work to be done.

Luskell crossed the broad ledge and leaned against the cliff face. She extracted her fiddle from the special pocket she'd sewed into her cloak.

"Well, Aku—here I am. How about a tune?"

THE END

About the Author

Karen Eisenbrey lives in Seattle, WA, where she leads a quiet, orderly life and invents stories to make up for it. Although she intended to be a writer from an early age, until her mid-30s she had nothing to say. A little bit of free time and a vivid dream about a wizard changed all that. Karen writes fantasy and science fiction novels, as well as short fiction in a variety of genres and the occasional song or poem if it insists. She also sings in a church choir and plays drums in a garage band. She shares her life with her husband, two young adult sons, and two mature adult cats.

Find more info on Karen's books and short fiction, follow her band-name blog, and sign up for her quarterly newsletter at kareneisenbreywriter.com

Special Thanks

... to Benjamin Gorman for starting a publishing company that so perfectly fits my writing; and to Viveca Shearin for her sharp-eyed editing.

... to the whole Not A Pipe family of authors for their support, encouragement, and example.

... to Angelika, Nan, and Yvonne, my invaluable beta readers.

... to Amy and Tim, my writing group that willingly listens to chapters out of order, some of them more than once.

... to Steve Scribner for help with the map of Eukard.

... to Keith Eisenbrey, my example for doing the creative work that needs to be done in spite of everything else. He has read countless drafts (of this and other projects), listened to me fuss over ideas, welcomed the host of fictional people who live in my head, and kept a roof over our heads all these years. I couldn't do any of it without him.

CPSIA information can be obtained
at www.ICGtesting.com
Printed in the USA
LVHW111837030220
645675LV00005B/74/J

9 781948 120326